I0653617

DEATH

SETS

SAIL

A Mystery

Dale E. Manolakas

Kallias Publishing

All Books on Kindle Unlimited

Books by Dale E. Manolakas

Legal Thrillers
The Russian
Hollywood on Trial
Rogue Divorce Lawyer
Box Set of Rogue Divorce Lawyer & Hollywood on Trial
Lethal Lawyers
The Gun Trial

Mysteries
Hollywood Plays for Keeps
Death Sets Sail
Box Set of Hollywood Plays for Keeps & Death Sets Sail

Author's Official Website
http://www.dalemanolakas.com
Author's YouTube Channel View Book Trailers
https://www.youtube.com/channel/UCac1mJynScdPGd2FVz1987A
Amazon Author Page with Book Trailers—Kindle Unlimited
https://www.amazon.com/Dale-E.-Manolakas/e/B00H0FMRX6
Sign up for a Mailing List [NO SPAM ONLY SPECIALS]
https://dalemanolakas.com/sign-up

DEATH SETS SAIL

A Mystery

Dale E. Manolakas

This mystery is a work of fiction. Names, characters, businesses, organizations, places, events, and incidents in this cozy mystery either are a product of the author's imagination or are used fictitiously. Any resemblance to actual persons, living or dead, events or locales in this mystery is entirely coincidental. All characters appearing in this mystery are fictitious. Any resemblance in this cozy mystery to real persons, living or dead, is purely coincidental.

PUBLISHED BY KALLIAS PUBLISHING

FIRST EDITION
Library of Congress Control Number: 2014922252
eISBN: 978-1-62805-006-6 (e-publication)
ISBN 978-1-62805-007-3 (Paperback)
ISBN 978-1-62805-008-0 (Audio)

DEDICATION

IN HONOR OF MY PARENTS FROM THE GREATEST GENERATION

I lovingly dedicate this book to my mother Betty Jane Heise Manolakas who taught me to write and with whom I enjoyed the most wonderful cruises, transatlantic and more. And with love to my late father George S. Manolakas, M.D. who, unlike his Greek ship-owning forbears on Chios, avoided the sea until World War II. Then, he crossed the Atlantic, seasick but courageous, to serve nearly four years with Patton's Seventh and Third Armies in Africa and Europe.

ACKNOWLEDGEMENTS

I want to thank my family for their support, encouragement, suggestions, and editing of this mystery: my husband Roy; our daughters Heather, Anne, and Kathleen; Bob; and James. Again, thank you to my mother Betty Jane Heise Manolakas who was the first published author in our family and my father George S. Manolakas, M.D., as University of Michigan football half-back, and a dedicated surgeon, from the old school, who always put his patients first.

I would also like to acknowledge my wonderful cruising partners: again my mother Betty Jane Heise Manolakas; Nadja Cherup, and my well-loved relatives Katherine Manolakas; and Angela and Nick Siokos. Our endless bridge games were so much fun.

"Wouldst thou, so the helmsman answered,
"Learn the secret of the sea?
Only those who brave its dangers
Comprehend its mystery!"

Henry Wadsworth Longfellow

PROLOGUE

"New York is a sucked orange."
- Ralph Waldo Emerson (1803-1882)

Thursday night in New York City, Professor Emeritus Otto Stein set two mismatched wine glasses down among the literary magazines strewn on his coffee table.

"Damn smudges!"

He grabbed each glass—this time by the stem—and rubbed the rim with the tail of his blue button-down shirt. Then he held each up to the nearby lamplight, filtered and dimmed by the yellowed dusty shade.

"There!"

As Otto re-tucked his shirt, he looked out at the wind-swept rain slapping against his sixth floor window. The tall buildings across Prince Street were checker-boarded with lit windows. The Big Apple had endured a snowy winter and a wet spring. June was no dryer; it approached the 2009 all-time record.

However, the drenching didn't matter to Otto tonight. Tomorrow, he was sailing away from his soggy city. He was embarking on the *Queen Anne*, a five-star cruise ship, on the Mystery Writers of the World transatlantic awards cruise. His trip was *gratis* because he was getting the coveted, world-renowned MWW Lifetime Achievement Award for his contributions to the writing profession. He had founded and, for over half a century, chaired the New York Greenwich University writing program. His cream-of-the crop graduates were a Who's Who of the writing world. And, over the years, he had calculatedly embedded himself in their lives.

Otto shivered and went over to the heat of his gas-log fireplace near the door. Since his early twenties he had lived alone in this West Village, rent-controlled apartment. Now, at eighty-three, he found it colder and draftier.

As he absorbed the warmth, he admired the mantel full of his university teaching awards, honorary trophies, plaques, and photos—photos that flaunted only his most famous graduates. With a grim, tight-lipped smile, Otto rearranged his treasures, making room for his new booty—his MWW award.

Suddenly, the old intercom's sputtering buzz announced Otto's guest downstairs. He reached over.

"Hello! You're here?"

"Yes!"

"Well, come up . . . come up! Sixth floor. Number 604. Take a right off the elevator. At the end of the hall . . . on the left."

Otto pushed the latch release for the lobby door. He shoved his packed suitcase aside on the worn wood floor. Then, he scanned the room for its guest-worthiness. To him it was presentable, especially at night when the low lighting and flickering fireplace masked its defects. His eyes stopped at the cluttered coffee table.

"Blast it!"

Otto rushed to his tiny galley kitchen. He returned with the missing merlot and plate of Brie with crackers. Just as he set them on the stacks of *New Yorkers* near the wine glasses, there was an up-tempo rap at the door.

Otto ran his fingers through his thick, white Einsteinian hair and smoothed his wild snowy eyebrows mounding over his pewter wire-rimmed glasses. He practiced a toothy smile as he headed for the door, but paused at the mantel to move his latest and largest addition forward—an oversized Oscar mockup. The Dean and his colleagues presented it to him last month celebrating Otto's graduate Frederick Larsen's recent, and second, Oscar for an original screenplay.

Otto's gray eyes ignited with anger as he fixated on the object—his smile vanished.

Then, a second hard knock summoned Otto.

"Coming!" He reset his smile.

Otto reached over and twisted the key in his three inch brass deadbolt installed when the area, now gentrifying, had gone from good to bad. Then, he turned the brass doorknob, shiny from use.

Suddenly, when the latch released, the door thrust open— slamming Otto full-force to the floor and banging into his suitcase. Although thin and active, age had made Otto frail. Pain shot up his back.

Otto was stunned, limp, dazed, and disoriented.

As the door shut, he peered through his crisscrossed glasses in a haze of confusion. Before him was a wet figure pooling water on the floor and dressed all in black—from the hooded rain coat down to black leather gloves and black umbrella. The right hand gripped Otto's faux Oscar.

Otto adjusted his glasses. When his gray eyes melded with the visitor's, his confusion turned into recognition and then fear as the black figure raised the Oscar.

"No . . . no . . . please!" resounded through the apartment.

Otto struggled to get up, but the Oscar came down hard down on his head, splattering blood. Otto's right arm failed to block a second blow. He fell back half-conscious, into his own blood and pooling rainwater. He rolled over and got on all fours. He fought to stand, but his shoes slipped in the pooled red mixture and his stricken arm gave way.

The faux Oscar slammed into the back of Otto's head. Otto collapsed unconscious and face down. The blood oozed through his wild white hair. The black figure hit him again and again, threw the Oscar down, and then left—door ajar—Merlot untouched.

Otto was stilled.

Forever.

⌘

CHAPTER 1

Anticipation and Alarm

Friday morning in Santa Monica, California, as usual I woke to four a.m. darkness—a time when I routinely immersed myself in crime. Not committing it, but creating it. I am Veronica Kennicott, a mystery writer extraordinaire with four unpublished—but excellent—books.

However, today, instead of writing or wrestling with my absent muse, I was waiting for an airport shuttle. I was flying to Kennedy International Airport in New York to sail on the *Queen Anne* for the biennial awards cruise for the Mystery Writers of the World—the MWW.

The world-renowned awards had more than twenty coveted categories, from best unpublished mystery book to best first published literary author and even best new graphic novel. The eminent Otto Stein was getting the lifetime achievement award. The *Queen Anne* would carry everyone who was anyone in the literary and mystery worlds—including authors, film writers, agents, publishers, and novices.

It was my first time going and I was excited. I had been packed for days and this morning was ready with an hour to kill. I went to my study, my writer's lair. I booted up my laptop to productively kill time, like the rest of the world, on the Internet.

When my screen Googled-up I was horrified. Highlighted on my home page was a murder, a murder amongst us—the MWW. Last night Otto Stein, a neighbor found the beloved patriarch of the writing world, in his New York apartment bludgeoned to death. The police called it an aborted burglary.

Of course, I didn't know Otto personally. But, naturally, since I was an up-and-coming writer of Southern California stature, I claimed him as my patriarch, too.

I needed to share my shock and grief. I needed communal mourning, but blogging would not suffice. I had to "have voice" with someone.

I speed dialed my cell for Mavis Osborne, my writing teacher and mentor for years. She was slightly older and a real professional who had made her living writing books her whole life. She was a collegial friend, even though I was as yet unpublished. She had convinced me to take this cruise at the last minute and honored me by asking me to be her roommate. I had accepted on the spot.

CHAPTER 2

Memento Mori

"Mavis, it's Veronica. I knew you'd be up."

Mavis had my same early morning writing routine and, besides, it wasn't that early in New York. Mavis had flown there two days in advance with Esther Nussbaum, the longtime MWW president and cruise organizer, to help with program details. Esther was now only an intermittent mystery writer, but because of her tenure as president she rubbed elbows with every writer worth knowing.

"Yes . . . for hours."

"Then you know about Otto Stein?"

"Esther and I heard last night at dinner."

"Did they catch anyone yet?"

"No, and the burglar took nothing!"

"That's odd." I turned on my crime solving brain.

"Not when a burglary goes bad and the neighbors hear it. But what's odd to me is Otto being burgled at all! What academic has anything worth taking? I personally suspect it wasn't a burglary, especially after reading the blogs!"

"Really?"

"The key is the bludgeoning. You'll learn with more experience that a brutal murder like that is typically personal . . . very personal. I don't like to repeat gossip . . . but it's all over the MWW chat room and mystery blogs anyway."

"What is?"

I knew Mavis well enough to know that, once encouraged, her Achilles heel was showing off, name-dropping, and unabashedly gossiping.

"They say he had problems. His colleagues were fighting over who would get his funded university chair and some of his ex-students, like Frederick Larsen, hated him taking credit for their successes."

"I never heard about any of that before."

"And, not to speak ill of the dead, there was more to Otto than met the eye. To be honest, I never saw any evidence of it, but . . ." Mavis hesitated.

"But what?"

"Well . . . people are saying he was a womanizer . . . or worse!"

"Really! At his age?"

"The MWW chat room is buzzing. And where there's smoke, there's usually fire."

"Who would have thought?" I reveled in Mavis's professional trust.

"But then, you know mystery writers . . . a theory around every corner. There's the psycho unhappy-graduate scenario. Another is a disgruntled ghostwriter . . . evidently he brokered them to our colleagues with writer's block . . ."

"Did he?" I thought of my own prolonged writer's block and wished I could afford a ghostwriter, or even a good editor for that matter.

"Ghostwriters are a shameful way around writer's block if you ask me."

"Of course." My thoughts were reprimanded. "Is there any credible lead?"

I used the word "credible" to establish my discerning crime-solving expertise.

"Not yet. But if there is, we MWW's will be on top of it. Otto was one of our own. I'd expect nothing less."

"Me neither." I bounced to another level of elation every time she used the words *we* and *our*.

"Such a useless tragedy. A wonderful person . . . so witty."

"You knew him?"

I was thinking I should have been more solicitous about his death.

"Of course, without him I wouldn't be where I am today. He was a genius . . . so helpful . . . and always a gentleman to me. He was a true friend. And, Esther will tell you that the MWW would not be the powerhouse it is today but for him."

"I'm sorry that I won't ever meet him."

"Esther and I worked most of the night replacing him in the programs and panel spots. We got Helga Brodsky and some other big names to step in. Now, of course, his Lifetime Achievement award is posthumous. We created a memorial theme for the programs . . . a celebration of his legacy. We actually got a few of his most successful graduates on the cruise, last-minute, to pay homage."

"Wonderful . . . for the memorial." I was excited to be sailing with even more biggies in the authorial world, which I coveted.

"We are a family, after all."

I heard the clicks of call waiting on her phone.

"Hold on a second." Before I could respond, Mavis relegated me to second choice in the silent world-of-hold we all inhabit—unless, of course, we have the power always to be first choice. "I'm sorry. It's Esther. I have to go. We have to get Otto's obituary up on the MWW homepage."

"Wait! Did you get my email about the storm crossing our sailing route?"

"Yes, I got Dramamine."

"Me too and packed extra. Do you need anything else?" We had not become fast friends yet, but I expected that to happen on the *Queen Anne*.

"No, I'm ready for every contingency." Mavis was gone.

I was happy I had reached out to Mavis.

* * *

Out my bay window, the early sun burnt through the misty marine layer called "June Gloom" that spread itself as many months as it pleased. I surfed the Internet on my laptop about Otto's death—and, of course, his life.

Otto's death had made our awards cruise even more newsworthy and popular. The entire community of writers was sprinting to New York at the last minute to join the cruise and commemorate his life, celebrate his death, or just have their say.

In his twenties Otto was a teaching assistant in the Greenwich University English department and published a book—his one and only. With that one publication, his PhD in literature, and a lot of politicking, at twenty-eight he became a tenure-track professor in that same department. Soon he founded his own writing program there which grew and had produced most of the prominent writers of the last half-century. He mentored them and publicly extolled them—the successful ones, that is. In fact, it seemed they were his life—his only life.

The long list of Otto's graduates and other mentees topped bestseller book lists and were winners of Pulitzers, Hollywood Oscars and Emmys, New York Tonys, and some London Lawrence Oliviers.

Mavis was not on the list. However, I expected that if I had started younger and had received Otto's help, I would have been.

On the MWW homepage, Mavis and Esther had already posted an obituary. It was literally plagiarized from the Internet article I read before—but then they were both under time pressure. Mavis was right about the chat rooms. Rumors were flying! But she hadn't mentioned it was a wholesale professional character assassination.

Was this sour grapes—or had Otto's death given license to tell the truth about this icon?

I was now late, but informed. I shut down my laptop and double-checked the doors and the timers on the lamps and televisions. As I left, I set the alarm system. Organizing my life for a long week's absence was hard. My dear departed husband had contributed more than I thought to the order of our lives. He had, unfortunately, died several years ago after an over-full, productive, and chaotic life.

Just as I got to the sidewalk, the shuttle arrived. I was on my way and reveling in the expectation of soon becoming a part of Mavis's inner circle and being vetted by her amongst the greats.

On the way up Lincoln Boulevard to LAX airport, I imagined that I would have become Otto's fast professional friend if he had sailed with us, especially with Mavis's introduction. I didn't care about his alleged past personal shortcomings—even if they were true.

CHAPTER 3

Clouds of Many Kinds

I endured the pre-flight security invasion and noted the unlucky people who were *randomly* detoured for *special treatment.* After x-rays bulleted me with their probable cancer link, I reached for my shoes knowing my valuables were safe—because I brought none.

I finally stuffed myself into my mini coach-class seat for the flight to Kennedy International. We were held on the tarmac, but I didn't care. I was on my way to fulfill my destiny on the MWW awards cruise, and my aisle seat had some air circulation—albeit the oxygen-deprived passenger mix.

During the flight, I studied the MWW program schedule and was delighted with all the big names in the writers' world participating. I liked several panel discussions: "How to Kill Quietly or the Poison Pen," "Characters to Live For," "Plots to Die For," "How To Self-Publish," and "Self-Publication Pitfalls." The self-publication part was intriguing. Maybe it was simpler than I thought. One panel about Octopus Books, the largest e-book self-publisher Internet retailer in the world, particularly interested me: "Octopus Books: Pimp or Publisher—Stealing Authors Royalties". Did that mean what I thought it meant? Were authors Octopus's whores after all the years of writing, editing, and advertising? I had heard about Octopus's surprise unilateral royalty changes that yielded pennies to authors for their books. I needed to know more.

I put the program away and leaned back. The only fly in the ointment on this trip was that my classmates Jody Thurston, Agnes Granchelli, and Herbert Frutlander were coming on the cruise. They were not writers of my skill and promise, but insisted, despite Mavis's dissuasion, on accompanying us.

The three had never completed any books, unlike me. And, over the years the chapters they shared in class showed they were fossilized writers stuck in their own mistakes, forever. They would never be amongst the published and they would never fit in on the cruise. At the moment, I was just glad they were not chewing my ear off on the flight. They had flown early to New York for the one-day tour of famous writer's sites.

After the cruise, I was going on the three-day tour of British writers' sites in London and Shakespeare's Stratford-on-Avon. I was a theatre arts major in college and had always wanted to visit Stratford-on-Avon. It would give me even more theatre cachet in my acting circles and social material for future MWW events—which I planned to attend when I came back.

As I sat there with the drone of the airplane engines, I dozed off satisfied and happy in that thought.

* * *

During the flight, the pilot made up some time, but not all. We landed late in New York. I was anxious about logistics because I hadn't traveled alone since my husband died. However, when I exited the jet bridge, there was a Wessex Cruise Line sign held high with a young man's friendly face beneath.

I magneted over with my roller carry-on trailing. The bag had everything I needed for my first night on the ship. Mavis had warned me that on her last cruise she had to borrow a dinner dress because her checked bag did not get to her cabin on time.

"Hi. I'm Veronica Kennicott for the *Queen Anne* sailing."

"Good morning. Welcome to New York and the Wessex Cruise Line. A group is waiting for us. I'll take your carry-on."

"Thank you."

I followed him through the crowd to ground transportation. As we wound through the airport, I touched up my lipstick and straightened my cherry red shirt collar over the lapels of my navy linen summer suit. I had bought it just for the flight and boarding. It was a loose size eight now. I had purposely dropped five pounds in preparation for the crossing. I had read about the famous Wessex gourmet meals and wanted to enjoy every one.

Down the escalator in the luggage area, three men and a woman were loosely grouped near another Wessex sign held high by a woman.

"May I have your claim check?" My escort held out his hand.

"What?"

"Baggage claim check to get your luggage?"

"Oh, thank you."

He disappeared, still in charge of my carry-on safety net.

* * *

As I approached my group, a tall, toned man with brown hair, graying temples, and sunglasses stood with his back turned. He was having an intense "thing" on his cell phone. I slowed and listened.

"Wait a minute. I'm here, aren't I? Any more threats and I'm not going to sail on that ship! You'll have to come yourself and do the Otto-adoration dance. The guy was a monster. He deserved what he got."

I was shocked. I stared open-mouthed at him. He glanced around to see if anyone had heard him and caught me full face. He turned back and lowered his voice. He was less audible, but still uncontrolled.

I kept walking, but even under his sunglasses I had recognized him. He was none other than Frederick Larsen, the famous film and television writer, and a graduate of Otto's. His antics were Hollywood tabloid fodder at my grocery store checkout stand and he had just been on television getting an Oscar for his independent film script—it was his second. Twenty years ago he had received his first for best original screenplay.

This year Otto had presented the Oscar to Frederick. Intriguingly, Frederick didn't shake Otto's hand or thank him in his acceptance speech. But, when Frederick finished, Otto stepped forward and put his arm around Frederick's shoulder. He spoke about Frederick's great talent and their enduring friendship until the music-signaled time was up and drowned him out.

The news the next day touted it as the most moving moment of the night. I realized now, after my eavesdropping, that Frederick had intentionally ignored Otto both on stage and in his speech.

* * *

As I joined the clustered Wessex group, a tall, striking, exquisite middle-aged woman snapped at me.

"We've been waiting an hour."

The woman's short, seamlessly highlighted rich jet-black hair showed her colorist was an artist and expensive. It encircled her pale pancaked face which was crayoned with bold

15

black eyeliner around her dark eyes, blushed cheeks, neon red lips, and a thin penciled black brow arched above her depilated natural one, gone missing.

I recognized her as well. She was Helga Brodsky, the most prolific and best selling female mystery writer in the last decade. She used several *noms de plume*, but each one was well known now. Everyone sought out her twenty-five books regardless of the names she had used early in her career. They loved her fast-moving plots and intense, if not distorted or, I would say, psychotic characters. Mavis and Esther had gotten Helga to take over some of Otto's roles on the cruise. Helga had agreed to moderate his panel on agents and to be the keynote speaker at the awards, as well as to present Otto's posthumous lifetime achievement award.

"I'm so sorry." I extended my hand as I smiled up at her. "My plane was delayed. I'm Veronica Ken . . ."

"Let's go." Helga interrupted, ignoring my hand, and headed to the double glass doors labeled "Ground Transportation".

I was stunned. Helga not only looked just like her pictures on her book jackets, but she acted just as the tabloids depicted— rude and hideous. I recollected the news coverage of her marriage to old Puritan and Boston Brahmin stock from Cape Cod several years ago, and her rancor at the press characterizing her as a "cougar". She had to be at least fifty now, but looked thirty-five thanks to a skilled plastic surgeon.

Helga strode away, not quickly but determined in her haute couture red tailored silk suit. The short coat was tight across her broad shoulders. At her side, her hands with long red nails marched away with her. The straight short skirt was loose through her narrow hips and displayed her long muscular legs bottomed-out with red four-inch heels perfectly matched to the handbag swinging at her side. She was an imposing person, even from behind. But a noticeable totter on her spiked heels, born of age, as they carried her through the double glass doors, flawed her exit.

The Wessex woman followed Helga with her Wessex sign bouncing overhead.

"Too bad she doesn't fall over," I murmured.

I looked to make sure no one had heard me. They hadn't. But an attractive, very tall man to my right smiled and stepped over.

"Sorry. It's been a long night for Helga. I'm Brent Hawthorne . . . Helga's husband." Brent extended his hand.

I noticed a slight Bostonian accent as he spoke. He was part of the Hawthorne family based in Boston, but himself living in Cape Cod. His ancestors included a judge at the Salem witch trials and the famous 19th century American author Nathaniel Hawthorne. He was taller, younger, and nicer looking than his news coverage. I hadn't noticed him there. No one would have, given her machinations.

"I understand." I shook his hand and smiled. "Veronica Kennicott. Nice to meet you."

Brent was not particularly embarrassed or surprised at Helga's rudeness. He smiled politely and handled the situation smoothly, suggesting this was routine for him.

Brent's suit hung loosely on his tall, thin body. His hair was done jet black like Helga's. His complexion was that of a man who spent a lot of time in the sun. He was attractive, animated, and charming, but his blue eyes were incongruous. Despite the facade, his eyes could not hide a disturbing hollow sadness. They had the worn look of a "non-person."

I surmised the grocery checkout tabloids were correct. After he had squandered the family inheritance, he had married Helga for her money. It and she allowed him to keep his Cape Cod lifestyle and do his tabloid-touted competitive sailing.

"Brent, come!" Helga glared at me.

I instinctively cowered. Brent instinctively obeyed.

"Yes, dearest." Brent neoned a detached smile.

When Helga swiveled her head back around, Brent's smile fell from his face and his eyes narrowed. But he heeled after his wife without another word, like a well-trained big dog.

I stared in amazement.

* * *

My Wessex man came back rolling my large checked bag with my carry-on perched on top. With his sign dangling at his side, he followed Brent.

Frederick walked past me whispering loudly on his cell.

"Gotta go. And when I said no speech, I meant it. Don't bother me again."

Frederick put his cell in his shirt breast pocket as he fell into step behind the others. He was Hollywood-attractive in his light washed blue jeans and black linen shirt, extensively wrinkled from his flight. He trailed along slowly with his camel leather jacket over his arm.

I usually loved a parade, but this one was a bit too intense for me.

I followed, shadowing these professional writers who I knew were my colleagues-to-be.

* * *

After several steps, a deep voice with an intoxicating base tremolo spoke to me from behind.

"Going on the *Queen Anne*?"

I glanced back.

Behind me was a tall man wearing a midnight blue business suit, white shirt, and maroon, cream, and midnight blue stripped tie. His deep eighty-five percent cocoa eyes twinkled as he fell in step with me and smiled down at me. He appeared to be in his mid-forties but had a stunning head of gray hair with traces of his former dark brown. He was over six feet tall, and filled out his suit jacket nicely around the shoulders and chest.

"Yes."

I smiled. In fact, I had to arrest a sloppy grin in the making. He was so good-looking and so friendly.

"I'm in the mystery writer's group. Are you?"

"No, as a matter of fact. But it sounds like fun."

"I'm Veronica Kennicott."

"Curtis Mihaly. Nice to meet you."

He held out his large hand. It encircled mine gently. I looked up into warm, friendly eyes.

The trip might be more exciting than I had planned.

⌘

CHAPTER 4

Vanities

At the van, the driver piled our suitcases and carry-ons in the back, Helga's on top as was her command.

Helga and Brent took the entire four-person center seat. Brent's head skimmed the van roof and his long legs were pretzled against the front seats and still blocked the walk space to the back seat. Helga simply spread out luxuriously next to him displaying her bare smooth crossed legs.

I tucked my head down and squat-walked past Brent's knee into the narrow rear seat book-ended by the wide wheel wells. When Curtis Mihaly started to follow me, the driver stopped him.

"I can't believe I got three of the tall ones. Sit shotgun. It'll be more comfortable for you." The driver threw his lunch and papers off the seat.

"That's kind of you."

"No, it wasn't," I thought, disappointed to be separated from Curtis and hoping he was, too.

The bus driver then turned to Frederick.

"I am sorry, sir, but would you be more comfortable in the middle or the back?"

Brent retracted his legs to make room for Frederick, but Helga spread out more.

"Thanks, the back is fine."

Frederick instinctively knew that a scene with Helga would accompany any attempt to sit in the middle seat. Actually, we all knew it and were grateful for the reprieve—especially the driver, whose face notably relaxed.

Frederick squeezed into the back seat and put his jacket over his knee.

He greeted me through his sunglasses. "Hello. I'm Frederick Larsen."

"Nice to meet you."

"Sorry about the phone call back there. Just agent problems."

"I understand."

I lied. I literally had no understanding about agent problems and, furthermore, I knew full well the phone call was not about agents, but instead about Otto.

"Are you an MWW cruiser?"

"Yes. Veronica Kennicott."

"Veronica Kennicott? I can't place the name."

I knew the dance-of-the-published-book-titles was coming. I had my excuses on the tip of my tongue, but knew this would be a very sophisticated volley and not something I was used to. Worse than that, the entire van would be the audience and potential participators, including Helga.

"Oh? I . . ."

I was happily interrupted.

"Yoo-hoo . . . Yoo-hoo."

An energetic plump woman called and waved as she ran up to the open van doors in her sensible white heels as her large white purse pendulumed at her arm. Her white and blue pin stripped seersucker dress had ridden up, exposing her bare white chubby thighs.

Trailing in her wake was an out of breath, older, stocky man in khaki slacks and a bright blue short-sleeved golf shirt.

"We made it. You didn't get rid of us." She teased the Wessex woman as she leaned on the van to catch her breath— her ample white and thoroughly pilled cardigan bunched under her generous arms. "You were supposed to wait while we went pee."

Her high-pitched squeal was incongruous with her substantial stature.

"I'm so sorry. I . . ."

"Forget it, dear. I'll grab that seat there in the middle." The seer suckered mass started to move again.

" . . . thought you could see us."

The Wessex attendant apologized to the backside of the harried, hard-breathing woman thrusting her heavy body into the van. There was, of course, no seat per se between Helga and Brent. However, as the determined sizable woman jostled across Brent's long legs, Helga's defensive slide to the window quickly created one.

The woman plopped herself down between Helga and Brent. She perched her purse on her knees and what was left of a lap at the end of her stomach.

"That's my Dior you're sitting on." Helga grabbed her red handbag peeking from under the seersucker.

"Oops. Sorry."

The woman adjusted her seersucker down over her knees and straightened her cardigan. Her brown and gray bun loosely pinned on the back of her head bounced as she adjusted herself.

"Where shall I go?" The older, stocky man boomed with a deep voice and heavy accent that I could not place.

He peered into the van at me with his dark sparkling eyes. I smiled and scooted as far as I could toward the window.

"Thanks, I'm coming in." The man started his crawl across Frederick.

"Let me move, too." Frederick's tall body slid agilely over to me in the middle, giving the older man the seat near the wheel well.

"Thank you, sir." The older man plopped down.

Frederick actually had more legroom now spreading out in between us two shorties.

"I'm Elias Vlisides, gourmet Greek cook and mystery writer." Elias grabbed Frederick's hand and shook it. "You're Frederick Larsen. One of Otto Stein's Oscar-winning students."

"Ex-students. That was a . . ." Beethoven's Ninth Symphony sounded on Frederick's cell in his pocket. He grabbed it and started texting.

I leaned forward and smiled at Elias.

"I'm Veronica Kennicott. Nice to meet you, Elias V . . . li . . . si . . ."

Elias laughed with his sparkling dark eyes dancing and his gray moustache smiling over his bright white teeth. "Almost! You pronounce it Ē-lē-ĕs. And then Vlĕh-sē-dēz."

"Ē-lē-ĕs . . . Vlĕh-sē-dēz?"

"Yes. Very good."

"Obviously Greek." I engaged playfully.

"Yes, my parents brought me here when I was young, but not young enough to lose this accent."

I recognized Elias Vlisides's name immediately from the bestseller lists. Of course, the accent was Greek and definitely a marketing tool. He wrote Greek food murders. The protagonist is a retired Greek surgeon who solves murders, all kinds of murders: *The Grape Leaf Murders*; *The Moussaka Murders*; *The Tiropita Murders*—all with recipes included.

"Take this." Elias handed me his business card with his name and web site next to a figure of a dancing Greek man on it. It added his last name phonetically spelled in brackets for people like me. He also handed one to Frederick, who slid it in his shirt pocket between thumbing his texts.

"Thank you. I love your mysteries."

I put his card in my purse and proceeded to shower him with all the white lies authors wanted to hear; the unreserved praise of their books. In reality, I had read only half of one of his mysteries because, although I found the characters interesting, his plots were thin and inherently unbelievable. Giving him the benefit of the doubt, perhaps his plots, based on the rampant disposability of females to premature deaths, were acceptable to him. There was, after all, a deep-rooted Greek heritage that instilled the adoration of the male, particularly sons.

"How's your next one coming?" I asked.

"Etsy ketsy. So. So." Elias shrugged his shoulders and cocked his head to one side. "Soon."

I understood too well that an author's reference to "soon" could mean someday or never. I suspected from Elias's body language that he was not going to have another book out this year. I sensed writer's block and a kindred spirit. To me, naturally, writer's block was nothing to be ashamed of. But maybe it was different for a successful author of a marketable series. I, of course, wouldn't know.

Elias turned to Frederick to change the subject. But Frederick was still two-thumb texting with the intensity of a concert pianist reaching a crescendo.

"Texting is a challenge . . ." Elias chuckled to Frederick. "Those tiny little letters are made for elves' fingers."

Frederick did not even look up.

There was silence in the van.

* * *

24

The awkward moment was thankfully saved by the cardigan-clad woman who had plopped herself between Helga and Brent. She rotated around and thrust her ballooned white face—dotted with red cheeks from the run and too much blush—as close to Frederick's as she could.

"Frederick Larsen?" Her shrill soprano voice reverberated. "Mary O'Connell. I am so glad to meet you. I am a fan."

Frederick glanced up and produced a rigid, obligatory smile. Then, he went back to his texting.

I started to chuckle, but feigned a cough cover-up.

This woman, like Helga, was another example of what linguists call a "heavy presence," and in more ways than the physical. Her energy filled every inch of the world she and those around her inhabited. She was going to engage Frederick, whether he wanted her to or not, because he was a captive audience for her.

Mary O'Connell was a force to be reckoned with. She even got Helga to cower. I scrutinized and enjoyed Helga's distress from my perch behind. Helga steadfastly faced forward and scooted as far away from Mary as she could. It was futile. The more Helga scooted, the more Mary turned to fill the vacancy.

"Congratulations on your second Oscar," Mary beamed, oblivious to the fact—or not caring—that Frederick was ignoring her. "I said congratulations! Well deserved."

"Thank you."

Frederick stopped texting. He was trapped and he knew it.

"Very well deserved, but . . ." Mary telescoped her face as close as she could to Frederick's and lowered her volume attempting, but not achieving, intimacy. "I saw you on the Academy Awards with Otto Stein. How could you forget to thank your old professor? He was so proud of you."

Frederick didn't respond. Instead, his analytical eyes studied the woman as if he was microscopically memorizing her for a future character, a character to kill off.

"You must be upset about Otto's murder." Mary force-fed Frederick without pausing. "I understand you owe everything to him. I wish I'd had a mentor like him. I might not be writing sex-slashers today."

Mary laughed loudly.

"Doubtful," Frederick muttered under his breath and went back to texting.

Mary either pretended not to hear, or actually did not hear, the comment—either way, she did not react.

Just then, I put two and two together. This dowdy, roly-poly middle-aged woman was "the" Mary O'Connell. The famous Michigan housewife and mother of four who had a degree in journalism, but stayed home with her kids and wrote sex torture-murder books in her spare time. She had four best sellers and one high-grossing film. The tabloids had pictures of the magnificent home she traded up to in elite Farmington Hills near Detroit. She had moved there from the ravaged, low rent Highland Park neighborhood. I was in awe.

Elias ignored Frederick's re-engaged texting. "My condolences, too. Lifetime friends like Otto Stein don't come along every day."

Frederick took a deep breath and stopped texting. I could tell he'd had enough. He turned to Elias and responded softly and slowly and coldly.

"Otto took credit for everyone's successes because he had none of his own."

Frederick went back to texting—or pretended to.

"Hear, hear," Helga chimed from the middle seat. "Well said. And accurate."

"I see." Elias swept his fingers over his salt and pepper moustache that was not yet the silver color of his hair. "Well, no matter. We should not speak ill of the dead."

He took his right hand and made the sign of the cross in miniature in the center of his chest. I recognized it as Orthodox, Greek Orthodox, and the reverse of the Catholic sign of the cross, which goes to the left first. I shrugged my shoulders at Elias and he did the same to me. We knew there was definitely no love lost between Frederick and Otto. And, it was clear Helga had her issues, too. I knew then there must be a basis for the vicious blogging I had read about Otto.

"That's a matter of opinion," Helga scoffed and then barked at Mary. "And can you please turn around."

Helga was retaking possession of her rightful share of the seat back.

"Sorry." Mary obeyed. "I was just going to . . ."

"Ready to take off! Buckle up!" The driver interrupted as he hopped into the driver's seat.

We were all buckled up, all but Mary.

"The other end is hiding." Mary fished for it under Helga.

"What the . . ." Helga jumped.

Brent hopped-to and found the other end for Mary under Helga. "Here it is."

"Thanks." Mary buckled up over her seersucker dress and white cardigan. Then she studied Brent for a long moment. "And who are you?"

"I'm Helga Brodsky's husband."

"Oh, my goodness. It must be exciting being married to such a genius," Mary gushed. "And what do you do?"

"He does nothing," Helga announced. "Nothing at all."

"Oh."

Mary was muted, cut off at her chubby knees, so to speak. There was no response to cruelty.

Helga had won the battle and the war.

Silence resonated through the van as we pulled out from the curb.

CHAPTER 5

A Stormy Calm

It was mid-morning and the ride over the New York expressway was mercifully fast, but not quite fast or smooth enough for Helga.

Helga fought with the driver until she finally forced him to turn up the air conditioning full blast, even though the late morning air was not hot, or even warm. Then, she attacked him about the bumpy ride. That had merit. We were all being jostled by the van's old shocks and the driver's "infamous" New York driving—sadly, I'm sure, spurred on by the thought of disposing of Helga quickly.

"The crossing better be smoother than this," Helga spit at Brent after finishing with the driver.

"I checked the weather. It will be."

"No storms. I hate storms."

"No bad weather, dear. I promise."

I wondered how Brent could promise that. Mavis and I had checked and stormy, rainy seas were predicted for at least a few days of our sailing.

I kept my mouth shut. With Helga's silence, I again enjoyed listening to Elias chatting about his Greek recipes with Mary. The exotic names of the Greek dishes alone made me hungry, but the descriptions that followed made me ravenous: koulourakia, kourabiethes, pastitsio, galaktoboureko, kalamari, tzatziki, and avgolemono.

Mary was still leaning into Helga, but interestingly, Helga no longer even tried to possess her share of the seat. Instead, she retreated toward her window, slowly seething to a boiling point. Brent moved closer into his armrest to give Mary his space and stem Helga's impending blowup.

Frederick remained engrossed in texting and Curtis faced forward reading a Wessex Cruise Line booklet.

I was just thrilled to be there, amidst tension or not, with some of the biggest names in our business.

"Our business." I tickled myself with the thought. For me that is what it really was, or soon would be, with Mavis's help and contacts. This crossing would make me a true part of my profession. I studied the creative trust that surrounded me. I fantasized that I was receiving the MWW award on the next cruise for the best first published book. My acceptance speech wouldn't be a boring string of "thank-yous." It would be original and funny. But how? I started composing my speech. My mind ground so loudly that I looked around to see if anyone had heard. They hadn't. I kept composing until we arrived at the piers in the middle of the city.

* * *

"Thank God." Helga's bellow resounded through the van. "Finally, we're here."

As we approached the piers, I saw the *Queen Anne*. The ship was like a white mountain range sitting in the middle of a gray New York City. I had seen cruise ships—and even been on a West coast weekender down to Mexico—but I had never seen a ship of this size juxtaposed onto the skyline of New York City. It dwarfed New York City's own magnificence.

"We'll never get in a van again, even if it is 'included,'" Helga snapped at Brent. "And the cruise better be smooth. I've had it."

"The *Queen Anne* has state of the art stabilizers. You'll be fine," Brent reassured her.

"I don't know why I let you talk me into this."

There was a dense, tense silence until the van pulled up to the embarkation site. Then, we peeled out one by one. I was just as glad as Helga was to get out of the van, partially because of my impending motion sickness from the back seat jostling, but mostly because of Helga, herself.

The porters grabbed our large suitcases and carry-ons. I remembered Mavis's cautionary first night tale and kept possession and control of my carry-on, not that I needed reminding. Everyone else let his or her luggage and carry-ons go to chance. But I remembered fondly a train trip in Germany I had taken with my late husband some years before. There was only one other passenger in our first class compartment, a tiny old German lady who had seven pieces of luggage with her, all linked by cords connected in a knot she held in her hands. When an attendant went to help move some of her luggage in the racks above her, she looked daggers at him and barked "*Nein!*" He backed off. I turned to my husband and remarked at her resolve to maintain "The Power of the Luggage." It was something I never forgot, and something I always maintained myself thereafter.

I took a few deep breaths to dispel any motion sickness and looked around for Curtis.

He was gone and there were only hasty, polite good-byes amongst us remainders to our adjacent van mates. Then, everyone disappeared into the pack of passengers going into the pre-boarding building.

I was disappointed that Curtis didn't acknowledge me, from near or far, before he left.

But then I knew he would be on the ship for five days. With me—I mean, with all of us, of course.

* * *

I entered the cavernous warehouse-like boarding structure with masses of people waiting, mingling, coffeeing, and chattering. There were wood benches around the perimeter and a snack area with tables and chairs.

Dragging my small roller bag behind me, I searched for Mavis. I spotted her seated in the center of the snack area, sipping coffee. I started over, but abruptly stopped.

Mavis was with my classmates Jody, Agnes, and Herbert. Agnes was holding court. None of them saw me. I was not going to start my trip keeping company with my never-to-be-published classmates from home, especially after my van ride with the elites of the mystery world. I spun around to make a quick exit, but collided into a woman behind me.

"Oh, I'm so sorry. Are you okay?"

I was face to face with a petite, stunning woman who was golden from head to toe. She wore a light mustard pants suit and had at least three shades of honey blond mingled artfully and expensively into her shoulder length hair. Her eyes were hazel with a light gold rim that sparkled in the light. Despite that electric gold rim, her eyes had an intriguing stillness about them. Her face had delicate features; her skin was light and flawless.

Interestingly, her mature years were revealed only by her rose lipstick spidering beyond her lip in age lines and horizontal forehead creases peeking out from under her wispy bangs.

"Yes, no harm done."

She held her coffee away so that the drops which spurted out through the plastic lid's small sipping hole fell to the ground.

The woman then gracefully floated around me in her matching mustard heels.

It was the calm depth behind her eyes and her ballet-like grace that made me want to know more about her. I impulsively introduced myself.

"I'm Veronica Kennicott. It's going to be a wonderful cruise, isn't it?"

The woman glanced back at me, her gold-hooped earrings dangling through her hair. "Quite eventful."

I noticed she did not volunteer her name. An omission. I spoke before she could leave.

"Eventful? Then you must be with the mystery writers group, too?"

"Yes, I am. An agent"

"Small world."

"Why? Are you looking?"

"Looking?"

"For an agent?"

I sensed that she was approached too much and too often as an agent. But, God knows, I was not looking for an agent. In fact, I was probably the only non-published writer here avoiding the possibility of submitting a book to an agent.

"Oh, no. Definitely not." I laughed to myself and sidestepped the agent issue with an ambiguous response. "I'm here to enjoy myself."

"Refreshing." The woman extended her hand to me. "I'm Amy Miller."

"Veronica Kennicott." I stepped up, took her hand, and matched her firm grip.

"Nice to meet you, Veronica."

My ambiguity had won the day. I realized that even agents who are looking for the next best seller needed relief from the pitch, just like I needed relief from being grilled about my books. I did, however, decide I would name drop fellow travelers just to up my coinage. I was not immune to making friends and influencing people.

"Nice to meet you too. This is my first awards cruise and I think it's going to be exciting. I already met Helga Brodsky."

"Too bad."

"You mean she's always like that?" I chuckled.

"What do you think?" Amy's eyes scanned the crowd.

"No comment! But, fortunately, Elias Vlisides was also in our transport. He's a hoot."

"He is that. And very successful."

Amy smiled for the first time. Her smile displayed properly bleached teeth and two small evenly matched dimples on her cheeks. It was engaging. She was engaging as she looked directly at me with her hazel gold-rimmed eyes.

"He's actually one of my regrets," she said. "I passed on his query letters several times. What a mistake. Who would have known such silliness would catch on? But everyone loves Greek food and a happy, tubby Greek man, don't they?"

"Yes, they do. But I agree with you. Who would have guessed? I wouldn't have either." I glanced around to make sure no one would hear, especially Elias. "I picked up one of his books years ago. I liked it, but I didn't read another. Not my cup of tea."

"Very diplomatic." Amy shot me another charming smile.

Then, my eyes rested on Frederick walking quickly toward us. In his sunglasses, light washed jeans, and camel leather jacket over his black linen shirt, he stood out as "Hollywood" even more than he had at the airport.

"Oh, there's Frederick Larsen coming over. He was with us in the van, too."

"Frederick Larsen?"

Amy's smile dropped from her face. Her eyes narrowed. Her head snapped to where my eyes had rested on Frederick, her golden hairpin wheeling into her cheeks and then settling back into place.

Ignoring my presence and comment, Amy studied Frederick working his way through the crowd in our direction. I knew from the look on her face that they had a history; a history that did not engender even a modicum of warmth. I watched Amy glaring at Frederick as he approached.

Before Frederick got close, a short agile man in tan slacks and a cacao brown short-sleeve shirt intercepted him. The two men did not shake hands. Nor did they smile. The statuesque, calm Frederick looked down at the man who was as unattractive as Frederick was attractive.

The short man blocked Frederick's path. Under his receding, graying brown hair was a face contorted in anger, with dark eyes glaring up at Frederick.

"Let the games begin." Amy whispered under her breath.

⌘

CHAPTER 6

A Barkingly Contemplative Embarkation

Amy observed the men arguing and I, in turn, observed her. Her eyes were slits now, and her face was frozen in an intense but emotionless mask, with her jaw clenched and bulging.

I looked at the men. Their argument was escalating, but still indiscernible to us. Frederick gestured in our direction.

Then the shorter man thumped his finger on Frederick's chest and shouted, "I'm here. Deal with it!"

"So is Amy. Deal with that!" Frederick turned and pointed at Amy standing next to me.

"What?"

Passengers within earshot looked at them and then over at us.

"Get out of my way," Frederick ordered as he strode around the man and straight towards Amy.

"Wait." The thwarted man grabbed Frederick's arm and wheeled him back around.

"Stay the hell away from me!" Frederick jerked loose and pushed the man away.

The man caught his balance and advanced on Frederick, until they stood chest-to-chest, both poised to fight, like cocks posturing before a bout. Then he broke his stare-down with Frederick and glanced at Amy with a deep sadness in his eyes. A sadness at odds with the transparent hate darting from Amy's hazel and golden eyes. He turned and retreated into the startled crowd.

Frederick watched him. Then he saw how shocked his surrounding fellow boarders were. He also disappeared beyond the span of the disturbance into the morass of waiting passengers, his path to Amy abandoned.

"You know them?" I asked.

"Of course I do." Amy calmly eyed the ghost of their fight.

"How?"

"What?" Amy regarded me with a detached, artificial smile.

"How do you know them?"

"Who doesn't?" Amy said evasively. "Frederick Larsen and Mendel Weitzman They're Otto's legacy."

"Mendel Weitzman. I should have recognized him."

I caught a glimpse of the globetrotting womanizing tabloid-regular at the snack bar. He had regained his composure. As he waited to order, he tucked his cacao brown shirt back neatly into his tan slacks.

Mendel was a prolific thriller writer whose plots were driven by man's basest sexual appetites, purportedly mirroring his own. When it came to his characters' quests for sexual gratification, Mendel didn't discriminate as to gender, or any mixture thereof. He graphically satiated sequentially or concurrently each mainstream, deviant or criminal appetite. Two of his books were toned down and made into films, still rated "X." His fictional world was reflected in his parties, or vice versa, at his homes in New York, London, and the star-studded Malibu Colony on the beach north of Los Angeles.

Before I could ask Amy why they had pointed at her, the loudspeaker announced our boarding and detailed the procedures.

The mingling crowd immediately responded. It shifted and redeployed in accordance with the instructions toward the two wide entrances at the far side of the massive building. The cavernous space was shifting its density. Every inch at the entrances was swallowed-up by the passengers redeploying and herding to board.

When I turned back to Amy, she was making her way to the entrances and disappeared into the crowd.

As I stood contemplating the scene I had just witnessed, I felt a hard thump on my shoulder.

I spun around.

* * *

I was, regrettably, face-to-face with my classmate Agnes who was dressed in her usual wrinkle-free attire. This time it was new black pants and a black yellow polka dotted shirt. In class, her clothes were well worn and no longer wrinkle-free, yet still un-ironed, and she covered them with long, mismatched, obviously acrylic sweaters.

"Veronica! We found you. Did you see that fight between that nice Frederick Larsen and that horrible Mendel Weitzman?" Agnes slowly enunciated in her clear, elementary school teacher diction, inbred after twenty-five years.

Agnes, a big woman in her fifties, had married an Italian-American auto mechanic born and bred in San Pedro, California. Her great American novel was a generational saga about him and his big Italian-American family. Unsurprisingly,

38

it had a transparently false voice because she knew nothing about Italians, Catholicism, or the Italian-American experience. Agnes did nothing to make herself more attractive or charming. She was content with herself, her teacher persona, her relish of Italian food, and her usurpation of her Italian-American husband's life.

"Did you hear what it was about?" I asked.

"Yes, and . . ."

"I heard them." Agnes was interrupted when Jody rushed over." They were fighting about Otto Stein. Mendel accused Frederick Larsen of literally murdering Otto. Then Frederick laid into him."

"Frederick Larsen a murderer?" I was stunned. "No way."

As usual, Jody spoke with no social filters. She was too loud, too frank, and had no grace at all. Her social IQ was at the moronic level, yet her actual I.Q. was probably genius. But who would know?

"Jody is nuts. All I heard was Otto's name and curse words," Agnes corrected as any authoritative schoolteacher would. "No one actually accused anyone of murder."

"I heard the word murder," Jody insisted.

Jody was thin, tall, thirty-something, and always looked the same. She had a squeaky clean pale elongated face colored lightly with blush and rose lipstick. Her dark long hair was always pulled back in a low ponytail and her hazel eyes always seemed open just a little too wide as if she were continually surprised. For eight years in Mavis's classes, Jody had been writing the same frontier American coming of age novel for teenage girls. Her perfectionism pushed her into the pitfall of endlessly researching every aspect of the old American West. In my more experienced opinion, she should write about something she knows, like me, and get it done. At least get it finished, if not done, which most authors defined as edited and out. "Done" defined by me, was naturally just completing a first draft and then moving on and shelving it for later.

"Agnes is right," Herbert confirmed in his annoying tenor nasal voice as he joined the group. "Jody, your imagination is too ramped up. Take a Lude."

Herbert smirked, showing his yellow overlapping front teeth as he peered at me through his thick black rimmed glasses, which magnified his eyes to a bug-like immensity. Herbert's long dark hair that he swept over his balding head had fallen out of place. His powder blue polyester leisure suit had been mothballed from the sixties and his unbuttoned white shirt oozed dark chest hair over the first closed button

Herbert, an older retired stereotypical pocket-protector engineer, lived an isolated existence. He wrote about sado-masochistic murders with marginal grammar, the depth of a celibate, and cardboard characters. In class, when he read the graphic sexual torture scenes, he got aroused. He breathed heavily and his sweaty hands gripped the pages too tightly. I never laughed, but it took all my self-control. One young woman walked out of class during one of his readings and never returned.

I looked at all three of the stooges and believed they were fictionalizing what they had heard for self-aggrandizement. I, naturally, recognized the animal because I was not above doing the same and, indeed, frequently indulged myself.

Mavis suddenly popped out from among the passengers swirling around us toward the boarding gates with her carry-on trailing behind her.

"Veronica, glad you're here."

"Hello, Mavis," I gushed, ingratiating myself to the woman who had made all this possible. "Good flight?"

"Surprisingly, yes. This is exciting, isn't it?"

"And getting more so. Jody says she heard Mendel accuse Frederick Larsen of murdering Otto."

"Really? Well, I wouldn't repeat that." Mavis ended the topic. "But, what I would like to know is who was that woman talking to you? Frederick Larsen pointed at her."

"Oh?" I did not want to share or engage in anything with my classmates on this cruise.

"Well, who was she?" Agnes asked.

"Some agent."

"An agent?" Jody repeated. "Did you get her card? I could use it, too."

"No."

"Why not?"

"Relax. We're all on the same cruise, Jody, and I'm sure there are agents galore."

"That's right," Herbert added. "Just chill out. We haven't even boarded yet."

"Yes."

I agreed with Herbert. Jody could get a million agent's cards, but was never going to use them since her book would remain forever unfinished. She had the opposite problem as me. Researching and over-editing every paragraph of her ever on-going book because of her compulsive perfectionism. I did not want that lovely woman Amy to associate me with Jody's unfiltered, ungracious, very loud verbal spews.

"Now children, no squabbling. Let's board." Mavis moved our little stationary island into the flow of the passengers. "Passports out?"

Mavis had her teacher hat on. In class, she endlessly traded on earnest enthusiasm for all her students and their writings, even though some were obviously more flawed than others. Her professional knowledge and charm blended to attract eager novices and keep them coming back, like me.

I grabbed my carry-on and Mavis hers. We fell in step behind the three who looked around quietly, in awe of the scene.

Far ahead of us, beyond the long row of check in stations, Amy went through the arches at the end of the hall to board the ship. She did not stop with the other passengers to have her ritual pre-boarding picture taken.

At Agnes's urging, and over my objection, the five of us took a boarding picture together. I knew I would never buy a copy. Upon boarding we were greeted by crewmembers decked out in crisp white uniforms, who welcomed us with even crisper British accents.

Then, thankfully, Mavis and I were directed to our cabin, located in a different direction than Jody, Agnes, and Herbert's cabins.

* * *

Mavis and I coiled single file through the emerald green fleur-de-lis carpeted corridors, our carry-ons trailing. We passed streams of fellow travelers, some like us wheeling carry-ons behind them. Everyone's eyes ping-ponged from their printed room cards to the gold-colored room numbers next to the doors.

There was general silence amongst the lost. A few of the friendlier and less focused souls greeted us with excited eyes and quick hellos.

I spotted a uniformed *Queen Anne* someone and held up our printed room card.

"Do you know where our cabin is?"

"Stateroom, madam."

"Ah, stateroom. Yes. Where our stateroom is?"

He gave us passable guidance and we did find our stateroom—an economy cabin gilded in name only.

To our surprise, all of our luggage had been delivered.

"Sorry." Mavis put her carry-on in the corner. "I guess we didn't need our insurance."

"But we could have."

We unpacked. Mavis took a nap. I stood alone out on the green AstroTurf balcony. The New York skyline fading against the dusk enthralled me. I could hardly wait to see the Statue of Liberty as we cruised out of the harbor.

As I leaned on the varnished walnut balcony rail, I couldn't forget Frederick and Mendel's argument and the look on Amy's face. I recalled Frederick and Otto at the Academy Awards and the next night in class when Mavis reminded us to mention her if we got an Oscar. Short of that she wanted to be in our acknowledgments—yet I had written my acknowledgements and not given her a drop of ink!

But then, our teacher-student relationship had only morphed to more when I recently gained notoriety solving the well-publicized Hollywood Valentine Theatre murders. That harrowing and newsworthy event put me on the map, justified or not, as a promising mystery writer and amateur sleuth. It also upped my coinage in the movie industry's wingspan that hovered over the megalopolis that is Los Angeles. I became recognized, justified or not, as an amateur but excellent actress. I was suddenly connected not only to the theatre, but also to the film industry and several "industry" personages with star power.

From the balcony, the New York skyline began to sparkle. I sat on the chaise lounge to rest a minute.

On this elite writers' cruise I had to navigate carefully through the minefield of not being published. It did make me a fraud of sorts, but fortunately not to my hometown fans in Santa Monica. They admired me and, in my mind's eye, I was an author. My gift was being detached from today's reality and visualizing more—much more.

I am well known at home as a professional writer because I act like one. I have books in progress, which I talk about incessantly. I wear old jeans and write from the heart about people I know or, more often, don't know. And, of course, I regularly have a case of the dreaded writer's block. In fact, I spent hours with other morning sojourners at my local coffee place talking about a cure for it, nursing an overpriced paper-cupped decaf tea.

I commiserate woefully about my writer's block with artists, actors, entrepreneurs, retirees, and the chronically unemployed. They all "speak" writer's block in Santa Monica. Everyone planned to write or finish writing something someday: screen plays, books, television pilots, or wildly embellished memoirs of common lives.

But, in point of fact, I speak writer's block with the most authority of them all because I have overcome it repeatedly and heroically, as is demonstrated by my several unpublished books. I am popular and missed when I actually stay home and write—which is rare now.

Today, however, if I were at my coffee klatch, I would not have complained about writer's block. Instead, I would have shared in collective sorrow about Otto Stein's death. After all, I knew Mavis, a personal friend of this newsworthy icon, and I was a member of his pet club, the MWW. Whether an unpublished student guest member or not, I had paid my dues, for years.

All this cachet for my fellow "coffee klatchers" would have to await my return though. I was here to seize my destiny and Mavis's friendship.

My mind meandered back to Curtis and I fell into a deep sleep.

* * *

"Veronica, wake up." Mavis shook my shoulder. "We're passing the Statue of Liberty and look at New York lighting up the sky line!"

Mavis's dark eyes twinkled, her graying light brown hair bobbed along her shoulders, and her freckles bounced on her cheeks.

"We're on our way."

"We are?" I stood.

I was hazy from my deep sleep. But not hazy enough to fail to marvel at the skyline and the illuminated Statue of Liberty across the water in the quiet light after sunset and before dark.

"Pictures! We have to take pictures!" I ran in and got my state of the art smart phone.

We took pictures of each other in the foreground with the Statue of Liberty behind. As we did, I thought of my first beginner's writing class with Mavis years ago at the local college extension program. She was a roly-poly bundle of energy then, too. I memorized every gem she taught us.

"Cheese." I snapped a great shot of her.

I was here on this balcony with Mavis because of my new mini-celebrity status earned from the Hollywood Valentine Theatre murders. I didn't care that, in truth, I was only at the right place at the right time. An old college fellow thespian and director gave me a role when his actors began to die. That led to the sequence of events resulting in my solving the murders. I embraced the accolades and, of course, repeated my ever more embellished story—often.

I had parlayed my fifteen minutes of fame into months of glory. My social functions and speaking engagements multiplied—not only as a writer and crime aficionado but also as an actress of some note. And, more importantly, this popularity gave me endless excuses to avoid writing, editing, and publishing. I had a fabulous life without subjecting myself to that self-abusive risk of rejection.

The Valentine murders also made my website, an authorial requirement, more interesting than my favorite best selling author's. And now, I had added my *Queen Anne* cruise amongst the "biggies" in the writing world. My website was exciting and dynamic. Like me! Like my life!

I do emphatically protest if anyone discounts my life as based on untruths. It is not. It is founded, at the very least, on half-truths waiting to be fulfilled. I understand my life has an element of hopefulness the average person might envy, but rest assured it is not a house of cards. It is a map to my future as a mystery writer. It is the path I follow.

* * *

Mavis went back in to dress for dinner. I gazed at the lights of New York City diminishing in the distance. We were now a floating island unto ourselves crossing the Atlantic Ocean.

I was excited, focused on my MWW companions and rubbing elbows with the best in the world. To me this was better than making it in New York City. It was making it in the worldwide writing arena, now afloat for five glorious days.

I rushed in and dressed for dinner—my first one with my new colleagues.

I regretted never publishing. I could have gone indie and self-published an e-book on Octopus Books. It was the steroid ramped-up near monopolist for e-book self-publishing that was appropriating ever more royalties from authors. But it was the only real game in town—anti-trust violator or not. It just looked like too much work to me though: formatting, browsing, downloading, creating covers, choosing fonts, marketing my own material on dot coms or social networks—Booksie, Nooksie, Facebook, Twitter, and whatever other permutations there were for the disconnected to connect, at minimum, with a cyber life.

What did I know about any of that? Besides, I had heard authors made a pittance while Octopus Books made millions.

Nonetheless, in my mind's eye, I am what I believe myself to be—an author—an author about to have dinner with my new colleagues.

⌘

CHAPTER 7

Table for Ten

Mavis and I headed out early in search of the dining room for our eight o'clock dinner seating. I was hungry, but that was secondary to my excitement at meeting our table full of possibly famous professional writers—our dinner companions for the entire cruise. I thought of my table assignment in my evening bag as a lottery ticket. However, if Helga were seated at our table, she would be the booby prize, world-renowned or not.

On the way to dinner, we met several wandering hordes of hungry passengers also searching for the dining room for the first time. Confused, excited, dressed to the nines, and mostly charming, we all chattered our way in the right direction. I was surprised at the large British and European contingents. I recognized them only by their array of accents ranging from upper-class British to working-class Cockney, and from German to French to Italian.

An older, modestly dressed Scottish couple joined us in our elevator quest.

"Good evening." The man nodded with formality and spoke with the unmistakable Scottish brogue of his people.

The wife didn't speak. He had done their duties.

"Good evening," we replied in unison.

I enjoyed the Scottish-ness of him. The Scots were a proud people and were offended if you called them Brits. After a bloody history, by the Act of Union in 1707 England took Scotland's parliament and self-rule away. But the Scots remained fiercely Scottish if conflicted, with a last violent gasp in the Jacobite Rebellion in support of "Bonnie Prince Charlie", which failed in the bloody battle of Culloden in 1746. After centuries, in 1999 they got their own parliament, for domestic matters only, yet still took an oath of allegiance to the British Crown. They were still ruled by Westminster for UK-wide-issues. In 2014 they volitionally voted to stay in the UK. The economic strings that tied them to the UK could not be ignored and corporate propaganda, an uneducated youth, dependence on the dole, rewritten history, and ignorance of their great heritage had diluted their fierce pride.

As the Scot held the elevator door for his wife and the rest of us, I flashed back to my husband and how much had changed since his passing. I had begun my authorial life to fill a void in the early morning hours when I was alone except for my television. For a time, too long a time, I joined the brain-atrophied populace in channel surfing, looking for something to care about in its transparent pabulum. I made the home shopping salespeople my buddies, talked to newscasters like they were friends, and slid into the world of old movies and television series. But no more, and this cruise was testimony to my new, improved way of living.

* * *

By the time we found our way through the ship, Mavis and I were no longer early.

We got off the elevator and saw a loosely organized line waiting for the eight o'clock dinner seating. The head of the line was up a majestic walnut paneled staircase leading to the dining room entrance. The line extended down it into a wide hall carpeted in emerald green. It was color coordinated with the fleur-de-lis in our "stateroom" corridors.

The Scots queued quickly, as was their national custom. We made our way to the end with the moans of American impatience.

The line buzzed with conversations and friendly introductions. The men were either in dark suits or tuxedos. The women wore short or long evening dresses or evening pants, many sparkling with sequins, beads, or rhinestones. Everyone's faces shone with expectation.

This MWW cruise was the most coveted event in the mystery writer's realm. During the five day trans-Atlantic crossing all the big name writers, agents, and publishers participated in daily programs, panel discussions, and presentations. Every mover and shaker in the mystery world was headlined, including film and television producers and writers in the "industry." Networking was the order of the day. Deals were made and careers launched.

Plus, I had to admit Otto's murder added to my interest, and I looked forward to being in the hubbub about it, too. I would be a part of Otto's memorial and mingle with his graduates who undoubtedly would have thoughts on his murder, solved or otherwise by then.

Mavis's long beige dress was perfect and so was my simple but elegant mid-calf black silk dress with a long sleeved, waist-length jacket.

"Here we are," Mavis announced, very teacher-like. "This is the end. Long way up there, isn't it?"

"We'll get there." I looked at the flood of passengers now behind us. "Do you know who is seated at our table?

"No, it's been . . ."

Mavis stopped abruptly.

"What?" I turned back to her.

To my surprise, Curtis was standing with us. He looked even taller and more handsome than he had this afternoon in his black tuxedo with a forest green cummerbund and tie.

Mavis stood silently, gawking.

"Veronica." Curtis smiled down at me. "May I join you?"

"Of course!" I instantly self-edited my excessive enthusiasm. "I'd like you to meet my stateroom mate and friend, Mavis Osborne."

I was so happy he had made the first move after taking leave of me at the transport van.

Mavis fluttered her eyes and in an unfamiliar girlish voice oozed, "Hello. I'm pleased to meet you. Are you with us? I mean do you write also?"

"No. Nothing so exciting. I'm giving a series of financial seminars."

"Oh? You're a professor then?"

"No." Curtis smiled with his winning smile. "I'm a financial advisor with American Financial Management."

"I've heard of that," Mavis syruped. "It's quite famous."

"I'm sailing with clients. Doing seminars. Business getting."

"How interesting." Mavis beamed. "Can we attend?"

"Of course, you both would add glamor to our little group." Curtis exuded chivalry and charm. "Plan on it."

"Wonderful."

"Yes. Wonderful," I echoed. I was disgusted with Mavis's palpable purring motor that was obvious, uninvited, and uninviting. "Where's your roommate?"

"I don't have one. I have to work."

51

"Oh?" I wished I didn't have this roommate interruptus, either, at this moment of expectant anticipations and possibilities.

But Mavis would not take her eyes off Curtis. Her eyelashes kept batting and she kept chatting about herself and the MWW.

I was more than annoyed.

* * *

The line moved quickly and efficiently. We finally reached the head of the line at the top of a mahogany staircase. We waited on the large landing overlooking the breathtakingly expansive dining room.

Too bad it didn't take Mavis's breath away. Mavis was still monologuing to Curtis about herself and her mysteries. Each of her books sounded like a literary masterpiece on the level of Joyce Carol Oates. Not! I had read a few of Mavis's "whodunnits" and I had never even finished her last one. Unfortunately, I knew who "dunnit" far too early in the book, and she had no strong character to hold my interest. Mavis made money with her books because they were pabulum for lonely elderly ladies. However, I did admire her immediate skill in redirecting all of Curtis's attentions from me to herself. I would have to be more careful of this pseudo-femme fatale.

At present, there was no upside in interrupting Mavis and vying for Curtis's attention. It was a done deal that would end with our parting for our own dinner tables. But it was an object lesson: keep Mavis at arm's length where interesting males were concerned—not that I considered her serious competition with her age-associated matronly shortcomings. But she was a gnat I had to swat.

* * *

52

On the landing, as Mavis noised on, I was in awe at the dining room below.

The main floor was polka-dotted with large round white-linen covered tables. They were amply spaced and popped out on the background of the green and cranberry herringbone carpet. Each table of ten was already filling with animated diners. The perimeter had two upper tiers with rectangular tables. All the tables had multi-colored rose centerpieces encircled by place settings of sparkling white china, silver flatware, and simple elegant stemware. Above it all, in the center of the gold leaf sculpted ceiling was an immense sparkling crystal chandelier.

When our turn came, a silver-haired, quite charming, and pleasantly portly maître d' greeted us with a highbrow British accent, just as he had the couple before.

"Good evening. I would like to personally welcome you to the *Queen Anne* and our exquisite dining experience. We'll escort you to your assigned table this evening."

Then quickly and efficiently, white-coated servers stepped forward to inspect our seating cards. The couple behind us did not have cards, but the maître d' found them quickly on the tablet he carried.

As Curtis started to follow his server, he turned back to me, leaned over, and whispered, "Would you like to have a nightcap later?"

"Sure." I was audibly calm, but my heart jumped.

"The main bar by the casino after dinner?"

"I'll join you there."

I watched him going down the sister mahogany staircase inside the dining room to the main floor.

A hesitant young woman in a black skirt and starched white coat then took Mavis and me to the right. She led Mavis single file up the narrow stairs to the mezzanine level. I trailed after them, disappointed at not going to the main floor. We wound through the mezzanine with its tables for two or four, and some for eight, abutted to the wall with four chairs on each side, ill-configured for true sociability.

When we reached the end of the mezzanine, the server stopped and talked to a white-coated older man. He pointed down to the main floor. We followed her and she followed the direction of his point down a flight of steps.

"Good," I murmured, anticipating being deposited on the main floor.

We wound past several tables now filled with elegantly dressed diners. They were smiling and introducing themselves to their tablemates and dining companions for the five-day sail across the Atlantic.

I held my breath as we walked by Agnes, Jody, and Herbert seated at their table. As we thankfully passed by the few empty seats there, Agnes, making mileage as usual, was talking about her husband's big Italian family. Her dining companions were actually engrossed. I was happy for her that she had a good shtick going for a couple of dinners.

Agnes caught my eye, waved, and called, "Yoo-hoo! Yoo-hoo!"

Because of her twenty-five years of teaching, elementary school behavior infused her every action. I nodded in recognition to shut her up and kept walking. That acknowledgment satisfied Agnes and she turned her attention back to her table. I knew they would eventually get tired of her prattle, but then they were a captive audience for five nights unless they chose room service or the cafeteria.

Ahead, Amy was at a table seated across from Mary O'Connell and near our MWW president Esther Nussbaum. Esther was diminutive and her impeccable shoulder length blond hair sparkled, incongruously youthful around her late-forties face. I had never met her, but recognized her from MWW newsletter pictures.

At that table, Mendel stood behind the empty chair between Amy and Esther commanding everyone's attention with a bombastic speech. He was swaying, but it wasn't from the ship's movement. The *Queen Anne* was sailing as smoothly as Brent told Helga it would. The empty Martini glass in Mendel's hand flaunted the reason for his instability.

I noted that even his tuxedo could not make this man attractive or taller. Energetic charisma? I gave him that, but that was all. The entire table enjoyed his story, whatever it was. I observed him as he swept back his receding, graying sandy brown hair. He picked up a fresh, green-olived Martini from near Amy's wine glass and took a drink.

As we passed, he lifted his Martini and gestured sloppily with it as he orated. He then lifted it higher in a toast.

"And that was the Otto I knew and hated!" Mendel proclaimed with his raised glass sloshing Martini down onto the table. "May the marvelous bastard rest in peace."

Everyone at the table laughed uproariously, everyone but Amy who glared up at him. Mendel took another drink of his now halved Martini, popped the olive in his mouth, and signaled the waiter for another.

"Your table." Our guide redirected my attention.

* * *

My hope was fulfilled. Our table for ten was on the main floor amongst the elite. It was near Amy and Esther, but strategically away from my classmates. The table already had four diners and one of them was Elias. I was delighted. I was even more delighted when I noticed Curtis at an adjacent table. It was populated with attractive, animated elderly couples.

He nodded at me. I nodded back.

As the guide left us, Mavis scanned the four diners already seated. She sat with a portly tuxedoed man who she chatted up immediately, as she had Curtis. I took Mavis's cue and deserted her for Elias. I knew I enjoyed him and would the entire cruise. Also, I didn't want to risk the roulette wheel of seating with unknowns.

I put my napkin on my lap decisively. I had also chosen that seat with a secondary objective in mind. It had a direct line of sight at Curtis.

I thought "out of sight, out of mind" and I did not want to be out of Curtis's mind's eye—even for a second.

CHAPTER 8

Almost All Present and Accounted For

"Veronica!" Elias boomed. "How wonderful. We have to stop meeting like this."

"Never." I bantered.

I was proud that this pillar of mystery writing was vetting me to the group.

"I'm so glad to see you again." I milked the moment.

Mavis eyed us and eavesdropped on our jovial and familiar interchange. She scrutinized me quizzically, obviously curious, surprised, and I believed envious at my connection with this nationally known writer.

"We are going to have a fun table." Elias leaned toward Mavis. "And you are?"

"Oh?" I was gratified to be the one making the collegial introductions. "Elias Vlisides, this is my friend, author Mavis Osborne."

"Hello." Mavis was obviously thrilled to meet Elias. "I loved your *Tiropita Triple Homicide*."

"Thank you." Elias ate up the recognition. "And I certainly recognize your name. Nice to meet you."

I knew full well Elias was lying. He didn't recognize Mavis at all because he didn't mention any of her books by name. That would have been the standard-and-proper acknowledgment decorum with writer-on-writer introductions, but only if he actually knew of Mavis and her works.

"Let me introduce both of you to our other dinner companions." Elias moved on quickly to cover his lack of Mavis-publication knowledge. "Everyone, this is Veronica Kennicott and her friend Mavis Osborne."

The three other seated diners turned their attention to us. I was ecstatic that Elias introduced me first and then referred to Mavis as my friend, instead of the other way around. I momentarily felt like a professional writer—an author-in-print amongst the same—or, at least, an indie e-book author in the distribution chain.

"This is Anne Thomas, British mystery writer extraordinaire from Bath." Elias referred to the elderly woman on his other side.

"Good evening. Nice to meet both of you. It's going to be a lovely cruise."

Anne had a refined and upper-crust British accent. She was a small, thin woman with gray unruly short hair and sparkling blue eyes that matched her blue evening dress with blue beads sewn around the collar. I recognized her immediately from her book jackets. Her famous international best-selling British murder mysteries were based on gardening themes. I had read *Pushing Up Daisies*, *Under the Roses*, and *Splitting the Agapanthus*. It was her humor that made them so saleable.

"And next to Anne is Heather Edison, an Otto alumna. Science fiction now, but looking at changing to one of us because we are more fun." Elias gestured to the striking beauty next to Anne.

Heather smiled at both of us with shimmering pink glossed lips. Her long straight natural blond hair hung like pale silk over her pure white skin that had a touch of blush on her high cheekbones. Long dark luxurious lashes framed her round, deep sapphire-blue eyes. I didn't read science fiction, but I did recognize her name. She was touted as a brilliant, creative science fiction writer. I was curious as to why she was interested in mystery writing, but perhaps she had simply run out of science fiction plots. I had days to find out.

Elias then turned and introduced me to the man Mavis had chosen to chat up.

"And this is Sean O'Flarity . . . a former NYPD homicide detective who immediately started writing his mystery books when he retired. Once a novice, but now the premier, most authentic detective writer on the scene."

Sean O'Flarity wore a tuxedo, wrinkled from his un-artful packing. He held his napkin in one hand, stood, and reached across Mavis with the other to shake my hand. When he stood, he exposed his paunchy white-shirted belly spilling over his displaced black cummerbund. He had an aged but not unattractive square, wrinkled face with reddish hair and graying temples.

"Hello. Any friend of Elias's is a friend of mine." He shook my hand vigorously.

I was pleased that he regarded me as a friend of Elias. I also noted the phrase "once a novice" Elias had chosen for him. I knew Sean actually had achieved instant success when he came on the scene with writing as a second career and, interestingly, from a non-writing background. I had read one of his books. It was a good plot driven man's man book that apparently women loved, too. I hoped his success story would take the attention off my unpublished status. It had certainly attracted Mavis. I understood her choice of seats now.

I shook Sean's large but gentle hand. His greenish blue eyes were sparkling and his cheeks were red. I surmised he had been celebrating the voyage even before we sailed by the Statue of Liberty.

"Mavis and I already introduced ourselves." Sean reseated himself, jostling the table.

"Well, it looks like we have Frederick Larsen, our Academy Award winner, joining us too." Elias observed Frederick approaching our table led by the same white-coated young lady who had escorted Mavis and me. "He always has wonderful stories. And, he will have useful advice for our transitioning science fiction lady."

Heather smiled. "Good."

I was right. I would escape focus, at least for now.

Elias was pleased with his role as unofficial host and, after Frederick was seated, he began introductions yet again. He appeared to enjoy it.

First, Sean, the detective-turned-writer, and then Mavis.

"Pleased to meet you," Mavis oozed as she stretched her hand across the table.

"A pleasure." Frederick touched Mavis's hand politely but briefly.

Frederick was very Hollywood in his tux. He had a pink cummerbund and his shirt, *sans* bow tie, had three buttons open, exposing his impeccably waxed chest. In my mind, he surpassed his glamorous tabloid pictures at the grocery checkout.

"Pleased to see you again," I volunteered, knowing my familiar greeting choice would elicit more envy and curiosity from Mavis. From the look on her face, it did.

"Nice to see you again, Veronica." Frederick was relieved to be extricated from Mavis's gawking. "And, I am acquainted with everyone else, I think".

Frederick nodded across the table at the other dining companions, who uttered a smattering of cheery greetings.

When Frederick's ice blue translucent eyes got to Heather seated one chair over, they stopped. "Everyone but this charming lady."

"Heather Edison," Elias chimed in immediately, again in his happy-host role. "Science fiction."

"Interesting." Frederick extended his hand and took Heather's, gently shaking it and then holding on long after the ritual ceased. "And why would a science fiction writer be here with us mere mystery mortals?"

Everyone at the table laughed. Frederick was charming.

"I'm incorporating mystery into my science fiction, actually."

"Really?" Frederick encouraged her.

"I think it's a fresh idea. I've started a series that I think is unique, but I'm here to learn and I was going to meet with . . ."

"Me?" Frederick volunteered, still holding her hand and grinning. "I'll tell you right now I think there is real money there . . . think film rights. Have you sold any film rights for your science fiction books yet?"

"No." Heather smiled awkwardly, looking at her entrapped hand. "I haven't yet, but Otto wanted me to come on the cruise. He had contacted me about . . ."

"Otto?" The smile dropped from Frederick's face.

"Yes, I'm an alumna. We were in touch again."

"Really?"

"Yes, we had been talking about my new series. In fact, the evening he died he said he'd help me with the film rights for my other books here . . . on the cruise."

61

"I'm sure he did." Frederick grinned lecherously. "Poor man. But don't worry, I can step in. I can show you the ropes better than Otto ever could have. After all, I'm in the industry. We'll have a drink later and . . ."

Suddenly, Mendel staggered up, knocking Heather and Frederick apart and freeing Heather's hand. He reached for the empty chair between them.

"My seat."

Mendel grabbed the chair for balance as his Martini slopped over.

If looks could kill, Frederick's would have put Mendel in his grave.

Barely visible and to my observation unnoticed by all but me, Heather wiped her now Frederick-tainted and Mendel-Martini-covered hand with her linen napkin.

Who could blame the young woman?

⌘

CHAPTER 9

Grated Expectations

"Greetings all." Mendel saluted everyone with his Martini and then downed his last drop.

As I watched his antics, I noticed Amy in the background at her table. Her eyes were riveted on Mendel with the same intensity I had seen at boarding. She didn't stop glaring until Esther turned and chatted her up.

Insensible to his spectacle, Mendel pulled out his chair and sat down, causing the water glasses to imitate a tsunami as he bumped the table.

"Careful, buddy." Sean steadied the table.

"I'm back, my dear Heather." Mendel ignored Sean and ogled Heather with his dark eyes. "Would you like a Martini? I have another coming."

Mendel glanced around to see where his fresh Martini was. It wasn't. Yet. He refocused on Heather, putting his arm on the back of her chair and leaning his face into hers. His eyes overtly perused down the neckline of her black evening dress.

It was cut high enough that it should not have invited such transparent lechery, but for the fact Mendel was Mendel.

"And we have new dining companions who you may not know, Mendel." Elias diplomatically gestured to Mavis and me, attempting a rescue of Heather in the process. "Mavis Osborne and Veronica Kennicott. Fellow mystery writers."

"Nice to meet both of you."

Mendel nodded at us quickly. He then turned back to Heather and whispered something in her ear that made her pale face flush pink.

"And so." Sean turned to me. "What is your forte in this mysterious group of authors extraordinaire?"

"My latest is about a theatre murder." I gauged how to dodge the inevitable publication issue. "And the . . ."

I stopped mid-sentence as Helga was deposited at our table with Brent in tow.

"I'm Helga. And this is my husband Brent." Helga announced perfunctorily, presuming everyone knew who she was and, obviously, not caring who anyone else was.

"Nice you are joining us," Elias lied.

Mavis made the error of attempting to introduce herself.

"Yes, I'm sure you are," Helga grunted without even a glance in Mavis's direction.

It was hideous seeing Helga at our table, but it was not hideous being interrupted. I was not up for the not-in-the-bookstore sidestep with Sean or any of the others.

"Good evening. We're pleased to join you." Brent held Helga's chair and then took his own.

"You need no introduction, Helga." Elias fed the insatiable Helga the recognition her ego demanded for the good of the order.

I had deduced in the short time I had known him that Elias read people well and was adept at giving them exactly what they needed and wanted. Elias, wanting to give the table its due, quickly went around the circle with all of our names. Helga settled her napkin on her lap and ignored Elias, but Brent dutifully greeted each person in turn.

When Elias came to Heather, Brent's face lit up.

"I've read all of your books. They are wonderful," Brent flattered. "Really original science fiction." Heather blushed. "Thank you. I'm . . ."

"But what are you doing here amongst us earthbound mystery writers?" Helga snapped.

"She beamed in to spy on us," Mendel interloped, laughing alone at his own joke.

"She's creating a niche for herself blending science fiction with mystery," Elias observed. "She's brilliant. And, if this book series is as good as her science fiction, she's on her way to our MWW award for best book of the year next year. But now, with Otto's untimely passing . . ."

"It's been done before and ridiculously so." Helga's dark, heavily lined eyes glared at Heather with an intensity that could have bored through steel. "Otto was just a dirty old man who wanted a toy on the cruise."

Brent opened his menu and retreated to its neutral safety, unwilling to challenge his wife.

Heather sat, nonplussed and open-mouthed.

After a moment of awkward silence, Elias commented on the good weather for our launching from New York and Anne joined in with a stiff upper lip.

I dreaded being subjected to Helga's theatrics and marital discord every night, at every dinner. Any hopes I had that her transport van horrors were an aberration were dashed. I was relieved when Helga engaged Frederick in a dialogue with a pleasant smile on her face, congratulating him on his Oscar. At least she left us alone.

I quietly studied Amy's prestigious and sedate table for a moment. A server delivered a Martini to Amy; presumptively the one Mendel was seeking. I would have been delighted to be seated at that table, but here I was. Then, I observed Curtis at his table, engrossed and animated. I fantasized sitting next to him. As I scanned my table once again though, I was satisfied. I just wished Helga would fall overboard. However, given that wouldn't happen, I planned on flying under the radar and staying out of her crosshairs.

My eyes rested on Mendel and the uncomfortable Heather. Beyond, I saw Amy call a server over. She had the fresh, green-olived Martini sent over to our table.

The server brought it over on a small tray. He quietly placed the Martini near Frederick, who was engrossed in Helga's flattery. During a break in the ego-stroking dialogue, Frederick picked it up.

"Hey, Mendel, I think this is yours."

"About time. Pass it over."

"Sorry, sir." Our head server signaled to his assistant.

The assistant scurried and carried it on a tray to Mendel. Mendel grabbed it off the tray over Heather's head.

"You're spilling." Heather wiped her hair with her napkin.

"Oops." Mendel stroked Heather's long hair feigning to help. "Soft. Natural blond?"

"Please, don't."

"She's fine." Anne zeroed in on Mendel with the evil eye of a protective matron.

Mendel ignored Anne, but did stop stroking Heather's hair—only to take a drink of his Martini. He then popped the olive in his mouth. As he chewed loudly and open-mouthed, he asked Heather about her writing.

Before Heather could answer, Helga asserted her dominance. She called across the table and interrupted Mendel's *tête-a-tête*.

"So, Mendel, what are your thoughts about who bludgeoned old Otto to death? That is, if you can tear yourself away from Otto's leftovers."

Heather blushed and looked down.

Mendel's head swiveled in Helga's direction. He took another drink of his Martini.

"To anyone with half a wit, it's obvious that old letch was the victim of an angry woman. A woman who was good at batting practice." Mendel laughed, took a slurp of his Martini, and then gave his full attention back to Heather.

"Well, if anyone would know, it would be you." Helga's pointed and blunt character attack did not draw Mendel's attention away from Heather.

"Once a womanizer, always a womanizer. Right, Mendel?" Frederick validated Helga's comment and then looked at Heather. "Careful, young lady."

"Still beating the same old drum I see, Frederick." Mendel snickered and then stood and held his Martini up to toast.

"Here's to the two time Academy Award winner, the great Frederick Larsen, who persists in throwing stones even though he lives in a glass house . . . a glass house of debauchery."

Mendel drank to his toast. No one else raised a glass.

"You son of a . . ." Frederick jumped from his chair and leaned into the table at least a head higher than Mendel.

"Hold it, guys."

Brent stood imposingly to stop the combat, verbal or otherwise. He dwarfed Mendel and more than equaled Frederick in height and size.

"You can do this later, gentlemen. Let's enjoy the evening."

I saw the dominating, raw power of male size and youth cowing both of the other men. I also saw the surrounding tables, including Curtis's and Anne's, shocked at the impending combat.

"Yes, the menu looks lovely." Anne encouraged civility amongst the well-decked out rabble that was our table.

"Someday I'm going to . . ." Frederick muttered settling into his chair again.

"What?" Mendel laughed and flopped back into his chair, sloshing his Martini on himself.

"Let me order some wine for the table. My treat." Elias offered, glancing at the fellow diners eyeing our table. "First night and all."

"I'll do the second day," Sean volunteered.

"Elias and Sean, that's too kind of both of you." Anne acknowledged in her British accent. "I'll get it the day after tomorrow."

"Count me in for the fourth," I said.

"I'll split the fourth night with Veronica," Mavis joined in, obviously not wanting to be out done, but also not wanting to do more than half since she could have volunteered for the fifth day.

"Give me the fifth by myself." Helga glanced pointedly at Mavis. "I don't need to split it."

Mavis buried her head in her menu.

"The fifth is the banquet." Elias said.

"Well, I'm off the hook." Helga laughed and Brent parroted her on cue.

The tension dissipated and the surrounding diners went back to their own conversations at their tables. Elias had rehabilitated the moment.

Our table's attention turned to the menus with *Queen Anne* beautifully printed in gold on the maroon faux leather covers.

* * *

As I opened the menu, I decided I was just as happy that Mavis had spoken up to share the fourth wine night. It would be expensive from the looks of our already too-lubricated table. Elias did as promised and the wine flowed readily.

I studied the pages inserted with tonight's menu. I was overwhelmed at the gourmet selections. Each of the four courses had three individual five-star gastronomical dishes described in detail. One selection of each course had a small red heart next to it, footnoted with the words "Heart Healthy." I naturally ignored those. I hadn't lost my extra pounds to engage in anything healthy on this sailing to the U.K.

Time motivated us as the server pushed for our orders. I decided on the wild mushroom Brie en croute to start and then the arugula and pear salad with mascarpone and toasted walnuts. For my main course I got the beef Wellington with roasted vegetables, and finally two desserts. Why not? I couldn't decide between the lemon tart or the coconut ice cream with a chocolate raspberry cookie. And why should I choose? It was all free! Well, it was all included in the price of the cruise, that is.

After we ordered, the conversation flowed as the server brought a lovely basket with a variety of rolls, seeded flat crackers, and interesting thick cheese-drizzled bread sticks. I took a bread stick and a dark seeded roll and passed it on. After I poured olive oil and balsamic vinegar on my bread plate, I passed them on also. Only Sean reached for the butter.

Helga passed on the carbs, literally, as she listened to Frederick's pitch to write the screenplay of her latest book. Her pale pancaked face crinkled in a pleased smile. Her dark eyes riveted on Frederick, crayoned bolder with black liner for the evening, sparkling with expectation and lust.

When Mendel got the basket, he set his depleted Martini down and the basket on his plate. Then, he rested his elbows on the table and leaned forward holding his head.

"Mendel, I want the bread." Frederick glanced over from his pitch. "We haven't eaten all day. Pass it on."

"Neither have I. So . . . just back off, you son of a . . ." Mendel glared glassy-eyed across at Frederick.

I expected an escalation to hand-on-hand combat when Mendel stood up, knocking his chair back onto the floor. But instead, he swayed and held onto the table for balance.

"I . . . don't feel good. I need to . . . lie down. I'll just . . ."

Mendel abruptly turned his back to us. He side-winded haltingly toward the dining room stairway knocking into the backs of diners' chairs.

"Shouldn't someone help him?" I asked as we all watched the Mendel spectacle.

"He can handle it. It's his thing," Frederick scoffed and then turned back to Helga. "Your books do lend themselves to the screen. You write almost like a screenwriter anyway. Your books are exciting."

"You think so?" Helga purred.

"I think I should help Mendel out." Brent volunteered. "He looks . . ."

"Forget it," Helga's blood red lipsticked mouth barked as she swept back her black hair with her diamond-laden fingers tipped with long red nails. She leaned forward and ignored Brent seated between them. She smiled invitingly at Frederick. Frederick smiled back, but less invitingly.

"The dining room is lovely, isn't it?" Anne initiated civil conversation.

"Yes, it is. I remember . . ." Elias was stopped short in his response.

Suddenly, screams exploded and dishes clattered near the mahogany stairs at the dining room entrance. I turned to see Mendel sprawled on a large round table between a man and a woman, crushing plates of salads and jettisoning glasses of wine and water.

One woman shrieked and the man next to her pushed Mendel off the table.

As Mendel flopped to the floor, he held onto the tablecloth, dragging the ten place settings, food, and drinks with him to the floor.

The elegantly dressed, wine-spattered women at the imploding table cried out. The tuxedoed men grabbed them off to safety.

⌘

CHAPTER 10

Boozeterism

The dining room rang with chaos. Passengers stood, spectated, and opined. Some ran over and joined in the cacophony of distress and confusion. Servers at each table tried to quiet the passengers and asked them to remain seated. Most didn't.

Amy got up from her table and ran to Mendel splayed on the floor. Esther followed and the less sprightly Mary O'Connell brought up the rear. She trotted along in her sensible shoes with her graying bun bouncing at the nape of her neck.

"Go help." Helga elbowed Brent.

"Let's go!" Brent echoed to Frederick.

Mavis got up instantaneously. She came over and tapped my shoulder from behind. "Come on. Let's help Esther."

I followed Mavis, who trailed behind Frederick and Brent. If she wanted to ingratiate herself with Esther with my help, I didn't mind. It looked exciting.

Curtis got up from his table and intercepted me. "Need help?"

"Yes. That's Mendel Weitzman, the author. He's in our group and he's had a little too much."

"No kidding! Let me help you out."

Curtis took my arm and wove through the unseated, unsettled gawkers behind Mavis.

* * *

When we three reached the scene, we had to elbow our way through the encircled passengers. At the core of the muddle of humanity, two male servers stood over Mendel doing nothing.

"Oh, my God." I looked at Curtis. "He's out cold."

"He sure is. Small guys can't hold their liquor."

Apparently, the male ego was ceaseless, endless, and ever ready to rear up. I excused Curtis and every male that particular unfettered, transparent, and usually ill-timed privilege. I had concluded years ago that men had no idea how silly they sounded; how "elementary-school-playground-rewind" their behavior patterns were.

"Of course," I agreed, but then I would agree with anything Curtis said—or almost anything.

Curtis was pleased with my validation. I was pleased that he was pleased.

I turned my attention back to Mendel lying on his back on the herringbone carpet. He was spattered with wine and a touch of salad. Esther leaned over him. Amy announced to everyone within earshot the number of Martinis Mendel had downed.

"Make sure his airway is clear," Mary yelled in her shrill voice as she pushed the man in front of her aside. "Once the airway is gone, it's over. I've slashed enough of them to know."

There were gasps through the gathering crowd.

"In my books. Slashed in my books." Mary shook her head, causing her double chin to undulate. "I'm an author."

Just then from behind, I felt a hand on my shoulder. I turned and was eye to eye with a steely gray-eyed, gray-haired man in an officer's white dress uniform. He was pasty white with a receding chin.

"Stand aside. I'm the chief doctor," he commanded with a well-heeled British accent and strong whiskey breath. "Let me have a look. I'll sort this out."

With some balancing difficulties of his own, the doctor knelt over Mendel and examined him.

"He's drunk," Amy volunteered to the doctor. "I saw him downing Martinis at my table."

"Yes, me too," Esther echoed critically.

"Ah, Martinis," the doctor repeated barely moving his lips to form his posh British accent. "They get the job done."

"Mendel never could hold his liquor," Frederick broadcasted over the doctor.

"Mendel?" The doctor quizzed Frederick.

"Yes . . . Mendel Weitzman. The author. Or should I say washed up author and asshole."

"Ah! I thought I recognized him. The globetrotter extraordinaire. But, evidently, not as extraordinary as his reputation would dictate."

The doctor studied Mendel as if he were a priceless work of art. Then, he observed the crowd leaning over him. He blatantly took time to relish the cleavage bursting from the evening dresses of the female observers. By upper crust public school British standards his present shipboard work-a-day job would dictate that he was a failure amongst his class.

"How is he, doctor?" One ample bosomed, middle-aged, striking woman batted her eyes at him.

The doctor stood, balance-challenged again, straightened his uniform and gave his undivided attention to the inquiring woman.

"Don't worry. I'll attend to him. Miss?"

"Mrs. Gwendolyn Chertoff. Gwendolyn."

"Of course." The doctor was visibly unenthused once the word "Mrs." popped off the woman's tongue. "You should go back to your table, Madame."

The doctor turned to the crowd and definitively announced his diagnosis.

"Ladies and Gentlemen, this man has simply had one too many. Don't worry. We'll take care of him. Go back to your dinners . . . please." The doctor turned to the servers close by. "Get these people seated. You two, come here. Get his stateroom number and get him back there to sleep it off. He's sloshed."

I whispered to Mavis, "It takes one to know one."

"What a mess," Mavis replied. "I hope Mendel can do his panel discussion tomorrow morning."

As the crowd ignored the dispersal orders, the maître d' ran up. "Sorry, doctor. I just heard."

"Nothing wrong. Just the usual. Trollied. We are getting him to his stateroom."

"Ah. Well, good. And I'll sort this out." The maître d' turned to supervise the cleanup.

"Are you sure he's just drunk?" Brent asked the doctor.

"Yes, I'm sure he's sloshed. I'm a ship's doctor. I'm experienced."

"Yes, obviously." Brent waved the doctor's whiskey breath away. "But he's white as a sheet. I'm concerned. Shouldn't he be flushed?"

"I think you're right," Mary agreed.

The doctor ignored both Brent and Mary.

I looked down at Mendel. "Now that you mention it . . . look at his jaw. It's twitching, isn't it?"

Brent leaned over and studied Mendel's face. "It is."

"Curious," Mary leaned in too. "I've read about that before. But I can't quite place it . . ."

"Back to your seats, people. The man can't hold his liquor. That's all," the doctor barked, enjoying his authority and especially the wide-eyed, well-endowed women watching him exercise it.

Several people standing around chuckled. Few left. One man took out his phone and started to videotape Mendel on the floor.

"That man's taking a video on his phone." Esther alerted the doctor and stepped forward to block the recording.

"What?" The doctor whirled around, unstable, but still in charge. "Sir, get back to your seat."

"Who's with Mr. Weitzman?" The doctor called out.

"I guess we are," Frederick replied.

"You'd better get him to his room now to sleep this off."

"Shouldn't he go to the infirmary?" I asked the doctor. "He looks awful."

"I'm not going to wet-nurse a man all night who simply doesn't know his limits. My nurse and I would spend all our nights with sloshed passengers in sickbay. This is a cruise ship, not a nursery."

Amy looked at me. "Don't worry. He's been this way since I've known him. He'll sleep it off."

"So you do know him?"

Amy ignored my question.

* * *

The white-coated server who went to get Mendel's room number made his way back through the crowd. He whispered Mendel's stateroom number to the doctor.

"Let's get him to his room," the doctor commanded.

"But . . ." I still thought Mendel looked ill.

"He has a steward," Amy cut me off. "He'll just have to leave a bigger tip."

"He can afford it." Frederick smirked. "Besides AA is the only thing that can help him."

Amy looked at Frederick. "Get him to his room, Frederick. You owe him that much. He handed you your career."

"What!" Frederick scowled at Amy.

"This is a circus. Do something." Esther finally lost her equanimity. "MWW can't have this. Frederick, help us here, please."

"Sure."

Frederick forgot Amy's comment. I didn't.

Frederick started to get Mendel up with a steward's aid. Then, unexpectedly Mendel opened his dark piercing eyes.

"What happened?"

Mendel looked around, his eyes locked on Amy, and he reached up. "Amy, my little love."

Mary looked at Amy. "My little love?"

I understood Amy's behavior at boarding. If they had been close acquaintances, perhaps too close, I would have behaved the same.

"He's out of it." Amy stepped back away from Mendel's sight line.

"Doctor, he's coming to," Frederick said. "Take another look and make sure we can move him."

The doctor kneeled back down reluctantly. "Sir, have you been drinking?"

"Sure! Who are you, the Martini police?" Mendel shouted. "Read me my rights."

Everyone within earshot chuckled.

"How many did you have?"

"Who's counting? I'm not driving the boat, am I?"

There was more laughter.

"Are you hurt? Are you in any pain?" The doctor was getting more annoyed, but well aware of the questions he had been trained to ask to protect the cruise line from liability. "Do you want to go to the infirmary to get checked out?"

"Give me a break." Mendel flipped his hand dismissively at the doctor. "I want my dinner."

"Sir, we'll take you to your room and get you some dinner." The doctor stood.

"Yes, just get him to his room. This spectacle isn't good for him, doctor," Amy smiled with her delightful dimples. "He'll sleep it off."

"This is not good for the MWW, either." Esther stepped forward with calm authority. "Can you get him up, Frederick? Please."

"Yes, this is too public," Amy urged.

"Fine." Frederick agreed.

"Yes," Mavis parroted Esther. "Can some of you men get him up?"

"Get him out of here," the doctor ordered, pleased his course of action had been validated by Mendel's colleagues.

"Let's get him to his room." Brent stepped into a leadership role and reached down to get Mendel up. "He's three sheets to the wind."

"More like nine. The steward can get him dinner there," the doctor added.

A ship's server stepped forward to help and Curtis stopped him.

"I'll help."

"No, I'll do it." Frederick glanced over at Amy and then started to help Mendel up again. "You lead the way."

"Sure." Curtis cleared a path through the observers to the stairs.

As Frederick and Brent lifted Mendel, Frederick asked Brent, "You said three sheets to the wind? You sail?"

Brent looked pleased. "All the time. I race."

"I race too, whenever I can get on a crew."

I marveled that male bonding was always catalyzed by booze or sports.

Mendel mumbled as the two giants rousted him to his feet.

I caught a glimpse of Mendel's face as his head flopped forward. He was pale and drool crept down the side of this mouth. I had never seen a drunk like him, not even in the epic college binges I had observed. Only observed, of course.

CHAPTER 11

A Lush in Luxury

Curtis led the way through the still-gathered gawkers dressed to the nines. Brent and Frederick followed with Mendel rag-dolled between them and continued to compare sailing experiences. They had bonded.

Further ingratiating herself to Esther, Mavis took charge. "You go back to your table and I'll take care of this."

"Report back?"

"Of course."

"And I'll go with her." I intentionally took advantage of the moment to introduce myself to Esther. "Veronica Kennicott. Mavis's stateroom mate."

"Oh, I didn't realize." Esther acknowledged me for the first time. "Esther Nussbaum."

"Yes, my stateroom mate." Mavis's tone was too neutral for my comfort level. "Let's go."

"Nice to meet you," Esther auto-piloted as she turned to go back to her table. "Come people. Everything's taken care of."

Esther was poised and controlled. She spoke with a slow cadence signaling the importance of every mundane word she uttered. She was a leader who people followed. I wasn't certain why.

Mary and Esther went back to their table, Mary chewing Esther's ear off.

Our other MWW people followed suit, and soon the rest of the diners dispersed.

* * *

As we left, five servers directed by the maître d' descended on the table Mendel had decimated.

Mavis, intent on reporting back to Esther, followed Mendel's entourage quickly up the dining room staircase. Wanting to be with Curtis, I followed Mavis.

I looked back from the stairway landing and saw the annihilated table was up, new clean linens in place, and being set, as if Mendel had never fallen on it.

Our unlikely little band proceeded quietly down the hallway to the elevator. Only Brent and Frederick chattered, still about sailing, as they propelled the smaller unsteady Mendel by his shoulders.

Curtis led the way into the elevator. The uniformed doctor strutted dutifully along, periodically glancing at Amy. Mavis and I brought up the rear.

In the elevator Curtis introduced himself to Brent and Frederick and joined in the sailing exchange, but from a Southern California, Marina del Rey perspective. Curtis's cocoa eyes sparkled as he talked about sailing. I couldn't help but notice again how striking he was in his black tuxedo with his contrasting rich gray hair, showing only whispers of his former dark brown. The men were in a world of their own far apart from the confines of the elevator or Mendel's mishap, a sailing world.

"I like it best when the sail is skimming the ocean and you're leaning over the rail balancing it," Frederick said. "I have to admit I've been deep-sixed over that rail a few times. On occasion, being a little heavier would help! Of course, I also love calm days when we hoist the spinnaker to take in as much wind as possible. Seeing that sail balloon out, especially if there are other nearby boats doing the same thing, is truly wonderful."

"I know what you mean." Curtis flashed a smile at me as I listened. "At this height my center of gravity has put me over those rails, too. But I admit our usual group manages to dump the spinnaker in the water as often as not when we try to raise it. Height makes little difference there."

"Yeah, the smaller boats like Solings are built for midgets. I've gone into the drink too," Brent admitted. "It annoys all the shorties. But they always invite me back. We can really leverage the lean with our size."

"And aside from the spinnaker, we can still grab anything with our wingspans," Curtis laughed.

Brent laughed with him. "I will admit that my favorite way to sail is solo, and indeed in a Soling because of its deep keel for stability. The boat's that is, not mine. Best of all are the days when the sea is rough, maybe even during a storm. I love taking the boat out in the open ocean then. Just me against the elements. No other people involved. A great way to release the tensions and frustrations of my daily life."

Curtis and Frederick exchanged knowing looks.

"We don't get much rough weather in Marina del Rey," Curtis remarked. "But when we do, I find it is often a stress reliever to take a small boat out past the breakwater, fight the swells and the wind, just me versus Mother Nature. Even better if it's stormy enough that I have to reef the sails. It takes all my ability and all of my senses to keep afloat and on course. Really an exhilarating experience. In addition, stormy weather hides the 'aroma' of all the bird guano that covers the marina breakwater, always a good thing."

Frederick nodded approvingly.

As the men "sailored" and "jolly-giant'ed" at each other, I noticed that the doctor had zeroed in on Amy to engage, even though she had no cleavage popping. He broke the ice, but not hers, by talking about the problems of drinking too much at sea. It was Mavis who responded sympathetically.

I chuckled to myself that this was one subject he appeared to know both personally and well.

Mavis impatiently punched the already lit elevator floor button. She thrived on attention and was getting none.

All the players in this troupe had their functions, and I was pleased Curtis had decided to help out.

* * *

When we got off the elevator, Mendel began belting out "Ninety-Nine Bottles of Beer on the Wall." He stopped at ninety-seven.

"Waiter, another Martini with an olive." Mendel slurred at the doctor who wore the only white coat in proximity.

"Sure." The doctor was annoyed at being taken for a waiter and being interrupted in the midst of his attempted *tête-a-tête* with Amy. "When we get you to your room."

"I don't think that's a good idea," Mavis called, from the rear of the group where we followed.

"He was joking," I whispered to Mavis.

"Oh."

By the time we got to the room, the two tall men were literally dragging Mendel. The doctor turned his attention from Amy and opened the door with his passkey.

Mendel's stateroom was huge. His appetites and money obviously extended to ostentation here as well. There was a dining area with faux-eighteenth century table and chairs; a large living room with a sofa bed and elegant coffee table; a refrigerator, obviously fully stocked; and flower arrangements, tastefully displayed. The stateroom had floor-to-ceiling windows with glass doors opening to a private balcony. The bathroom door was wide open, with clothes strewn around, and we could see it was all done in marble, with a whirlpool tub as well as a shower. A half-empty bottle of gin stood on the counter next to the marble sink.

Frederick and Brent continued to drag Mendel over to the king-sized bed with a thick blue and red bedspread inscribed with the insignia of the *Queen Anne.* Curtis pulled the bedspread and sheets back. Then, Frederick and Brent flopped Mendel onto the bed.

Mendel was limp and quiet.

"He's passed out." Brent took off Mendel's jacket.

Curtis followed the lead and took off his shoes. Frederick unceremoniously removed Mendel's tie and opened his shirt collar. I marveled at the unspoken coordination. It was a male ritual—to take care of their drunken, fallen comrades—that they had all practiced infinite times before. This male rite of passage started early in life.

"Is that a rash on his neck?" I asked Curtis, turning on the lamp on the nightstand.

Amy stepped up before Curtis could answer and looked closely at Mendel's neck. "His collar's been rubbing."

The doctor gave the rash a cursory glance and nodded, smiling at Amy.

"She's right. Let the man sleep it off, ladies. For God's sake, quit fussing."

"All right." I backed off.

I had been amply reprimanded with sexist overtones, which I accepted quietly under the circumstances. I had invaded the male post-drinking ritual. And rashes, after all, do come and then go with a little Cortisone.

I glanced at Mavis, who was observing impatiently. I had overstepped my bounds. I was an interloper paired with Mavis who, in point of fact, only had a tenuous color-of-authority from Esther. Moreover, Mavis obviously wanted to get back to dining and Esther.

"I'll get the steward." The doctor stepped outside leaving the self-closing door ajar by flipping the bar of the privacy lock resting between the jamb and the door.

"I've got to report back to Esther as fast as I can," Mavis whispered to me. "Don't bother the doctor anymore."

"Of course." I watched Amy zeroing in on Curtis across the room with her charming dimpled smile and coquettish body language. "Maybe we all need to leave?

"Esther and I have to plan a backup for the panel tomorrow. My guess is Mendel won't be up in time after this," Mavis gnawed on.

The doctor came back with the steward in tow and interrupted Mavis's self-important prattle.

"Check on him and get him something to eat later."

"Yes, sir." The steward was exasperated at the drunk who would multiply his duties that night and rumbled in a nasal working-class accent. "Shouldn't he be in sick bay, guv?"

"Do your job, man," the doctor barked, noting he had lost Amy's attentions to Curtis. "I'll do mine."

The doctor leaned over and peered down at Mendel. He reached to lift Mendel's eyelid. The minute the doctor touched Mendel's lid, Mendel's eyes popped open wide.

"Bloody Hell!" The doctor jumped back.

"What happened?" Mavis stepped forward and I shadowed her.

"Nothing," Frederick chuckled. "He's just out of it."

Mendel looked at the doctor and tried to speak but couldn't control his tongue. He slathered something low and inaudible. The doctor ignored him, but Mendel's eyes caught mine. His pupils were small, like pin heads. Something flashed across his eyes. It was unmistakably fear. Then Mendel's eyelids closed slowly.

"Did you see that?" I asked Curtis, concerned but also intentionally and calculatedly distracting him from Amy.

"Drunk as a skunk," Amy shrugged her shoulders and walked towards the door.

"Yeah, he's really tied one on," Curtis shook his head. "I've got to get back to my clients. Coming, Veronica?"

"I'll stay with Mavis." I hated to leave Curtis with Amy, but my instincts were telling me that something was just not right. "Thanks for the help."

"Interesting group," Curtis whispered in my ear as he walked toward the door behind Amy. "Later . . . in the bar?"

"I remember." I smiled, comfortable that Amy was not making any headway.

"Let's get out of here," Frederick said to Brent. "Hold on, Curtis, we'll go back with you."

"We all will. Let's let him sleep it off." Amy held the door open. "Coming, doctor?"

"Yes, one minute." The doctor took a last look at Mendel lying quietly on his bed.

Mavis walked over and took the door from Amy, holding it open for me.

"Let's go, Veronica. I have to fill Esther in." Mavis was annoyed that I was not moving fast enough for her. "He's passed out."

Amy, Frederick, and Brent waited with Curtis in the hall. Amy formally introduced herself to Curtis and engaged him in banter. I didn't like the competition.

As I moved toward the door, I glanced back at Mendel. His eyes were closed, but he was struggling to sit up, leaning on one elbow. His arm was shaking as he tried to support himself.

"Just lay down and sleep it off," the doctor ordered, giving Mendel a push on his chest.

Mendel flopped back down.

"Doctor," I asked. "Don't you have a nurse who can stay with him?"

"Of course, we have a nurse. A registered one. But she mans the infirmary . . . excuse me 'womans' the infirmary at night."

The doctor hurried past me and out the door, determined, I was sure, on getting Amy's attentions back from Curtis. I could smell the testosterone radiating from his thoughts.

I looked at Mendel for a moment. His eyes were shut, but his tongue fluttered between his parted lips and drool slid down from the corner.

"Doc," I called, but the doctor was already out the door.

"Come on," Mavis insisted, still holding the door open. "He'll be fine."

"I'm not so sure. Did you see him shaking?"

"Of course, he's plastered. He'll be fine, Veronica." Mavis signaled me to come. "You heard the doctor. There's nothing else to be done."

I joined the doctor and Mavis outside the door. "Doc, shouldn't we try to get some food or coffee down him?"

"No, we should get back to our dinner and . . ."

Amy interrupted, deserting Curtis and taking the doctor's arm, "Doctor, can you lead us back to the dining room? I'm afraid we might get lost."

The doctor smiled at Amy and then turned to me.

"Let him sleep it off. The steward will check up and feed him."

I looked away from the doctor as he spoke. The smell of whiskey on his breath was overwhelming. "The blind leading the blind," I thought. More precisely, "the drunk leading the drunk."

"Let's go. We've done everything we can do." Mavis started down the hall with the slowly migrating group.

"Yes." The doctor leered at Amy, who pulled him down the hall, too. "There's no antidote for drunkenness but sleep. A nice long sleep."

The doctor, arm-and-arm with Amy, took the lead for the troop of do-gooders who followed him down the hall. The three other men continued to "sailor" all the way back to the dining room.

I hesitated and then followed—unsupported in my concerns by anyone.

CHAPTER 12

An Anticlimactic Dinner

Back in the dining room, the world of eating and drinking and conversation not only had regenerated, but had even gained momentum.

Mendel's plight and person were forgotten. Frederick and Brent were back at our table post-bonding and talkative. Mavis, Amy, and I stopped to report to Esther. Esther, however, was more interested in her wine and bantering with the male seated next to her than in Mendel's status.

Over the years Esther had produced a fairly successful, but cookie-cutter, L.A. female detective series with less-than-graphic sex. She had enjoyed the status and sociability of the MWW presidential office for years and had recently married well. She had always been a part of the strong L.A. Jewish community, and her husband was a very prominent member of that community. They were, or to be precise, he was, a major donor to Wilshire Boulevard Temple, the oldest Jewish synagogue in Los Angeles. His father had been close personal friends with its most famous rabbi, Edgar Magnin. Esther had come from decidedly more humble origins, and occasionally it showed. Now, though, she displayed on her fingers and around her neck the diamonds that signaled her newfound freedom from the necessity of publishing and promoting books for a living. Indeed, her productivity had waned.

I concluded that this woman, whom I had looked forward to meeting, could be described with one word—boring.

Mavis cut her rendition of our Mendel excursion short. "Bottom-line, the doctor said Mendel was inebriated and had to sleep it off."

Only Mary O'Connell was listening to Mavis and called from across the table, "You mean the plotzed doctor's learned opinion was that the plotzed Mendel should go to bed. Did he prescribe two aspirins?"

The table chuckled and so did I.

"Mendel was too out of it to take two aspirins." Mavis responded to Mary, the only person actually paying attention to her report.

"This is nothing new for Mendel," Amy volunteered to the entire table.

"You know him well?" I probed, because after all Mendel had called her his "little love."

"Not that well, but enough to have seen him do that before." Amy's hazel golden eyes bored through me and belied her casual voice.

Amy strutted away without another word and took her seat at the table. She ate her waiting salad and buried herself in Mary's irritating soprano rendition outlining her latest sex torture book set at a Lake Michigan summer cottage.

As Mavis and I walked back to our table, I was even more curious about Amy and Mendel and, for that matter, Frederick and Mendel. What could a man like Frederick possibly owe a man like Mendel?

* * *

As soon as Mavis was reseated, she took it upon herself to deliver the Mendel report to our table. She recited the same Mendel update she had given to Esther. It was endured politely, but impatiently.

I ate my mushroom Brie en croute and started on my pear salad, which were both waiting for me.

"I can guarantee Mendel has no Irish blood in him or he'd be sitting here like a man now," Sean laughed, reaching for the wine. "All the more for us."

"Right," Frederick approved. "Pass that bottle over. Mavis, you need to catch up, too."

"Thank you," Mavis beamed as Frederick reached over and filled her glass.

"Veronica? Wine?"

"Please."

Frederick poured my wine and then more generously filled his own glass.

Sean immediately took center stage and entertained us with a humorous arrest he had made that went awry. Then he told us how he had modified it and used it in his latest book. I had actually read that book. It was fun hearing about the incident it was based on. As the laughter faded, I took the opportunity to ask Frederick about Mendel.

The Mendel incident had activated my detecting juices, justified or not. I found the comments and looks, apparently lost on others, curious and a catalyst for my inquiries. Admittedly, inquiries into nothing of moment, but interesting to me.

Humanity and its foibles fascinated me. I studied the frailties of human beings with interest: the justifications, the excuses, the seemingly uncontrollable passions, the envy, the laziness, the mistakes, and the choices wrongly made—choices that form lifetimes of regret and sometimes financial and emotional ruin. I guess I enjoyed judging people without condemning them. Or, in some instances, condemning them too.

"Frederick, it was kind of you to help with Mendel. Do you really owe him your career?"

Frederick stopped his merriment and sat up straight. He looked at me without saying a word. I could see his mind racing behind his icy blue eyes. After a short hiccup in time, he smiled amicably.

"Where did you hear something like that?"

"When Amy asked you to get Mendel out of there."

"Oh, that." Frederick's eyes softened and he leaned back in his chair. "It's nothing. We all studied under Otto together. It's all in the family. Why?"

"No real reason." I ducked-and-covered. "I just gathered that Mendel has had this drinking problem for years."

"I think that's common knowledge," Frederick turned abruptly to Sean. "Do you think being an actual homicide detective helped you become a writer? Because it seems to me that seeing so much would have made you too jaded to write. It didn't?"

* * *

At our table, not another word was said about Mendel the rest of the evening.

Helga repeatedly snapped at Brent and also repeatedly referred to the killing her last book was making. Brent took refuge outside the circle by leaning back in his chair and talking to Frederick about sailing. Frederick leaned back too—literally behind Helga's back. That is, until a peeved Helga put an end to it by scooting her chair back, blocking their interchange.

Helga made sure she was the arbiter of conversation and the center of attention, especially Brent's.

For the rest of the evening, I took on the role of a charming listener as Sean and Elias vied for the floor with Helga. I was content to fly under the radar . . . for now.

I did attempt subtly to catch Curtis's eye several times, but he was busy with his table of clients. I had to admit that our table was the lively one, and after Helga had a few glasses of wine she—quite pleasantly—started to laugh loudly at Sean's detective escapades, too.

I surmised she was interviewing him, that is to say pumping him for detective information for her books.

Our table lingered after dessert with aperitifs. I guessed that was a benefit of the second seating.

I intentionally ordered a second double espresso because I was meeting Curtis in the bar. I wanted to be alert and at my best, if I could be, after such a long day. I hoped he remembered.

Curtis's table lingered too, but broke up before ours.

We eventually got up and, in the hall just outside the dining room, I left Mavis sucking up to Esther. I made my way past the bright, jingly, and robust casino to the main cocktail lounge across from it. Both had inviting wide and open arched entries—wide and open, I assumed, to tempt the imbibed to gamble and the gamblers to imbibe.

It was half past eleven. I hurried.

CHAPTER 13

Bar Sinister

When I entered the large dimly lit bar, I spotted Curtis sitting on a barstool with two glasses of red wine. He was watching the door for me.

He smiled he saw me, picked up the wine glasses, and walked to greet me.

"Two fisted?"

"Yep."

We laughed together—the nervous laugh of expectation.

"I'm glad you remembered." Curtis said.

We surveyed the large room lit with soft flickering votive candles at each table.

"There's one." Curtis headed to a row of tables along the wall of glass separating us from the churning, dark night waves of the Atlantic Ocean.

As we stopped at the empty table, I looked out the window. The ship's lights bounced off the white foam and swells that lapped just below the window and intermittently splashed up onto it. A wall of blackness and the dark sea faded out beyond.

"A bit frightening," I said.

"What?" Curtis set the glasses of wine on the table.

"The sea so close below, with just that glass between us."

"That's not glass." Curtis held my chair for me. "That is as strong as any ship's hull."

"I hope so."

"I was beginning to think you weren't coming."

"No, our dinner just seemed never to end." Didn't he know that no sane woman would stand up this wonderful specimen?

"I did notice that you had a lively table." Curtis smiled across at me.

"We did. It was fun."

"My group was sedate."

"I saw."

"Oh, you did?"

"Yes." My admission was unqualified and unembarrassed.

I gazed into Curtis's dark eyes in the flickering candlelight. I was wrong. They were not eighty-five percent cocoa. Instead, they looked ninety-five percent dark cocoa or almost black. It was approaching midnight, but suddenly I was not tired at all.

"To a wonderful transatlantic crossing with all its possibilities."

Curtis clicked my glass and took a drink. I drank, too.

"Thanks for helping with Mendel."

"Hey, the poor guy was being videotaped. That's not fair. Famous or not . . . we had to get him out of there. Everyone deserves dignity."

"I agree."

There was a bleep in the radar of discourse and I began a topic that I knew Curtis would run with, until I got the lay of the land.

"So do you sail often?"

"I guess everyone knows that now. When we get back, Frederick and I may get together out at the Marina for some of the Cal Yacht Club's Sunset Series of races towards Malibu. He has a friend with a Hinckley 49-footer who could use another good man or two, though the races are more about socializing than winning. It's a shame Brent's on the other coast."

"I'm not sure Helga lets him off her leash, anyway."

"There is a bit of tension there, isn't there?"

"That's an understatement," I chuckled and drank my wine.

"But she has to lock herself away and write sometime. She's always got a new book on the shelves. That woman can write."

"Yes, in our circles she's what is known as prolific."

"Prolific and good. I've read quite a few of her books. Do you think she actually writes them all?"

"The word on the street is 'yes.' But who really knows. Some authors who turn books out one after another do use ghostwriters. They say that's where the has-beens go to make a living when their creative juices die—to ghostwriting."

"If I may ask? Do you?"

"Do I what?" I was truly confused.

"Use a ghostwriter?"

I stalled as my mind rummaged for a way to deflect his focus on my yet-to-begin literary career.

"No," I stumbled, telling a lie by omission.

I chuckled to myself. How could I possibly use a ghostwriter? I didn't even use myself at the moment. My muse was gone and I hadn't had a good idea, or any idea, for a book, a chapter, or even a sentence for months. I hadn't even written a word in my theatre mystery. In fact, not since I solved the Valentine Theatre murders and had a taste of local celebrity. I ate my celebrity up, and it ate up my muse.

My thoughts raced for a way to redirect the conversation's inevitable progression to my body of work. All of a sudden, I was rescued by a commotion in the bar.

* * *

Mavis, Mary, and Sean were going loudly from table-to-table asking for Esther.

They looked like penguins in a line flapping their wings to waddle faster. They moved their hands at their sides propelling themselves forward because their chubby, elderly bodies wouldn't carry them as fast as they wanted.

"Yoo-hoo," Mary called out and waved at me from half way across the room. "We can't find Esther."

All three fluttered up to our table and stood before us, ample-bellied to varying degrees and out of breath.

"He's dead." Mavis's freckles jumped on her animated cheeks in the candlelight.

"Dead as a doornail." Sean pulled out a chair and sat to catch his liquor-coated breath.

"It's unbelievable." Mary grabbed a seat too.

"Who's dead?" I asked, thinking it had better be someone really important, like a world leader, considering they interrupted my romantic rendezvous.

"Mendel." Mavis pulled over a chair and sat too. "The steward just found him."

"But how?" Curtis asked. "He was sleeping it off in his bed."

"We don't know. Had to be a heart attack," Sean opined.

"Or, maybe he aspirated on his own vomit," Mary volunteered. "It happens. I've used it in a short story or two."

Mavis ignored her companions' speculations.

"Have you seen Esther? I have to tell her."

"No." I looked directly at this now annoying habitual suck-up. "The last time I saw her she was talking to you in the hall. Don't you know where she went?"

"Obviously not," Mavis muttered, eyeing Curtis with inferences abounding in her gaze.

"I can't believe this," Curtis said.

"I can't either. Poor man," I echoed.

"Hello." Curtis reached over and shook Sean's hand. "I'm Curtis. With a financial planning group here. It's hard to believe the man died. He seemed okay when we left him tonight."

"Nice to meet you. You helped with him?"

"Yes."

"Curtis, you already know Mary and Mavis from Mendel's stateroom, I think." I rehabilitated my manners and identified them all as MWW members—naturally, under the circumstances I skipped their mystery writer's plugs as inappropriately timed.

"Of course." Curtis acknowledged.

Mavis stood and interrupted the very brief introductions. "Esther would want me to take care of this. I have to go to Mendel's stateroom."

"I'll help," Sean volunteered, standing at attention.

"Don't leave me out!" Mary got up, too.

Mavis, Sean and Mary stood regrouping into their threesome. Having amply caught their breath, they followed Mavis dutifully out of the bar.

* * *

As they marched away, I looked at Curtis and he looked at me.

"Let's go." Curtis stood.

"You read my mind." I remembered how ill Mendel looked when we left him.

"I feel badly about leaving him there alone."

"Me too. I need to know what happened."

As we trailed behind the investigatory body in the lead, I was happy Curtis was going with me.

I had to admit to myself though, even if the ever-chivalrous Curtis had not decided to join the group, I would have followed anyway. As any mystery writer will tell you, we all would choose an unexplained death to romance.

CHAPTER 14

Death, Dereliction, and Disappointment

On the way, Curtis and I brought up the rear. I was excited; morbidly so, I admitted to myself, but nonetheless excited. Moreover, I was on my way to examine Mendel's mysterious and sudden death in the company of a very handsome man.

Then, unexpectedly and unhappily, Mary dropped back and chatted up Curtis nonstop.

She was just like Helga; a giant sponge for information. I was getting an immersion into the habits of successful and productive writers. They spent every waking moment absorbing information, observing, and writing. Apparently, it was not a myth. I had seen enough on the cruise thus far to conclude that it was true. Not unpredictably, I now aspired to become an even bigger sponge than they were.

Mavis interrupted and reiterated intermittently that one of us should go to find Esther.

We all ignored her. We were on a path to adventure, with or without Esther.

As we hurried down the *Queen Anne's* corridors, Mary had elicited all the Curtis preliminaries; literally everything I would have wanted to learn about him on this first date if it had not been interrupted by Mendel's death. Listening to Mary's interrogation, I knew almost too much about Curtis, including that he was very polite and patient. However, I liked every bit of what I heard.

Curtis had an office in one of the Century City twin towers on the 22nd floor in West L.A. He was a very successful investment advisor for the extremely wealthy. He was doing the crossing with some of his firm's clients to promote business and afterward have meetings in London. He said nothing about a wife, girlfriend or children. And, I already knew he got his tan from his Marina del Rey sailing.

As we turned the corner to enter the hallway leading to Mendel's stateroom, the steward was halfway down, holding the door for Frederick and Brent as they entered.

"Hurry." Mary trotted ahead, taking the lead and waiving at us to follow. "He may not be dead? Let's hope not."

Although a blood lusting writer of torture murders, Mary wanted Mendel to be alive. Her values were more Midwest than she liked to show.

* * *

When we got to Mendel's, we single-filed in and hovered silently in a group with Frederick and Brent. The steward stepped inside and propped the door open a crack with the privacy lock's brass bar again.

Mendel lay on the bed where we had left him, except now on his side. He was pale and his face was turned toward the nightstand. His dark eyes were open and stared into the lamp.

101

Eerie jagged shadows were smeared across his face from the displaced lampshade.

Mendel's mouth gaped open with dry, caked drool and vomit streaming out at the lowest corner. Mendel's graying, light brown hair was matted and wet. His pillow was soaked where his head had been. Mendel's arm was fixed in a reach toward the phone on the nightstand.

"Too bad. He is dead." Mary was solemn. "Poor man."

Frederick was the first to break rank. "Steward, where's the doctor?"

"Coming." The steward cowered by the door, away from death.

"What does he mean 'coming'?" Frederick's ice blue eyes burrowed through the steward's anxious eyes. "My God. He should be here. A man's dead!"

"Precisely," the steward quipped in British understatement.

Frederick began to pace up and down at the foot of the bed.

"Why is his pillow so wet, and his shirt?" I asked.

I looked more closely at Mendel. After all, this was not the first real dead person I had seen. I had been initiated into dead bodies by seeing those strewn about the Valentine Theatre. That was my boot camp into discovering bodies and exposing murderers.

"Sweat?" Sean answered from his NYPD perspective. "Not unusual."

"What should we do?" Mary was clearly a woman of action. "We should do something."

"I agree. Shouldn't we do something?" Mavis echoed, looking back at the steward.

"Do what precisely? He's dead, madam. Looks like a heart attack."

"But someone has to try CPR." Curtis stepped closer to the bed.

"Yes, CPR, but it needs a hard surface." Mary pointed to the floor.

"She's right. I'll help get him on the floor." Frederick reported for duty with Curtis.

"Ready?" Curtis stood tall to do his responsibility.

Frederick grabbed Mendel's outstretched arm to slide him onto the floor for CPR. But Mendel's arm was rigid. Neither his arm nor his head, which was tilted toward the lamp, nor any part of his body moved. Mendel's eyes, now out of the shadows, were unmistakably lifeless.

"He's stiff." Frederick jumped back.

"Rigor mortis." Sean announced. "Leave him be. I've seen hundreds of dead bodies on the force. He's dead, Curtis; there's nothing to be done."

"God." Frederick grabbed a towel from the bathroom and wiped his hands.

"I don't believe this." Brent said. "He looks like he was reaching for the phone."

"For help." I concluded.

"Rigor mortis?" Brent came closer. "How long has he been dead?"

"Well, it only takes two hours to start in the smaller muscles like the face and neck. Then it works its way through a man like this in about four." Mary spewed information like a medical text as she took a seat in a chair. "That's how I show time of death in half my slasher murders. My last one, where the husband actually did a copycat murder, had . . ."

"What?" Frederick cut her off, "Then he died when we were still here! That's no heart attack. I didn't see anything like that."

Mavis took a seat on one of the chairs again.

"Well, it could have happened just as we left," Mary opined.

"This is so horrible. When did you find him?" Curtis asked the steward.

"Just now, when I brought him something to eat."

"That damn drunken doctor," Brent seethed. "He's been lying here dead this whole time."

"Do you think we could have saved him?" Mavis asked.

"Maybe," Sean replied. "But not if it was a massive coronary."

Suddenly, the door flung open, slamming into the wall.

The doctor ambled in, pushing the steward aside. All eyes turned to him except, of course, Mendel's.

* * *

The doctor was still three-sheets-to-the-wind, if not more. "Something wrong with our dear man again?"

"He's dead, sir," the steward reported at attention. "Heart attack, in my opinion, sir."

"Oh? Too bad."

"Yes, sir."

"Too bad?" Frederick blurted.

"Yes, a real shame." The doctor checked Mendel's outreached wrist for a pulse. "Stiff, huh? No pulse. Drank too much for the old ticker, eh? But not our fault. He was alive when we put him to bed."

"Certainly, sir," the steward agreed.

Curtis and I stared at each other in disbelief. Mavis immediately stood taking a position of authority in the absence of Esther.

"Aren't you going to take this seriously? A man died under your care. It seems to me that, at the very least, you should inspect the body before you pronounce his death and the cause. Or get him to the infirmary and take a better look. Seriously, this is awfully casual."

"Yes, I agree." Mary joined Mavis shoulder to shoulder. "There are things that need explanation. What is all that dried stuff down his chin?"

"That 'dried stuff,' as you so elegantly put it is drool and I smell vomit. Quite normal after you're properly sloshed." The doctor started to leave.

"He could have aspirated in his own vomit?" Curtis joined protestors, making it a trio. "Don't you think you should know?"

The doctor turned, studied the trio and then sized up all of us.

"You're all with that mystery writers club, aren't you?"

Brent started to object, but was cut off by Mary.

"So?" Mary threw back her shoulders and pulled her chin in until it went from double to triple with indignation.

"Well, we're not writing a mystery novel here. This is real life. People die on cruises, especially drunks. Overboard. Heart attack. You name it. I've seen it all. You should all go back to writing your little books."

The doctor strode back and threw the bed sheet sloppily over Mendel's head, leaving his one stiff arm pointing above it.

"And, if he aspirated, he wouldn't be on his side and the vomit wouldn't be there . . . outside his orifice." The doctor pointed at the mess as he lectured. "It would be inside his esophagus. Thus, by deduction . . . heart attack. What else could it be?"

"You make it sound like you lose passengers all the time!" Brent cross-examined.

"Do I? Sorry." The doctor headed for the door again.

"Wait a minute," Brent objected. "You're not just going to leave him here?"

"Uh, of course not," The doctor turned back, steadying himself with the doorjamb, and barked orders at the steward.

"Get security to take him to the infirmary for now. We'll put him on ice tomorrow."

"Yes, sir right away."

The doctor resumed his exit, steadying himself on the door jam.

"Wait," Frederick called. "Where are you going?"

"Back to my black jack table."

"Then that's it?" Frederick grabbed the doctor's sleeve.

The doctor turned and jerked his arm loose.

"What else do you want me to do? Bring him back to life?"

"Don't be an ass," Frederick seethed his face turning red with anger. "Do your job."

"I did my job. And to please you . . . all of you . . . I'll give him another look-see in the morning. Then, I'll write my report and send it up the proper channels. The usual."

The doctor marched out.

* * *

Our group, to a person, stood there incredulous. We watched the doctor exit with the steward on his heels as the door slammed shut. No one spoke.

Finally, Curtis spoke. "The usual? Evidently, his 'usual' is nothing. The 'usual' nothing."

"I hate to think we could have saved him," Brent replied.

"We'll never know. There is no process here." Curtis was dumbfounded as he surveyed the group.

Brent stood, thinking. "Apparently not."

"Yes, apparently," Frederick agreed.

Sean looked at them both and shrugged. "This is no New York City."

"I feel really awful about this," I said. "We should have paid more attention. I remember him trying to speak, but he couldn't. His pupils were small . . . tiny. But, I'm not a doctor."

"I didn't see anything. I just thought he was drunk," Mavis said. "And he was!"

"That goes without saying," Mary's impatience with Mavis was elevating.

"But half the people on this ship are . . . well, let's be honest . . . drunk," Brent said. "Does that mean they get no care and die?"

We all looked at each other.

"I saw him try to sit up, but he couldn't because his arms were shaking so hard. Is that a heart attack?" I asked. "And I remember the look in his eyes. He was afraid, but he didn't say anything. Oh no . . . maybe he couldn't?"

"You're reading too much into things. Imagining things mean something they don't." Mavis made slight of my input. "What do you know? You're . . ."

"What?"

I glared at her and she shut up. I knew what she was going to say: That I was unpublished. I didn't see what that had to do with my observations or my humanity and her lack thereof. I didn't like her discounting me.

"Couldn't speak? What do you mean?" Sean interrogated me in what I imagined from television shows was the good old NYPD style.

"His tongue was not working, like it was twitching or something."

Sean thought a moment and then pulled the sheet back, exposing Mendel's body again. "I've seen a lot of bodies. But I've never seen a doctor so casual about a healthy man dying . . . even if he was drunk as a skunk."

"Cruise personnel are useless. They are paid to cover up anything unpleasant," Brent said.

"We're on the high seas where it appears the rules are different," Curtis agreed.

I went over and inspected Mendel's body with Sean.

"This rash was here before. What is it, Sean?" I asked.

"I hadn't noticed it." Sean glanced at me with his sharp greenish-blue eyes. "You're very observant."

I lapped up the compliment in front of Mavis. I liked that Curtis and Sean were taking me seriously.

"Veronica may have something here. It's like a real case I worked years ago. The rash, the unexpected death. In fact, I used it in my first book *Death Trolls*," Sean said. "Actual sales were not that good, but I learned a lot about writing. I learned about plotting and . . ."

"Sorry, Sean, but the case? What happened?" Curtis interrupted.

"Oh, yes," Sean cleared his throat. "Sorry. It's the rash. And the shaking . . . the small pupils. Those are definitely signs of poisoning."

"No!" Frederick blurted. "That's absurd."

"Poisoning!" Brent was alarmed. "But how could that happen here? Couldn't it just be an allergic reaction to something?"

"Maybe," Sean pondered as the resident retired homicide detective.

"Interesting." I leaned in close. "Look at the eyes."

I wanted to contribute, so I stole a hackneyed phrase from the many mysteries I had read.

"The eyes tell it all," I added, hoping no one had read the same books.

I had actually sprinkled that phrase around my second book. I thought it made the protagonist sound smart. And as it turned out, in my book, she was. The eyes did tell her that the victim had been suffocated. In the end, the petechial hemorrhaging proved it.

Sean looked directly at Mendel's open eyes. "They do look a bit yellow and the pupils are small. Tremors, did you say?"

Mavis took a look too, but was close-mouthed. As far as she was concerned, her job was to report to Esther and nothing more.

"I don't like this." Mary got angry. "And I don't like the doctor's attitude. He can't dismiss us just because we happen to be mystery writers. What did he say? 'This isn't a mystery book.' He can kiss my Motown ass."

"Well, it may not be a mystery book, but it is a mystery," Sean said.

"Oh, my God. Don't be ridiculous. Maybe we've all written too many books and films. I know he's difficult, but who would . . . poison him? Really? Do you think . . ." Frederick leaned in to study Mendel's face and then backed away. "But you're right, that rash does look nasty and there's some swelling. But you don't die of an allergy as far as I know."

"You do if your throat swells and closes up." I remembered an allergy to tomatoes my uncle had late in life and how he was rushed to the emergency room to get his airway opened.

"Cover him back up," Frederick said. "I'll talk to the doctor tomorrow when he's sober."

"Good. Talk to him tomorrow," Sean agreed. "I think an autopsy's in order."

"Do you think it's an overdose?" Brent asked Sean.

"I've seen hundreds of those on the force," Sean said. "And I would say no. It doesn't compute."

"Then what?" I asked.

"I don't know. That's what autopsies are for." Sean shook his head in frustration.

"It's late. Let's go," Mavis ordained. "I personally think it was an overdose if reputations mean anything."

Mary glared at her, but didn't say a word.

Mavis had lost all interest in even discussing a cause of death, let alone investigating a real dead body. After all, she was just here to get information and then toady up to Esther.

"I have an early morning," Curtis apologized. "I should go."

"There is nothing more to be done now." Sean started for the door.

We followed. Sean was respected as the authority at this point.

Curtis said goodnight to me at the elevator and took it up with Frederick. I took the other elevator down with the rest of the group.

Death had trumped our date, but I hoped for another. Date, I meant. Not death.

CHAPTER 15

Scones and Scorn

The next morning, Mavis and I got our automated wake-up call and she grabbed the shower.

While I waited, I caught the *Queen Anne's* daily program on the day's activities and a run-down of all the facilities available on this massive, luxurious floating city: a hair salon, an Internet café, a library, theatres, an ice cream parlor, gyms, massages, spa treatments, jogging, a pool and hot tub, steam rooms, and outside sporting activities, including golf off the deck. Not to mention an array of high-end boutiques and jewelers. It was amazing. Much nicer than any other cruise I had been on.

Mavis became friendly and chatty as we got ready. I decided to forget her slighting me the night before in Mendel's stateroom. It was late, we were tired, and we had all had our fill of wine.

We left together, and timely, for the MWW welcome continental breakfast before the first program.

* * *

When we arrived, to my surprise, the large conference room was already full of MWW members standing about socializing and eating. It crossed my mind that all writers may be early risers, as I was. I chuckled to myself. Perhaps their literary careers began as mine had, killing time in the wee hours of the morning.

I admired the elegant continental breakfast laid out at the back of the room. Between the several multi-colored rose arrangements were scones with lemon curd and butter, pastries, coffee, tea, juices, decorative fruit platters, whole fruit jams, and the oh-so-British orange marmalade.

Unhappily, the minute we arrived, Jody and Herbert swept down upon us.

"Mendel Weitzman is dead," Jody ejaculated.

Her coffee sloshed over the rim of her cup, disappearing into the green and cranberry herringbone carpet identical to the one in the dining room.

"Oops," Jody took a drink of her coffee.

Agnes trailed up behind them, carrying a plate heaped with pastries and already buttered and marmaladed scones.

"Heart attack. Last night." Agnes pushed a half chewed piece of raisin scone back into her mouth, but kept talking with her mouth full as her elementary school students undoubtedly do. "A premature loss of such a creative mind. He was a genius. But I have to admit, I couldn't read his books."

"Why?" Herbert glared bug-like through his thick black-rimmed glasses

"Too much sex. Sex in the morning. Sex in the evening. Sex at dinner time. Yuck!"

"Speaking of yuck. Wait 'til you're finished chewing, Agnes." Jody turned to Agnes, again sloshing her coffee onto the carpet.

"Well, he was my personal hero," Herbert announced. "I read every one of his books."

"You would." Agnes bit into her raisin scone smothered with butter and marmalade.

"He was young for a heart attack." Herbert's nasal tenor voice was loud and serious as he watched Agnes licking the butter off her lips. "I don't eat butter for that very reason."

"It wasn't a heart attack according to Frederick Larsen." Jody challenged Agnes. "I heard Frederick arguing with security when I first came down. "He went to find the doctor."

"I should talk to Esther." Mavis bee-lined to Esther, who was talking to a security man on the other side of the room.

I followed, but just as we approached, the security man left.

"Good morning," I said.

"Well, not so good, Veronica . . . is it?" Esther retorted.

"Yes, Veronica."

"Mavis, what is going on here?" Esther turned her back to me.

I stepped back but stayed in earshot.

"Esther, I'm so sorry about Mendel," Mavis said. "I would have called you last night, but I didn't want to wake you and there was nothing to be done."

"Not according to Frederick . . . or Mary and Sean. They said the doctor was drunk and it might not have been a heart attack. But security just confirmed heart attack for the official report."

"That's just what I was coming to tell you. I was there and it was clear to me Mendel died of a heart attack. What else could it be?"

"An overdose," Esther whispered. "And, in that case, we don't want an investigation or autopsy. I mean that would not be good for Mendel or the MWW or, frankly, the cruise line. *Tsuris* we don't need."

"I see." Mavis nodded.

"So perhaps we don't need to stir things up?"

Esther was poised, even when she talked about a real murder. Her slow even cadence signaled no emotion or any urgency.

"It's up to you of course, but perhaps we don't," Mavis echoed.

"You were there?" Esther turned to me and asked. "What do you think?"

"Truly?" I stepped up. "I think an investigation and autopsy wouldn't hurt. I did discover an odd rash and his pupils were strange and I saw him shaking after dinner before he died."

I answered definitively before Mavis could discount me again like last night. I wanted to contribute and do my part as much as Mavis did—whether I was a published author yet or not. I, after all, had just solved the Valentine Theatre murders in Hollywood and, as far as I knew, Mavis had never solved a real murder in her life.

"What happened?" Esther was interested.

"His pupils were . . ."

"What Veronica means is that we really don't know anything beyond speculation," Mavis interrupted and got Esther's attention again.

I wasn't surprised that Mavis fought for center stage, but I was surprised at her blatantly untrue response in view of Esther's direct inquiries. It was clear her dialogue was aimed at giving Esther what she wanted to hear, and not the truth. It became obvious to me that Mavis was a "yes man" or "yes person." I was disappointed in Mavis yet again, and believed Esther wanted the truth. I spoke up.

"I have to say the doctor was definitely drunk and I think Mendel didn't die of a heart attack. I don't know why he died, but he had an odd appearance. Looking back, I think something was wrong when we left him in his room."

"What do you mean?" Esther asked.

"He had a rash and yellow eyes with small pupils . . . he was shaking and puffy or swollen . . . I'm no doctor, but it didn't look like a simple heart attack and I've seen one before, sadly."

"Really?" Esther said. "What do you suggest?"

"Hindsight is always 20-20. Looking back, it appeared to be some kind of reaction. I don't think any of us focused on anything but his drinking last night. And the doctor was so sure of himself. But I remember Mendel drooling and definitely in distress. I don't know exactly, but I think he tried to tell us what was wrong and couldn't."

Mavis stepped up and took the spotlight from me. She wanted to discount me to Esther again, even if I might be right.

"You're right, Veronica, you are no doctor. And the doctor was clear. Heart attack. Now, he could be wrong, but I truly doubt it. Esther, you have to understand Veronica is really a novice at these things. She's a beginner. She's unpublished."

"Oh? Really? So the truth is, you've got *bupkes*." Esther looked at me and raised her chin just enough so that I knew I was being relegated to the status of a second-class citizen.

Mavis had put me in my place again. I didn't like it. I knew I was right. I looked at Mavis through different eyes now. She was a suck-up, a glad-hander. She was a lapdog. I didn't like her. I might be unpublished, but I wasn't a novice. I was as much a criminalist as she was. More, in fact. I had written four books. One, as yet unfinished, was based on the murders that I had actually solved for the two inept Los Angeles detectives officially on the case. Furthermore, I had researched many medications, allergic reactions, and poisons to write one of my books.

In my mind, I was anything but a novice. Besides, my new friends who had bigger mystery minds than me, and much more experience, agreed with my assessment. After all, Sean was old NYPD.

"As long as it's not one of those ship epidemics. They happen too often for me," Esther looked at Mavis, purposely excluding me.

"That's so remote." Mavis assured Esther.

"We'll talk later, Mavis. Let's prepare the program."

It was clear I was not part of their club. The validation of publication had not anointed me.

I decided on the spot that I would spend the rest of the cruise substantiating my theory of Mendel's death to Esther and discrediting Mavis as she had me. It wasn't a heart attack and I knew it, and so did Sean, Mary, and Frederick. I would enjoy discovering the cause of Mendel's death and there would be plenty of time left for Curtis too. If, as Esther intimated, there were a ship-wide problem, we'd soon know anyway. We had all read the news of tainted food, noroviruses, and bad water on cruises. But the doctor couldn't cover that up for long.

Esther and Mavis walked toward the food tables.

I was left standing—feeling three inches tall.

I went to get tea. I would prove myself right and extricate myself from Mavis's clutches. Soon, she would be the one feeling three inches tall.

* * *

I got my tea and looked for a group to join. I saw Agnes, Jody, and Herbert, but refused to resort to that.

Beyond, Amy and Anne were by the assorted fruit, delicately cut and colorfully laid out. Amy was dressed beautifully yet again in a brown sweater and slacks. And Anne? Well, Anne was Anne, ever the Brit. She was in a nice light blue wool sweater and skirt ensemble that matched her eyes but a mismatched brown and green floral shirt underneath shattered the effect.

I headed over. Amy intrigued me. Besides, I knew she had a history with Mendel. A history that I could undoubtedly use in the rehabilitative independent investigation I had just launched.

"Good morning."

"Good morning, Veronica." Amy nibbled a small piece of pineapple.

"Good to see you again." Anne Britished through a tight-lipped smile. "I was just explaining to Amy how I started my book writing career despite believing that my destiny was to be a poet."

"Really?"

"Yes, I sat in my home outside Bath for endless hours and wrote what I realize now were marginally acceptable poems. I wrote one after another describing my prize garden. I wrote the 'Happy Yellow Rose' poem, the 'Sad Red Rose' poem, and the 'Primrose Proper' poem. Need I go on?"

Anne laughed. Amy smiled. I laughed too, but wondered if they had talked about Mendel's death. Perhaps that conversation was over, but I would bide my time for an entree to glean information from Amy.

"I was so self-assured poetry was my destiny that I self-published three short books of poems. *Blue Sky, Yellow Happiness ,*and *Red Heart.* They didn't sell. Looking back, I was daft."

"How did you get into mystery writing?" I asked.

"Easy. The money. My husband's accountant told him, and he told me, that if I liked writing so much I should make money at it . . . like Agatha Christie. It made sense to us. I wrote *The Red Rose Murder* and I haven't run out of flowers yet . . . there are hundreds of kinds of flowers. And then I can go to trees!"

Anne laughed. I chuckled mostly at Anne rather than with her. She was a delightful storyteller even about herself. I had read a few of Anne's books. Her sarcasm, irreverence, and sharp sense of wit came through in them, even in the titles. *Splitting the Agapanthus* was my favorite title and book.

"Speaking of vegetation, there was a garden tour of Central Park in the MWW New York writer's tour? Did you go?" I asked.

"No. I was on holiday visiting my daughter in Ithaca . . . upstate New York. She settled there several years ago . . ." Anne stopped abruptly when she saw Amy zeroed in on Frederick getting coffee. "Amy?"

"What?" Amy whirled back around.

"I'm so sorry. Frederick must be upset about Mendel. I understood they studied writing together with Otto."

Anne had inadvertently delved into the exact topic I wanted to. But Amy didn't answer. Her hazel eyes with sparkling gold rims were distracted.

"First, Otto murdered," Anne added. "And, now, Mendel's death. It is all so sudden and unexpected."

"Perhaps it isn't, though?" Amy had no reaction to my probing.

"Excuse me. I have to speak to Esther," Amy said. "She had me take Mendel's place moderating the first panel discussion today."

Amy left.

Anne looked at me and shrugged. "Have you heard anything?"

"No. Not really. I wish we would have helped him more."

"I'm sure you did as much as you could." Anne generously told me what I wanted and needed to hear.

"I imagine so. Did Amy say anything?"

"No. Just how Mendel's lifestyle predicted it."

"Ah."

"I'm going to get another tea and a seat. Join me?"

"Thanks, but I have to talk to Frederick. I'll see you later, Anne."

"Perhaps at lunch?"

"Sure." I agreed disingenuously as I made my way over to Frederick.

"Hello, Frederick."

"Oh. Good morning, Veronica. It looks as if it's true."

"What's that?"

"Life goes on." Frederick drank his coffee.

"Yes it does. A little less smoothly, but it does go on." I thought of my deceased husband and that life had gone on, then, too—rather quickly at that.

"You know . . ." Frederick said. "I . . . ah . . . spoke to Mendel's agent this morning . . . just to explain to him what happened. I thought he should know. He was the closest thing to family Mendel had. And he was shocked. He said Mendel was as healthy as a horse."

"Really? No heart problems?"

"No, none."

"Allergies?"

"No."

"That's strange," I said.

"Yes. So much for the ship's doctor!"

"Yeah . . . useless. Poor Mendel. Do you think it was a medication interaction with the alcohol?"

"Not prescription, anyway. Mendel's agent said all he actually took was Synthroid."

"Could it have been something in the water or the food?"

"Don't know. No one else is sick. I guess time will tell. I drink bottled water."

"I . . ."

"Excuse me," Frederick interrupted when his gaze fixed on Esther and Amy, coming our way in the crowd. "I have to catch Esther."

"I'll see you at dinner then."

"Yes."

I actually couldn't believe that Frederick had taken me into his confidence. I lauded myself for being so perceptive and outspoken last night. Frederick's call to Mendel's agent confirmed that I was being regarded professionally by at least one person here. It spurred me on to pursue my personal investigation of Mendel's death and countered my humiliation by Mavis.

I turned and left the meeting. I sacrificed hearing the panel discussions by the biggest names in the mystery world. I sacrificed everything I actually needed, including "Characters to Live For," "Plots to Die For," and "Publication Pitfalls."

"But duty calls!" I said to myself.

I left needed to research Mendel's symptoms and I knew just where to do it after watching the *Queen Anne's* closed circuit ship's guide this morning.

I headed for the ship's library. It had computers and Internet access. I decided the Internet café would be too busy and noisy. I hadn't brought my personal old laptop with me to use in my room because it was too heavy, but more than that I had, had no use for it in my current creative dry spell.

I needed to prove my worth amongst these published authors and my new friends. I also wanted to prove that Mavis was wrong about me. I was tired of being humiliated by her in front of everyone, including Esther. It was so cruel and so unfair. I was going to find the cause of Mendel's death, no matter what the cost—monetarily and personally.

I just hoped I could get on the Internet, because service was not guaranteed on the high seas. It could be affected by the *Queen Anne's* position and the weather.

⌘

CHAPTER 16

And Now We Were Nine

The library was large with walls and aisles of neatly arranged hardcover and paperback books for passengers to check out, hold in their hands, and turn the pages. It was a throwback to the world before electronic reading and e-books became so abundantly, economically, and conveniently available.

As it turned out, for Internet access there were rate reduction packages, but the savings was not much and there was no refund for unused minutes. All of it was outside my budget, but I was on a mission. A mission financed by my on-board account where the charges were posted and which I would pay.

I spent my entire morning on the Internet.

First, I scanned the latest news on Otto's murder. It remained unsolved, but the official cause of death was repeated blows to the head. There was a defensive fracture on his right forearm, his left cheekbone and jaw were shattered, and he had four broken ribs. The frustrated and embattled New York's finest still categorized the incident as an attempted burglary. Evidently, they had no other concrete leads. I checked the

MWW chat room and mystery writer's blogs. They were buzzing with exotic murder plots worthy of bestselling mystery books. The media fanned the flames by reporting anything scandalous short of defamation—sadly, filling their coffers at this icon's expense. But all the speculation just made the NYPD appear more rational in its conclusion.

Then, I got to work. I reviewed the effects of Mendel's prescribed Synthroid and its interactions with drugs and alcohol. Nothing was heart related or life threatening, even though the drug companies enumerated an abundance of side effects ranging from constipation to total insanity. The vast number of absurd and remote warnings, to me at least, invalidated any legitimate warning they could have given. I truly believed that someday a victim of side effects would sue and win because the courts would instruct a jury that the scattergun, catch-all miniaturized font warnings of hundreds of side effects constituted no warning at all.

I researched the symptoms I had observed before we left Mendel in his stateroom alive, but evidently dying, in his bed. I read about everything we noted after he died, including the time of death as Mary explained it. Mary was a very knowledgeable woman when it came to death and its symptoms. Her experience came from hundreds of deaths she had depicted in so many murder mysteries. I wondered if I would ever have her expertise. I feared I had started writing too late in life and, evidently, refused to devote the time it took to be like her.

Mendel's symptoms matched a conglomeration of side effects for an overdose of—or a toxic interaction with—hundreds of medications. When I studied the allergic reactions to medications, foods, and drinks the results were also manifold. All I could really conclude, after all the time and money I had spent, was that Mendel definitely did not die of a heart attack, as the good doctor would have had us believe. This research and learning the medical terms, at least, would make my conclusion more credible and help me express it clearly to whoever would listen.

I thought back to Esther's concern it could be something on board that would eventually affect other passengers—that Mendel was just the unlucky first. On other cruise ships, there had been literally hundreds of outbreaks of various illnesses over the years: most commonly a norovirus or a gastrointestinal disease, but also flu and even several dozen cases where passengers had contracted Legionnaire's disease. There were a number of deaths as well. We in the know had to keep our hands clean and our eyes and ears open, because it was obvious the *Queen Anne* staff and the Wessex Cruise Line were economically vested in keeping things hushed.

With all the variables, I needed to narrow my focus. I had to apply the mystery writer's process of systematically eliminating the possible causes of death. But there were just so many.

First, from my own observation, I saw Mendel drinking three Martinis that night and eat the olives. Then there was the half empty bottle of gin in his stateroom. And Amy inferred to the doctor that Mendel had been "downing" drinks at her table. So there were possibly more. The Martinis were served at two tables by the ship's waiters and, presumably, came from the ship's bar. And, Martinis were all liquor, which meant no tainted water or fruit juice—or anything other than the olives stuffed with pimentos—but they were a well-preserved condiment. Mendel ate nothing at our table before he got up to leave, not even the bread. And, he told Brent that he hadn't eaten all day. That could have been an exaggeration, but I believed not in view of the marked effects of the Martinis.

I was stumped. And a lot poorer for every minute I spent on the Internet. So I stopped using the expensive Internet minutes. It was 1 p.m. and I left the library. I took a walk around the ship's deck to reevaluate and analyze the facts.

The cool brisk wind was rejuvenating. I inhaled the thick salty sea air and felt it settle on my face. But unfortunately, all I concluded was that I needed more information. I also needed to know more about Mendel and Amy and Frederick. They were a trio that did not compute.

I went to the cafeteria up on the top deck before it closed for a bite to eat. I hoped I would see one of my new buddies to bounce some ideas off, hopefully Sean or Mary. I knew Curtis would be with his clients.

I wished last night had not gone as it did. Not only for poor Mendel, but because I had missed my chance at romance as well.

* * *

At lunch, I didn't run into anyone I knew. However, I enjoyed the spacious cafeteria alone. It had wonderful views of the vast Atlantic Ocean. There were dark clouds surrounding the *Queen Anne* with glimpses of sunlight shooting down, creating patches of sparkling water at the sea's churning surface. I thought how difficult it must have been for the Allies and Axis powers even to find each other in World War II. The Atlantic was endless, mountainous, gray, cold, and foreboding.

I meandered around the many food stations: Chinese, Italian, Indian, Thai, and American—even vegetarian. The fruits and desserts were inviting and every bit as gourmet as the dinner the night before. Finally, I chose Italian—crab-stuffed ravioli in white sauce. It was lovely.

As I sat with my warm decaf Earl Gray tea after lunch, I thought about what Anne had said at breakfast about Otto and Mendel dying so close together. It was tragic, but was it more? Was it too coincidental?

I had skipped the panel discussions I wanted to hear this morning to do my research. Unfortunately, this afternoon had all the MWW activities I dreaded. There were the groups meetings where authors read their works—presumptively for compliments, even though it didn't always turn out that way. Then there were the tables of book sales and signings in the main lobby—sales, naturally, were the key to the money pipeline. Most authors dutifully shopped the tables, contributing to each other's success. Lastly, there were critique sessions for new authors by assigned agents who were experienced authors or teachers. Mavis was in charge of one of them. I had purposefully not brought anything to critique. I didn't want to be assessed by anyone on this beautiful voyage, least of all Mavis, whose stature had now diminished in my eyes.

After my tea, I went out onto the deck. I stood at the rail, looked at the dark green sea, and thought about this evening and Curtis. I was soon chilled with no sun and went back to my room.

I took a long hot shower and washed away the salt in my hair and on my face from my brief sojourn on the deck.

I napped before dinner and, hopefully, before Curtis.

* * *

I woke to Mavis banging around the stateroom.

"You're awake?" Mavis was dressed and putting on her jewelry for dinner.

"I am now," I mumbled.

"Pardon?"

"Yes, I am. How was your afternoon?"

"Productive . . . but no time to talk now. I have to get down to the bar. Esther and a group of us are meeting with Frederick. Frederick graciously has volunteered to take over some of Mendel's panel positions and, just maybe, we can get him to do

Mendel's presentation at the awards ceremony on the last night."

"That's nice of him to pitch in."

I thought of Frederick's phone call in the transport van and his irritation at even taking the cruise. I also remembered his angry interchanges with Mendel at the table.

"I think he should be happy to pitch in." Mavis dabbed perfume behind her ears. "It puts him out there more."

"Out there more!" I thought.

I marveled at Mavis's strange and incongruous obliviousness to the politics involved and the pecking order of Frederick's popular and powerful position in the Hollywood world. Frederick didn't need to put himself out there more. But it wasn't my place to teach the teacher.

"Any more news about Mendel?" I knew Mavis had been with the group all day and was a gossipmonger.

"Not really. But Sean lodged a complaint with the cruise line about the doctor being drunk. It might make a difference but I don't know how . . . Mendel's gone. In my opinion, there is no use ruining our cruise over it."

Mavis was dressed in a sky blue silk dress and fabric shoes dyed to match. She looked like she was going to a prom in the sixties. I was glad I was not walking into dinner with her.

"I suppose not." I was appalled at her attitude. "But Sean has a point. The doctor might have been able to do more, especially if it wasn't a heart attack."

Mavis did not jump to the bait.

"I've got to go. Esther may have me do one of Mendel's presentations if Frederick can't do them all. What a coup that would be! I'm so excited."

"Well, good luck!"

"Thanks."

I thought to myself, "You'll need it."

"Speaking of good luck, are you seeing your friend tonight?' Mavis asked. "What a find he is."

"Don't know."

I didn't want to share with Mavis, not my research, theories or my personal life, let alone "girl talk."

Mavis left.

"Good riddance," I grumbled.

I was awake now, so I got up and got dressed.

I wanted to talk to Sean about my research, anyway. I was intent on rehabilitating myself in Esther's eyes and possibly making a name for myself on the cruise—just like I had at the Valentine Theatre.

* * *

As I approached the dinner line, I spotted Amy waiting alone. I rushed to take advantage of the opportunity to probe.

"Amy, hi!" I slipped into the line next to her.

"Hello. Did you enjoy the panel discussions today?"

"I didn't get to many." There was a cheeriness in Amy's voice that had been absent before.

"Oh, too bad," Amy said. "I was on three. I provided the agent perspective. I have done this so much that I was just on auto-pilot."

"I would imagine."

"But I was a reader for one of the new authors critique groups this afternoon, too. That was interesting."

"Do you actually discover new talent that way?"

"Surprisingly, yes. And I did hear a very interesting chapter read. The young man had a very unique, dark voice. I gave him my card."

"That's good, especially for him."

I noted Amy's unusual chattiness as the line moved forward—more quickly tonight because everyone knew where to go. The faster pace made me push to take advantage of Amy's unguarded sociability.

"Have you ever thought of writing instead of being an agent?"

"I'm published. Many years and a lifetime ago." Amy was uncharacteristically candid. "But I like being an agent. Who's yours?"

"My what?"

I knew full well I was about to do the agent-two-step again with her as I had at pre-boarding.

"Agent?"

"I don't have one yet," I admitted bluntly without excuse. "To tell you the truth I haven't bothered. I will someday."

Amy looked at me surprised. "From our conversation at boarding I thought you had one."

"No."

"Humph, usually novices without agents do nothing but hound me about their books. You haven't. That's refreshing. Aren't you interested in an agent?"

I had no rhetoric at the tip of my tongue. There was silence. The conversation was not going the way I planned or wanted.

"Well, look . . . here's my card," Amy smiled with her bleached white teeth and two small evenly matched dimples.

"Send me something! I think you may just have a good mystery under your belt."

"Thank you."

I put the card in my evening bag, but knew I'd never use it. I was wary of her and didn't really want any kind of a relationship with her. I was content being the voyeur peeling back fascinating layers of her onion-like personage to see what made her tick. One of those layers, the most important of course, was her time with Otto and why she appeared to dislike

Frederick and Mendel—the latter now deceased, with the definitive cause as yet to be determined.

We were approaching the dining room and time was short. I pushed my agenda.

"Did Otto help you get started as an agent after you gave up writing?" I delved quickly, and I thought artfully, into her background at Otto's program.

"No. Not really."

"You must have tried to land Mendel or Frederick as clients." I needed to know if her observable hostility toward them was professional or personal. "They would have been the plum prizes."

"Plum prizes? I suppose so."

Amy's voice was neutral and detached, and she turned forward as we reached the front of the line. She had closed down, but I still pushed.

"I think any agent would put it that way."

"Ah, here we are. Have a pleasant dinner." Amy took her leave without looking back at me.

Amy went toward her table—I to mine.

* * *

I side-winded through the people and tables to the bustling MWW area. Diners were greeting each other, inter-table and intra-table. Groups were blocking the aisles as collegiality brimmed over. I spotted Mavis hovering over Esther, who was already seated. Esther ignored Mavis and spoke intently to Frederick nearby.

"Hey, where have you been? I popped my head into a few of your meetings and didn't see you."

I turned in the aisle to see Curtis's dark eyes sparkling down at me.

"You didn't?" I smiled—it was nice to be missed.

"Fess up. Did you have another date?"

"No," I laughed as we now bottlenecked the aisle. "I was indulging in mystery and intrigue."

"Writing?"

I wished. But now was not the time to have a conversation about writer's block or my recalcitrant muse.

"No, I did my own research about Mendel's death," I whispered. "It was no heart attack! And I ruled out food poisoning, or any poison for that matter . . . no stomach pains."

"I think we know all that, Veronica."

"Do we?"

"Of course . . . it's an overdose. The doctor is simply being discreet."

"What? Discreet . . . by covering up a drug overdose?"

"I don't know for sure, but I do know an overdose wouldn't look good for Mendel, Wessex or the MWW, would it?"

"No."

"Just a theory from a finance guy. I never underestimate corporate greed. But then, of course, I don't have your credentials when it comes to bodies or mysterious, untimely deaths."

I was pleased Curtis thought well of my credentials, no matter how tenuous they really were in the face of the accomplished, published, and successful writers here. And, I would say nothing to the contrary—not tonight—not ever. I believed that unabridged and voluntary honesty is overrated. Especially, when it comes to relationships, particularly budding ones.

"But Mendel was drinking, not taking drugs! He . . ."

"Who knows without an autopsy and a tox screen?" Curtis interrupted me as diners squeezed by. "I watch cop shows and you write this stuff!"

"True . . ." I rehabilitated myself. "But the drugs dissipate and . . ."

"Excuse me." A portly man's cummerbunded stomach pushed by.

"Now is not the time. The bar after dinner?"

"Sure."

For a moment, my gaze followed Curtis to his table. He was so tall and so distinguished with his graying hair and his tuxedo. I wanted a date tonight, not a debate about Mendel's death.

As I went to my table, I decided tonight with Curtis we would talk only about him and a possible "us."

* * *

My table—our table—had no place setting for Mendel. Now we were nine. But despite the loss of Mendel, we carried on as usual—hungry, happy, angry, flirtatious, brooding, and boozing.

Sean studied the menu. Brent leaned over and chatted up Heather, who was giggling and enthralled. Brent, happy with Heather's attentions, laughed at his own wit and looked down her gently scooped black dress, much as Mendel had done.

Helga finished her champagne cocktail and ordered another as she, in normal form, gave Brent the evil eye. Brent ignored her glares and Helga occupied herself with her fresh champagne cocktail.

Mavis, who had deserted Esther, enthusiastically described Mendel's body to Elias.

I took my seat and scanned the menu.

"Good evening," Elias greeted me. "Mavis just filled me in on poor Mendel."

Mavis turned to the brooding Helga.

"It was horrible." I replied.

131

"Is it true the doctor said it was a heart attack and there's some doubt?" Elias asked.

"Yes."

"I suppose I'm not surprised. All he cares about is what he's paid to do . . . make Wessex look good."

"That's the bottom line. He was just too quick and cavalier. He didn't account for any of the strange symptoms."

I described what I had seen in detail.

"Those aren't heart attack symptoms!"

"Mary agrees, and so does Sean."

"They do?"

"Yes, nothing computes. So, I spent the day researching the symptoms. I don't know what killed him, but it was definitely not a heart attack."

"You should have come to me straight away." Elias stroked his moustache with his forefinger thoughtfully.

"What do you mean?"

"Behind this exciting Greek-cook exterior and mild-mannered mystery writer lies the wisdom of Socrates and the skills of Sherlock Holmes."

"Really?"

I was curious at the claims made by this recipe-writer. I assumed he was exaggerating and puffing, as we all know Greeks love to do.

"Yes, my dear. Really!"

"Then what did kill him, my master?" I chided, not expecting an answer.

"Prolixin," Elias whispered. "Since you asked."

"Prolixin!"

"Tasteless, odorless, and clear."

"The symptoms?"

"They all fit. I believe it was an allergic reaction to his Prolixin prescription. In fact, I will stake my reputation on it. Many novices would mistake it for a heart attack."

"But a doctor, too?"

"Well, he's not really a doctor's doctor, is he? He's a Wessex Cruise Line toady."

"I have to agree, having seen him in action. But how? How do you know so much about Prolixin?"

"Simple. I had the killer in my *Mousaka Murders* put liquid Prolixin in his wife's wine to kill her," Elias winked at me. "It did the job. And, it did it with the same symptoms you have told me. I researched it thoroughly. It's an anti-psychotic drug and knowing Mendel's ego there is no way he would think of himself as psychotic . . . or ever admit it."

Elias chuckled and then added, "We all think of ourselves as normal don't we?"

I was impressed. I also sadly realized that I was, actually, not as knowledgeable as these published writers. And, clearly not even the equal of the lower echelon of food mystery writers like Elias. He made his money on silly cooking plots and I had always looked down my nose at that contrived conceit. But evidently it took a stockpile of research and fine-honed knowledge to have a character commit murder-through-food in a book—and not get caught for over ninety-five thousand words of running, covering-up, and avoiding arrest until the climax.

Then my imagination soared, my suspicion of wrongdoing against Mendel now intensified. I probed the superior brain next to me.

"And, in an article I read today Mendel's agent denied Mendel took *any* drugs, except prescribed Synthroid, and also said there was no history of heart trouble."

"Interesting . . ." Elias held me in suspense for a long pregnant pause. ". . . very interesting."

"Talk, Elias! Tell me what you are thinking."

"First, we can assume Mendel did recreational drugs and the agent is covering up like they all do."

"Of course." I agreed, after all I lived in the orbit of the film and music scene in Santa Monica and was a part of the acting world—a small part, but a part.

"More significantly I believe that the agent was being candid about Mendel's health. Those folks scrupulously monitor their meal tickets. If Prolixin is the culprit, it obviously was not a voluntary ingestion," Elias leaned over and whispered in my ear, his mustache tickling through my long hair. "So . . . it has to be murder any way you cut it . . . murder amongst us!"

I gasped at Elias's clear and unequivocal validation of my own thoughts. "But . . . who? Why? How?"

"Well, therein 'lies the rub' as Shakespeare would say. Doesn't it?"

"Yes, but . . ."

"I did this exact research for my book. First, you have to be bipolar to get it prescribed, so with a little acting you can get a prescription and doctor-shop with another identity. Second, and most importantly, it's even easier to get on the Internet . . . for anyone with a brain. It comes in a little orange pill or liquid. Liquid's what I used it in my book. It is accessible and perfect to put the person's food or drink."

"But you say anyone can get it. So why . . . would . . .?"

"You ask just the right question, Veronica. *Why* . . . we need to know the *why* to discover the *who*! Simple."

"Not so simple if you . . ."

I was going to bring up Otto's murder being so close in time then suddenly, the table shook as if struck by the 6.7 Northridge Earthquake in 1994 that hit Santa Monica, too. Helga had jumped up, slammed her fists on the table, and zeroed in on Brent and Heather exchanging business cards.

"What the hell are you doing?" Helga shrieked and charged over to them, her feet barely touching the floor.

Helga leaned down into Heather's beautiful face. Heather's round sapphire eyes opened even bigger than their natural luscious size. Her white skin turned red down to her decoupage peeking from a modestly scooped black top adorned with a delicate gold chain. Helga grabbed both cards, ripped them up, and threw them in Heather's startled face.

"Get the hell away from him!" Helga spat. "He's mine! And no plump, fertile piece of ass is going to . . ."

"Helga!" Brent pulled her back. "Stop. Heather's husband is an entertainment lawyer in New York. An up and coming associate in a prominent and highly respected entertainment law firm there. She says he loves your work. We were only talking about you becoming a client!"

"Oh . . . I . . ." Helga stood up straight and adjusted her shimmering silver evening blouse back over her black silk skirt.

"Well." Helga thought a moment and then she pasted a red lip-sticked smile across her face for Heather. "Sorry, dear."

Heather sat frozen staring at Brent calming Helga with exaggerations; Heather's husband had only just started at his law firm and actually had never read Helga's books—just Heather had.

"Give her another card, Brent." Helga, unfazed at the spectacle and staring diners, strutted back to her seat. She ordered a third champagne cocktail.

"I'm so sorry, Heather."

Brent obeyed and put another card on the table. Heather sat frozen. Brent looked sheepishly around the disturbed dining room, held his head up, but not as high as usual, and followed Helga back to his own side of the table. Brent slid in next to Helga. He quietly drank his wine and buried himself in the menu.

"Excuse me." Heather stood with tears brimming in her eyes.

She grabbed her velvet black evening jacket and evening bag. She made her way through the tables to the staircase and out of the dining room. She left Brent's card next to her plate.

135

"I'll take care of this, Elias. Order for Heather and me if you have to." I followed Heather.

I went because I felt for the young woman, but my motives were not altogether altruistic. I wanted information about Otto's program and his last days. I also wanted insight into Mendel's background. The two deaths were too close to be independent. In this emotional, vulnerable moment I was confident that Heather would be unguarded and open. I was in search of the *why* that Elias had stated earlier was the key to finding the *who*.

In point of fact, what mystery writer hadn't written this emotionally charged scene with a beautiful woman who knew something she didn't know that she knew? It had been written a million times to further the plot and to elicit otherwise unreachable and seemingly unimportant facts.

Truly, at the very beginning of suspicions lie the creative impulses that make an investigation bear fruit. I had concluded that after my few encounters with crime.

CHAPTER 17

Anticipation and Consummation

I caught up with Heather at the elevators. Her long blond hair shimmered down her back set off by her black velvet evening jacket.

"Wait! Don't go."

Heather turned gracefully like a cat. Tears streamed from her round sapphire blue eyes past her waterproof mascara down her face. She wiped them away.

"I'm going back and ordering room service."

"Don't. I've only known Helga for two days now, but I've seen her behave just as badly several times. No one takes her seriously and she's forgotten it by now."

"But I can't go back."

"Please. You can't let her ruin your evening. Cruelty is a knee-jerk reaction with her . . . in case you haven't noticed. We all condemn her, but, like Brent, we can't stop her. What can any of us do? Don't let her spoil your evening . . . or ours."

"That's so sweet, but how can I face her?"

"Easily. We all know she is paranoid when it comes to Brent. It wasn't you. It's her. And we like you. Which is more than any of us can say for Helga."

"Thank you." Heather took a deep breath.

"Let's sit over here a minute."

"Alright."

We headed for the alcove seats.

"There isn't one of us Helga hasn't attacked, or will attack, before the cruise is over. We all have to just let it roll off."

We sat in an alcove near the elevators with a large window looking out into the blackness of the Atlantic Ocean at night. I looked down at the foam churned by the ship and dramatically lit by the ships lights. I had her alone. I planned my entree into a discussion of Otto's program and Otto's last day.

Then, Heather made it easy.

"You know," Heather said. "I signed up for the cruise to celebrate Otto's life and then he died. But I came anyway . . . to share my loss."

"I didn't know Otto, but his death is a tragedy."

"It really is, at least to me. He believed in me and helped me get my first book published while I was in his program five years ago. And, even though my husband does some entertainment law, truthfully, he's really new at it. Otto had contacts to help me sell my book for a movie."

"That's wonderful. You were young to publish."

"Twenty-one."

"Really!" As a glorified imposter I was impressed that she had published at all, let alone at twenty-one.

"Amy Miller was younger . . . twenty." Heather smiled.

"Oh?"

"I ran into her our first day out of New York. She's an agent now. I didn't get a chance to ask her why she stopped writing, but I'd like to know . . . being kindred spirits."

"Of course." I prodded for more insight.

"And now she has to deal with Mendel's death, too."

"What do you mean?"

"I think she was close to him. There were old-time pictures of her and Mendel and Frederick together in Otto's office. They looked like the three musketeers together . . . and happy."

"I didn't know that." But one thing I did know was that they were definitely anything but close now.

Heather chatted away and became calmer as she did. Her eyes lit up when she talked about Otto's program.

"I know I've published a lot since the program . . . science fiction you know . . . but Otto truly empathized with me about my science fiction rut. A lucrative rut, but a rut. I know that sounds silly, but I always thought I had more in me as a writer . . . and Otto . . . well . . . he agreed. He inspired me to test my boundaries."

"He inspired a lot of writers."

"You know that I came on the cruise because I was thinking of moving into mysteries or combining soft science fiction with a mystery overlay?"

"Yes, I heard. It's a good mix. The structure of mystery, I imagine, is easier than science fiction—with the crimes and then the solutions to them. But, it may bore you after the complexity of science fiction."

"No. Not at all. I would emphasize character development. It's hard to do that in science fiction. Doing mysteries I feel I could be more authentic . . . more creative. Human nature is what really excites me and that comes out more when you get away from science fiction . . . I think, anyway. Otto agreed with me."

"He advises writers after the program . . . forever it seems." I was trying to get to my questions.

"Yes."

"You were in touch with him his last days. Did the police ever speak to you?"

"No, why would they?"

At that moment, I knew then she'd never make it as a mystery writer. How could she not see that murder began close to home—almost always. She was not only in his home near the end; she seemed to be part of his family. She had to have some insight, some facts about his death.

"Oh, I don't know. Was he helping anyone else? Anyone who would know more about his death? Someone in your class, maybe?"

"Good thought."

Echoing silently through my head was a silent, sarcastic "You think, Ms. Science Fiction?" But I bit my sarcastic tongue and said, "Just brainstorming."

"I still have friends from my class, but they avoid Otto."

"Why?"

"They don't like him. They don't like that he takes credit for other people's successes and don't want him taking any credit for theirs. But, I say give credit where it's due."

"Oh, me too," I agreed disingenuously. "But there must be other reasons, too."

"Maybe. My best friend, Anita, from my first year . . ."

"Anita?"

"Anita Valdes. She won't even talk about him or the program. But I think that's because she doesn't write any more. She says her muse is gone."

I, of course, didn't bring up my own recalcitrant muse or my belief, born of hope that muses do return. Some writers thought that absent muses never returned, especially if trauma interfered or made it dormant for years. I knew that my poor muse was just starving for me to give it my full attention and stop playing author out-and-about in the real world. It wanted

140

me to get back to the lives of my characters in the printed and the fictional world of words being created in my books.

"Why is it gone?" I asked.

"I don't know. I think she's jealous of my success and my close relationship with Otto. Of the close relationship I had with Otto, I mean."

"Interesting." I thought of the womanizing angle Frederick had alluded to. "Did they have a personal relationship?"

"What do you . . . oh! No. Of course not! He's older."

I let it go and didn't say that men are never too old. "What about the days just before he was murdered? Did he say anything to you?"

"Wait! Do you think one of his students did it?"

"Oh, no." I hedged because I knew now that animosity, if not hatred, graduated with many of his students in the program. "I was just curious because you spoke to him that evening. Maybe someone saw something."

"Ah."

I was nonplussed again. How could Heather not see the relevance and be probing into Otto's death with her proximity to him in the last days of his life? I now was even more convinced she would never be a mystery writer, like me. She might get published, but it would be a mere "halo effect" rubbing off from her reputation as a science fiction writer. It would be undeserved.

"What did you talk about the night he was murdered? Do you remember?"

I was getting impatient with this wide-eyed adorable woman who appeared to be an idiot savant unaware of normal life. And, certainly, unaware of the proper and instinctive concerns ingrained in all suspicious and trained investigators of human foibles and evil—namely, mystery writers.

"Just me going into the mystery genre. But now that we're talking about it, I . . . I think he was expecting someone, because he did cut our conversation short."

"Who? A woman or a man?"

"I don't know. He didn't say. But, from my end of the phone I heard him pop a wine cork and clatter around with a couple of glasses." Heather dismissed the subject. "But I feel better now and you're right, I'm not going to let Helga ruin my evening. Let's go back.

"All right."

"How's my face?"

"Perfect." Sadly for all of us less fortunate, that was literally true. "Just wipe a little under your eyes."

I knew this conversation was a dead end. Heather was candid and couldn't add much more about that night because she was, at heart, just exactly what she had always been—a science fiction writer —an unsuspicious, unobservant, obtuse science fiction writer, whose imagination was her real world.

"Good thing I wear waterproof mascara." Heather giggled.

"I'm surprised you wear any with those long lashes."

"Thanks, but we all need help."

Some more than others, I thought as we headed back to the dining room. In the back of my mind, I reserved the right to take another run at her about Otto at some other opportune time, if not about the night he was murdered.

"You know I spent my whole youth writing poetry in school instead of listening to my teachers," Heather confided in me as we walked back to the dining room. "Every year I would send five new poems into the Poetry Society of America to become a member. But they never let me in."

"That's precocious." I was genuinely impressed. "Are you a member now?'

"No. But I applied again this year. I'm going to knock on their door forever."

"You're tougher than you look . . . all that rejection . . . and going back, even now, after your successes. I don't think I could do that."

I actually *knew* I couldn't do that because—I hadn't. I hadn't even exposed myself to one rejection of even one of my books. I had never even mailed a query letter to either an agent or a publisher.

Heather smiled. "I view it as their loss."

"Good attitude."

As we walked back to dinner, I thought of my low threshold for rejection and admired her tenacity. But I realized that she didn't have the mystery writer's instincts or the skills to be a genre jumper—very few people did. And if they did have the instincts and skills, more often than not, their fans rejected their new-genre books. Many multi-million dollar legal suspense authors publish excellent literary novels that flop because fans just don't see them that way. This phenomenon is real but unexplained. Evidently, there is not a new fan base to be had under the same name. Some use a *nom de plume*, but still fail because their *nom de plume* is back at ground zero with the thousands of new authors at the starting gate. Building a reputation and name recognition is not easy.

I believed Heather would never make a true mystery writer like me. She was unobservant and not analytical. We mystery writers see the possibilities in all that is around us and presume evil—oftentimes where there is none—but, to us, it all deserves a look-see and an analysis. To Heather, it does not.

I contemplated advising her to go back to the genre from whence she came. But I didn't. Let her learn for herself.

* * *

Back at the dinner table, everyone was chatting except Brent. He was eating quietly and glowering at Helga. I had not seen him like this before. Up to now, he had handled Helga with good graces and humor. In spite of her tirades, he had always sprung back to enjoy the moment and the company. Tonight, I felt sorry for him. He looked truly beaten.

Naturally, Helga didn't even notice Brent's distress or, if she did, she didn't acknowledge it. She went from champagne cocktails to dinner wine and got louder and louder. She was charming to Heather the rest of the evening. After all, she believed Heather's husband could be good for her. Helga made sure Heather put Brent's card in her purse and she also gave Heather one of her own.

Helga never apologized to Heather, but did obliquely refer to much champagne with no food. The same recipe that apparently contributed to the demise of Mendel, except it was Martinis.

I thought to myself, "Too bad it didn't do the same to this shrew."

* * *

After dinner, I met Curtis in the bar. He was waiting with two glasses of Cabernet at the same table we had the night before. I sat as he held the chair for me. I knew more about him than he knew about me after Mary's interrogation last night, but that didn't make any difference to him. He sat across from me and gave me a monologue about *his* day—*his* presentations, successes, misses, strategies, and annoyances. I didn't mind, though. I had been married for too many years to expect that men were anything less than self-absorbed.

I gave him my undivided attention. His dark eyes were intoxicating . . . more intoxicating with every sip of my Cabernet. Just looking at him made the listening worth it.

"Excuse me a minute." Curtis slid out of his chair quickly. "I want to sign for my clients' drinks over there. I'll be right back."

While Curtis gregariously took care of his table of clients in a far corner, I glanced around the candle-lit bar.

I spotted Mavis, Jody, and Agnes across the room at a table listening to the bespectacled Herbert, who was laughing and flashing his yellow teeth. He was obviously enjoying the sound of his own grating, nasal voice. His harem was drinking wine quickly and quietly. All three were postured in good female listening mode, much as I had been with Curtis. However, I knew Herbert was a charity case because nothing could compensate them for his always-uninteresting exchanges and unattractiveness. I concluded that too much wine had already anesthetized them.

Beyond, there was Brent on a bar stool, leaning on his elbow and gulping wine. Near the center of the room, Helga, Anne, Mary, Sean, and Elias had pulled surplus chairs up to a small table and formed a raucous group with a few unknowns.

More curious to me was the group of odd-fellows nearby sharing a bottle of red wine. They were none other than Heather, Esther, Frederick, and Amy. Esther and Heather sat across from Frederick, laughing as he performed an animated story, gesturing with his arms flying about. I was glad for Heather because she needed to form these relationships in the mystery genre if she was going to follow Otto's advice. Amy sat smiling next to Frederick. She appeared to be happy. I didn't know why, but she did.

I recalled the first time I had met Amy at boarding, and the look in her eyes when she saw Frederick and Mendel. I decided Amy and Frederick could break bread after all and Mendel was the odd man out.

Curtis returned. "Sorry, I got caught for a minute, but I am not going to allow anything else to interrupt our evening. Not anything."

Curtis smiled and leaned forward in his chair until the candle's dancing light washed over his face. Then, as if a light bulb lit in his mind, he asked about *me*. However, unfortunately, it was the dreaded subject— my writing.

"I want to hear about your writing."

I stalled by taking a long slow drink of wine. I gazed into his eyes. I was drawn into them, into him.

Curtis reached across the table. My hand met his like a magnet. I forgot what he had asked and so did he.

* * *

We left the bar with no more conversation. We walked by the noisy casino taking money from passengers in full throttle. I knew where we were going and he knew where he was leading me—up the elevator to his stateroom. I was happy. And it was not because of the wine, which had flowed so generously that night, but because I felt desired and attractive and wanted.

When we got to his penthouse stateroom, I realized I was all three of those things to him—desired and attractive and wanted. Curtis turned on one lamp. It washed the large suite with a low light, including the bedroom through double doors.

The mating ritual began with Scotches from the bar and an offer of room service. Then, it advanced to the couch with seamless tentative tender touches and then breathless tongue dances.

"The bedroom?" He breathed into my ear with tongue

caresses radiating tingles down to my neck.

I heard myself say, "Yes."

Curtis stood and carried me to the bedroom.

⌘

CHAPTER 18

Immoderation

In the wee hours of the morning, I snuck back to my room. I woke late and Mavis was gone. I ordered tea before I hopped in the shower.

As I showered, Curtis swept through my mind and body. I could still smell him and feel him all over and in me. He was very experimental, for me at least. As I stepped out of the shower, my face felt hot. I looked in the mirror. The face I saw looking back at me was bright red. My thoughts had embarrassed me, but they had delighted themselves.

I hurried and dressed as I drank my tea. I chose a low cut red sweater and black slacks in hopes of running into Curtis during the day.

This morning, I was attending an MWW panel discussion on "Marketable Ways to Kill Off Your Characters." Frederick was the moderator and I knew he would be entertaining. I actually did want to improve my authorial skills on this cruise. I was, in fact, a writer, and even though I was delighted with this recent and unexpected opportunity to flex my investigatory skills once again, I did need to learn something. However, there was one series of panel discussions I would still avoid at any cost, anything to do with editing and publication. To me, it would be like going to church and having guilt drilled into my writing soul.

I grabbed my purse and room key and rushed to the conference room. I was twenty minutes late.

* * *

At the conference room I reached to open the door quietly, assuming it had started. Instead, I literally ran into Brent rushing out.

"Oops! Excuse me." Brent sidestepped just in time. "Sorry. Are you alright?"

"Yes, fine. You in a hurry?"

"On an errand for Helga before I get to Curtis's investment seminar."

"Enjoy."

As I watched Brent speed down the hall, I thought I might slip into one of Curtis's seminars tomorrow, too. But seminars were not really what I wanted from Curtis. My memories of last night burst into my mind. I remembered Curtis's dark, dark eyes in the dim light of his bedroom looking down at me. I paused and then snapped back into the reality of the morning. I didn't want my face flushing again here.

In the room, the program had not yet begun. The others were as late as I was. Although most people were seated, there was a group still mingling around the continental breakfast table at the back of the room.

On the platform were the three presenters who were each geniuses in their own right on "Marketable Ways to Kill Off Your Characters." First, Sean, who was, of course, the expert on murders in the Big Apple, the grotesque and unique deaths in New York City catalyzed by humans stacked on top of each other with anonymity until their inhumanity erupted. Then came Anne, who took the British reserve and peeled it back until common things became uncommon vehicles for murder, including pillows, stairways, scarves, automobiles, delicious food, or the ever-present English tea. And, lastly, Helga, who was so prolific she had done it all in her books, including scaring victims to death.

I went in and sat at the back next to Elias.

"Good morning." Elias was always friendly and displayed his signature broad smile from beneath his moustache.

"I guess I'm not so late?"

"You're late, but our panel moderator is later."

"Frederick?"

"Yes, Helga sent Brent to drag Frederick out of bed. I think we might need a curfew at the bar for our dear MWW membership, especially the panel members."

"As if anyone would be able to enforce it in this group." I scanned the audience and thought how I, personally, would not have given up my Curtis rendezvous—hopefully plural from now on.

My eyes rested on Heather and Amy diagonally across the aisle forward from us. I leaned over to Elias and nodded towards the two.

"It looks like our new inductee Heather has made a friend, or is trying to."

"Yes. And, of all people, Amy." Elias studied the pairing.

Elias was right. When I took a second look I realized Amy was staring straight ahead at the panel on the platform while Heather talked at her. Heather didn't notice, or didn't care. Heather had made a connection she wanted.

Mary suddenly plopped herself down with a thud into the chair next to me.

"I'm late." Mary whispered in my ear so loudly her words bounced around inside of my skull. Then, she leaned across me. "Good morning, my Greek friend."

"*Kalimera.*"

"I know what that means! Good morning."

"Correct! We were going to call out the cavalry for you."

Mary laughed. "Liar. You two didn't even miss me."

She was right. I hadn't even given her a thought.

Mary leaned up to the row in front, said good morning to anyone within earshot, and explained how she hated being late. I thought to myself that while she might hate being late, she loved an audience empathizing with her for being so.

I spotted Mavis in the front row desperately sucking up to Esther. She was so transparent; I was appalled and embarrassed for her.

I studied the panel table beyond and up on the platform. They were all waiting for Frederick to come and perform his task as the moderator.

Helga sat on the end, talked to no one, and this morning she had a particularly sour look on her face. After seeing her in the bar last night, I suspected a hangover was enhancing her ever-charming self.

I sat back, relaxed and let my mind return to Curtis. I liked him beyond lust. I anticipated going with him to the California Yacht Club in Marina del Rey and sailing with him on weekends. I wondered if he would invite other couples. I started worrying about not having enough time to do my writing. Then I scoffed at myself. What writing?

"Earth-to-Veronica."

Elias blasted into and interrupted my very pleasant thoughts.

"I said . . . do you want me to get you a coffee?"

"Oh, I didn't hear you."

"What were you thinking of? Your mind was not in this room with us?"

"It was, really. I was thinking how much I like being with other writers." I offered him a big white lie and stood. "I'll go with you and get a tea."

* * *

At the rear, we got our coffee and tea. With the Frederick-imposed delay, a steady stream of fellow writers got up and followed our lead to fortify themselves with more caffeine or more continental breakfast calories.

Esther went forward to the platform, shadowed by Mavis. Esther went up to the front corner of the platform. Mavis remained below. Esther switched on the freestanding microphone.

"Testing." The word resounded throughout the room.

"Could we please stay seated everyone? Frederick will be here to start the program any minute." Esther spoke slowly and authoritatively. "We have a wonderful and very knowledgeable panel today and when it gets underway, it will be worth the wait. After, we'll announce an adjustment to the schedule to accommodate the late starting time. Those of you at the back, please, get your goodies and take your seats so that we can get started the minute Frederick arrives. Any questions?"

There were none. But no one returned to his or her seats.

Esther frowned at the non-compliance and shook her head with her well-prepped blond hair bobbing. She remained poised, but went to complain to Sean at the panel table.

With her retreat, the room got noisier. More people ignored Esther's request to stay seated and migrated back to mingle and consume. Amy stood and headed back as well. She left Heather seated and, literally, talking to herself. Surprised, Heather got up and followed Amy—still talking at her.

152

As Amy and Heather approached, I overheard Heather's rapid fire monologue. She was telling Amy in detail about her idea for her crossover-genre mystery book with an overlay of science fiction. An unexplainable, horrific snowstorm isolates the exclusive resort of Aspen, Colorado and vacationers disappear *en masse*. It sounded like something out of H.P. Lovecraft, and not in a good way.

I understood why Amy was trying to escape from Heather. Nothing is worse than listening to an author talk about a book instead of writing it.

To me there were only two kinds of books; those that were written and those that were not. I didn't bore people by talking at them about unwritten books. In my view, only a real beginner did that. It confirmed my conclusion that compared to me, Heather was less-than-a-novice in my mystery genre.

I approached Amy and decided to rescue her as a gesture of good will. Why not? I've needed rescuing before and I still believed that with more questioning, Amy could reveal something useful to my investigation.

"Amy, good morning."

"Good morning." Amy happily and immediately joined Elias and me. "Good morning, Elias. You both know Heather, of course?"

Greetings flowed all around. Heather's hellos were less friendly and more those of a thwarted and disappointed ear-bender. I knew Amy's plan was to dump chatty Heather on us, but with Elias's ear to relieve mine, I didn't mind.

"Of course." Elias said. "Frederick must have had a late night?"

"Yes, Helga sent Brent to drag him out of bed." I turned to Amy. "How late were you guys drinking?"

"What do you mean?" Amy snipped. "I wasn't drinking late with anyone."

"I'm sorry." I shrank from Amy's unexpected defensiveness. "I meant the group must have kept Frederick up late."

"I don't know about the group." Amy replied. "I personally left after one glass of wine."

"That's right," Heather intervened. "I left too, when Frederick started that sailing talk with Brent . . ."

"Not Frederick. Me." Elias jumped in, generously placating and appeasing the nonsensical ruffled edges. "Frederick was tired. He left, too. Brent and I talked about the sea until late. I'm from good Greek islander stock . . . mariner stock. If my grandfather's ships hadn't been blown up by mines in World War II, he would have been a shipping magnate like Onassis or Niarchos."

"Really?" I was fascinated.

"Another story for another time." Elias drank his coffee. "Where is Frederick? Come to think of it, Frederick should be here . . . I should be the one in bed after last night!"

Elias laughed at his observation. He really enjoyed his life and I enjoyed him. I laughed and added, "If they didn't have such a wonderful by-the-glass wine selection, I suppose we'd all retire earlier and soberer."

"They are really exceptional." Heather turned to Amy. "Don't you think so?"

Amy was staring over at the conference room door and ignored the question.

"Amy?" Heather repeated.

"What?"

"The wine. Isn't it exceptional in the bar?"

"Oh, . . .yes. It . . ."

Amy stopped abruptly when a boom resounded through the room. The double conference room doors had burst open and ricocheted against the walls.

All eyes followed Brent after his spectacular entrance—without Frederick. All eyes but mine, that is. Mine rested on Amy. She was startled, like everyone else, and focused on Brent.

As murmurs wafted through the room, Brent bee-lined with long strides up the aisle to the platform.

* * *

Amy saw me studying her and said derisively "No Frederick? He must have gotten really soused."

Heather moaned, "We'll never start."

The whole room was now silent and focused on Brent and Esther conferring up on the podium.

"What are they doing?" Elias glowered.

Suddenly, Esther's face turned white and her knees buckled. Brent grabbed her around the waist.

The meeting room was ripe with gasps and questions. But Amy looked on silently—stricken and apparently concerned.

⌘

CHAPTER 19

The Clock Strikes Two

"Get me a chair," Brent called to Sean at the other end of the platform. "Hurry."

Mavis started up the steps to help.

"We have her," Brent rejected Mavis's intrusion.

Mavis reluctantly stood below, but close and poised to help.

Sean brought a chair from the panel table. They helped Esther into it and then Brent spoke to Sean.

"Dead?" Sean exclaimed loud enough for the microphone to pick up and resound through the room.

The words *dead*, who, and when abundantly echoed in this milieu of mystery writers.

"Dead? Who's dead?" Heather gasped, looking from Elias to Amy to me.

"We don't know what's going on. Just wait." Elias put his arm around Heather's shoulders, giving her a little squeeze. "Relax."

Elias's answer was disingenuous. He knew it was Frederick and I did, too. Furthermore, this entire room full of mystery writers, with their well-honed deductive reasoning skills, knew it as well. Everyone in the room knew Frederick was dead because it was well past the time even a hung-over Frederick would have dared to keep his fellow writers waiting. Everyone knew, that is, but Heather. Her obtuseness convinced me yet again that she would never make a credible mystery writer. After all, Frederick was the panel leader, Brent was sent to rouse him, and Brent had returned alone. Who else could it be?

Sean took the microphone. "Please be quiet. Sit down."

Some members sat. Others didn't. Some were quiet, but most weren't.

Without saying a word, Amy walked away and sat at the back of the room, alone.

"Coming?" Heather asked.

"No, dear, go on." Elias fobbed Heather off on Amy. "I'm sure she needs your support."

Heather joined Amy in the back row. Amy ignored Heather who chattered at her—now, I presumed, about Frederick.

Esther stood. Brent and Sean reached for her arms to help her, but she waved them away. She went to the podium and Brent and Sean stood close behind her.

Esther looked down, took a deep breath, and surveyed the room. Her stature as leader commanded silence this time. All obeyed. I knew not so much because they wanted to listen to Esther's always self-important, slow cadenced speeches, but, instead, because they collectively knew it was the only way their suspicion of Frederick's demise would be validated. And every mystery writer in that room, as well as the parasites who lived off those writers, wanted that validation.

"I have some tragic news . . . Frederick Larsen, our friend and colleague, has passed away quietly in his sleep."

The room burst with the hackneyed utterances people exclaim when met with such news. Not that they aren't sincere, but they are always generic and predictable. Rumbling through the audience of writers, colleagues, and hangers-on was a mixture of questions, answers, and speculations—sprinkled with comments about the Hollywood lifestyle, deadly heart attacks, morally reprehensible drunkenness, womanizing, overdoses, and death-by-hard-living scenarios.

Sean leaned into the microphone. "Quiet, please. Let's settle down."

The gaggle of mystery writers did not settle down nor were they quiet.

Esther whispered to Brent. He immediately leaped from the platform and headed for the doors.

"Let's go." Mary signaled Elias and me. "Hop to. We've got another body."

Mary fell in step behind Brent. Elias and I looked at each other in disbelief. Elias was genuinely startled and saddened at another mystery writer's death. I, of course, was sad as well—but honestly I was more excited by my good fortune at having another mysterious death to notch on my writer's biography. If I couldn't list books, then listing numerous deaths I had solved would have to do.

"Hurry," Mary called back to us. "Foul play is afoot again. I know it!"

Elias and I deposited our spent cups and followed our "general" leading us into the fray.

As we left, Esther fought for control of the MWW members with Sean backing her up.

I couldn't help but think that Sean was too valuable an asset to leave behind in the trenches, but we had no choice.

* * *

We followed Brent and Mary out of the room and to the elevator.

"Don't worry," Elias said, literally reading my mind. "We'll fill Sean in later."

"Okay. But I wish he was with us."

"I do too."

We all filed into the elevator, and Brent pressed the button for Frederick's floor. We started down.

"What happened?" Elias asked Brent.

"Don't know. I went to get him. His breakfast tray was sitting outside, untouched. I got the steward. We went in and he was still in bed. We tried to wake him, but he was dead."

"Had rigor mortis set in?" I queried.

After Mendel, I now knew how to set the time of death. Of course, I also knew I had to go back and rewrite all my mysteries to add that element to the clues. I was exasperated because, as I well knew, editing was not my *forte*. But then, mystery writing is a craft that must be learned. And, apparently, I never did the appropriate amount of research for time-of-death quandaries.

"What?" Brent looked up quizzically at me.

"Was he stiff?" Elias baby-talked for the non-mystery writer.

"As a matter of fact, yes. He was. The steward was creeped out about that."

"Of course." Elias stroked his mustache.

"I can't believe this." Brent muttered as the elevator stopped. "Another one."

"Neither can I." I knew from my as yet-unfulfilled crime writing career that two bodies in two nights here and another in New York was not the norm in any small group. "How? That's the question."

"I don't know. He looked like he was asleep. Like he died in his sleep," Brent responded. "I don't like this. Last night I was with a body, too. And I'm not one of you!"

"I'm sorry. I know it's hard." Elias spoke for all of us.

We followed single file out of the elevator and down the hall to the stateroom in silence. There was nothing more to say.

None of us liked this.

Brent least of all.

* * *

When we got to the room the doctor, again in his officer's white dress uniform, was standing over the king size bed. The sheets were thrown back to Frederick's waist.

Brent was right. It looked like he had died in his sleep. There was a small defibrillator, opened and apparently used, on the nightstand. Next to it was an unwrapped bag to hand pump oxygen, apparently also used.

"Good morning," Dr. Witte said in his impeccably clear toff British. "I think we all may have met? Last night?"

He was commendably stone cold sober—after all, it was morning. But, "may have" was an accurate assessment of the doctor's recollections. I knew the doctor only vaguely remembered us from his inebriated condition the night before. We actually had not engaged in the formalities of introductions. Why would we have? Quite frankly, I for one never would have expected that another dead body would bring us together again. And, the doctor had not been concerned, or the least bit doubtful, about Mendel's cause of death. But this morning's event warranted introductions.

"I'm Veronica Kennicott. And this is Elias Vlisides, Mary O'Connell, and Brent Hawthorne. We're from the mystery writers group, Frederick is . . . was traveling with us."

I looked directly up at the doctor's steely gray eyes as I asserted our cloak of authority for being there.

"How do you do. Dr. Witte. Head doctor."

"Dr. Witless," Mary mumbled under her breath to me.

I suppressed a chuckle.

"Hello." Elias took the lead. "What happened here?"

While Elias and Brent spoke to the doctor, I signaled Mary and we inspected Frederick's body to see if it had the same indications that were on Mendel's body the night before.

Dr. Witte explained to Elias and Brent what he had done to revive Frederick.

"But nothing worked, gentlemen, as you can see. There are no marks or visible signs of any bruises. Nothing out of order really. Nothing to sort out. It looks like a simple heart attack. I'm sure of it this time."

"This time," I whispered to Mary. "What does he mean by that? He as good as just admitted that he isn't sure about Mendel's cause of death."

"And that means this one too," Mary replied. "Let's look for a rash like Mendel's?"

I looked closer for a rash on Frederick's neck and chest. Mary followed suit.

"None," Mary whispered.

"But look at his eyes." I studied his open, but now lifeless ice blue translucent eyes. "The pupils are just like Mendel's . . . pinpoints."

"And the whites are yellowish."

"I see." I leaned with Mary to look.

Mary grabbed a pen from her purse, got nose to nose with Frederick, and opened his mouth.

"If you don't mind," Dr. Witte protested. "Let the body alone, ladies, or you'll have to leave."

"Sorry, just need a peek." Mary probed further.

"Oh, my God," I said. "It's bruised."

"And cut! Doctor, look at this." Mary insisted. "Did you see this?"

The doctor stepped over and took a long look. "He bit his tongue. What's unusual about that in the throes of death?"

Mary and I did double takes at each other. Then, Elias came over.

"Doctor, don't you think you should do some tests to see what happened to this man? I mean, you must have some facilities here. Mendel and Frederick could have died of the same thing. We could all be in danger."

Everyone stepped back from the body.

"This could be ship-wide already!" I made my play to force the doctor into *any* action—beyond inaction. "If it is, we passengers have a right to know."

"Because he bit his tongue?" The doctor started for the door. "Don't be ridiculous!"

"Wait, doctor," I commanded.

To my shock, he obeyed. The problem was, I had nothing else to say. All I knew was that someone should be looking into these deaths. I wished Sean were here with his NYPD-knowledge and lingo to influence the doctor. Then, my mind raced back to my third book, where my victim died suddenly in his sleep and the medical examiner did blood tests for poisons.

"You should take some blood samples and test them." I salvaged the moment. "Or, at least, preserve some samples."

Brent stepped up. "I agree. Can't you do some tests to see what happened to this poor man and Mendel? I mean, two heart attacks in two days? Come on."

"I am concerned that we all could be in danger," I insisted.

"I concur," Mary added. "I think any reasonable medical professional who is responsible for an entire ship of people should also be concerned."

We all knew the doctor was a corporate whore and his motivation was the well being of the Wessex Cruise Line—

protecting it from bad publicity, e.g. mass death on board. This tack was obviously his only Achilles heel; the only way to light a fire under his company ass. It appeared one or two deaths were acceptable collateral damage in a five-day cruise.

"I know Mr. Larsen is . . . was part of your little mystery writer's club, but I can guarantee not one of you is a Sherlock Holmes. Just exactly what would I be looking for? Tell me that," Dr. Witte replied. "Look at it from my point of view. Of these hundreds of people, passengers and crew, there is no one else even ill."

"They may not be now," Brent interjected. "But . . ."

"And these men fit the exact profile for a heart attack!" The doctor ignored Brent. "It happens more often than you think on cruises with all the overdrinking and carousing. These aging coots, usually Americans, start acting like teenagers . . . their bodies give out. Talk to security. They'll tell you. Bloody hell, just read obituaries . . . listen to the news! Vacation deaths are high up there on the list, especially for this type of man."

"This is not . . ." Elias began, but the doctor cut him off as he had Brent.

"Now, I have my duties to attend to. I am sorry, but enough is enough! When we deposit the bodies on land, then you can do as you see fit."

"But perhaps . . ." Mary protested.

"Stop," Elias said. "He's made up his mind."

"If he has one," Brent murmured.

"I'd watch it, sir." The doctor was red-faced and offended. "The man lying there had a reputation for partying and drugs. I am not remiss in any assumptions I make under these circumstances. Besides, it is Ms. Nussbaum I confer with . . . not you."

"Should I deposit the body in the infirmary, sir?"

"No, take it directly to refrigeration. The unit where we put the other one. It's marked."

163

"Aye, sir." The steward knew the protocol all too well.

"You people rejoin your group now." The doctor walked to the door and held it open. "And for your information, Ms. Nussbaum wanted Wessex to protect Mr. Weitzman from any bad publicity. She is sure he had a heart attack. And I am convinced, once I speak with her, she will feel the same about Mr. Larsen . . . Academy Award winner or not."

We left as we were told, chastised and stripped of any authority.

Not one person spoke as we walked down the long hall, or as we waited for the elevator to go back to our meeting room. I felt my mind churning and thinking of any way to fight the powers that had taken control—self-serving control or, more accurately, in my view, cover-up control. I also intuited the power of the more schooled minds walking down the hall with me. There was not one of us, to a person—to a mystery writing soul—who would take this lying down. The minds that walked with me were churning and grinding as hard as mine. The weighty silence spoke for itself.

Finally, at the elevator door, our collective presence reached critical mass. Elias turned to our little band.

"This doesn't make sense. I propose . . ."

Elias stopped when an elderly couple rounded the corner and stood with us.

"Good morning." the man said with his impeccable schooled British diction.

His wife followed suit. We responded as the elevator opened.

"Is the lift going down?" The lovely white haired woman asked.

"Yes, it is. Are you?"

She smiled. "Somewhat against my will. We are taking in the promenade deck."

"It'll do us good. The fresh air."

164

"A little too fresh perhaps, dear?"

We packed into the elevator. We all exuded charm and sociability, chuckling and commiserating with the man's leadership and the woman's reticence. But, our abundant side-glances demonstrated only to each other that we were chomping at the bit to analyze and compare Mendel and Frederick's deaths.

Two floors down the British man led the charge for the couple exiting the elevator. "Bundle up, dear. Off we go."

"Good day." The woman stood straight and followed her man out to the overcast day and cold salty air.

We were alone. Finally.

* * *

As the elevator door closed, everyone spoke at once, but Elias took the floor with his booming Greek voice.

"Yes, we all agree. There is something wrong here. Mary, I stopped you arguing with the dear doctor because it's clear we're on our own."

"I know. I took the hint."

Brent added, "It's obvious Esther sealed the deal with Wessex, the corporate masters, behind the scenes to cover up anything amiss."

"Yeah," Elias smirked. "Anyone can die shipboard and the powers-that-be will close ranks to keep the ship afloat!"

"Well put." I was angry. "And the doctor . . . I use the term very loosely . . . will cover up anything that does not suit the corporate guidelines . . . stated or otherwise."

"And, imagine him saying not one of us is a Sherlock Holmes! That takes a lot of nerve," Mary said. "I fancy myself cut from the same cloth."

"That goes without saying." Elias grinned.

"That doctor is an ass basing his diagnosis on tabloid stories. I mean I've been in those tabloids and nothing they printed was true about *me*," Brent added. "Not ninety percent of it, anyway."

"Besides," Mary insisted. "Two heart attacks don't compute."

"I agree," I said. "It's easier for Esther than to believe Mendel and Frederick overdosed on drugs. And, giving her the benefit of the doubt, she may be trying to do them a favor."

"It would keep the MWW free of scandal as well," Mary added

"That's generous of both of you." Brent led the way off the elevator at our conference room floor. "I think she just doesn't want any bad publicity for the MWW awards."

"That, too." Mary said.

"But we can make her change her mind," I said. "Remember, last night Frederick and Brent literally had to drag Mendel to his room."

"Yes," Brent stopped and so did we. "I should have realized something was wrong. He wasn't a typical drunk . . . he never covered up by trying to act sober. I mean, I've been there. All drunks do that."

"And," I added. "He tried to talk, but he couldn't control his tongue . . . it was spastic. He was afraid."

"He had a rash and his pupils were tiny, like Frederick's," Mary noted. "And remember Frederick's tongue, he could have bitten it because it was spastic!"

"Yes," Elias agreed.

"I feel so bad," I said. "I should have put two and two together at the time. There was something really wrong with Mendel."

"We put him to bed to die," Mary said. "Poor man."

"Horrible!" Elias stroked his moustache nervously. "The doctor has written these deaths off as heart attacks to please

Wessex, and Esther's buying into the whitewash for her own reasons. Maybe nudged by her little shadow Mavis."

"But Esther is not doing either of them a favor, even if it's well meaning," Brent said.

"From my years of research and killing people on paper," Mary added, "I can guarantee there were no recreational drugs involved here. At dinner, Mendel had barely begun to party before he had to leave."

"It all makes no sense," Brent concurred. "Mendel left the table because he said he didn't feel well. Remember? But he fell into that table because something was really wrong."

"I can tell you Sean will agree." Elias insisted. "He's a cop. He's seen hundreds of overdoses in his time on the force. He'll know with one look at the bodies."

"You're right," Mary concluded. "We've got to talk to Sean. This is more than suspicious."

Like Ouija board fingers, we started to walk again slowly to the conference room.

"You're preaching to the choir," Elias noted. "Last night at the bar when Frederick came over to our table from Esther's, he hadn't had that much. He was way behind me, to be frank."

I recalled seeing Frederick with Esther and Amy and Heather. "He did look fine."

Mary avowed with gravity, "One of the reasons people get away with murder is because no one thinks it is murder."

Elias smiled a sly smile. "Murder at our little mystery writers' conference? You're such an optimist, Mary."

"Bite your tongue, Elias." I feigned a reprimand, but was really excited too.

I, and apparently my cohorts too, believed there was foul play afoot. And, I was in the thick of it. In on the ground floor. But more than that, my new friends valued my deductive reasoning abilities. I was an official sleuth amongst stellar sleuths who, in my mind, were the cream of the crop and should indeed be compared to Sherlock Holmes. I knew that I would be truly one of them when, not if, I published.

"Perhaps we are paranoid," Mary responded. "But even if coincidental heart attacks will out . . . at least we all have something to do besides listen to writers drone on and on about their craft and Esther bore us to death with her speeches."

"I do know two deaths are worth at least a second look," Elias agreed.

"If I can help, let me know." Brent started down the hall. "I'm going to get the end of Curtis's presentation. I might as well at this juncture."

"We will," Elias replied.

Brent left and we continued to confer—getting up a head of steam. Personally, I was more convinced than ever that Esther and Mavis were wrong, and I intended to prove it.

"I'll do my part too." Mary said. "I'm going to grill some of these so called security guys. I'll probably come up with a big fat zero. From what I have seen, these play-cops are only here to enjoy the cruise, too."

"Check out any security camera footage you can get access to," Elias said. "Sean and I will find that refrigeration unit where the bodies are. We'll take a good look at both again. It'll be much more interesting than the afternoon panel discussions anyway, even if we don't find something new."

"Can you get in?" I asked

"I'm sure we can. No one seems to care about much here. If we have trouble, Sean's badge will do the trick."

"Good," Mary said. "And Veronica, you get started on motive."

"Really?" I was honored to be assigned the most important and elusive element of our case.

"Of course," Elias agreed. "You are observant and analytical. Frankly, you're quite good."

"You'll have it," I said with the confidence of a pro, hiding the butterflies in my stomach.

"We'll meet before dinner in the bar," Elias said.

"Isn't this something? A real killer cruise," Mary laughed, but caught herself. "Sorry. Occupational hazard. I meant no disrespect to the dead."

I was excited about my new friends and my new imperative. I was more excited about our investigation than the MWW meetings. I was in search of a real killer, a murderer or murderers. But, ironically, where better to begin than in the meetings?

"Let's go assess the suspects, if we can figure out who they might be!" Elias reached for the door.

He and I slipped back into the room where the panelists were proceeding as if nothing had happened. It appeared that the routine of these authorial purveyors of death was not to be interrupted by real death.

However, I had no great interest in this panel discussion other than observing potential suspects. I spotted Mavis affixed to Esther for her own reasons and wondered if Esther's apparent motivations of protecting Mendel and Frederick's reputations from reports of an overdose were sincere.

I studied the players in the room and decided to damn the torpedoes and sail full speed ahead. The expression seemed appropriate since we were cruising through the Atlantic Ocean of World War II, even if it came from our Civil War. After all, this was now a war for me as well.

CHAPTER 20

Curiouser and Curiouser

In the meeting room the panel discussion was lively, despite Frederick's death.

Evidently, Esther and Sean had been successful in controlling the group and proceeding with the discussion on "Marketable Ways to Kill Off Your Characters." An enthusiastic and creative subject for the MWW members, who were the serial killers of the book world.

I surveyed the room and thought, "Why shouldn't the panel proceed? No purpose would be served by canceling it. Besides, leaving these book-bound criminalists with too much free time might lead to a herd panic if they discovered what Mary, Elias, Brent and I suspected. More than that, they could interfere with our investigation and my newfound friendships. I didn't want that."

Elias got a coffee and I a tea before we slid into the last row unnoticed. I sipped my tea and mused that if Esther had cancelled meetings based on body count, two mornings of instruction would already be gone.

At the long table for panelists on the platform, Amy and Anne sat attentively and listened to Sean describing the best types of guns to use for murders in mysteries. Helga listened with only half an ear. I scanned the room looking for motive amongst the mystery writers. Sean ended his presentation by describing New York gun favorites he had found in his years on the force.

"Thank you, Sean." Esther stood and led the applause. "That was a very good analysis of the best types of guns to use in different murder situations. Questions anyone?"

There were, of course, many hands up because all the lower echelon writers wanted knowledge from the premier earners who sat as panelists.

Esther called on Heather.

Heather stood. "What is the most marketable murder vehicle?"

"Thank you, Heather. A very insightful question. Helga, what is your answer to Heather's question about the most marketable murder vehicle. I presume other than guns."

"Yes." Heather smiled and sat.

"Helga, can you tell us what you consider the most marketable murder vehicle?" Esther caught Helga off guard doodling on her notepad.

Helga looked up startled through her dark, heavily lined eyes. "Oh, there are so many."

Helga thought and then smeared a grin across her face showing her white teeth surrounded with a cherry-red lip-sticked mouth. She put her left hand up to her chin. Her gigantic wedding diamond blazed in the lights as she thoughtfully tapped her chin with her forefinger.

"I personally use and adore surreptitious poisonings. They are people pleasers," Helga announced authoritatively. "Especially dosing over a long period of time. It builds suspense and makes the reader turn the pages to see if, or when, someone will discover the sequential acts. Of course, they never do . . . until it is too late."

"Follow-up!" Heather stood and addressed Helga. "But as a beginner, isn't that too hard to handle with all the clues a writer has to imbed over the long period of time? I know when I started my science fiction writing it took me several books to graduate to the tough stuff. I mean, might it not just be easier, and just as marketable, for a novice to have someone run over by a car or shoved off a cliff . . . something more spontaneous and simpler?"

As Heather stood waiting, Helga slowly tilted her chin down and dissected Heather standing exposed and vulnerable. The entire audience followed Helga's stare to Heather, including me.

From my observations, Helga was the antithesis of Heather not only in looks, but also deep into the marrow of her being. Helga was demonstratively bitter, ugly, and jealous. Heather was fresh, happy, and excited about blending science fiction and mystery to create her own niche. Helga showed no quarter to this burgeoning, expectant star.

Helga swept back her black hair, leaned forward, and said pointedly, "I suppose those who can—do. And those who can't—don't."

Heather's shoulders visibly slumped and she lowered herself into her chair as if the wind had been knocked out of her.

Helga crossed her legs, sat back in her chair, and crossed her arms. She was satiated.

"Well," Esther stammered, and then looked at Anne at the end of the table to rescue Heather. "Anne, do you have anything to add?"

Anne shook her head in the negative. She was not going to enter this fray.

Esther looked out into the audience. "Are there any other questions?"

No one dared put a hand up now. Helga had cowed Heather and her colleagues—just as she did her husband. And Helga hated Otto, too. I began to wonder what Helga's real relationship with Frederick and Mendel might have been.

"I'll release you for lunch early. Obviously, our afternoon panels can resume on the original schedule," Esther announced. "And by then we'll have an update on Frederick and his untimely passing. I know we are all waiting for some word."

I remained seated as the crowd filed out.

"Will you tell Sean I'll meet him outside to find the bodies?" Elias turned to leave.

"Sure."

I was left alone. Amy glanced at me as she made a beeline for the door. Heather puppy-dogged after Amy, but the crowd swept her out the other door. Mavis, the ever-present boot-licker, waited for Esther in the front row. Sean saw me and signaled from the platform to wait. He dutifully gave Helga his hand to help her down the raised platform steps, and then Anne and Esther in turn.

Anne and Helga left. But Esther, shadowed by Mavis, accosted me.

"Did you go to see the body with Brent?"

"Yes, Elias and Mary, too."

"Well . . ." Esther glanced around, obviously looking for a better source of information, but Elias and Mary had left. ". . . uh . . . the doctor was there too, wasn't he?"

"Yes, he was."

"Good."

I was silent and not forthcoming with anything. Dr. Witte's presence had been useless in finding the truth, but Esther apparently had her uses for him. They were joined at the hip to avoid bad publicity. Esther was well meaning, I presumed, but the doctor was merely a corporate lackey.

"Did he . . ." Esther continued her questioning, but was interrupted.

"Ladies, may I join you?" Sean closed the circle.

"Of course," I said. "We were just talking about the doctor and Frederick."

"Well, what did the doctor say?" Esther demanded impatiently. "I haven't been updated."

"I think the only diagnosis he learned in medical school is heart attack." I was sarcastic. "He's like a broken record. I think . . ."

Mavis interrupted. "So the doctor has diagnosed a heart attack?"

"Yes, but . . ."

Sean interceded. "What Veronica is trying to say is that two heart attacks in . . ."

"Let's go find the doctor, Esther," Mavis interrupted Sean. "We need to talk to the authority in this matter."

"You're right, the expert, not these self-proclaimed *mavens*," Esther agreed.

Esther and Mavis left. I certainly didn't mind being slighted and, in fact, expected it from Mavis. I knew, however, that Sean should have been treated with the regard a seasoned NYPD homicide detective and prominent published mystery writer deserved. Sean knew it too. He was flushed and his greenish-blue eyes flashed with anger.

"Good riddance." Sean had recovered his dignity. "They would just muddle things over to avoid problems. Give me the dope, Veronica—figuratively speaking, I mean."

I filled Sean in.

"And Elias told me to tell you he's waiting for you outside. He wants you two to have another look at the bodies."

"Two heart attacks. That's ridiculous. I've examined more bodies in the morgue than I can count. There's something not right here and we'll find out what. Want to come?"

174

"No, we divided tasks." I shuddered at the thought of being with bodies, yet again. "I'm researching motive."

"Ah, perhaps the most important element and the often most difficult to find. We're in good hands with you. Let's get on it, then."

As Sean walked left down the hall, I was proud. I was in charge of the key element of the probable—no, not probable—in my mind definite murders.

I wanted to deliver motive on a silver platter to my fellow sleuths, my published and popular new writing friends. My new cohorts who were, I believed, just like me in all respects, except for my aversion to publication. I knew after the cruise I had to address that one flaw in my otherwise illustrious writing career.

But right now, I had to deliver the goods—for real.

⌘

CHAPTER 21

No Good Deed Goes Unpunished

I raced to the library and the Internet again. Yes, the rates were outrageous, but so was murder. The difficulty factor of this task was amplified because I really was an amateur, but it was the most important thing in my life—along with meeting the geographically desirable and perfect Curtis, of course.

Finding motive would solidify my new MWW friendships. The Internet price tag daunted me, but did not dissuade me.

The library was a room full of temptations for me, like a candy store is to a child. I started to look through the mystery section to see whose books were stocked on the shelves. I wished I had one of my own to sneak in with them, but I didn't.

Since only one of the six computers was unoccupied, I thought better of my detour into the mystery shelves and took the last one.

I readied myself to glean motive by researching relationships because murders by strangers were much rarer than those by friends or relatives. Besides we had two, possibly three interconnected dead people. I was committed to paying the exorbitant Internet rates to buy credibility and respect. And, indeed, to solving my piece of the puzzle at hand.

The computers were beautifully placed in the library with expansive views of the endless ocean. I was entranced by the rolling Atlantic with its white caps, at this moment sparkling with tenuous patches of sunlight. There were dark, stormy clouds in the distance, and I thought of my seasickness patches.

Then, I snapped to. I contemplated an approach, a word search, to find a common thread for Mendel and Frederick's lives. I believed emphatically that Agatha Christie was right in observing that murders do go unsolved because no one believes they are murders.

When I signed on, I read the news flashes that scrolled in a frame at the top of the screen. The President was doing something cute with children at the White House, there was still starvation in North Korea, and there was a fire raging near Durgin Park, a well-known restaurant in the Faneuil Hall marketplace in Boston. Just as I poised my fingers on the keyboard to enter my search terms and begin the task at hand, a picture of Frederick popped up with a lead line under it about his death.

I clicked on it before it carouseled away. There it was, a UPI article about his death:

"UPI- Frederick Larsen, celebrated two-time Oscar winner and popular fiction writer, is dead. Mr. Larsen's agent Howard Edelstein and Esther Nussbaum, the President of the Mystery Writers of the World, confirmed today that Oscar winner Mr. Larsen died from heart failure on the *Queen Anne,* a Wessex Cruise Line luxury liner. He was to be a keynote speaker on the celebrated mystery writer's award cruise across the Atlantic. The Wessex Cruise Line expresses its regrets that shortly after the *Queen Anne* sailed from New York Mr. Larsen passed from a cardiac event in his stateroom. Mr. Larsen's agent states that funeral plans are pending."

Naturally, I thought, the official cover up. And, there was no mention of Mendel's death. I supposed that his death was not banner-worthy news like Frederick's; after all Mendel's career had waned. I did a search and discovered a buried, "back page" similar release about Mendel—again stating death by heart attack.

I put my anger aside and started my uphill fight to prove our theories. I read Frederick's and Mendel's biographies on their respective web sites. They had grown up on different sides of the country. They were never in proximity nor did they even meet until they attended Otto's writing program in New York. That is where their paths first crossed.

Interestingly, both of their biographies glossed over their years in Otto's program. That was a red flag, along with Frederick's slighting of Otto at the Academy Awards. I was sure, if there were a common ground for their deaths, it would be connected to Otto's program. That was the intersection of their lives. An intersection with a dead end so to speak, because Otto was also dead.

Since I knew Amy had been in Otto's program with them, and she was still alive and breathing, I looked at her agency site for clues. Interestingly, in Amy's biography on her agent's website she didn't mention she was even in Otto's program. I searched Otto's program and found that Amy was in an entering class, but was not an alumna. She had never graduated. That fact, and her lack of enthusiasm about Otto, tweaked my interest.

I recalled Heather had told me a picture of Amy, Frederick and Mendel together was in Otto's office. I looked at the university yearbooks online. I found one obscure picture of Amy, Frederick, Mendel and Otto on a collage page from Amy's first year in the program. I studied it closely.

The photo showed the four at a party with holiday decorations and a Christmas tree in the background. They all held their wine glasses up in a toast. Frederick and Amy smiled and had their arms wrapped around each other's waists with their heads touching. A much younger Otto was next to Amy with his arm around her shoulder. He had a broad, goofy grin and the glassy eyes of a person having celebrated too much. Mendel stood soberly and somberly next to Frederick, looking up at him. I looked closer. On Amy's left hand there was an unmistakable small diamond engagement ring.

I surmised that Amy either was, or had, the key to these three men's deaths. This was not a momentous leap for a sleuthing investigative mind like mine because, after all, she was the only one in the picture left alive. More importantly, she was here to question.

Suddenly, I was afraid for *her* life. Whether she liked Mendel and Frederick or not, my first instincts were to guard against another death. And she was so attractive that she could easily be a target for Helga if there were any hint that Brent was having any interaction with Amy at all. I struggled to find some thread that would link Helga to the quartet in the picture. Meanwhile, I had to dress for dinner and get to the bar to talk to my fellow investigators-at-large.

As a copy of the picture printed, I noticed the sea had changed during my research. It churned with huge white caps under a stormy layer of clouds coming towards us. I took my picture and left.

* * *

As I made my way to the stateroom, I activated my sea legs because the *Queen Anne* was dancing with the Atlantic. I hoped the worst of the weather would bypass us.

When I got there, Mavis, with a coat and scarf on, was on the balcony looking out into the building storm over the Atlantic. It was dark and overcast beyond her.

The door slammed shut with its tight spring.

Mavis glanced over and then looked back at the dark murky sea with its menacing rain.

I thought it would be a long voyage if we were at odds. With my newly discovered information and the picture, I decided to convince her that Frederick's and Mendel's deaths were connected and that they had not died of natural causes, but at someone's hand. I wanted to get her to have Esther pursue an investigation.

I knew Mavis was supporting, if not encouraging, Esther's commitment to ignoring the obvious because she wanted to be important to Esther. But, bad publicity or not, I believed these men were murdered and that now Amy was in danger.

Right then I made my unilateral decision to give Mavis a chance to join our unofficial investigation. With Mavis on board, we could get Esther's ear. That alone would meet the approval of my fellow investigators and advance our cause.

* * *

"Hi," I called through the open sliding glass door. "Did you enjoy the afternoon?"

"Yes." Mavis was actually friendly as she came in and shut the storm-churned air out with the sliding door. "I didn't see you at any panel discussions."

"I took the afternoon off."

"Really? With Curtis?" Mavis off her coat and was dressed for dinner underneath.

"No, but that would have been nice." I shared my personal life to the extent I had to.

"I'll say."

She took a chair by the small table, removed her scarf and fluffed her hair.

"So what interesting thing did you do that didn't include Curtis or our illustrious panels?"

I went for it. Partly, I still wanted Mavis's friendship, but more importantly I cared that Mavis had Esther's ear. The white-washing UPI news reports were a public avalanche covering up the truth. It was worth being late reporting to the bar, if I came with Mavis in tow. I thought if Mavis truly understood these were not overdoses, then she would convince Esther that she was not protecting these men's reputations, but instead impeding a murder investigation, a justified murder investigation launched by her fellow mystery writers.

I explained my research and what our group was doing. Then, I took a deep breath.

"In my mind, there is no explanation other than murder."

"I suspect, in your mind, that is a reasonable conclusion. Evidently, in Mary's too. I had a good chat with her this afternoon. All about your theories and your foursome."

I felt validated that Mary had used my same approach— to get Esther on board through Mavis. But, I was also wary of Mavis's use of the phrase *in your mind.* I hoped Mary, with her superior experience in crime, had opened Mavis's mind to the possibility of murder. And, I was hopeful with my new piece of evidence she would want to join our group tonight at the bar.

"Well, I found something very important." I reached for my purse with the picture in it.

"And what is that? A justification for your group's unofficial activity, unsanctioned by Esther?"

"She would sanction us if she knew about this."

"About what?"

"I'll show you."

"I'm sure you can just tell me succinctly. You're a writer, after all."

I sensed sarcasm but chose to ignore it. I needed Mavis on board for my group of sleuthing aficionados. I took the picture out of my purse.

"Amy, Frederick, Otto, and Mendel were friends in Otto's program and I think Frederick and Amy were engaged."

"That's it?" Mavis smirked, showing her true colors again. "Frederick has been engaged repeatedly and *ad nauseam* his entire life. People say that is how he got the best out of his women until he dumped them."

"But . . . this is different . . . I know it." She had knocked the wind out of my sails, but I unfolded the copy of the picture and handed it to her anyway. "I know this picture is the key. The common denominator between Frederick and Mendel's murders."

"Murders! This picture?" Mavis studied it.

"You see the engagement ring and the looks on their faces."

"And I suppose Otto's death can be explained by it, too?"

I paused. "Maybe."

There was a long silence.

"Oh, for God's sake, Veronica. Do you realize how farfetched this is?" Mavis blasted me. "I've had it! That's ridiculous. You base all this on a grainy picture? Everyone knows Frederick and Mendel studied together. And who cares if Amy was food for Frederick's engagement fetish. He wanted her and that's how he got her."

Mavis threw the picture on my bed. I was speechless. Mavis had sucked me into her confidence just to shoot me down.

"Don't you know that Esther is just trying to protect the MWW and these men's reputations? We all know they were druggies and drunks. They overdosed. We're lucky the doctor's playing ball. Do you think Esther wants this to be publicized as the MWW "overdose cruise", especially with Otto's murder? I mean what kind of a pall do you want over the group?"

"But . . . I . . ."

"I'm not listening to any of the amateur crap coming out of your mouth."

"But, if you would just listen . . ." I doubted if she had dared to cut Mary off like this.

"You think you're a writer just because you spew words onto a page. You're not. That's not what a writer does. They plot, they write, they rewrite and rewrite and rewrite. They edit, they promote, and they sell. They work at their craft and their career. You're a dilettante, a hanger-on, an amateur just like Herbert and Agnes, and Jody. You're all wasting your time."

"But . . . you . . . invited me here!"

"I invited you because I lost my cabin mate and you were the only one who said yes whom I could tolerate. Correction. Whom I thought I could tolerate. At least, it appeared you had manners. I was wrong. You are a hanger-on who thinks it's appropriate to bite the hand that tried to feed it at our dinner table. My hand."

"I see." I sat on the bed with my back to Mavis. "I do see, now."

Mavis didn't say anything else. She stood there for what seemed like an eternity. Then, she touched up her hair and makeup in the bathroom. When she emerged, she grabbed her purse off the dresser and left without a word.

I was shattered.

* * *

I sat unable to move. The wonderful life I had created and believed in was crushed. My mentor had just called me a phony—a groupie. Worse, she had compared me to Agnes, Herbert, and Jody. Was it true?

I treasured my new friends, especially Sean, Mary, and Elias. I trusted they didn't think of me as a phony. I believed they respected me. They had included me as part of their team. Indeed, I was an integral part of their team—our team. They assigned me to unravel the all-important motive for the murders and I believed I was well on my way to doing just that, despite what Mavis said.

I sat up straight and assured myself that my friends would embrace my theory of the murders with this picture. I had been careful and methodical like any good mystery writer. Any good tactician. Any good detective. I had come up with a common thread amongst the dead and the one left living—Amy.

The view of the Atlantic was dark now. Rain pelted our balcony and the ship was swaying.

Deep down, I knew Mavis was wrong about me. Well, not completely wrong, but wrong enough. More wrong than right. Besides, anything she believed about me I could correct with simple discipline—by simply engaging in editorial and publishing behavior.

My books were excellent. I had read enough books in my lifetime to know that. I just hadn't engaged in the business of being a writer and selling. Perhaps because I didn't desperately need the income . . . at least, not now, not yet.

I got ready to meet my sleuthing team in the bar. As I went through my ablutions for dinner, I felt my heart beating at half-mast because it had been ripped apart. I'd had so many setbacks in life, and this one would take the help of my cohorts and time to mend. But emotional discipline was a learned skill, along with everything else in the world.

I didn't save the new red killer outfit that I had brought for the awards banquet; I put it on tonight. It was a deep red, very fitted long silk dress and matching short red and black striped jacket. Of course, *killer* was a poor descriptive word choice under the circumstances, but that's what it was. I looked great in it and I needed it tonight—for me. And, I admitted to myself, for Curtis, too. It would be wasted on both of us if I waited for the last night and the actual awards dinner. I placed the picture back in my black evening bag.

Dressed to kill, so to speak, I left for my meeting with my friends who valued me. As I started down the hall, I widened my stride to match the sway of the ship in the now rocky seas. Evidently, the state-of-the-art stabilizers could not negate everything.

Stepping off the elevator, I wished I had won Mavis over to our side. But I was still armed with the photo—the evidence of the trio-of-intimacy. I was sure Amy was the next target; after all, Mendel had called her his "little love."

CHAPTER 22

The Gathering Storm

I was late. On the bar level, the ship's rocking was worse since it was on an upper deck. I held onto the proscenium arch, looking for my cohorts and, I admit, Curtis.

The bar was packed. While the first-seating passengers dined, the second-seating passengers cocktailed away.

As I scanned the tables, eyes gravitated to me—the lady in red. I immediately stood tall, took a long breath, and owned the moment. I truly was in a superb outfit and a very Curtis-worthy ensemble. I felt rehabilitated after Mavis's attack. Now, I just had to search out my fellow investigators and solve Mendel's and Frederick's murders—and possibly Otto's.

I spotted Curtis near the entrance to the left hosting his oldies table. I lingered longer under the proscenium in his plain view. When our eyes met, Curtis nodded and smiled. The dress had done its job. I knew we would meet at the bar after dinner as usual—that is, if another dead body didn't interrupt.

Then I saw Esther, my nemesis, seated with Mavis and laughing with a crowd of eight in the far corner beyond Curtis. Surprisingly, the center of attention was Agnes. She was entertaining Esther and the others *sans* Herbert and Jody, and very well.

Helga and Brent were to the right at a table for two. Brent was tuxedoed up and Helga decked out in a black sequined gown with a black ostrich feather wrap draped on her chair. They were statues, silent and fixed, in front of an expansive window being slapped by storm waves. In the distance beyond the ship's lights, the ocean faded to black. Their faces were as black as the view beyond.

One table away from Brent and Helga, a chubby arm, housed in pink floral chiffon, reached high and waved at me. It was Mary, sitting with Sean and Elias. I hurried over before she could amplify her unceremonious beckoning by adding a verbal component.

* * *

The ship continued rocking as I weaved between chairs. Man was no match for Mother Nature in the North Atlantic.

"Hello." I sat next to Sean across from Mary and Elias. "We're really starting to rock."

"I know," Mary said.

There were greetings all around.

"But it's nothing compared to the crossing two years ago, the last awards cruise." Mary said. "You know the ship has a weather forecast just to let you know when to put on a motion patch."

"I think we can tell when we need one!" I chuckled.

"Right." Mary shoved a wine glass towards me on a white napkin embossed exquisitely with *Queen Anne* and Wessex

Cruise Line in gold and maroon. "I got you a glass of house Chardonnay like mine."

"Perfect. Thanks." I tasted the Chardonnay. "Mmm. It's nice. Anyway . . . I'm sorry I'm late. I was talking to Mavis about our investigation. I had hoped to get Esther's ear through her. But she deep-sixed me."

"What did you expect?" Sean said.

"She did the same to me this afternoon," Mary added. "I can't believe I was sucked in. The old 'looking for information to use against you' routine. I'm smarter than that. I do that all the time to the characters in my books and it works, but only with really stupid characters. I guess I'm one of my *really stupid* characters."

I shook my head. "We both should have known better."

"Forget it," Sean said. "She's not worth our time."

"I agree," Elias said. "Let's move on."

The words *not worth our time* shot through the pleasure center of my brain. I was beyond pleased at Sean's assessment of Mavis. It validated my Mavis-damaged, needy ego.

"So where are we with the ship security people?" I asked Mary.

"Like I told the guys already . . . nowhere. Security has a real conflict of interest when it comes to balancing this kind of thing and Wessex's public relations interests. They are tight-lipped and are focused on protecting the cruise line, corporate profits, and their jobs. They just stone-walled me with passenger-privacy baloney at every turn."

"You mean you got nothing?" I asked.

"As far as I'm concerned, they will cover up anything for the sake of dear old Wessex . . . even murder. And, like I told Elias and Sean, the security cameras on board tape over themselves in less than twelve hours."

"That's outrageous."

"And convenient." Mary drank her wine.

"Keeping the system cheap and outdated is a calculated decision," Sean interjected.

"They didn't preserve anything?" I asked in disbelief.

Elias looked at me and shrugged his shoulders. "Why would they? Then they can create any scenario they like without the tapes. Maybe they should join us . . . the creative, fiction-mongering souls at MWW."

"It's unbelievable!" Mary said.

"What about the bodies?" I asked Sean and Elias. "Did you at least get into the make-shift morgue, or whatever you want to call it?"

"That we did! And with no need of my retired NYPD status." Sean sat up proudly. "It's sad to say that it was unlocked and unattended. No one noticed or cared that we were in there."

"So much for the integrity of any forensic evidence," Mary said. "Without the proper chain of custody, my detectives in my books could never nail my slashers. I always . . ."

"How you nail your slashers doesn't matter," Sean interrupted. "We hit pay dirt anyway."

"I knew it. What did you find?"

"We verified everything you told us about the rash, the tongue, and the pupils," Elias began. "And then . . ."

"And then, we put that together with the other symptoms," Sean interjected.

"Not mincing words, we concluded that I was right. It was an overdose of a prescription drug that simulates a heart attack," Elias announced.

"But interestingly," Sean vied for the spotlight, "if Mendel hadn't had an allergic reaction to the drug the first night, we might never have figured it out. The symptoms you saw that night, Veronica, were the ones that helped us determine what really happened."

Elias raised his wine glass for a toast. "To you and your discerning eye, Veronica."

"To all of us." I ecstatically raised my glass and clinked everyone's at the table. "What drug was it?"

I ended the self-congratulatory interlude that literally erased my Mavis-shattered ego.

"It *was* Prolixin," Sean proclaimed. "We knew it because Mendel couldn't walk, had a spastic tongue with a rash, and irregular pupils."

"It had to be," Elias decreed.

"Yes," Mary said. "Sean knows because he investigated a real New York murder by Prolixin before he retired. An old guy, who did not kick the bucket fast enough for his kids, was helped along with liquid Prolixin."

"They got it over the border in Canada," Sean explained. "They would have gotten away with it too, but for a sharp doctor and the old man's allergic reaction to the drug, like Mendel's, but not quite as bad."

"And . . . that brings us to the motive?" Sean looked at me intently.

With perfect timing, Amy entered the bar.

"Motive?" I said. "The key just walked in. She is the last alive-and-kicking common denominator amongst the three dead men. Yes, Otto included."

My friends all turned and zeroed in on Amy.

Amy stood in the foyer, a picture of yellow from head to toe. From her golden hair down to her lemon colored, sequined spaghetti strap blouse and raw silk pants. She balanced agilely with the ship movements in her open-toed gold high heels. She joined Heather at the bar with Heather.

Heather had attracted a bombastic older man who was using her as an audience and obvious ego stroke. But as soon as Amy got her glass of wine, both women took their drinks over to Esther's table where they were welcomed with more chairs dragged over to accommodate both of the attractive women.

"Amy?" Elias looked back at me as did Sean, both speechless.

"I don't understand." Mary questioned.

"I have proof," I said. "I think all three murders are linked and she could be the fourth, yet to come."

"What?" Elias leaned forward. "But why?"

"You'll see." I reached for my evening bag. "I think she could need protection."

Before I got the picture out or could explain, there was a commotion nearby. It was Helga. Although her words were inaudible to us, the now familiar look on her face left no room for interpretation. She was mad—mad as hell.

* * *

Helga stood and grabbed her black ostrich feather wrap from the back of her chair. Brent jumped up and put it over Helga's shoulders before she charged out of the bar.

"Like hell," Helga yelled. "You said there would be good weather all 5 days!"

Helga tottered out of the bar between tables.

"But I . . ."

Brent followed closely on Helga's exit trail. His arms were poised, ready to catch her as she fought the movement of the ship in her spiked black heels and tight black sequined dress.

"You what?" Helga shouted back at Brent. "You liar! You didn't even look at the weather."

"I did! I did."

They disappeared through the proscenium arch.

* * *

Sean shook his head. "I don't know how he puts up with it. Money or no money."

"I don't either," Elias agreed. "And now he is supposed to guarantee the weather? In the North Atlantic?"

"If he could do that, he wouldn't need her pocketbook." Mary turned her attention back to me. "What did you find out, Veronica?"

"Take a look at the group photo I found."

I milked the moment just as I had on stage as an amateur, but excellent, actress. I slowly opened my evening bag, ceremoniously unfolded the photo, and placed it on the table.

Mary grabbed her drug store magnifying glasses, commonly called cheaters, from her purse. "That's Otto there."

"And, if I'm not mistaken," Elias took out his glasses too and squinted. "Right there. A young Frederick and Mendel."

"Right," I said. "And look at the woman. It's Amy with an engagement ring on her finger."

"Wow, you're right." Mary removed her cheaters.

"They are connected. Could Amy really be in danger, too?" Elias wondered out loud. "But why? What is the connection?"

"I don't know. That's as far as I got. But there is a connection . . . a definite correlation. Don't you think?"

"I do . . . but Elias is right," Sean analyzed. "What is the common thread? I mean the others were famous, successful, and powerful. She's not."

"True enough," Mary confirmed. "Amy's an agent no one has heard of, in a small start-up agency. I think she could be in danger too!"

We all sat silently for a moment.

Then Elias put his glasses away and looked at us. "You know when things don't make sense, it means a piece of the puzzle is missing. We need to dig deeper. That's all."

"Then we'd better keep an eye on Amy in the meantime," Mary added. "She could be a target."

"Should we warn her?" I asked.

"No," Sean insisted. "Warn her of what? An unsubstantiated theory? We hold off on that . . . at least for now."

"Sean is right," Elias agreed. "At least for now. She just doesn't fit the pattern. We'll keep an eye on her . . . talk to her . . . see what we can learn."

"Yes. I concur. She may know something that even she doesn't know she knows," Mary said. "By the way, when I ran into Esther on the way here, she wasn't happy about our activities and I didn't even tell her the half of it."

"Good. Don't. Keep her out of the loop from now on," Sean said. "I think she's well meaning, but she's not a complex thinker. You can tell by the drivel in her books."

"Yeah," Mary snickered. "And she hasn't put one out in years."

"Well, she's busy being president." I said.

"Sure," Sean scoffed. "Not that busy. She's hiding from the death of her muse."

I drank a gulp of Chardonnay. Instead of being smug like my cohorts, I was appalled. Is this what happened to you if your muse deserted you? Are you dead to everyone? Do they mock you, even if you have had a good run? Maybe writing, which I always thought of as an intellectual haven where thinkers found refuge and collegiality, was actually as unkind and brutally competitive as any other profession.

"Anyway," I interrupted the Esther-bashing, "we don't say a word for now to anyone. Not Esther or Amy. Agreed?"

Everyone agreed.

"And none of us should approach Mavis again, either," Mary said.

Once again, everyone agreed.

"Just remember, loose lips sink ships," Elias added.

"And if Amy's murdered, there will be no great regret, anyway," Mary chuckled. "She's a parasitic, judgmental agent who is on the ten percent 'dole', just like the rest of them."

Elias laughed loudly and so did Sean.

I smiled because I was a part of the group, but thought, "No wonder Mary can write such gory torture mysteries. She has a real dark side."

Deep down I knew that I would never get to editing and publishing without an agent pushing me. None of these veteran authors appreciated their agents. I identified with Esther, hiding behind being the MWW presidency like I continually hid behind any pretense I could conjure up.

The bar started to empty. It was time for our dinner seating.

"Let's get going," Elias said. "And keep your eyes on Amy."

"Yes." Sean stood. "The murderer got away with a heart attack and a sequel. So they'd never try another. Amy's not a good profile for that type of death, anyway. We have to keep our eyes out for other things . . . unusual . . . out-of-place things."

As I followed our quartet out of the bar, even with the ship's rocking, I walked proudly and confidently. I had performed my mystery writer's duty with skill and stellar results. I had pointed us in the right direction—Amy's direction. But how were we going to protect her?

CHAPTER 23

Inquiry and Ignominy

During the parade into dinner, the ship continued to sway as the line of diners along the foyer worked its way toward the dining room. Some unescorted women passengers stayed near the wall, periodically reaching out for balance. Men in their flat and practical shoes chivalrously helped the women, both the attractive and the impractically high-heeled.

I saw Amy ahead. It was easy to spot her sparkly blond hair and her standout evening ensemble of yellow from head to toe.

"I'm going to stand with Amy," I whispered to my friends.

"Good idea," Mary rubber-stamped.

I worked my way up to Amy. What closer eye could I keep on her than being with her?

"Amy?"

"Hi." Amy donned her charming, dimpled smile. "A little rocky!"

"Yes."

She was receptive to company and her hazel eyes were permeated with an animation I had not seen before. I surmised the cruise was doing her good. She actually seemed happy. After some obligatory small talk, Amy appeared unguarded enough for me to side-wind into the heart of our investigation.

"It's a shame about Frederick. He seemed to be a very likeable person."

"Yes." Amy had no emotion and no tell. "But then, if you abuse your body it's bound to give out."

"You were engaged to him, so I guess you should know."

I blatantly dropped the bomb and studied her reaction. If my theory had credibility, I was convinced her life was in danger too. But, if it was, she didn't appear to know.

"Who told you that?"

"Common knowledge."

Amy stopped and the line bulged behind.

"I doubt it. That was for an instant and so long ago. Who told you?"

"I forget."

Right there and then, I decided not to mention the picture or warn her about anything. She might still know something she did not realize she knew that would point us in the right direction.

"I barely even remember it." Amy released me from her visual bullets and chuckled nervously. "Did Frederick tell you before he . . ."

Amy moved forward, freeing the line of diners from her disruptive bottleneck. All was in sync again with the objective of reaching the communal nightly dining ritual.

"I don't think so." I walked with her.

I was uneasy. I had been too frank, too forthcoming. I was not going to learn anything from her tonight. I changed the subject.

"Are you getting a lot out of the conference?"

Amy sized me up with a glance, regained her composure, and smiled. I wanted to withdraw, but we were fused at the hip until the dining room seating would separate us to our respective tables.

"Yes, of course. I'm looking for contacts, perhaps new clients." Amy oozed with obvious superficial gaiety. "People are always ready to jump ship, so to speak, for a better deal."

"Of course."

I continued to agree with anything Amy said, obviously having absolutely no knowledge about agents or their representation.

"Authors need the best representation they can get," I said. "A match is a match."

"Are you getting what you wanted from the conference, too?"

"Yes, it's great." I was gratified that Amy at least continued a polite dialogue with me.

"Well, I'm pleased that I found an author this afternoon who didn't have an agent and might be promising." Amy didn't miss a beat—her voice and demeanor had no signal, no tell, that anything was wrong. "You know, as I told you before, if you wanted to send me one of your books, I'd be happy to look at it."

"Really?" I was again surprised and disarmed at her offer.

"Of course. I know how hard it is to break in. Seriously, send it to me."

Amy reached in her small yellow cloth evening bag and handed me a card.

"Thank you."

I began to think I had misread Amy's guarded, if not hostile, reaction to my question about her engagement. No one could fake the equilibrium she displayed now. At least no person I knew, or any character I had written or read about in my literary life. I decided to take one for the team and probe one more time. Why not? She was being friendly again. Besides, we were near the stairs to the main dining room floor. I could leave her and depart to my separate table in a second.

"You didn't have trouble getting your book published?"

"My book?" Amy looked at me, surprised, and paused. "My goodness, that thing. I'm surprised anyone has heard about it. It was a lifetime ago. I dabbled."

Amy stepped ahead of me on the stairs, held onto the rail for balance as the ship swayed, and then turned back. "Send me something."

"All right. I will."

I watched Amy wind ahead of me to her table. I didn't see why anyone would want to take her life. Maybe a jilted lover, or a person jealous of her relationships with Frederick, Mendel and Otto? Because I still trusted my instincts about the significance of the picture.

As I passed Amy at her table, she was unusually animated and greeted her dinner mates enthusiastically. I hoped Mary had the presence of mind to take advantage of Amy's chattiness. There had to be a clue.

In point of fact, every sleuth knew listening and observing were the most important skills they possessed. I reiterated that over and over again in by mysteries. Perhaps too much. I would have to check that.

* * *

I made my way to my table.

"Veronica, tonight? The bar?" Curtis tapped my shoulder from behind.

I turned and tottered with the motion of the ship.

Curtis caught me by the shoulders and laughed. "Careful!"

198

I didn't laugh. I smiled with pleasure at his moderated

grip, calibrated to be gentle when with my smaller being. He was sensitive and aware and handsome. "Where did he come from?" I wondered to myself. How had I been lucky enough to cross his path?

"After dinner." I was balanced and now de-shouldered by Curtis.

"By the way, great outfit."

"Thanks."

I knew that the premature use of the gala-night outfit had been worth it and, obviously, effective. It had achieved its purpose—my purpose.

"Until later."

Curtis flashed a charming smile and made his way to his table of investors.

* * *

As I approached my table Elias stood and held my chair for me. "Last but not least!"

"Good evening." I smiled.

I was pleased with the array of friendly faces until I caught sight of Mavis. She was whispering to Helga while Helga pierced me with her evil eyes. I took my chair. I knew Mavis was getting even with me for not being her lackey.

As I settled in, I noted how roomy the table was. We were now eight—not nine—not ten. We were spread out, but as I soon learned, not enough to ignore Helga. She was in rare, particularly "Helga-esque" form.

"Anne, it's your night for wine. You'll have to get a white for me. I'm going to have the Chilean Sea Bass," Helga ordained from across the table.

"Oh?" Anne peered up from her menu and over her cheaters. "Yes. That'll be fine. I'm sorry, I don't know much about ordering wine. Is white fine with everyone?"

There was a quiet, mutual acquiescence until Helga exposed her fangs.

"Hardly, dear. You English are true teetotalers. You might know a good 'cuppa,' as they say, but you know nothing about dining. We need a nice cab, too. Don't we, Brent?"

"I don't." Brent looked sheepishly around the table.

"Yes, you do," Helga insisted. "You're having the sirloin tips."

"But . . ." Brent protested, but was censored by Helga.

"Waiter." Helga signaled with her left hand flashing a huge diamond ring and wrist bejeweled with a five-row sparkling tennis bracelet. "We'll have two bottles of the 2012 JJ Prum Wehlener Sonnenuhr Riesling Auslese Goldkapsel and two of the 2009 Lindstrom Stags Leap District Cabernet Sauvignon. There, Anne. It's done, since you don't really know that much."

Brent glanced shamefacedly at Anne.

"Thank you, Helga." Anne escaped back into her menu for long enough to process the insults quietly and with grace.

There was an awkward silence amongst all of us. I certainly did not want to speak. I didn't know whose head Helga would put on the chopping block next and I didn't want it to be mine. Besides, I became fascinated watching Amy at her table—so animated and conversational. Strangely, Frederick's death seemed to have lifted her spirits—or given her nervous energy. I didn't know which.

"What are you ordering?" Elias brought me back to our table's milieu.

"Perhaps the rack of lamb."

"Ah, me too. You know us Greeks and our lamb."

200

"I do, actually. We . . . I have a neighbor who taught me that." Whenever I thought of my home and the years I had with my husband, there engendered a "we of me," a very pleasant but now long gone use of the word "we."

As our dinner progressed it slipped further into a Helga-phantasmic nightmare.

Helga's complaints escalated from the wine tasting through the appetizers and salads. Nothing was smooth enough, cold enough, or hot enough for her. Her wine glass was either filled too full or becoming too empty. We heard in detail about Brent's guarantee the sailing would be smooth, how the storm and the swelling Atlantic were interfering with her writing, and how her seasickness patch must be defective.

I sympathized, ever so slightly, because I felt queasy myself from the ship's rocking after finishing my onion soup.

Helga ordered a third bottle of the Riesling. Anne was unhappy. It was unfair, too expensive, and grossly impolite. Helga drank most of it with the exception of the portions she poured into Mavis's glass. Somehow, they had become fast friends and engaged in several *tête-a-têtes* as the evening imploded in on itself.

* * *

By the time the waiter cleared the entrees, the dinner had degenerated into a pall. The rocking hadn't gotten worse, but Helga insisted it had. Every time Brent spoke, she threw a barb at him. Finally, Brent gave up and sat silently drinking, or more aptly guzzling, a third bottle of the Cabernet, generously ordered by Helga on Anne's dime. Sean resorted to the same behavior. He talked with no one.

Everyone else tried to enjoy his or her entrées and keep the conversation neutral in the face of Helga's drunken menace. We chatted quietly, and carefully, walking on eggshells. Helga was like a spider waiting to pounce and we were in her web—the obligatory assigned dinner table.

"It seems like you are enjoying your Cabernet, dear," Helga slurred at Brent as the waiter cleared the last dinner plate. "And why are we so quiet? Pouting?"

Helga took a gulp of wine and then blasted Brent with a pent-up frontal assault.

"I see we are indeed pouting. Is it because we didn't get our allowance this month?"

Brent glanced around the table shamefacedly and then down. Even Mavis, who had been graced with Helga's intimacies at dinner, could not meet his eyes.

Elias tried to deflect Helga. "Is anyone going to the wonderful reprise of Broadway musicals in the main theatre tonight? I'm sure it will be a night to remember."

"I'm sure they'll put up a proper show." Anne encouraged the change in subject. "I plan on attending."

But Elias and Anne could not derail Helga's verbal battering of Brent.

"Are you unhappy because you couldn't bring your girlfriend on the cruise?" Helga paused and then shouted. "Or are you unhappy because you did bring her and I have been keeping you too busy?"

"Helga!" Brent pleaded. "Be quiet. You're drunk and making a fool of yourself."

"That's it, isn't it? She's here," Helga snapped backward, rotating her head unnaturally to scan the tables around her. "And you don't want me to make a scene."

Then, Helga zeroed in on Heather, sitting there wide-eyed and open-mouthed at the Helga spectacle. "Or, have you substituted her for some fresh meat?"

"What? I . . . We . . ." Heather turned red and was unable to speak.

Sean interceded. "Helga, I think that's enough."

Brent turned to his harridan wife and gently touched her hand that pinched her wine glass stem. "Stop this now, dearest. You're making an ass of yourself."

For an eternity of silent intensity, Helga remained poised to pounce on Heather. Heather remained a deer frozen in Helga's headlights, vulnerable and waiting for the impact.

Then Helga broke her stare. She sat up straight, took a deep breath, and turned to Brent.

"Give us a kiss, Brenty-baby." Helga leaned into him sloppily.

Brent acquiesced and gave her a peck. Before he withdrew, she trampled his face with an open-mouthed marathon lip sucking and tongue-drilling kiss.

After she was satiated, Helga sat up, victorious in her humiliation of Brent. Brent stared at his plate.

As Helga checked her lipstick with her compact mirror, the table collectively began to breath easily again. Dinner was more relaxed. Elias engaged his social skills, but not with his normal ease. He was agitated and angry with Helga.

However, the evening was gradually salvaged thanks to Anne's and even Mavis's efforts. I tried to stay out of the crosshairs and so did Heather.

"We had an interesting afternoon." Elias said. "Sean and I."

"Oh, really," Helga sneered, not wholly satiated with her humiliation of Brent and still trolling for another victim. "And, what did you do?"

"I don't think we should be talking about this," Sean whispered to Elias.

"Too late. It's out of the bag now." Helga lobbed her head like a tennis ball from Sean and then to Elias and back again. "What did you do?"

I saw Brent relax as Helga's attention focused on other quarry.

"We had a look see at the bodies." Elias poured another glass of Cabernet. "Anyone else want a top off?"

With no response, Elias put the bottle down.

"Why?" Heather asked.

"Because these fools are pretending to solve a mystery aboard our ship," Helga laughed. "A mystery that doesn't exist!"

Helga was licking her chops. She acknowledged Mavis with a nod. Mavis had obviously spilled at least some of the beans in their *tête-a-têtes*.

Sean flashed a look at Helga that could kill and his Irish face turned red. He took a deep breath and withdrew from the conversation with the dignity and detachment of a man who had been baited his whole career by criminals—criminals he put in prison. He had solved crimes his entire life. I understood and admired him.

"And what did you find?" Helga teased.

"Murder." Elias did not mince his words and rehabilitated his ego—however injudiciously and dangerously. "Double murder!"

"Elias!" Mary reprimanded.

She and I recognized that he was angry enough to divulge prematurely too much of our clandestine investigation.

"Murder?" Anne said. "You mean Frederick and Mendel!"

"Oh, my God," Helga turned to Anne. "Shock from the flower child who has daisies strangling her victims at picture perfect, tranquil English country houses!"

Helga laughed loudly, distorting her painted red lips.

"I beg your pardon," Anne retorted.

"Helga, please." Brent put his hand again on hers again, hoping it would calm her as it had before.

"Shut up!" Helga slapped his hand off. "Never do that again."

"Wait, did someone murder them?" Heather turned to me, ignoring the Brent-and-Helga-show.

"And why are you asking Veronica that question?" Helga interrupted and then, without missing a beat, turned to me and spit with wine breath. "The impostor. The unpublished. The interloper. The pretender."

I glowered at Mavis. She had done her dirty work here tonight at my dinner table through Helga. Brent was red-faced at Helga's unnecessary and cruel degradation of me. I wanted to "Helga" Mavis face-to-face right then and there for what she had done. I was not to be disregarded just because I was unpublished. I had a better crime-solving reputation than she did, and in a famous locale. I was more recognizable than she was, especially in my community, which was neither undiscerning nor small.

Instead, I sat in silence—in shock.

Elias, imbibed and ego-bruised, tromped into my hiccup of silence. While I was still formulating a response to Helga, he answered the lovely Heather's question. After all, she was a rare female specimen. At least, at our table. Young, plumped, ripe, and wide-eyed.

"Heather . . . the answer to your question is yes." Elias felt the power of wine and seized the moment for his Sherlockian-reveal, as all well-written protagonists would. "And there is a group of us who are going to prove that. We could use your help. But we must not spread the particulars around until we are through gathering our proof because . . . there is apparently a murderer amongst us."

Heather went white. "A murderer amongst us? The MWW?"

"Elias, I think we should cool it." Sean whispered, giving up his isolation policy of the evening. "You've already said too much."

"Yes," I chastised Elias too, ignoring Helga glaring at me with cold malice.

I glanced at Mary and she back at me. We had to shut down Elias strutting his stuff in an obvious attempt to one-up Helga. I couldn't blame him, but it was untimely and would be detrimental to our investigation. His rally-to-arms had to be stopped. Fortunately, Mavis's self-importance did it for us.

"Elias, this is not a melodrama," Mavis said. "Esther and the doctor have looked into Mendel's and Frederick's deaths thoroughly and have concluded they died of unfortunate heart attacks."

"So you think . . ." Elias interjected.

"So I know," Helga glared at me. "Some little people's imaginations have gotten the best of them. And they should remember there are consequences to their actions . . . liabilities. The MWW and the Wessex Cruise Line have put this to rest."

"Put this to rest?" Heather queried.

"Oh, put it anywhere you want, sweet young thing." Helga tried to stand. "I'm done. And I'm going to use Brent's allowance with abandon at the blackjack table. Want to watch, dear little Brenty?"

"Helga, let's talk." Brent stood and held Helga's chair dutifully. "Careful. Your heel's on your hem."

"I don't know how you talked me into this cruise." Helga yanked at her dress. "It's bad enough being cooped up with these people, and now I'm on a high seas roller coaster. You're a fool."

"I apologize." Brent looked at us sheepishly and whispered. "I'm so sorry."

"Oh, shut-up, you little kiss-ass," Helga shouted, as she literally ripped her black sequined hem free and strutted away.

Helga worked her way through the tables fighting for her balance in her tight sequined gown. The long piece of her now-ripped hem trailed behind her, scattering black sequins over the herringbone carpet.

I watched Brent watch Helga. If eyes could have pierced her flesh and ripped Helga's heart out, Brent's would have.

Finally, Brent grabbed Helga's black ostrich feather wrap and dutifully followed. He was statuesque and steady, his head held high. His large strides easily caught up with Helga as she sidestepped for balance.

He didn't take his eyes off her, nor did he make one move to help steady her.

CHAPTER 24

Harridans

We all observed Helga's drunken exit from the dining room with Brent in tow. Mavis now had to get along without her confidante. I for one was not going to make her comfortable.

As relieved as we were the table was now *sans* Helga and Brent, the waiter appeared even more relieved. Why wouldn't he be? This wasn't a British Royal Navy warship and he didn't receive combat pay. He flittered around our war-torn table dropping off our dessert menus and briskly removed all signs of Helga and Brent, including the stray breadcrumbs.

I ordered a double cappuccino. I was flagging and wanted to be perky when I met Curtis. I got sherbet for a palate cleanser and skipped all the other condensed caloric goodies. Everyone else indulged, Mary twofold because she *loved* the flourless chocolate cake and *adored* the Napoleon.

"You know." Mary swallowed a big bite of her cake. "I could put them in my next book as the couple from hell who slash each other to death."

Everyone laughed, including Mavis who was ever the suck-up, apparently to all indiscriminately. All but me, that is.

Anne forked her lemon tart. "And I could murder them in my next book, too, and have their bodies fertilize the rose bed,"

There was a reconstituted chuckle around the table.

"I wonder if it's worth it?" I asked Sean.

"What?"

"Brent staying with Helga?" I sipped my cappuccino and expected a resounding negative response from this hard-core, independent retired homicide detective.

"To him?" Sean answered thoughtfully. ". . . Yes. I've seen it work well when the man learns his place. Brent just hasn't done that yet. He still hasn't had all his self-respect beaten out of him . . . and, it's eating him up."

"Will he leave her?"

"He'll leave her or learn to get over himself. No man can live like that . . . without making that choice once and forever."

"Or woman?" I added.

I lived in a rarified wealthy corner of the world where trophy wives spawned babies to win the ATM jackpot. If it doesn't work out, then they fight like rabid animals for their support orders and community assets to maintain their lifestyles and marketable bodies for their next victims.

"Yeah, women too. Being NYPD homicide, I've seen some of those marriages end in well-planned murders."

"I've only read about that," I remarked. "But, in my neighborhood a block away, a very wealthy husband did die suddenly and left a charming child-wife with a hunk of change. Who knows?"

"Exactly."

"In my books," Mary forked her Napoleon, squishing the cream out onto the plate. "Spousal murder is one of my favorites. But, take it from me, Helga's smart enough to have a bullet-proof prenup. Brent's dead in the water. And, in my view, murder is a non-starter for him."

"You never know. Prenups can be changed and challenged." Elias winked. "Money pilfered and hidden. More agreeable, lonely ladies found. One never knows. But let's get on with the murders at hand instead of speculating about marital discord. Perhaps these ladies, with their fine analytical minds, would like to join us in our clandestine investigation?"

"I for one would be honored," Heather said.

"I'm at the climax of my new book. I have no time, but I'll lend some advice where I can." Anne took another bite of her lemon tart.

Her excuse was polite and British. But she was clear; she had sufficient doubt in our little band to decline out with grace.

Mavis glanced approvingly at Anne. "I don't mean to be rude, Elias. But I have no time to waste either. I have MWW duties that are paramount. I can't join in your murders-on-the-high-seas illusory endeavor. Plus, as you all know full well, Esther has made the MWW position clear. There was no murder or suicide or anything irregular about these unfortunate deaths. It's for the best."

Mavis applied her lipstick and put her napkin on the table to leave, but lingered to hear what Elias had to say.

Elias pushed on, ignoring the uncommitted and the naysayers, and filled the table in on our findings—but only selective ones.

Mavis listened intently and, as the protector of Esther's presidency, would be reporting everything. I was worried until I heard Elias altering and strategically selecting facts. He knew what he was doing and what would get back to Esther through Mavis, and from Heather to her new friend Amy.

Elias was a tactical genius, revealing with sleight of mind our theory explaining Otto's death too and suspecting a danger to Amy.

Unfortunately, he gave me full credit, which engendered a Mavis frontal assault on her way out.

"Since this is all based on an amateur's suppositions," Mavis pronounced. "I can't take it seriously. As Veronica may not have disclosed to her new friends, she is my student and has been for years and years. In my opinion, she never will be published and her mysteries, as well as her investigative skills, are amateurish."

"Oh?" Anne was as usual polite. "Well, we all had to start somewhere, didn't we?"

"I think Veronica's research and analysis are stellar." Heather spoke up. "My husband's law firm has Hollywood connections and Veronica did single-handedly solve the Valentine Theatre murders not long ago."

"You heard about that?" I was surprised my crime solving reputation extended from coast to coast and, now, over the high seas.

"Sure. The entertainment industry is a small community with long tentacles," Heather smiled. "Stephie Sevas, the film star, told one of the partners at his firm. Stephie's protégé was in the play."

"Fascinating, Veronica!" Anne's interest was piqued. "We must have tea before the cruise is over."

"I'd love to."

"Valentine murders or not, this so called theory is full of holes." Mavis was now discredited and on the defensive.

I was careful not to share my suspicions, or at least my questions, about Helga's possible role in all of these events.

"It's a better theory than two heart attacks," Sean scoffed. "That's absurd."

"It's not unheard of though, and their lifestyles can't be discounted," Anne waffled diplomatically and placed her tea bag in her individual pot. "One has to be careful . . . very conservative where real people's lives are going to be affected."

"Well . . . my father did die of a heart attack . . . young . . . too young," Heather added.

"Precisely!" Mavis peacocked with glee.

Heather looked over, startled.

"An early, sudden death is hard," Anne intervened sympathetically, rehabilitating the moment. "What a shame."

"Thank you," Heather pushed her dessert away after one bite. "I'm tired and I'm afraid a bit motion sick. If you'll excuse me?"

She left.

"I hope I didn't offend her." Mavis looked to Anne for support.

"Of course not." Anne was conciliatory—but lying. "It's the rocking. We're all feeling it."

I saw British politeness at its best in Anne. But she was so diplomatic that I personally found it offensive. I would avoid any tea with her. The invitation had served its purpose without needing to come to fruition because I knew Mavis took it as a slap in her face.

I looked around. Most tables were still nursing after dinner drinks or desserts like us. However, Curtis's table was starting to break up. He stood and I caught his eye. He nodded at me. I decided not to be late for our date tonight—a rocky Atlantic Sea notwithstanding.

"Mary." I leaned over to her. "I'm going to the bar. Can you keep an eye on Amy?"

Mary glanced at Amy, still embedded in sociability over liquors and dessert at her table. Then, she saw Curtis looking my way.

"I'll take over tonight. We'll see you in the bar . . . or not!"

"Thanks."

I left the table of well-fed and well-imbibed authors to their conversation and Mavis, who remained seated, to her mean spirited demolition of my character. Amongst my now

212

fast-friends and cohorts, she sounded silly. I, after all, had discovered the common thread amongst the murders, even Otto's.

I was confident that together with my quartet, I would prove Mavis and Esther wrong. But I didn't care if it was tonight. I had other things on my mind.

* * *

The ship was still undulating, but I had gotten my "sea legs." I made my way to the bar with more equilibrium.

On the way, I stopped outside the casino. It enticed passengers with its camaraderie and bright-lit slots jingling away, intermittently ringing out for the winners.

If I had not been meeting Curtis I would have joined the hottest craps table piled three deep with passengers putting down bets as they cheered spontaneously. I loved the sociability of craps. To me, it had the ups and downs of a roller coaster ride, the players screaming and moaning with each roll of the fickle dice. I usually played simple pass or no pass bets and rarely ever got fancier than that. When I did, I always lost.

To the right were the quiet, serious blackjack and poker tables where passengers were taken for a further ride, a quiet somber one.

As I scanned the room, I caught sight of Brent and Helga at a blackjack table close by. I drifted in among some potential gamblers loitering around to find their courage. I was curious about Helga and Brent in the aftermath of their dining room scene. And about Helga for other reasons as well.

I inched in where Helga was perched statuesquely on a high leather stool with her drained Martini glass harboring a lonely tooth picked olive. Before her on the green felt were colorful chips piled high. Meticulously arranged in a semi-circle were a short stack of red five-dollar chips, one tall stack of green twenty-five dollar chips, and three midsized stacks of black one hundred dollar chips. She had a queen of diamonds and a card face down. She slid ten black chips, a thousand dollars, into the circle.

Brent was next to her with a full Martini glass *sans* olive and four green chips, a hundred dollars, before him. He had just been dealt a king of spades and a card face down. He slid his last chips into the circle.

The dealer stood with sixteen showing in the cards before him. At sixteen, he would deal himself another card. All the players at the table knew this was the house rule, but, of course, didn't know what the card would be. Each had to decide whether to go for twenty-one or stay and hope the dealer got a high card sending him over twenty-one and out. It was, after all, a game of chance.

The dealer summarily disposed of the players in order, leading up to Brent and Helga. One stayed, not taking any risks. One with a soft hand at eleven took a hit from the shoe, the box where the shuffled cards are placed. He got a four—giving him fifteen. He hit at fifteen, got a ten point face card, and lost with twenty-five. The other two players stayed. They hoped for a high card when the dealer took his hit with his sixteen points.

It was finally Helga's turn. Her cards left her in a similar conundrum.

"Eighteen. I feel lucky." Helga scratched the table for another.

"Are you nuts?" Brent blurted. "You have eighteen and that's a thousand dollars!"

"It's your allowance, though. Remember?" Helga laughed as she looked at her new card.

It wasn't hard. The dealer hit her with a two.

"Twenty . . . I'll stay." Helga turned to Brent with her faded red lips. "Coward."

Brent glared at her.

"Sir," The dealer pushed Brent.

Brent turned over his card. "Twelve? Damn it!"

"Coward?" Helga again goaded Brent.

Twelve was low enough to take a gamble. The dealer could be lucky. The house always was. That's why they are in business. They win.

"What'll it be?" The dealer asked.

"Yeah, what'll it be, Mister Big Mouth!" Helga smirked.

Brent gave Helga a dirty look and then he scratched the table for a hit.

A ten came from the shoe—twenty-two. Brent was out. He sat quietly as the dealer took his cards, his chips, and his pride with them.

The dealer hit at his sixteen and got an eight. At twenty-four, he was over and paid out the remaining players, including Helga. The dealer added to Helga's castle of chips.

Brent got up to leave. No chips meant no money and no seat at a black jack table.

"Stay!" Helga commanded.

Helga shoved her tall stack of green chips over to Brent. He obediently sat back down, as would any well-trained dog.

When Brent reached for the stack of green chips, Helga laughed and grabbed them back with both hands.

Brent seized her forearms. She stopped laughing. Helga winced with pain. She tried to pull her arms away but couldn't. Brent stood up and leaned his face into hers.

"Never again," Brent spit at her.

"Let go, you ass!" Helga screamed, still clenching the chips despite the pain.

The dealer nodded at the uniformed security man in the pit.

Brent looked at the dealer and then at the security man. His face was red, contorted, and angry. I had never seen him out of control.

Brent threw Helga's arms down. They hit the edge of the table and the green chips scattered on the carpet.

Brent's feet crunched on them as he charged out, not noticing me.

He headed to the bar.

Helga watched Brent with eyes of flashing anger. She rubbed her forearms. Security picked up the scattered chips. She looked around at the gawkers and quickly composed herself. When she turned again to the blackjack table, all her fellow players had left.

Helga sat alone. Her rigid body vacuum-packed in her black sequined dress was no longer statuesque. Instead, it looked lonely and stiff against the flowing, chiming, and colorful background of the casino.

The dealer dealt. He looked up at Helga to play her hand, but otherwise avoided any interaction.

CHAPTER 25

Roiling and Romancing

I went to the bar. I was as upset as I had been at dinner by Helga's cruelty. Brent was trapped, at least in his own mind, and she knew it. Their lives were condemned, condemned by each other to each other.

I stopped at the bar entrance. It was crowded, even with some of my fellow second seating passengers still at dinner. Its popularity had spread. It would thin out when some of the bar-goers, who were waiting for the main stage show, left.

At the far side of the bar, heavy rain pelted the thick glass, mingling with the ocean spray from the high waves. Beyond was the white-capped sea reflected in the ship's lights and the darkness beyond. I suddenly realized the profound aloneness of the *Queen Anne* in the pitch black of the stormy Atlantic. We had hit bad weather. The ship felt it and, therefore, we did, too.

I spotted Curtis settling with his financial clients at a large table.

I waited for him at the bar, as he had for me.

I sat next to Brent, partially out of sympathy but also out of curiosity.

"Hi, there."

"Oh, Veronica!" Brent had his calm public face back after his blackjack scene. "How's it going? Bearing up? Or do you get queasy like Helga?"

"I'm okay for now." I ordered a white wine, astounded by Brent's quick recovery from the casino scene. "And you?"

"I'm a sailor. Remember? The rougher the sea, the better."

"That's right. I do remember. It's just been a long evening." I gave him an opening to talk about more than the pitching sea.

"Yes, it has been. Very long." Brent's voice was tired and he slid his empty Martini glass over, signaling the bartender for another. "This time two olives."

"Whoa, buddy." The bartender caught the Martini glass before it toppled. "Are you sure you want another?"

"Yeah, I promise I'll catch a cab back to my room." Brent laughed.

The bartender didn't crack a smile as he left to get our drinks. I did, however, a big broad one.

"How do you do it?" I asked.

"What?"

I overstepped because I felt entitled after seeing Helga crushing this poor man for two days. I felt like I knew them intimately—like married neighbors on the other side of a very thin apartment wall whose bedroom life you have essentially shared for years.

"Live with Helga." I blatantly talked about the elephant-in-the-room.

"Oh, that . . ." Brent chuckled. "'Live' is not the word I would choose."

"At least you still have a sense of humor."

"Yeah." Brent observed me. "And do you still have a sense of humor?"

"What?"

Brent smiled big and bright. "Come on. You've been outed by Mavis. It appears we are both here under false pretenses."

"Ah . . ." I took a deep breath.

The bartender brought our drinks and we both drank.

"That bad, huh?"

"Indeed, but that's a long, boring story." I deflected because I was focused on Helga and him. "Why'd you make Helga come on the cruise if she hates the sea?"

"Who said that?" Brent looked at his Martini and played with the olives.

"Helga at dinner."

"Oh, right." Brent took a healthy drink of his Martini, downed one of the olives, and played with the other nervously. "She has meetings in London and it was really her idea. She wanted to get in touch with her colleagues again. She just turns the tables and blames me when she's not happy. Too bad you're all subjected to her."

"We're fine." I figured the truth of them taking the cruise was somewhere betwixt and between.

"She's seasick and the patches haven't helped, so she's worse than usual."

Suddenly, from behind, Helga's voice bellowed over our heads and through our ears, vibrating into our brains.

"Turn off the charm, you gigolo. She's too old to fuck and too poor to screw."

I twisted around and looked up at Helga. She was a five-foot-ten, thin-as-a-stick harpy—an *haute couture* virago of unbridled rage wrapped in her black ostrich feathers.

All eyes around us turned our way.

"Helga!" Brent stood and shook his head hopelessly. "We're having an innocent drink."

"Nothing is innocent with you." Helga's contorted mouth was rimmed with worn red lipstick barely defining her lip line.

"Let me get you to your room. You're out of control." Brent took her arm and tried to muscle her away from the sideshow she was giving for the bar. "You're drunk."

"I'm sober as a judge! And don't think I don't know about the money you've been pilfering. I'll prosecute you for theft, my prolonged little play date."

Brent glanced around. I faced forward, absenting myself from the spectacle now tentacled as far as Curtis's table.

"Get her out of here or I'll call security," the bartender ordered Brent.

"Sorry. She's just had too much. I'll get her to our room."

The bartender watched, poised to take charge if he necessary.

Brent pulled Helga's arm, moving her forcibly toward the door.

"Stop . . . someone stop him!"

Helga struggled to free her arm, but couldn't. There was no intervention. Helga was a mean drunk and Brent, the dutiful husband, was following the bartender's order—as he apparently had many times before.

No one cared that Helga was being dragged away. Why should they? We all hadn't spent our good money to watch the very disturbing Brent-and-Helga freak show for five nights and four days.

* * *

In the hallway, between the casino and the bar, the combat continued as Brent pulled Helga to the elevator.

Before Brent could get her there, Helga yanked herself free. She tromped away alone, swaying with the ship, back into the casino. Brent followed her. But outside, he hesitated. Then, he turned and retraced his steps alone to the elevator.

"Hey, beautiful." Curtis came over and rescued me from the lingering effects of the scene Helga had made.

He found us a table. I was still shaken. With Mavis's dinner authorial attack and now Helga's even more public pronouncement that I was the *other* woman, I was viscerally upset. I couldn't be charming. I felt hollow and the increasing rhythm of the stormy sea was making my head thick and my stomach unsettled. I was sure my face had turned green.

Curtis flashed his winning smile. "The rocking getting to you?"

"A little." I didn't admit to anything else.

"I know what will help."

"Really?"

"A little of the bubbly."

After a sputtering start, we clicked again and the conversation flowed about seasickness, sailing, and the MWW deaths. But before I got a chance to update him that the deaths were murders, I was interrupted by a couple of his female clients who came over and pulled up chairs at the little table. One unattractive woman with a large diamond on her left hand and one very attractive woman with short gray hair and a left hand *sans* wedding ring. She pulled her chair next to Curtis. She dominated the conversation and was very knowledgeable in finance and investing. Curtis was hers, at least for now, whether he wanted to be or not.

I excused myself after a short but polite time with a case of motion sickness.

I tottered toward the elevators and my stateroom hoping Mavis was not there.

The storm was making the sea rougher. All I wanted now was a motion patch and my bed. Wessex's state-of-the-art ship stabilizers were still no match for the North Atlantic. And, apparently, the North Atlantic was no match for Helga either; I saw her still in the casino gambling.

Me? I was just as glad to call it a night.

* * *

When I got to the stateroom, Mavis was mercifully absent. I was glad. I took a quick shower and put on my navy blue jogging suit to relax. I slapped on a motion sickness patch and sat in my bed with pillows stacked comfortably. I turned on the news, but I didn't listen. The only news I would have liked was that Mendel and Frederick's deaths had been ruled homicides. And that didn't happen, so I ruminated about the evening.

After my seasickness waned, I regretted not staying to fight for Curtis. This was the third night of the cruise.

I turned to the cabin phone on the nightstand next to me. I hesitated, but then called Curtis's stateroom.

There was no answer. I didn't leave a message. Perhaps I should have.

I watched more of the news half-heartedly and then reached for the phone again. Just as my fingers touched it, it rang loud and clear. I was startled, but had an idea who it was. I let it ring just twice—just long enough, but not too long.

"Hello?"

"Veronica?"

"Yes."

"It's Curtis. Where did you run off to?"

"I didn't feel well. I'm relaxing."

"I saw you were a little green around the gills."

"I'm better now. Besides, you looked busy."

"Business. It always interrupts."

"Business?"

"Yes . . . only business."

"I get it."

"Good. Let's have a nightcap."

"Oh, I'm already in bed."

"So am I."

I laughed a sophisticated laugh. Curtis was smart. He gave me his locale and didn't let me get another word in.

"I'll see you." Curtis hung up.

* * *

At four am, I startled awake in Curtis's stateroom. I felt him wrapped around me, warm and strong.

"I've got to go," I whispered.

"Stay." Curtis didn't move.

I gave him a long, sensuous kiss.

"I can't. Mavis is after me enough now. I don't want to give her more gossip to monger."

"Alright . . . but let me walk you back."

"That's so sweet and chivalrous. But really, it's the twenty-first century. I'll make it."

"As you wish." Curtis tightened his enveloping hug.

"I've got to go." I freed myself from the warmth of his body, but only after he relaxed his steely arms.

"Tomorrow?'

"Tomorrow."

I had to be in bed when Mavis woke to avoid giving her more grist for her mill. I hurried down the wee-morning, empty corridors.

Mavis was snoring loudly as I slipped into bed in my same jogging suit.

⌘

223

CHAPTER 26

Exercized

The next morning the storm had passed. I hoped all the storms had passed—particularly the Helga-and-Brent one.

I woke at seven, ship-time. The cruise line turned the shipboard time forward one hour from New York toward London time every midnight of the cruise. It helped ease the "jet" lag when we finally docked.

This seven o'clock might have been my normal four o'clock biological wake-up time. I didn't care to analyze it. I could see there was daylight through a crack in the curtains. That's all that mattered to me.

I snuggled under my covers and thought about Curtis and the moments that were ours. I hoped, no believed, that this was more than a shipboard romance. I liked his company. And I had never experienced something like him before. So experimental, for me at least, so passionate. Not that I had experienced much before I was married or, unfortunately, during—or after, for that matter.

I heard a snort and rustling sheets. Unhappily, Mavis had walrused into my lovely morning daydream. But she was still dead asleep with earplugs and a sleeping mask over her eyes. I realized "dead asleep" was just wishful thinking.

I lay back, cozy and comfortable with happier thoughts for a minute. Namely, that we had gone one night without a death. Most certainly, there would have been a knock at my door because my friends were keeping an eye on Amy, the next likely target.

I chuckled to myself. I was glad there had not been a knock at my door because I was not here. It would only have given Mavis something else she could use to malign me. Then I panicked. Could there have been? I quickly glanced at the phone. Happily, there was no message light blinking and no note on the pad next to it. I had not missed anything. I relaxed. I would have gladly missed anything, including a murder, for last night with Curtis.

Still in my navy blue jogging suit, I put on my tennis shoes to take a turn around the walking deck. I escaped unnoticed. Saying "good morning" to Mavis would have been such a downer. I hoped she'd be gone when I returned.

I had planned a walk around the *Queen Anne's* promenade deck once anyway. It was a must. And this was the last morning at sea before we docked at Southampton near London tomorrow. This experience was important for me because the great stars in the 1930's movies always strolled on the promenade decks of luxury liners during their trans-Atlantic crossings. The old movies were etched in my memory from my all-night sleepless vigils after my husband passed. I grabbed my red cashmere hat, just in case, and stuffed it in my pocket.

I thought of calling Curtis to join me, but then I didn't know his waking habits. I Cheshire-cat-smiled to myself, however, because I certainly knew his sleeping habits—they were nearly nil when I was there.

I wondered if he woke early like I did. When we returned to Southern California, I was sure I would have the opportunity to find out. We did hit it off.

* * *

Up on deck, the Atlantic haze filtered the sun. The sea was calm again with low crests, intermittently dotted with white splashes. I stepped across the deck to the rail and looked out into the distance. It went forever.

"Watch out," a gray haired and gray sweat-suited jogger yelled.

He was going at a fast clip and unavoidably bumped into my shoulder. I leaned into the wood varnished rail and grabbed it. I looked down into the foaming sea at the base of the ship. It was a long way down.

"Sorry," the man shouted back.

I stepped back away from the rail. The drop was scary. I watched the man jog away. He looked nothing like the wealthy promenaders depicted in Hollywood's movie classics, nor did he have their manners.

"My fault," I called.

"Coming up on the right," a woman called from behind me.

I jumped back toward the rail. She and another woman in bright shorts and sweatshirts topped with blue and yellow baseball caps passed at a jog near me. Any further romantic illusions I had about my stroll were dispelled by the visual of the one woman's ass—sweaty bare white buns jiggling below her blue shorts. The other woman's broad butt bounced too, but stayed in her red shorts. The pairing was enough to kill any nostalgic remnant I had in my mind about old-movie sailings across the Atlantic.

I should have asked the deck etiquette before I embarked on my adventure. Evidently, there were no longer the chatting strollers one saw in the 1930's movies. Not dissuaded, I staked out a path along the rail in the cold air and crisp winds. I took out my red cap and put it on. I walked in the wake of an older couple going at a slow pace and talking. They could have been the couple we had talked with in the elevator. They were in leisure wools. They renewed my original vision of the scene on the promenade deck, which apparently had become more of a track stadium in the twenty-first century.

As I walked, I scanned the expanse of the now gray-green sea with small white caps trickling into the distance. I thought of the movies about the Atlantic theatre of World War II on my oldies television channel: the submarines, airplanes, supply convoys and destroyer escorts rattling around its immensity with no satellites to pinpoint their locations with ease. Primitive.

I ruminated about Amy and the fact she had published a book. I knew she was the key, the last living member of the group of four. Perhaps the Amy connection was a dead end, but I believed in it, and evidently so did my seasoned friends. Besides, it was all I had, and as any good mystery writer knows, when that's true, you go with it.

I took one turn around the deck and my Southern California lungs objected to the frosty and salty wet Atlantic air. My nose was starting to freeze and I put my hands in my pockets. I felt the salt air cling to my hair and my red cap. After another quarter turn around the deck, I decided to go to the gym. I needed exercise and, in any event, had to kill more time to assure Mavis had vacated our stateroom.

* * *

In the gym, the more practical passengers filled the jogging machines and stationary bicycles. This was never a scene one would see in the thirties movies.

My body sucked up the warmth in the room, boosted by the body heat the exercisers generated. I removed my cap and stuffed it into my pocket again. Brent was working out with weights in the distance, intermittently chatting with Sean. Then, I spotted a stationary cycle next to Heather in the far corner.

I grabbed a small workout towel from the stack by the door and bee-lined over.

I beat out an older man who had eyed the same cycle, but was slowed by his age and associated impediments.

"Hi." Heather smiled as I climbed onto the seat and started peddling. "Gray day!"

"It is." I set the bike for the least effort I could see on the settings, one hour at low resistance on simulated flat land. "It must be lonely without your husband here."

"It is, but he's busy."

"What firm is he with in New York?"

"Blumberg and Hutchinson. He just started really. Brent exaggerated."

"It took care of the Helga moment!"

"He does a lot of work for a partner who has authors for clients. Mendel was a firm client and my husband did work on his publishing agreements."

"Really? So did you get a copy of his latest before it went on the shelf?"

"We always do. The partner gets every associate working on the agreements an autographed first edition. He thinks it's their due. He has some old rare ones from the beginning of his career."

"So you've read Mendel's latest?"

"Yes. My husband brought it home. I have to say that it's not like his others."

"How so?"

"A woman is the main character, for one thing. And it's sensitive, sad, and poignant."

"That is different."

"You should read it. It's done really well. You wouldn't guess the author was a man . . . let alone Mendel."

"How interesting. It's been a couple of years since he published. They say his creative juices had dried up."

"Well, they came back. Either that, or he channeled someone's tragic life."

"I'd like to read it."

"I'm sure it's online. It's probably for sale in the lobby with everyone else's books."

"Right!"

Everywhere authors gather they sell their books to each other, in an incestuous ritual. On the ship, I had avoided running that money-sucking author's gauntlet of autographed books. But now, I would seek it out.

"I'm sure someone is manning his table," Heather said. "And plugging their own books."

"Right. Thanks. You know, I think I've had enough. I was jogging on the deck before this."

I lied. I had to get a look at Mendel's book and see if it revealed anything we needed to know to solve his murder. Getting to my investigation was more important than avoiding Mavis. I also needed to head to the library and spend more computer time on the foursome who had more than "crossed paths" so many years ago.

"The promenade?"

"Yes." I got off the cycle.

"Wow, you're brave. It's a speedway."

"I figured that out."

"Ah, it doesn't take long to learn. I made that mistake, too."

I didn't admit that I naive when it came to the promenade deck.

"See you at dinner." I hopped off the bicycle.

"Bye."

The older man, who had missed getting my stationary bicycle, was still waiting. He smiled when I left. He undoubtedly wanted the cycle next to Heather to chat her up while he exercised.

* * *

When I got back to the cabin, Mavis was just leaving.

"I'm late." Mavis gathered her things. "Esther called. That damn Helga hasn't shown up yet for her 'Agitating Agents' panel discussion."

"Oh?"

Mavis was chatty despite submarining me last night at dinner. My immediate choice was to accept her as she was this morning. Some drinkers didn't even remember the night before. I didn't know if she was one of them. I didn't care. I was polite because her openness was to my advantage. Information flow was my objective, no matter how trivial.

"Is it chilly out there?" Mavis asked.

"Yes, take a wrap."

"Thanks."

"What do you mean Helga hasn't shown up? She must be awake. I just saw Brent in the gym."

"Awake or not, it doesn't matter. Esther says when Helga starts writing she tunes the world out and does no-shows for meetings, lunches, you name it. Evidently, she won't answer her cabin door or the phone. She's probably holed up there with her muse." Mavis paused and then added with a bitter edge to her voice. "She isn't known as 'Ms. Prolific' for nothing."

"That's a gift." I recognized Mavis's writer's envy, but carefully did not reveal mine.

"She's self-centered and egocentric to be leaving us in the lurch." Mavis grabbed her short black coat from the closet and her purse. "Esther and I have to deal with this. I might take over. I have my own agitating agent."

"Good solution."

"Of course, you wouldn't know what that was like." Mavis's fangs came out. "Dealing with an agent."

I did not jump to the bait. Evidently, last night was fresh in her mind and her attacks on me were to be repeated whenever she felt like it. I let it go. It was more interesting to me that Mavis was in a tizzy about the Helga-drama of the moment. It made her important to Esther and she thought she might get something out of it.

Without another word, Mavis headed out to vie for the spot on the panel.

"Good riddance," I mumbled.

I got dressed and balanced my desire to look smashing for Curtis against my need to get on with my investigation. I had to get my research done on the outrageously expensive shipboard Internet and brave the book gauntlet to buy Mendel's new—and last—release.

⌘

CHAPTER 27

An Open Book

By the time I got ready, I was hungry. I dropped by the twenty-four-hour coffee bar on the way to the library and picked up a tea and a raisin scone. This was a British cruise line and I wanted to have at least one authentic scone. I had seen kippers on the breakfast menu, too, and planned to go to the dining room open seating breakfast and try them as well before the cruise ended. Kippers were strewn amongst the old British movies.

The library was nearly empty. I sat overlooking the ocean again and sipped my tea and ate my scone as I did Internet searches. I looked for information on anyone in our growing and complex drama.

I read everything I could about Otto, Frederick, Mendel, and Amy.

Finally, the information became inbred with every search leading me to the same pages and repetitive information. Then,

I decided to look at information on Mendel's new book that Heather had found so interesting.

She was right. The reviews were stellar. They touted the realistic vengeful female main character and the intricacy of the plot. But of more interest was the setting. It was a depiction of Otto's writing program, but disguised as an acting program. I needed the book. I decided I would search for Amy's outdated published book later and left for the book fair.

* * *

At the book fair, the long tables of books were manned by five of our authors. They were promoting their books and signing them for a surprisingly sparse, but eager, group of passengers.

Mavis sat at the end of one table with no comers. I wondered if she had been allowed to grace the panel discussion in Helga's absence. Certainly, if so, it had done nothing for her sales here. Not even my classmates were buying from her.

Agnes and Jody were waiting together at Mary's table. Mary was signing copies for a chatty, elderly woman who bought a whole bag of her books. Herbert was at Sean's signing table, which had a group of animated men talking and laughing. Sean was a real man, and it showed. Too bad Herbert wasn't. That showed too.

Elias was across the way, surrounded by women. He was signing his books and charming them all with his mustached smile and gleaming teeth. I went to his table.

"Elias, when are you through here?"

"Why? What's wrong?"

"Nothing, but we need to meet," I whispered. "I have new information."

"Sure, lunch? Give me at least an hour. One-thirty?"

"Yes, in the dining room. I'll tell the others."

I told Mary and then Sean over at his table.

"What meeting?" Herbert interrupted and glanced from one of us to the other through his thick-rimmed glasses. "I want to come."

"It's just a book meeting," Sean placated him. "I'll tell you about it after I sign this for you."

Herbert was pleased. He believed Sean's subterfuge.

"Right on, Sean," I muttered as I left.

I was irritated at myself for not being more circumspect around Herbert. He was a bother.

I bought a copy of Mendel's book from an author I did not recognize. He was manning Mendel's table to piggyback his sales in on Mendel's reputation. I hurried to my cabin to read it. I was convinced it held the key to his death—and maybe more.

* * *

In the elevator, I reveled in the potential irony of Mendel helping to solve his own murder. But then, I thought, what in the book could have been the catalyst for his demise?

In my cabin alone, I skimmed through the book quickly.

The main character was a thinly disguised Amy at a premier graduate acting school. And the male characters were none other than Otto, Frederick, and Mendel—by other names. It was a plot of female revenge for rape, betrayal, and the destruction of her acting career. Did Mendel think that this rendition of their pasts would go unnoticed by the woman who had paid the price—Amy? How arrogant he was if he thought so!

Every paragraph confirmed that this book was autobiographical and depicted Amy's horrific background. To me the guise of an acting school was transparent. Mendel had taken Amy's life story, her true and tragic life story. The rape scene was graphic, brutal, and perverse. It had a victim participatory element that made it equivocal—made it a he-said she-said with overtones of desires that were just not believable for a young, inexperienced female. Frederick was there too, not in name, but in context. He was weak, opportunistic, and evil.

Had Mendel run out of plots? Or, was he so jealous of Frederick's Oscars and commercial Hollywood wealth that he had to get even?

The public at large would not know the true biographical nature of the book. Amy would–and now me after delving intimately into the obscured past and also having seen the interaction between Mendel, Frederick, and Amy.

The book clearly depicted Amy's strength and capacity for sustained anger. I was right that she was the last of the four standing. But had I been mistaken? Was this slender, reserved, elegant woman's life in danger, too? Or, was her new-found light-heartedness a product of delayed but successful revenge? Had I gotten it wrong? Was Amy the murderer, not Helga? A triple murderer?

I looked up at the clock. I was just going to make it to the lunch meeting. I grabbed my purse, put the book in it, and headed out.

* * *

In the dining room Elias, Mary, and Sean were waiting at a table for four in a far corner. The dining room was not full and had groupings at other tables on the main floor, but not in the tiers above.

"Sorry I'm late." I sat down.

"We just got here, too," Elias said.

"We all ordered Salade Niçoise and got you one, as well . . . and that's your iced tea," Mary said. "Hope that's fine."

"Wonderful. Thank you." I grabbed Mendel's book from my purse and put it on the table. "Have any of you read this?"

"No." Mary picked it up and leafed through it. "Not yet."

"Sadly, his last," Elias said. "I haven't read it, either."

"I bought it yesterday afternoon," Sean said. "After you told us about those four being in Otto's writing program together. I started it last night and I finished it a couple of hours ago. Now, I have to say I'm not afraid for Amy . . . I'm afraid *of* her."

I leaned back in my chair, let out a sigh. "Then you see the same thing I do?"

"Yes." Sean put his elbow on the table and leaned towards Mary and Elias. "Amy's revenge."

"Amy's what!" Mary exclaimed. "I thought she was in danger."

"What is going on here?" Elias insisted. "I don't understand."

The server brought our lunches and we all hushed until he left.

"It's about a graduate acting program and has four main characters." I leaned forward again.

Sean and I explained the plot and the characters. Then, I related it to the actual picture I had found.

"But the acting program in New York is transparently a duplication of Otto's writing program. The setting, really everything, is the same," Sean added. "And the characters are the promising and talented female acting student in the program, her boyfriend, his best friend and teaching assistant, and the head of the program. In other words, Amy, Frederick, Mendel, and Otto."

"Mendel barely changes their physical descriptions!" I interjected.

"You'll recognize them immediately when you read it," Sean added. "The female graduate student is raped by the teaching assistant and goes to the police."

"But in the book the rape is ambiguous and makes Amy's character appear to want it rough and has her begging to be sodomized and degraded. It's horrible."

"Oh, my God," Mary said. "That elegant little thing would never invite that. Not at that young, tender age anyway. I write enough of that stuff to know."

"And I've seen enough on the force to know that as well," Sean agreed.

"Yes," I said. "And that makes this book a real slap in the face to her."

"I can see why she's irate," Elias said. "But murder?"

"It gets worse," Sean went on. "Her boyfriend and the head of the department coerce her into dropping the complaint she had made."

"Yeah," I added. "The department head gets the boyfriend a big film part in Hollywood for his part in the betrayal."

"Anyway." Sean was getting annoyed at my interruptions. "She gets pregnant from the sex . . ."

"Rape," Mary corrected.

"Okay. Rape." Sean was impatient to finish. "She drops out of the program and has the kid, but it dies suspiciously of SIDS. Then . . . she learns the boyfriend had traded her for that job in Hollywood. That is where the book takes a different turn. She becomes a successful movie actress and systematically tries to destroy the men's acting careers and marriages. But in the end, she doesn't exact catastrophic revenge because the three men join forces in time. She doesn't kill them or even try to kill them."

"That's because Mendel wrote it instead of Amy. He underestimated her," Mary said. "On top of that, just imagine her seeing Mendel's book come out. Reading it and its twisted ending."

"And then watching Otto and Frederick at the Oscars, splattered across the news and Internet," Elias said

"It would be the final straw," I said. "That's when she decided to confront Otto."

"I'd whack off their manhood, like the women in my slashers. Then, I'd slowly skin them alive," Mary smirked.

"I'm sure you would." Elias chuckled. "Remind me not to cross you, because that mind of yours is beyond normal."

Mary laughed. "Thanks, Elias."

"Let's be serious for a moment." I quieted the authorial banter. "Not only is this autobiographical for Amy, but it distorts the reality she has lived all these years. She is depicted as a woman who initiated rough sex and then cried rape and then killed her baby. I mean this book is really bad."

"I agree," Elias said. "And what better place to dispose of Frederick and Mendel than on this isolated cruise across the Atlantic where there are no cops, no forensic teams, no coroner . . . no anything."

"Just a hack doctor, used for Wessex cover-ups, and a brain-dead security team," Mary said.

"Don't forget Esther and Mavis getting in bed with them, too." I got my digs in.

"Yes," Sean agreed. "FYI, I had a copy of the police report Amy made when the rape happened transmitted to me this morning. It doesn't match the book . . . it was rape. The cops took it seriously. Mendel was lucky she withdrew it."

There was silence. Elias shook his head and stroked his moustache. Mary and Sean took a few bites of their barely touched salads as they thought. I started my own salad.

"How ironic that Mendel's book was probably the catalyst for all three murders. Without Mendel's book, life might just have gone on as it had before." Elias ignored his salad. "What do we do now?"

"I don't know," Sean said. "It's clear Amy doesn't need our protection. And I don't think at this point there will be any other bodies popping up."

"Unless she knows we are on to her." Mary shoved her food away. "There is no one to arrest her here and we don't have proof. If she finds out about what we really know we could all die of heart attacks. Who would know the difference? I am certainly tubby enough to be categorized as a heart risk."

"Oh, no." I objected to Mary's self-criticism, even though it was painfully accurate.

"Wait. That sounds ridiculous, but might not be." Elias got serious. "You can only be executed or imprisoned for life once. And she has nothing else to lose."

"Then we have to keep this to ourselves." I was frightened. "Right now, she has no idea what we have discovered."

"I'll make sure if we start dying she won't get away with it," Sean said. "I'm wiring this to my ex-partner who's still on the force. We need someone on the outside who can avenge us if need be, but more than that, we need to find proof against her while we keep our mouths shut."

"I agree," Elias said.

"We've already said too much at dinner." Mary looked worried. "And . . ."

"We are where we are. No recriminations," Elias interrupted. "We've got to get the Prolixin away from her, if she still has any and we can find it. And, Sean, do you think your ex-partner can trace any purchases she made?"

"Good ideas," Mary said. "Who would have thought that little Amy could have done all of this?"

"She probably wouldn't have," Elias said. "The matter was dormant . . . behind her . . . until the book and the Oscar."

"Mendel should have let things go," Sean said. "It was his book."

"Right," Mary agreed. "The rumors were true. His muse was gone and he needed something. Fiction can never beat the twists of real life."

"Dinner is going to be hard," I said. "We have to be careful, Elias."

"I agree," Elias said. "I'll watch my liquor."

"You'd better," Mary warned. "You start talking and don't stop. Look at you with Mavis."

"Come on," Elias objected. "I had an ulterior motive."

"We all have with her," I said.

"Look. Everyone just act normal," Sean suggested.

"Well, I for one am going to do something now," Mary announced. "I'm going to try to get into her stateroom. We need proof and to confiscate the Prolixin if she still has some in her stateroom."

"I'll go with you and stand watch in the hall," I volunteered. "Does she have a roommate?"

"We'll find out," Mary said.

"How are you going to get in?" Elias asked.

"I don't know," Mary replied. "Trick the steward."

"Too dangerous," Sean said. "I can pick a lock."

"What?" I blurted.

"Cops have many talents." Sean shrugged. "What can I say?"

"Good." Elias stood up. "We'll all go. Sean and I will stand post at both ends of the hallway and watch for Amy or any potential roommate. You two go in and get out fast."

As we four marched out of the dining room and down the hall, I was fearless. My chest swelled and my heart beat with pride, purpose, and belonging.

I was convinced I had solved the murders—well, Sean and I had.

⌘

CHAPTER 28

Oh What a Tangled Web We Weave

The halls were deserted after lunch. The MWW members were in meetings. Other passengers were at their groups' meetings, and unaffiliated cruisers were at the Wessex Cruise Line's daily movies, card games, and programs. I presumed early risers were napping before four o'clock High Tea. High Tea was of course a tradition on British cruise ships.

Elias had confirmed that Amy was attending the after-lunch MWW panel discussion on literary agencies by agents. It was a highlight of the MWW program for writers. It revealed the inner workings and thoughts of that parasitic layer between the book and the public, the statistical health of the book business, and trends.

In fact, my cohorts were afraid that as a grouping they would be missed. It went without saying that I, of course, would not be. But we all agreed we would work quickly and then slip in at the back of the panel discussion.

With his detective skills, Sean found Amy's stateroom and that she had paid almost double for her stateroom to sail *sans* roommate. We all agreed that, with her less-than-stellar career, she could not easily afford it. It confirmed to us that she had paid that dear price to achieve her true goal in secrecy—murder.

* * *

Sean knocked on Amy's door with a plausible story on the tip of his tongue. With no answer, Sean waved us up and did his work picking the lock. Mary and I hurried and stood sentinel with Elias down the hall near the closest bank of elevators.

"There it is. A piece of the proverbial cake." Sean cracked the door open. "Have at it and leave everything as you found it except any evidence we'll need—the Prolixin, notes, calendars. Mary, I've read your books. You know the drill. Veronica, follow her lead. I'll go down to the other end of the hall."

"Move aside, Sean. We're ready." Mary stood poised at attention.

"I'm ready too," I whispered. "But you guys have to stop Amy if she shows up . . . no matter what!"

"Believe me I know what to do, and so does Elias." Sean turned and scooted down the hall quite agilely for a man his size and age.

Mary pushed the door open and started in. I panicked and froze in my steps.

My good girl kicked in and I couldn't step over the threshold. How could I break and enter? Well, how could Sean break and I enter? How could I be involved? This was absurd! I was Veronica Kennicott, aspiring author from Santa Monica, California in the good old U.S. of A. Had the isolation of the high seas and salt air gone to my brain? Was it truly the rule, rather than the exception, that anything goes on this floating conglomeration of people ruled by the questionable and the imbibed of the Wessex Cruise Line—at least anything that did not threaten Wessex's corporate bottom line?

"Come on." Mary broke my brain streaming and dragged me in by the arm.

"Shouldn't we at least put out the *Do Not Disturb* sign in case the maid shows up?"

I looked to her for leadership, but then laughed at myself. Her qualifications might be superior but they were still only derived from my same experience—none other than the printed word. We were alphabet graduates in the school of crime. Suddenly, I was even more afraid.

"No, it could cause complications. Shut the door. The guys will take care of us."

I shut the door to the room's daylight-darkness filtered through the drawn curtains. I held my breath as Mary turned on the lamp.

"Thank God." I breathed out in relief. "She's not here."

"Of course not, she's at the meeting. Don't be such a Nervous Nellie. Let's get to work. You take the bathroom. Call me if you find something. Anything you move put back just like it was. Be very careful. We don't want to tip her off if we don't find the goods . . . and, even if we do, we need time on our side. I'll start with the dresser."

I turned on the bathroom lights and went over every inch—not that there was much. I searched Amy's make-up case and toiletries. Her make-up was top drawer and her face creams expensive. I personally bought middle-of-the-road all the way. I ignored the hard sell for the pricy creams, as I aged and slid further over the proverbial "Hill".

On the way out, I looked under towels piled on the floor for the maid.

"Nothing. No Prolixin." I turned off the lights and left everything as I found it.

"Go through the nightstands. I'll take the closet." Mary slammed the bottom drawer of the dresser. "Oops!

While we searched, every second was an hour. My hands were shaking and my forehead was hot with sweat. I concluded I would never be a good criminal. I was just a criminalist, or really, a criminalist who really simply wanted to create clues and evil in print. The only real, live chasings-of-evil I had done involved the petty thieves and barking dogs in my neighborhood. Of course, there were the notable Hollywood Valentine Theatre murders I had solved, but in the end, I had tracked down that killer to save myself from arrest. Suddenly, I transformed into a calm exacting sleuth. After all, we were here to save our lives! Our foursome was a threat to Amy and she had nothing to lose. I steadied my hands and remembered the Valentine Theatre as Texans "Remember the Alamo."

I opened the last drawer of the second nightstand.

"Mary, look. Medications. Containers of them," I announced as I started to read the labels. "Well, this one accounts for her placid affect. She's drugged all the time."

"Let me see." Mary came over and read the labels. "Wow, this is a whole pharmacy. Pills to wake up with. Pills to stay awake with. Pills to make her want to stay awake. Pills to go to sleep. And pills to counteract the pills."

"How do you know all that?"

"Just years of living with my killers, killees, and cowards. A writer's life." Mary rummaged away. "Everything but Prolixin."

"Look here." I held up two containers. "These are from a pharmacy in Canada."

"The Internet!" Mary grabbed them. "And look, two different doctors. Interesting. She could get Prolixin from there, too. And Sean said there's a liquid form."

"Do we take these?"

244

"No, she uses them. She'd notice." Mary got the ship's pad and pen from the adjacent desk. "Write down the info. Get the prescription numbers and pharmacy names, too."

"I'll just snap a picture with my phone."

"Oh, yeah, I forget technology. I even forget it in my books sometimes." Mary put the pen and pad back carefully.

"Easy to do." I sympathized, of course, without any personal authorial experience in that vein at all. I noted, though, that when I edited my books I should check on updating technology references.

"Snap anything that will lead us to the Prolixin. I'd go through the closet, but she might have it with her."

"What for? There's no one else we can predict from the book." I lined up the Canadian pill containers and snapped pictures. "And we're all here."

"Not funny."

"But considering we're in here, her purse might be the safest place." I studied the labels. "Guess what? She misspelled her last name by one letter on some of these. Sean's partner could never have traced these purchases."

"Great catch. Amy's a tricky lady. Double check it and then help me with these suitcases." Mary opened the sliding mirrored closet doors and struggled to take down the stored luggage in the closet. "This is where my delightful murderer in book number eight years ago hid his knife on a very bloody family vacation."

As the large black suitcase submitted to Mary's pulling, she whispered, "Bingo. Hear the stuff rattling? You take the small one. Don't forget to check the small pockets and the lining."

"Did you look at the safe at the back of the closet?" I grabbed the mismatched and tattered navy blue carry-on

"Yeah. It's open and empty, just as I expected. In my experience, murderers want to be clever, not obvious. That's how I write them, anyway."

"Ah, I'll remember that." I threw the carry-on across the bed next to the large suitcase that Mary was fighting to unzip.

"Damn, this zipper is touchy. It's like mine that I overstuffed once too many times," Mary said.

Finally, and suddenly, the zipper gave way. Mary rummaged through what amounted to a laundry bag of clothes used so far on the trip and a large stash of the small toiletries the maids place every day in our cabins.

"Nothing."

"Too bad." I had mine unzipped.

Mary ran her hands along the lining and in the two small side compartments again. "I'll put this back."

I flipped open my lid as Mary put the unhelpful large suitcase back up on the upper shelf of the closet.

"Look at all this stuff. And here's Mendel's book."

"Jesus, Mary and Joseph!" Mary looked at my find. "His book."

I grabbed the book from amongst the news clippings, magazines, small boxes, and clothes in large sealed baggies.

"Freeze." Mary whispered.

"What?"

"Shh. Just freeze."

I looked at Mary and didn't move. I didn't even twitch and eye. I thought she saw a trap or bomb trigger wire or something. My knees started to buckle.

"Put it down just like it is," Mary commanded. "Fingerprints. We want her fingerprints."

Mary made her way over. "We have to preserve anything we can."

"Oh, my God." I sunk into an adjacent chair. "You scared me to death. I thought you saw a booby-trap or something."

"No, sorry. Get some tissues from the bathroom. It looks like there's something stuffed in the book."

I was irritated, but got the tissues.

"See . . . There." Mary took a tissue.

"I see it."

Mary flipped the pages of the book with the tissue. As she did, we saw meticulous notes in the margins. It looked like the textbook of an average student competing with gifted ones for an "A" in a college literature course. I remembered those college days, trying to make up with ink and time for what God had not given me in gray matter.

"Look here." Mary pointed. "Amy has notated Mendel's embellishments and lies."

"Here's an envelope." With a tissue I slipped an envelope out of the book. "A law firm."

Mary opened it laboriously using tissues. The law firm refused to represent her for a defamation case. They said there was no defamation, actual or by innuendo.

"I know what the actual means, but what is that innuendo?" I asked.

"It means indirectly, from the context." Mary put the letter back carefully. "The reader would need outside facts to recognize that the book was about Amy's life."

"Anyway, the bottom line is that she couldn't sue?"

"Yes." Mary put the letter and book back and then examined a clear plastic baggie with hot pink underpants and a bra. "Look at this. Holy Mary . . ."

"Are those the underwear garments she was raped in?"

"They've got to be. Look at the ripped side." Mary was unable to take her eyes off them. "There's some blood. Look. On the bra."

"Maybe." The keepsakes repelled me. "What the hell did she bring them here for?"

"I think to get her anger up. Her courage. A reminder."

"Are you kidding?"

"No. Way back, in one of my first books, I had a man do that with his wife's hair to stir him up for revenge. The murderer had ripped it out of her head during the rape-torture-murder. I got the idea from a psychology book with a chapter on revenge."

"Huh." I was amazed by Mary, but immediately tried to look as professional and savvy as she did. "I think she was planning a ritual burial at sea with this stuff too, after she got her revenge."

"Possibly." Mary looked at me with a smile. "You're good. I'm going to work that into the book I'm writing now. With your permission, of course."

I preened. "Have at it."

I knew there was no stopping Mary, anyway. Besides, I had taken that plot point from an obscure but very good mystery I had read a decade ago. I turned back to my hunt through the rest of the artifacts.

"There it is. The Prolixin. With Kleenex around it." I took a liquid vial from an inside zipped pocket. "But it hasn't been opened."

"My God." Mary dropped the underwear on the bed and grabbed the bottle with a tissue. "You're right. Look, a different name, an anagram. May Rellim. Canadian. And a different doctor. Internet. We never would have found this doing research."

"Depends where she had it delivered." I impressed even myself.

"Good again. I'll read your book when it comes out. I bet I'll get some ideas."

I smiled on the outside but gasped on the inside at the growing pressure I felt to publish.

"But why isn't it open?" Mary muttered to herself.

"Because it's a refill. A back-up. Look at the bottom of the label. One refill remaining."

"Of course, refills. Excellent again. We've got to find the opened one, too."

"She has it with her. I'm sure of it."

"I agree. Get a picture of all this stuff with your phone. Can you?"

"Sure, but we've got to get out of here. I'm getting really nervous."

"I think we should take this stuff. It's evidence."

"But she'll know. And she'll guess it was us."

"Maybe not . . . at least, until we dock in South Hampton. I'm going to ask Sean and Elias. Stay here."

"I don't want to stay here alone. What if she comes back?" I looked at the time on the digital clock. "The panel discussion's almost over."

"I'll be back in a minute."

"Wait."

Mary ignored me and hurried out the door.

* * *

I was alone. Alone after Sean's breaking, and Mary and my entering into Amy's cabin.

My heart raced. I quickly snapped some pictures of everything with my camera. As I rearranged things to get more pictures, I found three memory sticks nestled with a CD and a folded paper. I scanned the paper. It was an untitled synopsis of what appeared to be a book Amy was writing. After the first few sentences I knew from the title and short synopsis I had found in my Internet research that this was not the book she had published in her twenties. I assumed the memory sticks had copies of that book on them.

I flipped through layers of magazine articles and Internet blurbs about Mendel and Frederick and Otto. I finished my pictures and then made a command decision and slipped one memory stick into my pants pocket.

All of a sudden, Mary laughed and talked boisterously outside the door.

I inched toward the door and listened. It was Amy and Mary, together. My heart stopped. Obviously, Elias and Sean had been unable to stop Amy in the hall.

After I repacked the small carry-on, I lifted it back onto the top shelf quietly. I prayed Mary could lead Amy away.

I smoothed the bed and took a quick look around. Everything seemed in order.

Suddenly, Amy's electronic key card slid in the door.

I panicked. I remembered the lamp had been off when we came in. It was too late. I had no time to turn it off. Without Mary's boisterous warning, I wouldn't even have gotten the carry-on put away.

As the door handle turned, I dove into the closet, hitting my head on the open safe.

I quietly crept behind the clothes, knees bent and head tilted. I arranged them neatly.

I reached for the sliding closet door and started to close it. Mid-slide it jammed. I looked down. Nothing. Then I looked up. It was the larger suitcase. Mary had placed it cockeyed.

There was nothing I could do.

I melted back into the wall of the closet behind Amy's clothes.

⌘

CHAPTER 29

Out of the Closet and Out of the Bag

Amy's closet was economy class, ship speak for very small. I pressed against the back wall so hard I felt my vertebrae bruising my skin. I held my breath too long and then desperately started shallow quiet breaths.

I prayed Amy's didn't remember the lamp was off and that her clothes were not bulging—screaming that I was behind them. If caught, my hope was that if Amy could get away with two murders shipboard then I would not be thrown in the brig for "mistakenly" being in Amy's stateroom either. Somehow, I would reconcile hiding in the closet.

"High tea will be so much fun," Mary called from the doorway. "Seating is in five minutes."

"It'll just take me a second to get ready."

"All right, but you look fine."

"I wonder if they really serve crumpets, and what they actually are?" Amy laughed, but from inside the cabin now.

"I think they're these little English muffin-y things." Mary toned her voice down. "My feet are killing me. I'll come in and wait."

"Sure. Grab a chair. I thought I left that lamp off? Huh . . ."

Mary distracted her. "I'm so glad we ran into each other."

"I didn't know you were on my floor."

"It would be a shame to take this crossing and not go to English high tea at least once." Mary sidestepped Amy's query. "Also, we haven't had a chance to really chat. I wanted to talk to you about your agency. Confidentially, I haven't been thrilled with the representation on my last two books. Just because I'm successful doesn't mean they can ignore me."

"I agree." Amy jumped at Mary's bait. "I can't believe any agency would ignore you."

I stood in the shadows behind the clothes thinking greed was, as always, a blinding monumental motivator. Mary was tapping into Amy's professional lust to distract her. She was dangling her ten percent agent's cut in front of Amy's nose. Amy had no idea that Mary's urgency, baiting, and invitation to high tea were just subterfuges—a way to save me. I was grateful, so grateful.

"I'll get my black velvet jacket." Amy walked towards the closet. "I . . . uh . . . that's funny."

There was silence as Amy stood at the closet door half opened and the large suitcase above misaligned against the door.

"Too dressy for tea, really. We should go." Mary was desperate when she saw her mistake replacing the suitcase. "We want to get a main floor table. There's plenty of time to change for dinner after."

"No I'll just grab it."

I saw Amy's arm reach up and push the suitcase above back into place. I felt for a velvety jacket in the dark, hoping it was toward Amy. I found it half way to me. I lost all hope.

When Amy opened the closet door, more light streamed in. I froze. My back hurt and my thighs burned from my semi-squat position. I held my breath as Amy started to hard sell her agency, riffling progressively my way through her clothes.

I turned my face and shut my eyes so that my dark hair would blend into the shadows. Time stopped for me. The fraction of the second Amy searched in her closet became an eternity.

I waited in terror. But nothing happened. I was sure Amy couldn't miss seeing the top of my head. But Amy didn't break the rhythm of her search or chatting up her agency.

Mary was desperate. "We'd better go."

"My floral silk, that's more English tea time."

Amy's hand stopped its march toward me and rested on her floral jacket—still away from me. She paused for what seemed to me to be an hour. My thighs and back ached.

"Great! Let's go." Mary pushed.

"Who is your agent?" Amy finally pulled the jacket out and rearranged the adjacent clothes where the void was created.

"I'll fill you in on the way." Mary got up and headed for the door.

Amy put on the floral jacket and then slid the closet door fully closed. I believed she had seen me. She had evaluated the situation and decided a confrontation was of no benefit to her.

My legs felt weak. I was left in the dark closet waiting for the cabin door to sound their departure.

* * *

After Amy and Mary left, I took several deep breaths and shook my legs out. I felt steady enough to get out of the closet. I arranged the clothes as neatly as they had been. Obviously, it was an exercise in futility, but I did it anyway with a last ditch hope that Amy had not seen me.

I had to get out of there, but I didn't know whether to take any of the evidence we found. I decided if Amy had seen me she would dispose of it all immediately. Her survival instincts would take precedence over her compulsive hoarding of her justifications for murders. If she hadn't seen me, Mary was right; there was no reason for her even to look at it until we docked. It was my call. So—I grabbed it all from the carry-on— the Prolixin vial, the papers, notes, Internet printouts, clippings, and articles. I even took the book with notations. I stuffed everything in one of the several white plastic dry cleaning bags stacked on the upper closet shelf. I put the carry-on back, made sure the closet was neat as a pin, and slid the door shut.

I believed, if Amy had seen me, she had gambled I would just flee the scene after her closet intrusion. But she was wrong. I knew crime analysis and killers. I knew opportunity and how to take advantage of it. I valued hard evidence above all. I was on an adrenaline high. I was also memorizing this entire ordeal to put in a future book. Real life really was more amazing than fiction. At least, mine was.

On the way out, I stopped at the door and scrutinized the scene of my crime—my first real crime—breaking and entering and burglarizing. Everything was in order. And this time Amy had left the light on herself.

Even though I had the last bottle of Prolixin, I was still worried for Mary at tea. The open-and-used vial of Prolixin had to be in Amy's purse—the vial Amy had used on Frederick and Mendel.

* * *

When I walked out into the hall, Sean and Elias descended on me.

"You're okay?" Elias asked. "I couldn't stop her."

"Yeah! I know! If Mary hadn't done her routine at the door, it all would have been over."

"Why? Did she catch you? Where did you hide?" Sean asked.

"In the proverbial closet. Where else?"

"Good choice" Sean laughed. "So she didn't find you?"

"I don't really know. I thought she had . . . but then she didn't say a word."

"Huh," Sean mumbled.

"But she sure noticed the lamp was on and that Mary left one of her suitcases out of place."

"Why did Mary leave you in there alone?" Elias asked.

"She wanted to ask you what we should take."

"Nothing," Elias answered. "Amy would know."

"Too late for that." I held up the bag of evidence. "And I snapped phone pictures too."

"A right plonker you are! You sure don't fool around . . ." Sean turned serious detective. "And for the best. It's done. We need the evidence, especially if we've been compromised. Good decision, Veronica."

"Fine . . . I guess. Let's get out of here . . . now." Elias led us down the hall. "We can go to my place and look through the stuff."

"Yes!" I followed. "Do you have a roommate?"

Elias laughed, "Of course not. I'm too noisy to get along with anyone and too old to change my ways."

"I know what you mean," Sean commiserated as we reached the elevator. "It would have been worth the money not to be bothered with anyone. I didn't think of it. Next time."

"Well, now we know why Amy didn't want one." I said.

"And, I guess we didn't have to worry about protecting poor little Amy, Veronica." Elias shook his head.

"That's pretty clear." Sean patted my shoulder. "But don't worry. We've all gone up the wrong path many times."

"Thanks."

"We're on the right one now." Elias led us onto the elevator.

We shared the elevator intermittently as we traversed decks, but Elias was so gymnastic in his sociability that he immediately switched gears, exchanging pleasantries with our transient elevator companions. My heart was still beating too hard to engage and Sean, being ever the detective, looked quietly and covetously at my bag of goodies.

* * *

I liked going up to the more expensive decks. Writers like Elias and Helga do really well with their mystery series, and reap the rewards. I committed myself to preparing my books and finding an agent to sell, sell, sell.

As Elias led us off the elevator to his upper level expensive stateroom, I again thought about Mary and the vial of Prolixin Amy still surely had in her purse.

"I'm worried about Mary. I'm positive Amy has the vial of Prolixin she used on Frederick and Mendel is in her purse. It wasn't anywhere in her room."

"Does Mary know that?"

"Yes."

"Then Mary can take care of herself," Sean responded. "Do you think Amy saw you?"

"I just don't know." I described Amy's search in the closet and her settling on the floral jacket.

"This is bad." Elias opened his door. "If she knows, she could do something desperate."

256

"But proving anything to the security here is going to be an uphill battle," Sean entered the stateroom. "They won't do anything and there is but one day left. We have to hide this stuff until we get to port and just stay away from Amy."

Elias's stateroom was elaborate and beautifully decorated in green and peach. It had a bedroom alcove off to the right and a breathtaking balcony.

"This is gorgeous." I placed the bag of evidence on the coffee table.

"Sit down. Should I order us a drink or coffee?"

"Sure," Sean answered. "Let's get some wine to wash this evidence down."

We all laughed; I more than either of them, because I was so relieved to be safe.

"Good idea. It's almost that hour," Elias agreed. "Veronica?"

"Great." I actually needed something stronger after my close encounter in the closet, but I settled for wine.

* * *

I took the evidence out of the bag and put it on the coffee table. I set my phone there, too, with the pictures up. I showed them Mendel's book with Amy's notations and expletives. Sean studied it.

"This is motive . . . guilt served up on a silver platter."

Elias looked at the pictures on my phone. "Most of these are out of focus."

"I was in a hurry."

"No matter. We have the real things here, thanks to Veronica," Sean said.

Elias looked through Amy's collection of magazine articles about both Mendel's and Frederick's rises to stardom. "Interesting. Otto rose right along with those two."

257

"That must have eaten away at her." Sean scanned the papers too. "Their lives hounded her, especially since she stayed in the book game. Every bestseller Mendel wrote reminded her of what they had done to her."

"And Frederick's proclivity for collecting Oscars drove her over the edge," Elias added. "Especially the last . . . with Otto there, preening,"

"I've seen real-life murders done for less, much less." Sean scanned an article. "I have to say I feel for her."

"I do, too." I grabbed the memory sticks. "Oh, and I picked up these. If you notice there is a synopsis of a new book in the pile and I think this memory stick may have the full draft on it."

"Great job!" Sean grinned. "This is amazing."

The wine came and the tension of the last several hours faded.

"Can we just go to security now and at least try to get Amy thrown in the brig until we dock in Southampton?" I asked.

"First there probably is no *brig* . . . and we have too many holes. Especially with this unprofessional bunch protecting the Wessex Cruise Line." Sean topped our glasses. "First, we'd need to show that Amy doesn't have a medical reason for having the Prolixin. And that's impossible here in the middle of the Atlantic."

"And then we'd need to prove Prolixin killed Mendel and Frederick." Sean added.

"Not going to happen out here, either." Elias shrugged his shoulders.

"And then how do we prove Amy killed Otto?" Sean asked. "Because, in my mind, there is no doubt that she did."

"Mine either," I agreed.

"But we have even less for Otto's murder and my buddies closed the case with their burglary-gone-wrong theory. They had no suspects and nothing else panned out. I don't blame them with their caseloads, and I don't think can get them to reopen it without some hard evidence. It didn't help that all our colleagues and the media made a circus of it."

"But, it was a well-meaning circus," Elias interjected.

"Of course, but this is a real uphill battle now," Sean said.

"But closing it can be fought," Elias said. "I've put harder cases together in my mysteries and I do base them on research into real murders and real solutions. Granted . . . I wedded multiple murders and fictionalized them. But still, I think we can do something here."

"I guess I can have my ex-partner fight to officially reopen Otto's case based on the evidence our brave Veronica got." Sean winked at me.

"Thank you." I smiled.

"Let me get some of this scanned in and sent to him."

"Okay." Elias put the memory stick in his laptop on the desk and scrolled through it.

"I wish Mary were here. I don't like her being with Amy drinking tea with that vial in Amy's purse." I was worried for her.

"Take my word for it. Mary won't take one sip of tea this afternoon. Not with Amy around."

"Right," Sean said. "And besides, Amy presumes she has gotten away with everything. She won't risk another murder this afternoon because she doesn't know we have this stuff yet."

"I think you're right about that," Elias agreed. "But it will be another thing if, or rather when, she finds out."

"But did she know I was in the closet?" I asked.

"I personally don't believe anyone could be that cool." Sean said.

"Maybe. I hope so." I said.

"I don't think we can count on anything, though. We all have to be on our guard from now on," Sean said. "She'll discover we took the stuff soon. We are almost at Southampton. Who knows when she'll start packing?"

"This is interesting." Elias looked up from his laptop. "It's a book synopsis and a draft of a book by Amy. The plot parallels Mendel's book, but in reverse. He is the villain. And it's in a writing program."

"What?" Sean exclaimed.

"I'll read through it more before dinner," Elias said. "And then I'll put it in my safe."

"I'm going to send some documents to my ex-partner now." Sean stood.

"And I have a few other things to do." I had done my duty and wanted to go by Curtis's meeting room to see if he was finished for the day. "See you later."

"Okay," Elias said. "We'll meet an hour before dinner at the bar."

"At the bar it is." Sean chose several of the documents he had read to send to his partner. "These are about as much as I can do in one sitting."

I left.

I thought of looking for Mary, but the consensus was that she was not in danger. I started to the elevator to find Curtis and give him the opportunity to make a date with me tonight.

I had, apparently, solved two murders on the high seas and one in New York. Of course, I did it by now committing some of the crimes I had only written about up until now—but *c'est la vie*. I intended to take the night off and celebrate my triumph. There were other things in life besides solving crimes and writing them up as fiction.

CHAPTER 30

Helgatory

I missed Curtis at his seminar. It ended early. I went back to my stateroom to get gorgeous for dinner and hopefully post-dinner—if no more bodies piled up. Unfortunately, Mavis was there. My envy of both Elias and Mary having no roommates intensified. At that moment, I was truly motivated to edit, publish, and get a wad of money to be roommate-less two years from now.

As I entered my sardine can, I felt claustrophobic and vulnerable to Mavis's assaults. I was still unnerved because of this afternoon's scare. Naturally, I didn't share a thing about it with Mavis and only half listened to her self-absorbed chattering. I grabbed the shower and welcomed the steamy heat relaxing my whole body.

As we got ready for dinner, Mavis bragged nonstop about her possible new agent who might reissue her first murder series with new splashy covers and new names. It was her most popular book series with, in her words, a "marvelous" female protagonist—a Los Angeles detective who solved crimes others couldn't. As Mavis spoke, I decided she was talking this up to convince herself it would happen.

"But why re-issue?" I put my lipstick, money, and room key in my evening bag. "Isn't it more profitable to go on to the new series you announced last year in class?"

"It depends." Mavis called out from the bathroom where she was still in her robe and finishing her make-up. "If an agent gets a publisher to print my old series on demand and as an e-book, I think it would be great. It'll be money in the bank for everyone with no work . . . well for me, anyway."

"I guess so. Those were published in the paperback days, weren't they?"

I still did not understand why any publisher would reissue an outdated, already sold series. The books would be so stale, given the massive changes in technology and popular culture.

"Sure they're paperbacks. What of it? I have a following for all my books and I get e-mails about the ones out of print all the time. Besides, it's my agent who's pushing it."

"Well, congratulations." I knew then she had writer's block, just like me, and no new series to publish electronically. "I guess it is worth a try, but I . . ."

A loud banging on the door interrupted my next question.

"Who is it?" I called.

I heard a muffled response. I went and looked through the peephole. Brent was standing at the door looking up and down the hall nervously. I opened the door.

"Brent?" I was dumbfounded as to why he was at our door—and banging on it.

"Are you alone?" Brent whispered.

"No."

"Who is it?" Mavis called.

She came in from the bathroom still in her bathrobe, but makeup perfect. Her mouth dropped open. Then, it formed the flirtatious smile she reserved, consciously or unconsciously, for attractive males and sometimes the unattractive.

"Oh, Brent, good evening." Mavis twittered.

"Good evening." Brent transformed from nervous to pasted-on-charm with alacrity. "Just picking up Veronica . . . for that drink as promised . . . remember?"

I was confused. I didn't remember planning a drink with him. But, I took his cue. After all, I was ready to go, I liked Brent, and, from his initial facial expression, it looked like something was wrong. Besides, I could dump Mavis, who was still in her robe.

"Sure!" I grabbed my bag from the bed.

"Wonderful." Brent stepped aside as I made my way out the door.

"See you at dinner, Brent." Mavis purred.

"Yes, of course." Brent followed me out.

"Have fun, you two." Mavis called salaciously, rudely, and most of all, jealously.

The door slammed on its too-quick and too-heavy automatic closing spring.

* * *

I had shut Mavis out—shutting her out of anything was rewarding to me—but exactly what was I shutting her out of? Since it obviously involved the Brent-and-Helga saga, I was sure it would be interesting, but either way, I had been rescued from Mavis.

Brent sped down the hall and I followed. I didn't care if Mavis believed the Helga-delusional accusation at the bar last night that I was having an affair with Brent. It was, on its face, an absurdity for anyone who knew Brent's avaricious ways and my less-than-wealthy personal situation.

"Hey, slow down," I called.

"Sorry." Brent stopped.

"Brent, did we make plans? I'm sorry I . . ."

"I didn't know what to do." Brent glanced around to see that we were alone in the hall. He was upset and had turned off his auto-charm.

"About what?"

"I need help and I trust you. I've watched you. I know you're discreet and not invested in rising to the top like the others."

"Thanks . . . I guess." Whatever it was, it was not good—and it was also not good that Brent didn't think I was interested in getting ahead in the authorial world. "What's wrong?"

"She's gone. She's not anywhere."

"Who? Helga?"

"Yes, and I can't find her."

"I don't understand. What do you mean?"

"I need help. Help from someone who will respect Helga's privacy. And, I know you will . . . only you."

"I'm glad you have confidence in me, but I don't understand."

"I can't find my wife!"

"What do you mean you can't find her? This is a ship. It's in the middle of the Atlantic."

"Literally, I can't find her. I've checked but . . ."

"We should call security. . ."

The minute the words came out of my mouth I stopped. I knew it was a ridiculous suggestion in light of the incompetence demonstrated thus far.

" . . . or not."

"I think not . . ." Brent said. "Not yet, anyway. The publicity. Her reputation. I can trust you to keep this quiet, can't I?"

"Of course."

"I knew you were not one of them . . ."

264

"Them?"

"The hungry and desperate writers bloated with ego, trying to claw their way to the top by bringing down Helga. They would love to dethrone her. And you wouldn't. I can tell."

"Thanks." I wondered if that was really a compliment, but it was better than what he had said before. "Thanks for trusting me."

"I'm worried something is really wrong."

"Brent, you have to settle down. When was the last time you checked your stateroom?"

"An hour ago. I've been all around."

"Maybe she's back." I headed to the elevator. "Let's start there."

As we waited for the elevator, I wished I hadn't engendered so much trust in him. Enjoying a few murders amongst friends was one thing, but marital discord—or better put, spousal warfare, was entirely another. My husband and I had avoided it, both within our marriage and with friends, all our lives.

"Where have you looked?" On the elevator, I was, again, on the way to where the wealthy ensconced themselves shipboard.

"Everywhere. Literally. Well, everywhere I could think of, but there are so many places to go on this floating island. Besides when she gets . . . gets . . . well, this way . . ."

"What way?"

"Honestly?"

"Yes, if you want me to help you."

"Sometimes . . . no . . . often . . . Helga will throw fits and disappear for days."

"That would be hard to do on board a ship."

"Yeah, I figured that, but she missed her massage appointment. She wasn't in the gym. I couldn't check the woman's steam room . . . you can go places I can't."

"Did you check the library?" I asked.

"Didn't think of it." Brent got his cabin key out. "I don't know if a library would have entered her mind. But I did check the champagne bar and the casino."

"I see."

I hoped she'd just be in the stateroom and I could leave them to fight it out. I had seen her ire, especially her ire under the influence, and I didn't want it directed towards me ever again.

As we made our way down the halls, I wondered how this man could care so much after the humiliation I had witnessed in the last three days alone. In fact, I was through with her after the scene at the casino and the incident afterward at the bar where she named me as "the other woman".

* * *

At the exclusive stateroom, several decks higher than Elias's, Brent slid his magnetic card key in the slot. He straightened the do not disturb sign.

"Helga keeps it up and then calls housekeeping when we go to dinner. She likes to be left alone."

"I see." I could not have cared less about this horrible woman's habits and hoped she had returned on her own.

"Helga!" Brent went in. "Helga! Are you here?"

"She's not here?" I followed Brent in.

"Doesn't look like it."

"She might be somewhere writing. She isn't known as the mystery world's most prolific author for nothing." I hid my envy since my curiosity was now piqued and my passport into the intimate world of Helga-and-Brent depended on my non-competitive, amateur status.

"Come in. I just want to check her bathroom before we scour the ship."

266

"That's a good idea."

I admired the magnificent soft white living room suite with vases of spring bouquets thick with yellow and pink roses. There was a sweeping view beyond the large balcony of the changeable Atlantic, now sparkling after the stormy night. The balcony had symmetrically arranged outdoor chaises and chairs dotted with neatly folded red and navy plaid blankets. There was a large bedroom off to the right beyond the well-stocked, and apparently well-used bar. The king-sized bed was unmade and Brent's clothes were thrown on it. There was another closed door to the left behind.

"That's Helga's room." Brent responded to my gaze.

I saw that the handle was hanging and broken.

"I had to get in. I hadn't seen her all day."

"Of course." I hoped that Brent was being melodramatic.

"At home after our late night brawls I usually just let her sleep it off in her room."

"Her bedroom?"

"We have separate bedrooms at home, too. She keeps erratic hours writing. Sometimes all night. That's what it takes to be her."

"I see." I almost fit that requirement too, getting up at four every morning. If it were only more productive.

"She usually crawls out of bed late, has lunch, and we make up. But today I jogged around the deck, went to the gym, steamed, lunched, and then caught Curtis's financial seminars. When I got back to get ready for dinner, I knocked on her door. It was still locked and she didn't answer. So I . . . Well, you see. I was worried."

Brent opened the door to check the bedroom. I was shocked at what I saw.

* * *

Helga's bedroom was destroyed. Jewelry and clothes were thrown on the dressers, the bed, and the floor. The closet was open and full of sloppily-hung clothes. The bed was unmade, but I noticed it didn't look like the pillows had been used. They were fluffy and pristine.

"Did she sleep in here?"

"Of course." Brent followed my eyes to the pillows and added, "Unless she wrote all night."

The door to the *en suite* bathroom was open.

"Not here," I said.

I looked into the bathroom. It was pristine and all the towels were unused and hanging untouched, except one lonely hand towel draped disheveled by itself over one towel bar. I looked around for other used towels, but there were none. I felt the shower. It was bone dry. Unused.

I walked back into the bedroom. I joined Brent, who was looking out at the sea.

"This room is a mess." I said.

"Yeah, but she does that when she throws a fit. Our maid at home hates it. But we both expect it. She'll destroy anything if she feels like it."

"Uh-huh." What else could I say to that?

"That always means a big tip for the maid."

"This kind of thing is not unusual?"

"Well . . ." Brent started toward the living room. "I mean she doesn't do it that often. That's not exactly true . . . often enough. We should go . . . find her."

"Is it usually after you argue?"

"Argue?"

"I saw you in the casino last night."

"Oh, that. Believe me, that was not an argument. That was a spat."

"Ah." I kept looking around for any clue to help us find her.

"She throws things around a lot . . . even after she argues with her agent or editor or publicist. I guess it happens more often than not. Let's go."

Brent started for the living room again, but I did not follow. Instead, I looked at the balcony off Helga's bedroom and the gray sea beyond. I noted the blankets on the chaises were lumped in a pile and the chaises and chairs were not symmetrically arranged like the living room balcony.

"It looks like she was out on the balcony."

"I don't think so. It was storming last night." Brent looked at me and then out onto the balcony.

"Yes, the blankets have been used and the chaises rearranged." I started toward the sliding glass balcony door and Brent followed.

The door wasn't locked. I slid it open and walked out to the rail.

The bedroom balcony was separated from the living room balcony and also from the neighboring cabin by a solid white metal privacy walls. I looked out onto the post-storm cold, sun spattered Atlantic sea. Brent stood next to me and looked out himself.

We were amidships and there was a straight drop down to the white foam below where the ship cut through the sea.

"Helga hates neighbors, so she picked this stateroom. At least no neighbors underneath."

"It's nice."

"I think you're right. She must have been out here." Brent watched me look down to the foamy sea. "What are you thinking?"

"Nothing."

I stepped back. To me it was like standing on a cliff in an earthquake. I remembered my jogging incident on the promenade deck.

Brent stepped forward. He looked carefully over the rail coming to his hip height. The rails were made for average people; not for a man his size with his center of gravity so high.

"She couldn't have . . ."

"Fallen?" I completed Brent's thought.

"It was storming."

"No." I went back into Helga's bedroom. "Don't be silly. We'll find her. She's probably in the sauna or getting a facial. Let's go."

"It's a beautiful view. I feel sorry for the folks with just a porthole. Thanks for the help."

Helga's closed laptop was on the desk. "Did she write this morning?"

"I assume. She always does. Why?"

"Just thinking. May I open it?"

"Sure."

"It's off. Can you power it up? I'd like to see when she last worked."

"No she'd kill me if I touched it. Besides she has it password protected."

"Ah . . . Of course."

For the first time, I actually began to wonder where Helga was myself. She was eccentric enough to be anywhere doing anything. A hook-up crossed my mind. She wasn't unattractive and could be charming when she wanted to be. Then, I immediately came to my senses. I didn't care about this tremendously rich couple and their machinations or sexual appetites. I just wanted to leave and see if Curtis was at the bar before I had to meet with my cohorts.

"Maybe we should just wait and see if she shows up at dinner. She could have come and dressed while you were running around the ship. Did you check her evening clothes?"

"No. How could I tell? She has so many, and they're such a mess."

"You're right."

"Let's go. I'm sure she'll show up at dinner. She enjoys it so much."

"At our expense," I thought.

"Now that I've talked to you I feel a little silly." Brent was sheepish.

"We have a plan then."

"Right." Brent said. "But I owe you a cocktail and we can check out the bar."

"Great!"

Brent did a very agile 180-degree turn from being the distressed husband to acting the charming host. I wondered if it was my reassurances, or the fact that Brent was just ready for his cocktail hour. He, most assuredly, had forgotten about turning the ship upside down to find his *adoring* wife.

We left for the bar and even though Brent was actually a nice guy, I determined that I would divorce myself from any future Brent-and-Helga dramas. I didn't care if she came to dinner or not. I had other plans for the night. I had been abused by her enough and had been sucked into their rich-person spectacles more often and more deeply than I could handle.

⌘

CHAPTER 31

Desperation and Determination

The bar was devoid of Helga, and so was Brent's conversation as we sat at the same two barstools we had occupied last night when the Helga attack happened. My fellow investigators were not there yet and neither was Curtis.

Brent enjoyed two Martinis to my one wine. The whole time he was checking out an adjacent table of peppy young female passengers, generously displaying legs and breasts.

I wasn't enjoying any of this. I was bored with Brent's vapid conversation and wandering eyes.

"I'm going to the casino."

"Fine, I'll camp out here." Brent didn't take his eyes off the young women.

"Okay. But be careful. Helga may show up."

"Huh?" Brent glanced at me, oblivious to my warning. "Thanks for the help."

"Sure. I'll see you at dinner. Helga will show up. Don't worry." I was being facetious since his only focus now was filling his non-Helga time with the young things nearby.

I left, annoyed that he had involved me in his obviously ridiculous urgent search for Helga. The only redeeming factor was that it made Mavis curious and jealous.

I looked into the casino and decided I'd powder my nose first. I hated those feminine euphemisms, but they automatically came to me after many years of acculturation.

* * *

As I opened the nearby restroom door, I heard Mavis and Esther squabbling inside. I stopped with the door ajar and listened.

"But I need the work." Mavis was intense. "You don't understand. I can't pay my bills. I refinanced my house three years ago and the money's spent. Now I can't make the mortgage payment!"

"I understand, dear. Don't be so *verklempt*. I just don't use ghostwriters and I don't know of anyone who does . . . or would admit they do. Let's get out of here. We'll talk some other time."

"But . . ."

"Look . . . do editing."

"You know it doesn't pay enough."

"What about your agent reissuing your old series?"

"You know the odds of that taking off . . . besides, it will take too long even if he stops dragging his feet. I need money now."

"I can't help. Really."

"I've been in this game since before you started." Mavis shouted. "I'm good. I just need work to tide me over. Any work."

"I understand."

"You don't!" Mavis snapped.

There was a long silence and then Mavis moderated her tone.

"I'm sorry, Esther. Just hear me out, please. Asking you is hard for me. My last book didn't even make my advance back. And it was a book I wrote in my twenties, revamped. It was not good enough then and only got published because of my name."

"*Oy vey*. Did your agent approve of your little scheme?"

"No . . . he didn't. I tweaked it myself. But it doesn't matter anyway. The next one I tried to retool and get by him he rejected. He knows I'm dried up and so do the publishers. I have nothing left. No muse and no money." Mavis's voice cracked. "My agent avoids my calls. He's all but dropped me."

"It can't be as bad as all that." Esther was uncomfortable. "Your muse will return. It's just a dry spell. We all have them. It's late. I . . ."

"Esther, please! Wait a minute!"

"Let go, Mavis, you'll rip my sleeve!"

"Sorry . . . but you know everyone. You could help me on the Q.T. You can set me up anonymously to ghostwrite for someone. I know you can."

"*Bist meshugeh*? I won't be associated with ghostwriting! It could ruin my reputation!"

"Look, I know you use a ghostwriter."

"What! I . . ."

"And you could use me instead. I'm better. I'd be more discreet than they are. How do you think I found out? I would be confidential."

"How dare you? I don't use a ghostwriter! I don't use anyone but myself." Esther dismissed Mavis with an ordination of finality.

"I'm sorry." Mavis submitted to the reprimand. "But, please, will you ask your friends? It'll all be confidential."

"I . . . I'll think about it. But you start talking about any ghostwriting associated with my name and our friendship is over. Now let's go."

I knew Esther's acquiescence was disingenuous. She just wanted away from Mavis and her oozing desperation, and to control Mavis's implied threat of disclosure.

I took off for the casino before they caught me eavesdropping. I was upset for Mavis, even though I didn't like her. I had read articles that stated ninety percent of all writers earned less than $10,000 a year. It was so much work to write a book and, even worse, it took intense dedication to publish even one. I thought they deserved more. But all artists struggled, even those who became successful, now and through the centuries: actors, painters, sculptors, composers, singers, dancers, authors. I began to doubt my commitment to publish even if that commitment was born of non-monetary objectives. Would $10,000 a year be enough to dignify my efforts—even if it also gave me my interesting authorial life and solidified my friendships from this cruise? Ingrained in my psyche was the notion that only money was a validation for my work, as it was in the psyches of most Americans.

* * *

I went on into the casino, but I felt lost—devoid of purpose. I didn't want to think about Mavis any more. I knew playing blackjack would distract me—but I was not a true gambler. I was unwilling to risk money for what I considered a sure loss at blackjack. I bounced around through the chiming, colorful slots, like I was the shiny steel ball in a pinball machine.

I finally found a vacant, inviting well-cushioned red leather stool. I had a view of the bar entrance to watch for Curtis or my cohorts.

Perched on the stool, I tried to relax after the Mavis-Esther encounter. I believed Esther really did have a ghostwriter and that many other moneyed authors did, too. I fed the machine dollar bills and some tokens came back. I used the tokens on the slot machines, killing time along with my fellow passengers, which is to say donating money to the house before the second dinner seating.

My relaxation didn't last, though. Most inopportunely, my classmates appeared and accosted me.

"You'll end up losing your shirt. I did." Agnes blurted out, apparently having lost her quota of money.

"Yeah." Herbert trailed up to my other side. He patted his long dark hair swept over his balding head to confirm it was in place.

"That's an exaggeration, Agnes. You played three lines at a time and lasted thirty minutes." Jody corrected Agnes.

"The odds are against you, here and everywhere." Herbert stopped patting his hair. "Statistically, the house will win because no one can walk away when they are up."

"Thanks, but I'm just feeding it a few dollars. I'm about even."

"About even doesn't mean even," Herbert hounded. "If I were you, I'd . . ."

Jody interrupted with her brash loud voice. "Have you given up trying to make murders out of those heart attacks?"

"Who told . . ." I aborted my question—I knew it was Mavis who was discrediting me.

"Mavis did," Herbert ratted. "And, I might add, that she is right. The odds of two murders happening on the same cruise ship one day after the other are prohibitively high."

I stonewalled the discussion. I didn't want anything getting back to Mavis or Esther, which it surely would. I slid off the red stool.

"See you later." I took my tokens to another slot machine.

"You should put your imagination into finishing your last book," Herbert called after me.

He was rude. I had been, too, but I refused to engage them with respect to anything pertaining to our investigation. At this point, I owed allegiance to my new friends and myself. Our reputations, if not our lives, were at stake.

I played with the tokens as I lost them one by one—but they dribbled back to me in part, three for every five I lost. I liked their feel. Some cruise lines had gone to straight paper vouchers with bar codes for the winners to cash in. They said it was for hygiene reasons. I, of course, relished the good old germy days when real quarters and real dimes were used, along with silver dollars. I even remembered the nickel slots.

Five bucks into my intermittent and expected but fortunately slow losses, Heather wandered into the casino with Amy. They sat nearby at a blackjack table across the aisle. Amy was very different from the woman I had met at the ship's boarding pavilion in New York. Tonight, she was smiling as she responded to, and appeared to enjoy, Heather's bright-eyed chatter. Did Amy not realize our double-barreled investigative shotguns were pointed right at her—or didn't she care?

Was Heather Amy's next target? I didn't know of any connection or motivation. I wanted to join them and gauge Amy's reaction to me to see if she had seen me in her closet. Frugality, however, stopped me. I just couldn't afford to sit at a blackjack table where the stakes were higher and the losses faster.

Suddenly, three black bars popped one by one on my new slot machine, and tokens drained into the wide trough below. I was in the black by at least thirty bucks. I grabbed the small, used bucket that a previous loser had left next to my machine and gathered my winnings.

I could now afford the price of a seat near Amy and Heather at the blackjack table.

I got my tokens changed into chips for the blackjack table. On the walk over, I remembered the rule I had learned to hit on fifteen and stay on sixteen. Or, was it hit on fourteen and stay on fifteen. I couldn't decide, but it didn't matter because I never could resist getting another card anyway. Hopefully, my dealer would be of the same mindset, go over twenty-one, and bust.

I walked up behind Amy and Heather and heard the blackjack players moan as the dealer announced a natural. That is to say, twenty-one with a face card and an Ace. Across the board, he took everyone's red five-dollar chips, green twenty-five-dollar chips, and some black one hundred-dollar chips. Heather was winning and had stacks of red and green chips. Amy, however, had a meager stack of red chips.

"Veronica?" Heather noticed me. "Are you going to join us?"

"Sure." I sat in the stool next to Heather and put my short stack of five-dollar chips down. "Are you winning?"

"Not really. The stacks of chips you see are deceiving." Heather gingerly placed her one chip in the circle for her next bet. "I'm about even. It seems that's all I ever am."

"How are you doing, Amy?" I couldn't resist poking the bear.

"The dealer doesn't have a chance of nailing me." Amy leaned over and whispered with a cool evil glare from her golden eyes. "I'm too careful. No one does."

I shuddered. I regretted engaging her. I confirmed, though, that she did know Mary was not at her cabin accidentally and that she had seen me hiding in her closet. That was not merely a double entendre—it was an overt threat.

I got off my stool and turned to Heather.

"It's getting late. I'm going to the bar." I put my chips in my purse.

"We'll join you," Heather chirped.

"No. You two are having fun. See you at dinner."

I hurried away—from Amy.

I went to the restroom where I had eavesdropped. I was alone. I leaned over the sink to catch my breath and calm myself. Amy scared me. I looked at myself in the mirror. I touched up my lipstick and straightened my hair. I decided I would not be alone or near Amy the rest of the cruise. There was safety in numbers—and in distance.

Two chatty thirty year olds came in.

I left.

* * *

I rounded the corner into the main hall and went to the bar. Sean, Mary, and Elias were already seated at the far end. Their table abutted the massive windows framing the nighttime blackness, laced with reflections from the ship's lighting. Dribbles of seawater streaked the thick glass.

As I rushed over, I passed by Brent, still seated on his bar stool. He was now enjoying the company of the two young women I had left him eyeing. They had joined him and were loudly and obviously admiring his wit. The giggling bounced through my ears.

A quick scan showed me the bar was, as yet, devoid of Curtis and his client group.

"Here," Mary called loudly, unnecessarily waving her ample arm as I headed for their table.

"Good evening," Sean greeted me.

I sat and noted their depleted glasses of wine. They had been there for some time.

"Am I late?"

"Not really." Sean drank. "We're celebrating."

"Got this for you." Mary pushed a glass of red wine at me.

"Thanks. Any Prolixin in it?"

"Not funny!" Mary said.

"Celebrating what?" I took a drink of my wine.

"Sean got Otto's case headed in the right direction," Elias explained. "They are looking at forensics again and seeing if any security cams in the vicinity have Amy on them. They may reopen it officially if they can find something . . . anything."

"Yeah," Sean added. "No one knew about the Amy connection. My partner . . . ex-partner . . . liked it. He's getting back to me tomorrow."

"Good. Because Amy's on to us . . . or, at least, onto Mary and me."

"What?" Mary exclaimed. "What do you mean you she's on to us? I didn't think she noticed a thing. She was great at high tea. I mean . . . I did keep an eye on my teacup . . . but she was friendly and chatty. And she was the center of attention at the table."

"Well, I was just at the blackjack table with her and Heather. Amy threatened me."

"My, God," Mary mumbled. "I can't . . ."

"What did she say?" Sean interrupted.

"She got right up in my face, stared me down, and said 'The dealer doesn't have a chance of nailing me. I'm too careful. No one does'."

"That's as unsubtle as it comes," Sean said,

"There's definitely no other way to take that." Elias shook his head. "We're in trouble."

"Yes. And when I think of how reserved little Amy was when she boarded," I said. "She's changed. She's fearless, manic, and . . ."

"Satiated," Sean interrupted. "Like an animal full after the kill . . . satiated for now, but ready to pounce . . . ready to kill again. Especially if threatened."

"I'm sure she saw me in that closet. And it's getting around the MWW that we're making progress."

"Christ on a crooked crutch," Mary said. "In the stateroom I didn't see any reaction from her. I would have sworn that she didn't notice a thing."

"She's a good actress." I thought she was better than me, even with all my training and experience. "You know when I first met her in New York I mentioned the cruise would be wonderful and she said it would be 'quite eventful.' I thought she meant the awards, but obviously she didn't."

"She meant the evil events planned by her," Mary said.

"You know," I recalled, "When Mendel fell in the dining room that night, he called Amy his 'little love'."

"Evidently, it was unrequited," Mary said. "To say the least."

"My take is that she feels invincible now," Sean said. "She has two murders under her belt, probably three, and she has essentially gotten away with them."

"That's true." Elias stroked his mustache as he thought.

"I've seen it a million times when I'm questioning suspects who have gotten away with crimes. They don't even invoke their right to an attorney because they think they are untouchable. In Amy's case, she thinks she has committed the perfect murders."

"The perfect murders . . . maybe." Elias shook his head. "The NYPD closed Otto's murder case publically and they didn't even know about her relationship with him. And here, the Wessex and Esther did the greatest cover-up. For all the wrong reasons."

"You know, my partner said the video that guy shot of Mendel in the dining room was on YouTube with thousands of hits," Sean said.

"That didn't help," Elias said.

"We have to keep an eye on each other and stay away from her," Sean cautioned.

"But Mary's at Amy's table." I pointed out.

"I would suggest, Mary, that you don't drink anything tonight," Elias said.

"Can she eat?" I asked. "Wouldn't that be dangerous too?"

"Of course, she can eat," Elias answered enthusiastically, like a true Greek who could not imagine skipping a meal. "Amy can't mix that stuff in food easily. Just stay away from the soup."

"I wouldn't eat anything," Sean cautioned. "Maybe the bread. Just shove things around your plate. Just . . ."

"Look," Mary cut the discussion off. "I've already made up my mind to order room service later. I'm shoving the food around my plate like Sean said. I'll eat the communal bread and butter. Amy wouldn't dare knock off the whole table."

I snickered. "Let's hope not!"

"Hey, getting serious here, my partner said security won't do anything on board unless they're forced to," Sean said. "Like catching her in the act. That's Wessex's MO. And, he said, it's the same for all cruise lines. They protect their reputations first and foremost."

"Corporate greed knows no bounds," Mary interjected. "I've killed off a couple of CEO's in my books. It gives me great satisfaction."

"You should escalate to their torture-murder," I chuckled. "Maybe I will in my next book."

"Come on girls," Elias rapped his knuckles on the table. "Shh. Let's stay focused. This is life and death. And the death part is taking over."

"Anyway, my partner's going to talk to Scotland Yard as soon as he gets the forensics report back and looks at the surveillance. Amy's going to have a big surprise when we land on the other side of the 'pond' as the Brits would say."

"But doesn't he have enough right now for Scotland Yard to get these Wessex people to lock Amy up before we dock?" I wanted to enjoy the rest of the cruise.

"I don't think so. He'll contact me tomorrow morning with more. Maybe we'll be able to relax the last night for the awards ceremony. Meanwhile, act normal. Keep your eyes on your drinks. Everyone stay away from Amy. And Mary, be careful at dinner."

"Can't Mary switch to our table? God knows, we are minus two."

"No," Sean answered me. "Too obvious."

"Speaking of dinner, it's time to go." Elias waved for the bar tab.

"I'll get this one," I offered.

"No, I insist. You're not raking in the royalty dough yet." Elias flashed a big smile under his moustache.

* * *

At the dining room, Esther and Mavis were entering just ahead of us. They were talking like high school best friends exchanging secrets. Mavis had obviously refused to take "no" for an answer and was still ingratiating herself more to get ghostwriting dollars from Esther or one of her friends.

I would not have any relationship with Mavis when we returned or ever take another class from her. I knew she was in trouble, but she had made it clear we were not friends.

"Mary," I whispered. "If a writer had an agent interested in republishing an old series again as a print on demand and e-book, would that be a good thing?"

"No. It's usually the desperate act of an uninspired writer. Who is it?"

"I don't think . . ."

"Come on. Spill the dirt."

"It's . . ." I hesitated, but then decided turn-about was fair play here. ". . . Mavis."

283

"That's hardly news. We all expected that. Poor woman. If I were she, I wouldn't expect much revenue from that series. It didn't do well when it first came out."

"Ah, too bad." I was genuine in my sympathy for Mavis.

"It happens. Often."

"I guess."

"Wish me luck," Mary whispered, and then followed Esther to their table.

Mary bravely took her seat near Amy who shot her a smile tantamount to the Big Bad Wolf in *Little Red Riding Hood*, but with dimples. I wished Amy was locked up and hoped Mary stuck to her plan not to eat.

Mavis stood lingering at Amy's left. She was genuflecting while Esther seated herself. Mavis watched me as I passed with Elias and Sean behind me. Then, Mavis leaned into Esther with her mouth moving a million miles an hour. When Esther glanced over, I knew Mavis was spewing venom about my group and me.

"Hello." Elias greeted their glares cheerily as he made his way past the gauntlet to our table.

Neither Esther nor Mavis responded.

As we approached our table, Brent was seated, but without Helga. I looked toward the entry and then scanned the room for her.

Helga was nowhere to be seen. Or, more notably, heard!

⌘

CHAPTER 32

A Helga of a Mystery

At dinner Brent, floating on too many cocktails, gregariously led the conversation. He was uncharacteristically uninhibited because there was no Helga-downer by his side. He cheerily replaced the Brent-and-Helga Show with the Brent Show.

Mavis and me took our turn buying wine for the table. The server poured.

"Will Madame be coming?"

"Of course. Why not?" Brent snapped, then moderated himself and added, "She's just late."

Brent returned to his conversation with Anne about her gardening and spectacular roses. I had taken care of my own gardening and roses enough to catch that Brent had done nothing but smell the flowers, not cultivate them, in his lifetime. He was shooting from a non-gardener's hip or, worse yet, a hip that had not even frequented a flower shop. The closest he had ever gotten to rose-care was ordering them on the phone.

Our table had been noticeably sparse in the absence of Mendel and Frederick, and was even emptier now without Helga's heavy presence and unpleasant domination. Her full elegant crystal wine glass sat strangely untouched by her red, red lips, which regularly delighted in drawing red, red blood from those around her.

Mavis finally stopped sucking up to Esther and, undoubtedly, disparaging our investigation. She took her seat at our table. She was sullen. I now knew the personal pressure she was under and was not entirely unsympathetic—just mostly so.

Curtis came late and sheepishly took his seat at his dinner table. He avoided looking over at me even though I openly waited for his usual friendly smile. Had I done something wrong? Well, besides having dead bodies turn up around me, that is.

"Trouble in paradise?" Mavis smirked.

I wasn't surprised she had been watching me and even less surprised that she seemed delighted with the question.

"No."

I sat up tall and then joined her and Brent's conversation with Anne. It was about the rose's place in literature and love. Brent apparently did know something about that.

"I have one spot in my front yard that gets enough sun for roses," I volunteered. "I have planted . . . no . . . really overplanted with so many varieties and colors of roses. Every single rose bush is my favorite when I buy it."

"I understand," Anne agreed. "Every color is my favorite, depending on the day."

"I know. It's strange, isn't it? And you can't help but mother them—spray them for aphids and feed them rose food."

"They give you so much pleasure that you are compelled." Anne was delighted with my kindred spirit.

"In all honesty," Brent confessed. "I don't know about feeding them, but I buy them regularly for Helga . . . Blood red."

Mavis interrupted.

"Where is Helga? She's late. That's not like her, Brent."

I waited for Brent's response. I was surprised that he simply did not respond

"Yes." Elias topped off his Cabernet Sauvignon, did the same for his closest tablemates, and then passed the bottle to Brent. "Where is your charming wife?"

"My charming wife, as you call her, is writing, I suppose."

Brent then turned and charmed Heather into a flirtatious exchange about her day.

I studied Brent. Had he found Helga, or did he just not want to go public with her absence all day? I was surprised that he seemed not to remember that I knew she wasn't writing. We had found her laptop in her bedroom closed and apparently unused. And why would she start at dinnertime when she so enjoyed being an evil black hole in public?

I tried to catch Brent's eye, but he avoided looking at me. He had extended his good-times antics from the bar to our dinner table.

* * *

As the appetizer and salad courses came and went, I noted our little table had become a hybrid family. It had all the personality conflicts and annoyances that come with those kinds of relationships. In a way, I did miss the Brent-and-Helga Show, the venomous exchanges and tongue-lashings. She was an entertaining fireball and he was a practiced lightning rod.

Elias skillfully kept one eye on Amy at her table across the way. I did as well. Amy was chatting animatedly with Esther. Sean appeared unconcerned; he trusted Mary's survival instincts.

As we waited for our main courses, not too overtly but not quite furtively enough for Mavis's evil eye, I glanced repeatedly at Curtis. I wanted some sign we would have our date tonight. There was none. He had found someone else—I was sure of it. And why not? Bodies were piling up around me, and there were likely to be more if we couldn't get Amy under control. How attractive could that be?

Then, just as I had given up on Curtis, he turned and smiled at me. He raised his wine glass slightly and mouthed, "The bar?"

I very casually nodded, hoping he thought I had just momentarily glanced over. I discarded any doubts about our relationship and justified his preoccupation until now.

Mavis watched the interchange with a sour look. She was jealous, jealous Brent had showed up at our cabin and jealous of Curtis's attentions. I ignored her and rejoined the Brent, Heather, and Anne conversation. They were analyzing decomposing bodies and their nutritious effect on roses when buried in a shallow grave under them—as opposed to a deeper one.

"Aren't you two carrying this too far?" I laughed. "I don't think the reader cares about this minutiae. It seems obsessive and inbred."

"The reader cares about every detail," Mavis said. "But you wouldn't really know that, would you? You've never worked with an editor for publication."

I smiled pleasantly at Mavis and this time couldn't resist cutting to her core. I wanted to get even. I wanted to make her publicly admit her writing career was dried up. I had taken all I could.

"And what are you editing now with a publisher?"

"Several things."

"Oh, interesting. Share? We'd all like to hear."

"Not now." Mavis looked away and drank her wine.

The table was silent. Everyone knew Mavis had become an authorial shadow of her former self, and was not really on the publishing carousel with them. I felt cruel, but it was oddly and curiously satisfying. It was as if Helga had channeled through me and was present at the dinner—Helga was sharp and would have known Mavis's answer referred to her old series, too. I shamelessly used eavesdropping information gleaned from her and Esther in the restroom. Mavis wondered at my knowledge of her confidential conversation and then turned her attentions elsewhere.

The hiccup of my shameless attack passed and conversations went back to normal. And Brent, of course, went back to devouring Heather—verbally and visually. It appeared that the entire table knew about Mavis's fallow years and, evidently, the code of conduct, which I had transgressed, was "don't ask, don't tell." I didn't know that and seemed to be excused for my ignorance because, as Mavis had amply pointed out, I was unpublished, not quite part of their club, and, therefore, not ruled by their code of conduct.

Either way, I would never do that again!

It did not feel right to me, anyway. That just wasn't who I was.

* * *

Our main courses were served with clockwork precision and in unison. The presentation was beautiful and the gourmet plates were all steaming hot.

Just as I put the first bite of my crispy and creamy au gratin potatoes in my mouth, a security guard quietly advanced on Brent. He was quite clearly trying not to attract attention, and he achieved his goal—almost.

"We need you Mr. Brodsky." The security man whispered.

"It's Mr. Hawthorne. And stop whispering in my ear!" Brent took a drink of wine to wash down the large bite of filet mignon he was chewing. "Can't it wait until after our dinner?"

"I'm sorry, Mr. Hawthorne. But, no, it can't wait." The security guard stood straight and spoke softy in middle-class Queen's English. "Could you please come with me? It's important and personal."

"Important and personal?" Brent was loud and sarcastic as he stabbed another bite of filet and a slice of the raw onions he had specially ordered. "Then it must be my wife. Tell Queen Helga I am at dinner . . . and that she is late."

"What is it?" I intervened—I believed as of right—after this afternoon's trek with Brent.

"Never mind." Brent turned to Heather with a pleasant smile and then back to the security officer. "Tell my wife to join us."

"Sir, I can't. I need you to come with me . . . now."

Brent glanced up at the security officer and then down at his dinner plate. Instead of putting down his fork and knife, he cut another piece of his filet and stabbed at the pieces of raw onion.

I scrutinized Brent. He was not going to move. I thought this was odd after he dramatically drafted me into his domestic hide-and-seek game this afternoon. Why wasn't he jumping up?

At the table, everyone was irritated at Brent's behavior. Even if it was just Helga's nose being out of joint, they thought Brent should go. At the very least, if not for Helga, he should go for them and their own peace at the dinner table.

I suspected at this point that it was not about Helga being a pissant, but more than that. I spoke up.

"I'll come with you. Is Mrs. Brodsky in her cabin?"

"No." The security officer glanced at me, and then back at the top of Brent's head as Brent chewed his onion and filet and forked his next bite. "Sir, she's not . . . sir, she's had an accident."

"What?" Brent stopped his fork with a large piece of rare filet and onion—mid-air. "Is she all right?"

"No, Sir." The security officer was through being patient and obviously tired of Brent's arrogance. "I'm afraid she's not."

"She's not?" I interjected, horrified at the thought of another body.

The security officer ignored me—viewing me as an outsider, a non-player in this situation.

"Is she alive?" Shock and panic flash across Brent's eyes as he stood quickly. "I mean . . ."

Brent stopped in midsentence. I thought how presumptive and odd it was that he went straight to death. The others, of course, were not privy to my afternoon adventures with Brent.

"I couldn't say, sir."

He immediately regained his composure, looking around the table at us. "She's probably on one of her binges."

"No, sir, she . . . I think you'd better just come with me, Mr. Hawthorne. It's very serious. The doctor and captain are with her."

"The doctor and captain with her . . ." Brent parroted.

A clatter of questions arose from our table

"What kind of accident?" Sean asked.

"What happened?" Mavis simultaneously signaled Esther with a small wave, to no avail.

"Is she dead?" Heather asked with furrows across her smooth pale forehead and between her large eyes.

The security officer lowered his eyes. We all knew.

"Lord above!" Sean shook his head.

"This is too much." Anne held her hand up to her chest. "I don't understand. Our table is . . ."

"Getting smaller and smaller," Elias said.

Elias made the sign of the Greek Orthodox cross several times, looked gravely at me, and then eyed each member of our quartet—even Mary who had now turned her attention to our table, as had most of the nearby diners.

"But it doesn't fit the pattern," Sean whispered to me.

"No, it doesn't," I agreed, privately relieved that I had not shared my suspicions about Helga being the murderer with anyone.

As Brent got up to leave, I suspected another pattern now—a pattern of one—one miserable abused husband taking advantage of the wild-west deaths on the high seas—or, should I say, wild-Wessex deaths. One shattered and battered husband counting on the Wessex Cruise Line and Esther to cover up foul play at any cost. One degraded husband perhaps desperately trying to change the trajectory of his life. I wondered if he really had that mistress. Was she at home or on board cruising with us across the Atlantic as we quite literally collected bodies?

"Follow me." The security officer headed to the staircase out calmly, trying to curtail the mounting scene.

"I'm going with him," Sean stood. "Elias?"

"Let's go." Elias gulped the last third of his wine glass.

Without a word, I followed the parade out of the dining room. Mary joined us and I told her what I knew in a nutshell.

I glanced back to see Mavis hurry over to Esther. The nearby dining tables were no longer silently watching the activity at our table, but were instead buzzing louder and louder.

Our small, very subdued group waited for the elevator.

⌘

CHAPTER 33

A Lifeboat Too Far

As we stood waiting for the elevator, Brent remained quiet, oddly quiet. And not the least bit inquisitive. He asked nothing. Then suddenly, as if he realized he should be interrogating the security man, he forced out a question.

"Where is she?"

"Down below." The security officer punched the down call button several times again.

"Down below?" Elias repeated.

"A machinist found her on his routine maintenance checks."

"Wait a minute. What do you mean?" Sean interrupted. "A machinist found her? Where? What do you mean by 'down below.' Speak up!"

Brent joined the bandwagon of inquisitors that he should have been leading. "Yes, what do you mean '*down below*'? Where's Helga? What happened to her?"

"Look, all I know is what I was told. The captain and the doctor are with her."

"With her?" Brent questioned. "Is she alive?"

"I don't know, sir. I was just ordered to get you and . . ."

"Did she say anything? Did she ask for me? What is going . . .?"

"What in heaven's name is going on here?" Esther interrupted as she and Mavis dashed up to the elevator. "Is this about Helga? I am the head of the MWW and in charge. We can't have our functions and dinners disturbed like this every night!"

"Helga is evidently in trouble," I whispered.

"Oh." Esther settled down.

We all boarded the elevator, Mavis was the last and stuffed herself in, insistent on not being left behind.

Then, to my surprise, Curtis came around the corner. Mavis was only too happy to make room for him.

I smiled up at him and felt my mind wandering away from any concerns for Helga.

The elevator descended with this incongruous group of riders, much like any elevator would. But a unified mission bound this odd assemblage, and also, I was convinced, it housed evil—it housed Brent.

* * *

Brent was silent again on the short ride, oddly and inappropriately so for a supposedly caring, if always demeaned, husband. We all were silent, too, but then we were just marginally invested albeit very focused sojourners.

As we descended into the bowels of the ship, Sean and Elias watched Brent and I also studied him in profile. Brent's jaw was set hard, with muscles bulging in his mandibles. His eyes looked straight ahead. He was worried, but in my estimation, not about Helga. He didn't express any concern on the way down.

I could feel his mind twirling and fighting through the alcohol he had consumed. I believed he was steeling himself against what we would find, not because he was worried about Helga, but because he was worried about himself. He was calculating the ramifications of the situation in his mind.

There was nothing spontaneous about Brent's reactions. He was as controlled as he had been this afternoon with me. As controlled as he could be, with the copious amounts of bar drinks and dinner wine he had consumed.

I wondered if they should be called celebratory libations in his case.

* * *

Our bizarre group went down into the bowels of the ship until, finally, we arrived at a lower, non-passenger deck.

Curtis caught up to me. "Thought you could use some support."

"Thank you."

"This way." The security officer led us single file now down a narrow passageway. "Be careful. Watch your step. And your heads."

He led us through several magnetic card controlled access doors. Then, we went through an even narrower gray metal passageway out to the starboard side of the ship. At the end, he opened a small metal hatch in the bulkhead leading out onto a wooden deck, damp with sea spray.

The captain waited with a group of his security officers and the ever-present, but reliably useless, Dr. Witte. They stood encircling a lifeboat, hanging from its davits adjacent to the gunwales of the ship. There was a pool of very red blood near their feet.

As we approached, the men turned, exposing Helga's long, lean and bloodied body. Her black sequined gown from the night before was now wet from the sea air and spray. Her body was crumpled over the edge of the white lifeboat—her hair matted and caked with blood. Helga was obviously, and violently, dead. Her black ostrich feather wrap was absent and her black sequined dress was hiked up, exposing her well-toned thighs.

"Saints preserve us!" Mary made the sign of the cross beginning on the left side, like any good Catholic.

"My God!" Elias made the Greek Orthodox sign of the cross repeatedly, once again.

I was shocked by Helga's bloodied body rag-dolled over the edge of the white lifeboat surrounded by red splatter. Her head and arms dropped over the edge like frozen icicles suspended upside down. Her dark hair hung toward the ship's deck and her open, dull, lifeless eyes receded into her sockets. Her ever-red lips gaped open. Her black, spiked, sling-back open-toed shoes were below her on the deck. One had landed upright below her icicled arms.

"*Oy gevalt!*" Esther slapped her hand over her mouth to stop her cry and grabbed at the hatch handle to steady herself.

"I'm here." Mavis immediately put her arm around Esther's waist for support.

"Can we get her a chair?" Mavis asked a security officer, who immediately double-timed down the hallway in search of a chair.

"Just get her out of here." The captain dressed down the security officer who had led our parade to the bloody scene. "Get them all out of here. I told you to get her husband."

"Sorry, sir." The security officer cowered. "They followed."

"Go, take care of yourself, Esther." Dr. Witte knew the value of having Esther's cooperation for the Wessex Line. "I'll sort it out and meet with you later."

"Thank you, doctor."

Esther and Mavis left with the security officer.

"Where's that blanket to cover her body?" The doctor barked at another security guard in crisp upper-crust British.

The word "body" rumbled through our little troupe like a 10-point earthquake. The doctor had now confirmed another death. We knew he was at least talented enough to easily recognize death and this time the cause was obvious—a fall.

"Which one of you is Mr. Brodsky?" The captain scanned our group.

"Mr. Hawthorne," the security office whispered to the captain.

"What! What did you say?"

"He calls himself Mr. Hawthorne."

"Oh, well. Americans. What do you expect?" The captain turned to Brent, almost but not quite eye-to-eye with the tall man. "Mr. Hawthorne, we are very sorry, but your wife has had a terrible accident."

Brent, who had been standing stone still at the back of our group, now erupted into an animated tirade as if a director had shouted "action."

"Helga. My God, what happened? Helga. Helga. She's . . ."

"Yes." The captain stood at attention in his dress uniform as a sign of respect. "I'm sorry we couldn't get you in time. She's passed. You have our deepest condolences."

"In time?"

"We found her alive. She tried to hold on for you."

"What?" Brent was startled. "What do you mean? Hold on?"

"You are Brent, are you not?"

"Yes."

"We believe she said . . . murmured your name before she passed."

"Is that all?"

"I'm sorry, sir. Yes."

"Are you sure?"

"I'm sure." The captain feigned compassion as best he could. "I'm sure she was saying good-bye in the only way she could."

"What happened?"

It should be apparent, sir . . . your wife fell . . ." The captain's irritation bubbled up again.

"Yes, I see that, but . . ."

"Obviously, from her balcony and, as she descended, she was swept back into these lower lifeboats in the storm. The wind . . . the rain . . . the swells . . . the ship tossing. We hit a few big ones"

"Of course." Brent noticeably relaxed.

"There's only one thing." The captain paused.

"What?"

"What was she was doing out on your balcony in the storm?"

"I don't know. I was playing blackjack most of the night."

"But out there? In a storm like that?" The captain murmured.

"She . . . she loved weather. Real weather. Storms. Rain. She often walked in it. For inspiration, I think."

I glared at Brent. I had listened to Helga enough to know he was lying. Brent caught me. I looked away.

"Ah, understandable then. And, we . . . uh . . . we think her coat blew away?"

"I imagine." Brent agreed.

We had gone down an elevator aft from where Brent and Helga's cabin was located to get to her body. She had been swept backwards—a very long way. I knew Brent had to have thrown her off that balcony. But he had done so awkwardly, and she had missed the sea under their balcony, contrary to what Brent had planned.

Helga's body showing up onboard was Brent's surprise, not the fact that she was dead. And I distinctly remembered in the van when she warned Brent that the cruise better not be stormy and at dinner when she said she hated rough weather at sea.

"Are you sure she's . . .?" Brent asked the doctor. "Can we help her?"

"No." Dr. Witte stepped forward.

"Oh." Brent darted a nasty look at the security guard who had led him to believe Helga might still be alive. "Did she suffer?"

"No, she was more than likely disoriented from a fall that high." The doctor took the blanket from the returning security man and placed it over Helga's body. "She was not conscious for long, if at all, given that height."

"Thank God." Brent lowered his head. "Thank God. She didn't suffer."

Brent was suddenly calm and relaxed. The Captain and doctor thought it was because Helga had not suffered. They were wrong. I knew it was because Helga hadn't been conscious and able to reveal that Brent had thrown her off the balcony.

"The machinist who found her thought she tried to speak . . . your name at least. But as a doctor, I can assure you it was just air being released from her lungs when he moved her head to see if she was alive."

I leaned over to Curtis and Sean and whispered, "He killed her. I know he killed her."

Curtis looked at me, surprised. "No, that's not possible."

"Shh," Sean sputtered.

Brent glanced over malevolently. Had he heard what I said?

"Didn't you miss her when you went to bed last night?" Dr. Witte asked.

"Finally, a good question," I thought.

299

"She's a writer and keeps her own hours. I don't disturb her," Brent replied. "We have a suite so that she can . . . well, be alone to write when the muse strikes, which is . . . or was . . . erratic."

"Yes, quite," the captain said.

"I hadn't seen her all day. I tried to find her. In fact, I asked Veronica over there to help out. I suppose I was upset because we'd had a tiff in the bar the night before. But then, that was nothing new, as anyone can attest. She was a temperamental artist to the core."

I shivered. Not because of the cold, but because I had to be his witness—or I knew I would be his victim.

"Quite understandable." The captain cleared his throat again. "Long marriage and all that. Can't avoid the occasional disagreement, can we?"

"No, we can't." Brent stepped up close to Helga's body and buried his hands in his face.

"Oh, Helga . . . Helga . . . Helga . . ."

Brent stood sobbing like a baby with his hands over his face and his shoulders bouncing a rhythm with his sobs. He and his sobbing and his outburst were as phony as the CGI animation they shoved down our throats at the movies now. I didn't want to walk out on the theatre-of-the-absurd before me—and valiantly suppressed my urge to mock the Brent Show.

Sean put his hand on Brent's shoulder. I glanced around the sympathetic group. Sympathy wasted. This was murder, a third murder on board the *Queen Anne*. I scrutinized Brent, as any good criminalist would. Unfortunately, his hands were devoid of scratches or other signs that he had struggled with Helga before tossing her over her balcony.

"Dr. Witte, get him out of here," the captain said. "He's had enough. Give him a sedative if he needs it."

"I'll take you back to your stateroom." Dr. Witte doctor wedged himself between Sean and Brent.

Sean turned to our group. "Let's go."

"Yes." Mary turned to lead our group back into the bowels of the ship.

I lingered further to observe Brent. His face had no marks or scratches either. But, to my surprise, Brent's eyes were red and real tears flowed from them over his cheeks. Brent was a superb pretender and a shrewd murderer.

"Come on." Curtis took my arm.

As we left, the only question in my mind was whether Helga's murder was premeditated. Had Brent planned this before the cruise? Or did he just take advantage of the storm and Helga's own uncontrolled, public drunken spectacles? Proving this murder would be hard with no observable scratches or marks on him, his credible alibi, and the Wessex corporate machine burying everything not Disneyworld-worthy.

I was angry. I was offended. Brent had used me publicly to cover his tracks. He did it with Mavis as a secondary witness. He chose me not because he thought I would be discreet, but because he believed I was stupid, gullible—an amateur who was a cut below all these famous, published authors. He took advantage of me because of Mavis's dinner table disclosures and humiliation.

I was his dry run before dinner—his rehearsal to prepare for the big guns who observed him here: the captain, the doctor, and the published sophisticated criminalists like Mary, Sean and Elias.

Little did Brent know that he had made a mistake by using me.

I would not be his friendly witness, his patsy. Unpublished I might be, but I had no less an analytical mind than my new cohorts. I could compete with any mind on this

301

ship, including his. My past success in crime solving proved that.

Suddenly, my mind ground to a halt and I panicked. After my behavior at the Helga-discovery, did he now realize that he had made a mistake in using me?

I should have kept my looks to myself.

I should have been circumspect.

I should have kept my big mouth shut.

CHAPTER 34

The Mourning After

The captain and security officers stayed to facilitate depositing Helga's body with the mounting pile.

Brent, escorted by the doctor, followed us and a crew-leader as we all filed back through the entrails of the ship to the elevator. We waited.

"So, Brent, you played blackjack most of the night?" Sean, the ever-detecting homicide detective, probed at him.

"I'm sorry?" Brent looked cold eyed and steel-faced at Sean.

"Let the man be," Dr. Witte ordered.

Elias elbowed Sean who stopped the interrogation.

"I feel so badly I wasn't there for her, doctor," Brent said.

"How could you know?" the doctor soothed. "I'll give you something to rest."

I didn't laugh out loud, but I could have. In point of fact, Brent needed his rest after laying his wife to "rest" so brutally.

Brent and the doctor exited on Brent's deck. Brent dragged along behind the doctor, stoop-shouldered.

It was farcical to me.

* * *

"He killed her." Sean announced the minute the elevator doors shut.

Mary smirked. "Can you blame him? That woman was a monster."

"And he used me in his cover-up charade this afternoon."

I explained the afternoon and Brent's implicit threats just minutes ago.

"Well, he tossed her off, that's clear," Sean concluded.

"Yes," Mary agreed.

"What are we going to do?" I asked.

"Are we sure?" Elias asked, startled at the vehement, unquestioning consensus.

"Yes," Mary answered. "You're no amateur. Put two and two together."

"I have. I just don't want to believe that he did it."

"Yeah, that's what criminals trade on," Sean interjected.

"Then, what do we do now?" Elias asked.

"I think we have to keep our mouths shut." Sean said. "We have no proof."

"Yeah," Mary agreed. "And, God knows, we have enough trouble without taking on a man who tosses people off ships."

"Next time, he'll get the body into the sea." I said. "Practice makes perfect."

"What do you mean . . . not say anything?" Curtis spoke up. "Even I know he did it. I watched him. His eyes were cold and the tears well-done but without emotion."

"They sure were," Mary chuckled. "I smelled the onions he had on his fingers when he touched his eyes. And, I've put that scene in at least ten of my books. Who doesn't know that trick?"

"Are you kidding?" I exclaimed. "That's how he did it? They looked real to me and his eyes were red."

"An old trick," Mary went on. "Onions are particularly good, and fun, a little flavorful addition to spousal murder plots."

"Film actors use onions, too," Elias added.

"The raw onions he ordered for his steak!" I said. "I could kick myself!"

Curtis leaned over and whispered in my ear, "Veronica, your friends are fascinating. I think I may take up mystery writing myself."

I smiled at Curtis. His wonderful musky smell overwhelmed my analytical thoughts. As he whispered, his breath wafting gently on my ear reminded me of last night. His thick strong chest, iron shoulders, and lovely gentle biceps positioning me—first above him and then below and then doggy style. As we made love, the evening had become a *Kama Sutra* night of exploration for me. Exploration that I, at this late age, invited with hesitation, then fascination, and then wild participation.

Suddenly, I caught myself breathing deeply. I shook the images and thoughts off. I had to focus.

The elevator opened on the main deck, and we all gravitated to the bar like animals to their watering hole.

* * *

In the bar, we grabbed a couple of tables and put them together. Curtis held the chair for both Mary and myself. And then took a seat next to me. That pleased me. Curtis was enthralled with our group's never-ending pastime—solving murders—never-ending murders.

"That's number three." Mary settled in.

"Four . . . if you count Otto," I corrected.

"True," Mary agreed. "But either way, I personally didn't expect another body to pop up . . . or drop down . . ."

Mary chuckled and I couldn't resist.

"This is amazing." Curtis shook his head. "If I weren't with you all, I never would have suspected murder in any of the deaths."

Mary smirked. "Well, I thought the bodies were done piling up. I didn't know Brent would join in the mayhem at sea. Brent either planned this or decided no one would notice one more body."

"I don't think he planned it." Sean signaled a server. "I think he was just fed up and drunk and stronger than her."

"I don't know," I said. "I think he came on the cruise with Helga to kill her. I believe the two other deaths actually inhibited him. But then, she was such a horror he just cast caution to the wind. Her gambling with his allowance was the last straw."

"I agree," Elias said.

"I think Veronica has hit the nail on the head," Curtis said. "If I may express my opinion as a mere financial advisor."

We all chuckled at the needed levity.

"She has," Elias agreed. "At dinner, Helga said Brent talked her into the crossing. He was always planning n taking advantage of the storm. But Mendel and Frederick's deaths became flies in the ointment. Then, he went ahead anyway when Helga got so publicly out of control."

"I have to concur . . ." Elias shrugged. "It was set up too nicely for him to ignore."

"And remember the night Helga asked him if his mistress was on board?" Mary added.

"Whether she is or not, he has a lover at home . . . motive . . . along with the abuse," Elias added.

We were circumspect while we ordered—the women wine and the men hard drinks, neat.

"What do we do about it?" I asked. "Is he going to go after me next, because of my big mouth?"

"He used you to cover his tracks," Curtis observed. "He needs you."

"Curtis is dead right." Elias said. "Oh . . . just *right* will do. He needs you."

"But he knows I don't believe his charade," I said. "He has the captain and the doctor who believe him. And I didn't like the way he looked at me tonight."

"You're not going to be alone, anyway. You can't because of Amy," Mary pointed out.

"That's true," I agreed.

"I say we do nothing," Sean suggested. "We can't without proof. An autopsy will have to be done and something has to pop up . . . Brent's skin under Helga's nails. Some bruising from a struggle."

"The odds of either of those are remote," Mary supposed. "The only skin exposed in a tux is Brent's face and hands. There were no scratches there. I looked."

"I did too." I was proud of my seasoned-criminalist behavior.

"Good going." Mary reached her hand up and we high-fived. "In the mystery writing world, husbands often get divorced this way. At least, in my books they do."

"Well, in my world of real crime they do too . . . though not as often," Sean added. "But that doesn't change our position here . . . the fact that there is nothing to do right now. I'll e-mail my old partner and see what he can do with Helga's body and arranging an autopsy when we land. Or, maybe he can get it sent back for an autopsy before Brent can bury it or worse, cremate it."

"Good plan . . ." Elias paused as the server brought our drinks. " . . . but I think we had better focus on Amy now. Brent's not knocking anyone else off . . . even you, Veronica.

Too dangerous. And, personally, I can't think of anyone who deserved a little toss over the balcony more than Helga. I'm glad not to have her around."

"Elias," Mary reprimanded. "You sound like women deserve a good old fashioned stoning for misbehaving . . . like in *Zorba the Greek* or one of those Muslim countries? I think we should be less candid in our remarks. A woman has died."

"Been murdered," I corrected Mary.

"Right."

"I think we have enough problems with Amy right now," Sean took control. "If we have to make a choice . . . better to stop a serial killer than a wife killer. Let my partner take care of Brent."

"Speak of the devil," I remarked. "Don't look now, but Amy's here with Heather in tow."

Amy led Heather past several empty tables and took one adjacent to us. She sat facing us. She smiled and nodded.

Amy kept an eye on our group and, I believed, particularly me.

Curtis and I stayed for just the one drink. We left, but not until I was sure Sean and Elias would escort Mary to her room.

* * *

In Curtis's stateroom, we had another short drink before our ritual began—as it had before, slowly and tenderly.

⌘

CHAPTER 35

No Tea, No Sympathy

In the early morning, I went back to my own bed, unnoticed by the ear-plugged and eye-masked slumbering Mavis. It was hard to sleep thinking of Curtis—of us together.

I woke late, but still before Mavis. This was the last full sailing day before we docked in Southampton to disembark at seven a.m.

I fluffed my pillow and lingered cozily thinking of Curtis. I glanced at Mavis still in a deep sleep. Then, I forced Curtis to leave the pleasure spot in my brain. Instead, I thought about the dreaded day before me and my ongoing need to be vigilant against Amy. I was sure my cohorts were not thrilled with the prospect, either. But we had no choice. There was one thing we could not do in the middle of the Atlantic Ocean and that was to leave the *Queen Anne*. That is—leave it alive! To me, the MWW awards ceremony tonight had lost its allure. Murders could do that to an event. Murders—and Mavis and Esther's assaults on my character.

My only objective the rest of the cruise was to survive. I needed to avoid Amy's remaining vial of Prolixin and keep clear of Brent, particularly near ship rails.

I got up quietly, showered, got dressed, and got out before Mavis awoke.

I went to our MWW seminar room to get a strong tea and find Elias, who had Amy's memory sticks.

* * *

As I rounded the hallway corner, Jody, Agnes, and Herbert were chattering in front of the meeting room. An elaborate continental breakfast was set up outside the two adjacent seminar rooms. The gathered MWW members were milling around and talking about Helga's death. Some comments were quite nasty, but justified. Others were more sympathetic— obviously from writers who did not know the woman.

"Damn the high octane tea, full speed ahead to a coffee jolt," I said to myself.

I grabbed a big mug of java and all the uppers it afforded. It was hard burning the candle at both ends.

"Both ends." I smiled to myself.

I circled through the gathering to find my cohorts.

"Veronica." Agnes bounced over like she was on a school playground. "Did you hear about Helga?"

I did not slow my pace one iota. Instead, I kept scanning for Elias amongst the troop of writers all in a twitter. I ignored Agnes and grabbed a muffin.

"Did you hear the news?" Agnes trailed me with Jody and Herbert now in tow.

"News?" I feigned ignorance.

"Helga's dead. Dead as a doornail," Jody heralded. "She fell from the rail in the storm."

"Statistically unlikely." Herbert shrugged. "But they say it happened."

"Brent was here with Esther this morning and told everyone," Jody sympathized. "He's heartbroken."

"Brent was here?" I didn't see either Brent or Esther there now. "When?"

"I don't know." Then Agnes smiled slyly. "You know, I hate to say this but you do realize with her gone, the publishing world has a void that needs to be filled."

"Yes," Jody burst. "But I didn't even bring my book with me to work on."

"I did." Herbert smiled, yellow, crooked overlapping teeth and all. "I've plotted out three more short novelettes, too. I used these *Queen Anne* cruisers as characters. Amy is one of my victims. I called her Andrea and had her ravished in . . ."

"Write it. Don't speak it." In class I had to be an audience for his smut—not here. "Remember what Mavis said. If you talk a book, it doesn't write as well."

I knew now she said that so she wouldn't have to listen to all her students' drivel that would never be written or published.

"Oh, right . . ."

Herbert's disappointment at not titillating himself was written all over his face. In class, we were functionaries in his world of brutal fantasy sex. It never registered with him that we could shut him down out of class.

"I write everyday no matter what, and guess what? That includes on this cruise." Agnes ignored Herbert's shtick as she always did. "Prolific and terrific."

I laughed and my mug bounced coffee to the brim. But not one of the three hack hobby writers laughed with me. Evidently, they were not joking—my bad!

I couldn't believe my ears. These three had aspirations to jump into the fray and compete for Helga's crown? These abusers of the alphabet and abortionists of the writing craft were more delusional than I had thought.

"Good for you, Agnes." I mustered the phony enthusiasm of a carnival barker. "By the way, have you seen Elias?"

"No," Herbert answered. "But I think he's presenting. The schedule is posted over there."

"Thanks. I'll see you all later." I turned and muttered, "See you later . . . in your dreams!"

It was too early, too late, or, just too anything for me to put up with the three of them. I walked over to the posted meeting schedule to find Elias and gulped down my now-cooled coffee. I needed to get the memory stick and find out if there were any developments. I hoped Elias had come up with a new idea to prove up Helga's murder. And I also hoped Sean had heard from his New York connection about our triple murders. Quadruple, if you included Otto's demise.

I scanned the program. Elias, Sean, and Mary were not on the schedule until this afternoon. I looked in the MWW rooms and didn't see them or Esther or Mavis.

I set down my now-empty coffee mug and headed for Elias's stateroom. They had to be where the evidence was. As I rounded the hallway corner, Brent shot out in front of me.

I planted my feet but we collided. Brent grabbed me by the shoulders.

"Veronica! Just who I wanted to see."

I looked up at the big man and felt his massive hands clamped around my thin shoulders. I knew Helga had no chance once this muscular mass chose to get her over the rail.

"We need to talk."

"I am in a hurry. I have to go."

"Wait." Brent did not release me. "I want you to listen. I loved Helga. I would never have done anything to her. She was my life."

"I know . . . I know how worried you were yesterday when you came and got me." I soothed him because he did not release me.

Brent silently studied my eyes and then whispered, "You're lying."

I saw people crossing to the elevators down the hall and said loudly, "Let me go. You're hurting me."

Brent saw them, too. His eyes flashed anger as he dropped my shoulders so hard I almost fell.

"Veronica stop the bullshit, I saw the look on your face last night, I heard what you said to Sean, and I know you're lying now."

"What are you talking about?" I goaded him.

"Look. You're wrong. I need you to know that."

"Brent, I know you wouldn't hurt her."

"But you would kill her," I thought.

I bald-faced lied, and adeptly too, both for my preservation and my friends. I should have been more circumspect last night. I shuddered at the memory of being alone in his cabin with him—on the very balcony where he had disposed of Helga. Thank God, there was no balcony around now. I was even smaller than Helga. With one swoop he could scoop me up and be rid of me in the churning, changing Atlantic. I would simply follow the many other bodies that had joined her depths. The Atlantic was endless in the dark distance eastward. I was amazed at the Vikings, Christopher Columbus, the Pilgrims, and so many others who had challenged it in their tiny ships. Then, I thought of the centuries of dead who warred on, over and below its waters, always, of course, with God on their side—only their side.

"Good," Brent calmed down. "If you thought I killed her for her money . . . I didn't. Most of her estate goes to her alma mater. You have to believe me. You saw that I was looking for her all day."

I was cornered and frightened. I didn't want to be hunted by both Amy and Brent. Nor did I want my friends to be. But the operative word in his plea to me was "most." However, I was not going to debate with a killer about the monetary proportions in the will. He had tossed Helga over the balcony. Whether in a rage or by design, he had thrown her into the storm that night and had expected her to end up at the bottom of the Atlantic. But she hadn't.

He was guilty and had coopted me to use me as a witness to cover it up. That was his mistake. I did not believe his charade in his cabin and I did not believe him now. On both counts he had failed by judging me an idiot—that part of his plan made him the idiot. He shouldn't have involved me at all, because I will be a witness for the prosecution if it comes to that.

"Then . . . your conscience is clear." I stepped around Brent and started down the hallway.

"Wait."

Brent blocked me.

"Are you going to kill me, too?"

The minute the words filled the narrow space between us, I regretted blurting them out. My vanity had undone all the placating and lying that I just did.

"You little . . ." Brent's face was red and the words spit through his teeth. "You don't know anything. And if I were you, I'd keep my mouth shut. If you . . ."

Just then, Esther came down the hall.

"Brent, I'm so glad I ran into you. How are you doing?"

Esther took his hand and held it.

"Not well," Brent calmed himself, looking back and forth from Esther to me. "I was just asking Veronica if she knew where you were. I wanted to make sure Helga's presentations were covered."

Another lie.

Esther continued to ignore my presence and still held Brent's hand. "How sweet. Don't worry about that. But we do want to remember Helga tonight at the awards. I need you to help with some more intimate, charming memories about her in her honor."

"Sure." Brent retrieved his hand. "I'll have to get back to you."

"We need to do it now," Esther insisted. "There isn't much time. You need to meet with Anne, who's doing Helga's memorial speech."

"I have to go." I escaped.

As I hurried down the hallway, Esther chattered about Helga's accomplishments.

I knew, as Brent did, that Helga had one defining accomplishment, systematically creating a murderer—and I don't mean in her books. I mean the gradual creation of a real murderer—her own murderer—Brent, her abused caged animal.

CHAPTER 36

There Be Monsters Here

Near Elias's cabin, I passed two security guards talking in the hall. I recognized them both. They stared, but didn't say a word. I knew they recognized me, the troublemaker. I knocked on Elias's door.

Elias opened the door to Sean and Mary standing amidst a cabin torn apart. There were cushions on the floor, drawers emptied and hanging open, and in bedroom beyond clothes thrown out of the closet.

"Come in."

"What happened?" I shoved the Brent incident aside.

"Obviously, Amy happened," Mary replied.

"When? Last night?"

"No." Elias shut the door after me. "This morning early, when we were panelists."

"She knew it'd be clear," Sean said.

"I reported it to the security men outside," Elias said. "But just as a formality. They don't care."

"But how did she get in?" I asked.

"We figure the maid was cleaning and she slipped in. Hid until she left," Sean said.

"Or did the harried-lost-key routine," Elias added. "Works in my books."

"I don't even want to ask what she took." I looked at Elias.

"Everything important."

"I bet she got rid of what little evidence you left in her room, too." Mary threw the cushions back on the couch and then slumped onto it.

"What are we going to do?" I asked.

"Nothing to do," Mary answered. "I'm sure it's all overboard at the bottom of the Atlantic."

"Too bad I didn't transmit all of it to my partner in New York," Sean said.

"Too bad, indeed," Mary responded. "But none of us were thinking."

"I didn't put it in the safe, damn it. I was just in a hurry. I forgot," Elias said. "I mean I could have plotted her break-in from one of my books. But I was coming back after the panel. It wasn't that long."

"What's done is done." Mary replied. "We all didn't think."

"What about the Prolixin?" I asked. "Did she get that?"

"Sure." Elias threw cushions on the easy chairs and he and I sat. "And we know she has the opened vial in her purse."

"This is not good for us," Mary said.

"No, it isn't." Sean joined Mary on the couch.

"What was on the memory sticks? Did you have a chance to look at them?" I asked.

"Yes," Sean said. "They were circumstantial and would have bolstered our case, but we still needed hard evidence."

"He's right. It was drafts, including the final draft, of a novel. A very sad one, but still just a piece of fiction," Elias agreed. "I stayed up late and read most of it. It's a thinly veiled autobiography. It contextually exposes Otto, Mendel, and Frederick for what they were. But not by name. It's really masterful . . . with a fast-paced plot and unique characters. It is edited brilliantly. I understand now why she was published so young. She was a genius, a natural."

"Too bad she stopped writing about murderers and became one," Mary interjected.

"Do you blame her?" I replied. "The utter betrayal, by people she loved and trusted."

"The flash drives would only have helped put the nails in Amy's coffin if we had all the other stuff, but we don't now," Sean declared. "I think she wrote the novel before she decided to kill them. We'll still see what my partner says about getting her for Otto's murder."

"She should have just published it and not killed them," I said. "If she had leaked its origin in the circles that count, she would have at least ruined Frederick's career and any chance of Mendel's revival."

"I guess that wasn't enough for her," Mary replied.

"It doesn't matter now," Sean focused the conversation. "We are where we are."

"And speaking of where we are," I said. "I saw Brent."

"I thought he would hole up in his cabin until the cruise ended. Keep a low profile. Feign mourning," Sean said.

I told them what had happened.

"Well, it's not a confession, but he's a desperate man and you'd better watch it," Elias cautioned. "You should have played along more."

"I know. I made a mistake. I was just so upset about being used like that yesterday."

"At least we know if you go overboard, it's Brent," Sean chortled.

"And if you or Elias or I have heart attacks, it's Amy." Mary joined in with a nervous chuckle.

"They wouldn't dare at this point, would they?" I asked.

"Why not? The Wessex spin is working, and they have Esther teamed up with them," Mary replied.

"And desperation has its own momentum," Sean added. "People who are desperate can do anything. I've seen it before in my cases. Rational thought is not the foundation for actions of people trying to preserve their freedom. We have eighteen hours until we dock in Southampton. Eighteen hours to keep our eyes on each other."

"Let's have lunch in the dining room and then stay together at the afternoon panel discussions," Mary suggested.

"I think that's a good idea." Elias stood. "Especially for you girls."

"I hate to be sexist, but it is always the women who seem to go first in my mysteries." Mary headed out.

"And, in real life . . . excuse me . . . real death." Sean followed.

I fell in step behind them.

"Sad but true." Elias took a last look at his ransacked cabin and then trailed our troupe out the door.

* * *

Marching abreast down the hallway to the dining room, I felt safety in numbers, particularly after being held in Brent's vise-like, angry grip.

"We'll keep together," Sean recounted. "We'll have lunch together and go to the same events this afternoon. We'll escort you girls back to your staterooms to change for the awards. Then we'll pick you up again."

"I really can take care of myself," Mary objected.

"Mary, we have to protect . . ." I started.

"But . . . I'll do it." Mary interrupted. "But just because I like being referred to as 'you girls'."

"Me too, actually." I chuckled at Mary's reasoning, which reflected her writing style.

In Mary's books, the smallest of events or references often changed the victim's fate. It hit home with me, and from her sales numbers, obviously all of her readers. I tried to do the same in my books, but it was hard.

The thought that small events or inconsequential conversations could change the course of your life scared me now. Did life turn on the minuscule, not the monumental—a light turned off or not, a car parked in the wrong or right place, an unkind or kind word, a fight picked when it should or shouldn't have been?

"I'll escort you this afternoon, Mary," Elias volunteered. "Your cabin is near mine. And Sean, you take Veronica."

"My pleasure. But what about Curtis?" Sean winked at me. "I don't want him to think I am moving in on his territory."

I picked up the flirtatious cue and ran with it.

"Why not? He could use the competition."

Sean and I laughed. I had made the old man happy. I enjoyed it.

Mary interrupted our fictitious, but satisfying, *tête-a-tête*.

"I have to get my awards speech ready. Have you done yours, Sean?"

"Esther has me presenting for the best short story published this year," Sean answered. "It's the same thing I did two years ago. I just tweaked it a little."

"Mary, this is your first time, isn't it? Are you ready?"

"Holy sakes, yes. Esther trapped me when I was in a pliable mood. Best first time published book. Piece of cake. I'm a talker," Mary glanced at me. "But I wish I was presenting it to you, Veronica."

"Maybe next time!" Elias's mustache bounced with his encouraging smile.

320

"Yes!" Mary's eyes crinkled in her chubby face as she beamed. "Next time, Veronica."

"I hope so."

I smiled. But I felt like a deer caught in the headlights. I feared I would never get an award at the rate I was going. If I survived this cruise, of course.

The four of us got in the short line for the dining room single lunch seating. Most passengers lunched in the cafeteria on the top deck, in their rooms, or not at all.

"Each of us has to put our crime-solving brains to work. We have to get something incriminating and solid on Amy tonight. Let's be at the bar before the cocktail party to strategize and share our ideas," Sean whispered with finality and authority. "Lunch is open seating. Be careful what you say. There could be big ears around us."

"I'll be careful," I guaranteed. "Being in Amy's closet was no fun for me."

I actually looked forward to not rehashing the murders and meeting new people at the open seating lunch. It would be refreshing to get our minds off death. But I held that thought to myself. I didn't want to be less serious than the exalted writers with whom I was now associated.

"And having my room ripped apart was no fun for me either," Elias said.

We paused in the foyer. The view down to the elegant dining room was as breathtaking in daylight as it was at night. The chandeliers were lit and sparkled and the tables set as beautifully.

"We'll meet at the bar at six," Elias said.

"It's noon. That gives us six hours," Sean added. "Just think of some plan, no matter how outrageous. Think outside the box like me and my partner did when a case stumped us. We need a strategy to get Amy and now Brent."

"Okay, but I am more worried about the next eighteen hours until we dock than I am about the six until cocktails."

"Don't worry," Mary turned to me. "We'll be together."

"It'll be a long eighteen hours."

"We need it to catch these murderers," Sean said. "And it is not much time for that."

"You're right . . . even with the brain trust here, we'll have to move fast."

I hid my fear and feigned enthusiasm. Over the next six hours, and indeed the next eighteen hours, I was more concerned for my life—our lives. Those hours until we landed in Southampton would be the longest eighteen hours of my life.

The word *life* gave me the shivers. It was now too closely associated with the word *death*.

Was that the mindset of a professional writer? No fear in the face of adversaries? It appeared so. Evidently, that was set these multi-million dollar authors apart from the herd. It was also what being a professional meant; showing no fear—ever. Just stepping up and doing what needed to be done, however hard that might be.

⌘

CHAPTER 37

Mealtime Minuet

We were seated at a large round table for ten with two men already settled in. The waiter was just finishing taking their orders and removing their menus.

We quickly selected from the never-ending elaborate gourmet choices on the menu, which I had come to expect. They were as tempting as dinner. I was glad. I, for one, was hungry. Facing death on an empty stomach was not my first choice. Even death row inmates got their last meal.

Then, there were introductions all around. The men were Australians who had gotten partial financing in the United States for their software company. Now, they were on to London for more of the same. They were a couple—a charming one, who engaged in delightful banter and had social IQs that were one of their assets—perhaps their biggest.

Other interesting passengers, all non-MWW members, successively joined us. I enjoyed meeting them—most of them, at least. An American couple introduced themselves and within minutes showcased their wealth and prominent status in

Charleston, South Carolina. I had to admit their lifestyle was large and their pocketbook matched it, but who couldn't be big in Charleston compared to my competitive, exclusive spot in the glittering world of Los Angeles?

But the wife was a delight anyway—the giving, interested, relaxed superficial delight that came from being ensconced in affluence. She "just adored" the crossing, Elias's mysteries, Mary's bravery in slasher writing, and Sean's career at the NYPD. However, her husband was her unpleasant opposite. In fact, he was clearly angry that he was stuck on this cruise and particularly with this lunch table. Nothing was quite right and neither was our company. He made it clear he never read fiction. He was too busy and too important. He also mocked the two Australians' startup business, predicted its failure, and said their investors were looking for tax losses. But, after a glare from his wife, he arrested his remarks on their gay lifestyle. It appeared to me Helga's ghost had taken up residence in him, in all its aggressive, belittling, and cutting nastiness.

Then, thankfully, another couple came to fill the last two seats and stopped this man from continuing to lay waste to our lovely lunch.

They were the cute British couple we had all met in the elevator when they were headed for their trek around the promenade deck. The wife under protest, I remembered. They were led by the maître d' himself to their seats.

"Here you are, your ladyship," the maître d' held the woman's chair as she sat. "Anything further, your lordship?"

"No, thank you."

There were looks all around the table at the royalty references. They introduced themselves using their given names with no reference to titles. We acknowledged the elevator encounter with humor. They charmingly reported on the walk on the deck and it seemed the pleasure of it was in dispute between them.

Our male Helga was attentive and engaged the newcomers who, clearly, were worth his charm. The lunch became predictable and I wished shorter. Although the British royalty and other VIP's had a private dining room, they often came down for lunch and breakfast to enjoy their fellow passengers and the large dining room in all its elegance. Also, the common man was of course a fad in England after the late Lady Di and Prince William's commoner-wife Kate Middleton.

Whether the commoners were popular or not, I had read about the Wessex Cruise Line's Canterbury Club, the separate and very exclusive dining room for people of their ilk. The elite guests all traveled in AA category staterooms. The pictures of the exclusive art deco dining room showed a high ceiling with backlit decorative glass panels, a sandblasted decorative glass wall commensurate with the finest Lalique crystal pieces, and panoramic windows over the sea. Had our Charleston couple been *that* huge, *that's* where they would have been.

The lovely lunch was served. Afterward no one desserted, but we all cappuccinoed.

During most of the lunch conversation, in which verbal one-upmanship and social pecking dominated, I was quiet. I didn't want to compete with any of these people and, of course, I couldn't. Not in wealth, royal breeding, writing, business accomplishments, or, fair to say, nastiness.

I lost myself in thoughts of Curtis. I re-experienced his gentle and urgent intimacy in my mind.

"You look far away," Mary leaned over and whispered. "And pleasantly so. Curtis?'

"I wish!"

I coveted my privacy and added, "Actually, I was thinking of how to nail Amy to the wall."

"Of course," Mary respected my little white lie. "Speaking of that, we had better go."

I took the lead. "I'm sorry. I hate to be the first to leave, but I have a conference. Please excuse me. It was a pleasure meeting all of you and seeing you again, too."

I directed my last comment to our royalty just to one-up our new male-Helga with exaggerated feigned familiarity. It was real enough to irritate him. I was getting adept at lying without a thought at the drop-of-a-hat now. I started to admire myself for this expanded skill.

"As do we," Sean and Mary stood. "I'm so sorry."

Elias followed suit reluctantly because he, not unsurprisingly, was immersed in the lunch banter. Knowing him, as I was getting to, I appreciated that he was memorizing characters for new books—me included— and I hoped kindly. I suspected this whole trip was to get his juices flowing and another book out soon. I did wonder if he went back and made notes on the people he met or even wrote little scenes to use later. I might ask him at some point. But then, as generous as he was, it has been my experience that writers do not candidly share the deepest secrets about their real processes.

We left the dining room as a group for the first of our two two-hour panel discussions. As we had agreed, we were all four joined at the hip to assure we would survive.

* * *

In the first panel discussion, "Marketing for Money," Amy was a panelist. During the presentation, when she was fallow, her hazel gold-rimmed eyes were riveted on Mary. I only caught her eyes on me once, which is not to say they weren't there more.

I would have preferred to hide in another panel discussion on "Spicing up the Dialogue" down the hall without Amy. But we needed a united, strong presence. I didn't think this tactic was necessarily wise, but I followed the lead of the professionals.

The group, both in its demeanor and questions, was different than I had imagined. There was no frivolity. Amy, as an agent, bolstered with authority what the five other panelists, all hardworking professional writers, said. They were serious about publishing, serious about making money, and serious about the business of book writing. And the attendees were even more so, because of the bleak financial prospects most writers faced.

One very prolific and wealthy mystery writer took the lead on the panel, obviously because of his years of experience, longevity, monetary success, and probably his gray hair. He told the hungry audience that supporting oneself being an author was a seven-day a week, fourteen hour a day job. He did share some secrets with us, including the fact that he devoted one third of his workday to writing, another third to editing, and the last third to marketing.

My face dropped. I didn't know if I had that sort of discipline. I knew I didn't have the marketing knowledge. I should have gone to all the self-publishing panels and especially that one about Octopus Books being a pimp and we its writing whores.

Suddenly, my hand popped up like a spring to ask a question. The wonderful old author pointed at me before I could pretend that I was scratching my head, a grade school tactic when we acted before we thought.

"Yes? Question?"

"The marketing?" I stammered, formulating my question so that I appeared to be a professional, published writer. "With all the advances in technology and self-publishing, what sources do you use to keep updated?'

I was satisfied that I sounded knowledgeable, not like an utter amateur. My real question should have been "How the hell do you even get started selling a product to the public and does it have to be Octopus Books?"

Interestingly and generously, however, the panelist gave a broad answer. He knew I needed more than updates on marketing. I needed a basic plan. I was amidst perceptive and intuitive people. People who made their living studying, with great skill, the human character and reading nuances of communication both verbal and physical. This man, this established popular author, instinctively knew my quandary. To him, I was Agnes, Herbert, and Jody all rolled into one. I shuddered at that thought.

"If I may, first let me give some basic guidelines for the novices amongst us. In point of fact, they are precious to us and must be nurtured. They will carry the baton after we are gone. This is sadly in the forefront of all our minds after the passing of our colleagues on this cruise. Then, of course, I will answer your question on updates specifically. Is that alright with you?"

"Yes, of course." I was relieved that this insightful man had been generous and respectful of my status—my non-status—and my privacy as well.

He gave a succinct outline of on-line, print, new media, social media, Internet podcast marketing, and interviews. He then balanced the cost in money and time of the various options against their effectiveness. He condemned agents and publishers as unable, or refusing, to help more—or at all—these days. He complimented indie authors, working entirely on their own, for sharing their tradecraft through chat rooms, YouTube, and blogging. He also analyzed the effectiveness and costs of hiring a publicist or marketing consultant and their limitations. Then, he offered his conclusions on the use of each and how to keep up with changes and update oneself for each.

None of it sounded like fun. Murdering people on paper in the wee hours of the morning was fun, but so different from the business of marketing. All of that seemed onerous and alien to me.

I looked around the room and down the row at my new friends. Could I discipline myself like they did? Maybe. At least I could give it a try, because I wanted to be part of this—of them.

I resolved to absent myself from the neighborhood coffee shop and gnawing at my muse. I also committed to editing my finished books, or at least one, and sending them, or it, out to agents and publishers. The indie route seemed overwhelming, and I wanted to be a professional, to publish, and keep my newfound friends. Also, non-agent, unassisted Octopus Books authors were ending up with an insignificant piece of their own pie after working so hard.

I wished I could take Amy up on her offer to read my work. But then, it was an agent I needed—not a murderer.

"Just my luck," I thought.

* * *

Mary picked the second panel discussion, "Octopus Books: Pimp or Publisher—Stealing Authors' Royalties." One of the panelists was an Octopus rep. Mary wanted to learn first-hand about Octopus Book's new policies. It was just the one I wanted, too—until I got there. Their power was complete. Their domination was unchallengeable, their programs, to me, tantamount to theft of product. In the room, however, the authors remained respectful, even through the questions at the end. It was akin to ignoring that "the emperor has no clothes." I understood why, as had many ordinary Germans in Nazi Germany and every serf who owed fealty to a noble with swordsmen at his side in feudal times.

But I had my answer. An agent it was for me—if I could get one.

* * *

After the second panel discussion, Sean escorted me on the elevator to go back to my cabin. At my floor, I jumped off.

"I can make it down the hall."

"Okay." Sean held the door a moment. "I need to get hold of my ex-partner in New York before the banquet. I'll come for you as soon as I'm ready for dinner. Wait for me."

"Okay."

"Promise?"

"I promise."

We parted ways.

As I rounded the corner to my cabin, Mavis and Esther were quarrelling in the hallway. I backed up and hid there. They were both already dressed to the nines for the awards dinner. When Esther walked away, Mavis grabbed her arm.

"Wait. I thought you said you'd ask around. I need to make a living."

"Excuse me." Esther pulled her arm away. "Desperation is not becoming in anyone."

"So what? That's what I am. God knows, I've done enough for you and the MWW to deserve help."

"Deserve? Deserve? Who do you think you are talking to? I run the MWW and I do all the real work, day in and day out. Week in and week out. Year in and year out."

"I know. I know." Mavis calmed down. "I'm sorry. Really I am. I realize I only help out and don't do anything compared to you."

"Well, at least you are being honest, now!"

"I don't want to upset you. Our friendship is worth so much to me."

"I understand." Esther's voice was as cold as the Antarctic.

"Thank you . . . but please . . . Esther . . . did you ask anyone?"

"I will." Esther had cowed Mavis and enjoyed the power, the scorched-earth unequivocal victory. "I will. Now, let's get to the awards banquet."

"Thank you. It means so much. I'm sorry I upset you before the banquet. I guess I am desperate. And you're right, I shouldn't be. I do have friends."

There was silence from Esther.

"I hope you never get in this situation," Mavis sucked up, personalizing her problems to Esther. "It's horrible."

"*I* won't. Now, I need to check on the awards banquet."

Mavis, with nothing to lose now, tried one final stratagem to boost her profile.

"Esther! Just a minute, please. I know I keep hounding you, but maybe you could at least let me get up on the podium . . . to speak. Helga was going to give Otto his posthumous lifetime achievement award and . . . and . . . you were going to . . ."

Esther gave Mavis an imperious, condescending smile. "Sean O'Flarity is presenting that award."

"That's great! I wouldn't *dream* of doing that . . . I just thought I could take your place . . . you know, as your assistant . . . and introduce Sean. It would be short and give my profile a boost. I'm re-releasing my series and I've thought of a great new mystery! I mentor writers, just like Otto. I'm a respected teacher, like Otto. And I knew him. He helped me . . . well, a little! My ties couldn't be stronger."

"Just stop. Stop exaggerating," Esther interrupted. "You're old news, dear."

"But, I've helped you for years. Can't you . . ."

331

"Stop hounding me! It's too much on me. I've already settled the intros, and that's that."

"What do you mean?"

"Amy will be introducing Sean."

Mavis glared at Esther walking toward the elevators—and me! I immediately strolled past Esther down to my cabin so she didn't know I was eavesdropping at the corner near the elevator.

"Hello," I said as Esther swept by.

"Good evening." Esther didn't even look over.

Then I heard her mutter, "Why would I pick a washed-up *nebbish,* a *nudnik to* do a presentation?"

I saw Mavis the *nebbish*—the *nudnik*—standing abandoned, a dejected look on her face. When she saw me, however, she stood straight, smiled and puppy-dogged after Esther. I slowed my advance. I felt badly for Mavis, but I couldn't help her and, more than that, I didn't want to. This trip had proven to me that she had never thought of me as a colleague or a friend.

"Hello," Mavis greeted me.

"Leaving for the awards banquet?" I fumbled for my cabin key and avoided her eyes.

"Yes, Esther and me." Mavis covered her Esther-encounter with cheerfulness. "I may help her during the program. It's so exciting."

"Good luck!"

Mavis was lying, but then, she didn't know I had overheard their encounter. I opened the door, but stood watching Mavis scurry to the elevators in Esther's wake.

All this certainly confirmed why Esther had been her focus since before the cruise took off. She needed Esther's connections for her own financial survival. This was like the acting profession. There were the elite moneymakers at the top and very little money trickled to the other ninety percent of hard-working professional writers. I equated it to Octopus

Book's new policies, taking more of the small slice of the pie most authors got.

Then, it sunk in. Mavis was arguing there were no murders because Esther was her financial life and death. Mavis's needs trumped the loss of human life—lives.

More than that, I believed now that Mavis had never cared about me, or any of her students, except as functionaries to make a buck—and that the twinkle in her eye when she praised our writing came from dollar signs. She analyzed our writing with feigned enthusiasm. And, her soft voice was the schooled affectation of a failure. Here, on the high seas amongst robustly successful authors, it was clear. She was envious and commanded no attention outside her classroom. She was obsequious and she had squandered her life experience because of her bitter jealousy. She now, to me, was a perfect example of an author who had never loved the art form and had failed at marketing—the business of being an author. Had she even edited? Maybe not. Maybe her publisher even took care of that.

It dawned on me that I had outgrown Mavis years ago, but never realized it. I had no authorial self-doubt any longer, in part, thanks to her betrayal. That was the greatest lesson she had taught me.

CHAPTER 38

Threats Can Come in Many Forms

I was happy to have the stateroom to myself as I rushed and got ready for the gala—and Curtis *après* the gala.

Thinking of Curtis, I saw that the phone had no message light on, and if Mavis had received a message from him, she hadn't said. Since I would not be in the main dining room tonight, I simply would go to the bar and meet as we always had.

I hoped Sean would have good news from New York and that I would not get another assignment from my cohorts. I had done enough. Now, all I wanted was one more night with Curtis before we docked. Perhaps I was only an amateur criminalist at heart, because my prioritization was in favor of love's lust instead of proving up the murders. But, I would argue, one night off would not prevent me from becoming a professional, published, money-earning mystery writer.

I showered the unpleasant day away. I dressed in my black silk pants ensemble complete with a black sequined cropped jacket and my tallest spiked sling-back, open-toe heels. It took a minute of tottering to adjust to them, but they were definitely worth the torture.

As I put on meticulous evening make-up, I bemoaned that the last night of the cruise might end up business—the business of staying alive—and not pleasure. Although I enjoyed Sean's company, I wanted and needed Curtis to be my bodyguard tonight.

I was ready early. I sat on the edge of my bed and waited for Sean to escort me to the evening's festivities.

I flipped through the television channels, and stopped at the closed circuit video explaining our landing procedures. Evidently, we had to have our luggage out in the hallway tonight if we wanted the staff to take it off the ship.

I grabbed my large suitcase stored in the top shelf of the closet and put it at the end of my bed. I packed as the woman on the television charmingly, and very clearly, finished her debarkation instructions.

Packing was always a pain, whether now or later. I put everything from my drawers I would not need in the suitcase. I had definitely brought too much and at least a quarter of my clothes, including three cardigan cashmeres, remained untouched.

When I went to the closet to cull through it, there was a knock at my door.

I glanced at the digital clock near my bed. Sean was early, too.

"Good," I said. "Saved by the knock."

I went to the peephole in the door. The hall seemed dim, but I caught a close-up of Sean's black tuxedo.

"Sean?" I called through the door.

"Yes."

I grabbed my small black sequined evening bag on the bed, turned off the lights and television, and hurried back to the door. I was excited for the evening.

* * *

When I pressed the handle down, the unlatched door swung open. I jumped back.

"Hold on, Sean. I . . ."

A male burst in, silhouetted by the dimmed hall light. He was not stout like Sean, but instead trim and fit. He lunged for me.

"Oh, God!" I cried. "Help!"

I turned and grabbed the large suitcase on my bed and threw it at him. The cashmeres splayed on the floor as he batted the suitcase aside. Any escape blocked, I focused on the phone. I retreated to grab it, but my coveted heels tangled in the cashmere sweaters. I struggled to balance, but plummeted down. My evening bag went flying and my head hit side of the bed.

I was dazed. I grabbed my forehead looked up in the dim light.

"Brent!" I gasped as I struggling for breath.

"Damn it." Brent bounded and shoved on the door, but my bag still wedged it ajar.

"Help! Help!" I stuttered, still dazed and struggling to get my footing.

"Shut up," Brent growled as he spun around, forgetting the bag and the door. "Shut up!"

The light slicing in through the cracked door emphasized Brent's eyes. They were wild with rage.

I grabbed my heels and threw them at Brent.

Brent stepped over my suitcase and charged at me. I had my footing now, but it was too late to run. Brent was between the hallway door and me.

"You should have left me alone," Brent lunged, grabbed me, and threw me over his shoulder like a rag doll. "Helga wasn't worth it."

His huge shoulder knocked the wind out of me. I lay limp and without any breath left to scream. My arms dangled down his broad back. The sliver of light still streamed into the cabin door because my evening bag remained lodged there. I fought for my breath to scream for any passerby, but it didn't come and they didn't come.

As Brent carried me further into the room, I caught a glimpse of his red, contorted face in the mirror, striated by the beam of hall light.

I gasped and a shallow breath came, then two, and then a deep one. I started hitting Brent's back and kicking. Slowly at first and then wildly as I got my breath and my adrenaline pumped through my body.

"Help." I croaked louder and then louder. "Help. Help!"

As I flailed wildly, Brent carried me to the balcony's sliding door.

I suddenly knew my fate. It was Helga's. I was terrified. Helga's body flashed through my mind. Should I hope for a clean fall to the cold Atlantic? They say that drowning in cold water is euphoric. I didn't want to linger on an obscure deck somewhere below, suffering like Helga until some crewman discovered my body. But there was no choice because there was no Atlantic beneath my economy balcony. I was smaller than Helga. Could Brent have the strength to pitch me out far enough?

As Brent struggled to open the sliding door and keep me on his shoulder, I grabbed at anything and everything. I grabbed the curtains, but they just came down limp in my hands. The ambient light from the ship's lamps filtered onto the balcony and into the room.

When I saw the balcony and my fate, a desperate screech came out of me that I didn't recognize. It was inhuman in its strength and potency.

"Help! Help! Help!" I screeched over and over again.

Brent got the sliding door open.

I grabbed onto the doorframe. I wasn't strong enough to keep my grip when he jerked me through out onto the balcony. I felt my fingers writhe in pain as they were forced to relinquish my hold on life.

I tried to reach anything I could, but was only able to grab at the black wet sea air in my frenzy.

"Help me!" I screamed again tasting the salt in gasps I took in. "Help!"

Then, I saw it over the balcony—the churning Atlantic's white-capped waves. The waves glared at me and I at them. I would relax to help Brent thrust me into the sea instead of having to suffer a close in painful plummet like Helga's onto a hard deck—crushing me or leaving me in lingering pain.

"Veronica?" Sounded from the hallway. "Veronica?"

The door opened and the hall light shot into the cabin. Sean's large tuxedoed body charged in.

The door, *sans* evening bag, automatically slammed shut. Suddenly, it was dark again except for the ship's ambient light filtering onto the balcony.

"Brent, stop!" Sean yelled.

Sean grabbed at me and pulled me. Finally, Brent released his grip and, suddenly, with a thud I hit the balcony's Astroturf, hard.

The two men struggled above me. I crawled for the open sliding door to call for help, but couldn't pass them. The chairs and chaises flew.

Sean and Brent collided again and again. In a flurry, arms wielded fists that thudded with body blows. It was stag against stag—pushing and pulling. I couldn't get to the phone. I sat balled up in fear.

Then, Sean charged Brent with the full force of his tank-like body. Brent flew towards the rail.

In an instant, Brent was over the rail. His high center of gravity and the laws of physics combined to force him to lose his footing.

"No!" Sean yelled.

He reached for Brent, but Brent just fell—headfirst.

Sean the victor was tottering over the rail, but grabbed on hard. In slow motion, his feet left the ground. He started to go further and further and his feet lifted higher and higher as he began to plummet and lose his battle to stay on the balcony.

"Sean!" I grabbed his thick muscular ankles.

My voice was drowned out by Brent's unearthly receding shriek on his way down.

"Sean!" I screamed again with tears flooding down my cheeks, desperate to save his life.

"Hold me!" Sean called. "Hold on tight!"

"I am! I am!"

I was being dragged across the sea-misted, slippery Astroturf and Sean's weight began to lift me up and off the green-bladed plastic.

A lifespan and moment later, my vise-like grip on Sean's ankles eased as I felt Sean's body tilt back into the balcony. But I still held on.

I looked up. Sean's white knuckled hands and my weight had teeter-tottered him back to the balcony side. He must have had epochal NYPD training, impeccable natural balance, and incredible strength to do a save like that. Or, it might simply have been fear and adrenaline—or maybe just my hold on his ankles made the difference. Whatever it was, I knew one thing.

I would not have been strong enough to hold him and myself if he had gone over. I was glad I hadn't had to decide when to let go, because I would have. That thought put a pall on my joy.

"You can let go now," Sean said with both feet firmly planted on the balcony.

"What?" I still gripped both of Sean's ankles.

"I'm safe. You can let go."

I looked up through my haze of tears and saw that he was.

"Are you hurt?" Sean reached down and helped me up.

"No, I don't think so." My cries and tears mingled with my laughter of relief and dark secret that I would have let him drop if I had to. "Thank you, Sean. Thank you. Thank you."

"It's going to be all right." Sean hugged me, big and bear-like.

I buried my head on his chest, happy to be alive. Happy we were both still here—happy I didn't have to release his legs. I could hear his heart beating double time. Joy at his life won out and my guilt at my probable choice was forgotten.

"Is he?"

"Dead? Head first? I think so! I just couldn't hold him. But you held me or I'd be with him. You were great, Veronica!"

"No. No. You held yourself. I just helped out." I looked up at Sean's sparkling Irish eyes.

"Don't be so modest. You're a quick thinker. Thank you. It was like old times on the force. You were my partner. You ever think of being a cop?"

I laughed.

Then we heard a loud scream from a woman several decks below.

We looked over the balcony rail. The black cold Atlantic sea was cheated that night once again, as it had been with Helga. There below us was Brent, hooked onto a balcony rail two decks below. He hung limp and still. We heard another scream from below.

"Good God! What's going on here?" A man with a thick Scottish brogue looked up at us leaning over his balcony. "Don't you two move!"

We were silent. Even in the aftermath and panic, I recognized him from the elevator ride our first night.

"Call the authorities, lass," the man barked at the whimpering woman as his eyes ping ponged between Brent's body and us. "Don't you dare move."

"Shall I get a doctor?" A woman called with the same Scottish trill but in a contrasting soprano register.

"We'd better," the man answered. "But I'm sure he's dead."

Sean and I stared down at Brent's body.

* * *

I had no feelings one way or another about Brent's death. I was just glad it wasn't Sean or me splayed down there or in the deep, cold, dark Atlantic.

Strangely, I flashed on my frog-eyed, enthusiastic high school history teacher who had shocked us all with the revelation that the Vikings came to the Americas before Columbus. It had shattered my lexicon of reality. Then, I thought of all the Americans in World War II who died in the depths of the Atlantic saving Europe from the Nazis. The aged veterans were dying off now, their individual sacrifices buried with them and most forgotten eventually—the years of their lives, the limbs from their bodies, and the mental peace they gave up to serve.

In a short moment, I was jolted back to my reality as a white uniformed carnival of ship personnel began fluttering about barking orders on the fateful balcony below. The Scottish couple looked up at us and pointed accusingly and emphatically.

341

They mouthed the condemnations and presumptions that were spewed by all witnesses who see half of an incident—half of the truth. These half-truths once born take on a life of their own as the witnesses' egos insist on their rightness. Thus, lies are born and grow to punish the innocent. All witnesses who observe after the onset of an act never know the genesis of a conflict and never believe they could be wrong. They become invested in being right. The proof of this lies in all our childhoods when parents punish the innocent sibling while the initial aggressor watches quietly or is theatrically crying.

"Stay there," a ship's security officer called up to us in the commotion.

"Get Dr. Witte down here," a higher ranking man ordered, but in working-class Cockney. "You, call for the captain."

There was a flurry of more white dots and upturned faces.

I dealt with my disheveled clothes and face in the bathroom. When I came out, white uniforms were surrounding Sean. The captain entered and the door slammed shut on crowd in the hall being told to move on. The white uniformed array around Sean peeled open to look at me. They stood at attention as the captain entered my stateroom.

Security confirmed Brent was dead. A quick and quite deadly broken neck from his head-first plummet.

"Veronica, how are you?" Sean asked.

"Fine." I stood with Sean. "I guess."

"This is Veronica Kennicott," Sean introduced me to the captain. "It's her stateroom. And I'm Sean O'Flarity."

"I recognize you both from last night's incident."

Sean explained that Brent was our dinner table mate and then began to tell the captain what happened, but the captain interrupted.

"It's Ms. Kennicott's stateroom. Let her tell us what happened."

I told my story. The captain listened with no reaction. His eyes could not belie his annoyance with Sean and myself and the bodies piling up during his trans-Atlantic crossing. He whispered something to his uniformed and apparent number-one man. I could not hear, but Sean did.

"What do you mean you don't want us on board again?" Sean yelled. "Someone just tried to murder this woman. It's not her fault. And it's not my fault I had to rescue her. If you would have detained Mr. Hawthorne last night on suspicion of killing his wife, none of this would have happened here tonight. We're both lucky to be alive and not on that balcony below."

"Or in the Atlantic," I added

"I mean what I said emphatically," the captain enunciated perfectly in his toff British upper-class quipped words. "As far as I can see, all you people apparently get your material from murdering each other. Take your inbred blood-bath to some other cruise line next awards cruise, because I'm going to see to it you don't sail with us again!"

Sean shouted, "Then you admit people have been murdered on board your ship?"

The captain turned and left.

The head of security stepped up to Sean. "We don't admit anything of the sort."

"Your captain just did."

"You're mistaken, sir." The man retorted, thumping Sean's chest with his index finger and our ears his loud middle-class Queen's English. "This is not your jurisdiction, Mr. Ex-NYPD Detective. Heart attacks, fights, suicides, accidents . . . those are the doctor's findings and everyone is satisfied with them. Talk to Ms. Nussbaum, your MWW president if you don't agree. My work's done. You want murders, you take it up with her or the authorities when we land. Just see how far you get."

"What do you mean by that?"

"Wessex's barristers have already sorted this out with the powers that be. And between you and me, mate, it would be easier to change the tides. Britannia hasn't ruled the waves all these centuries for nothing!"

Sean hit the officer's hand away from his chest. "Well, I've already contacted my buddies at the NYPD and they reached out to Scotland Yard. So we'll just see about that, you British stuffed-shirt rent-a-cop."

"Back off, you bloody American! And, inform your friends to keep their little mystery writers' minds to themselves. I am chalking this one up to self-defense and defense of others. That is, unless you want me to change my mind and call it out-and-out murder . . . committed by both of you two. Misplaced revenge for your fellow writer . . . premeditated revenge."

Sean, red-faced and angry, yelled, "Is that a threat?"

"Is it?" The head security officer shouted back. "Try me and we'll see if your machine is bigger than . . ."

The doctor burst into my cabin and interrupted the prelude to a cockfight. "I'm done. Let's get to dinner."

Even from a distance, I smelled the whiskey on the doctor's breath. He ignored Sean and myself. But to the doctor's credit he was not slurring his words or staggering—yet.

"He's dead. Cracked his neck. Fractured his skull," the doctor confirmed and then turned to Sean and I. "It seems this is the last night of our cruise and you are four for four. That's a record on the *Queen Anne*, the Wessex Cruise Line, and probably every cruise ship that ever sailed the ocean blue. It's a good thing we land tomorrow morning. Who knows who's next with all you mystery writers aboard? Quite exciting!"

The doctor chuckled and one security officer followed suit.

"That's enough." The head security officer glared at his underling. "Let's get the body bagged and below with the others. That is . . . if we're not out of bags."

"Yes, get the body below. Put it with the other three," Sean needled. "If you had done your job, this man would have been detained and would still be alive."

"You killed him, so I'd just count my blessings if I were you, gov," Dr. Witte whispered. "And don't prod a wasp's nest, if you get my drift. It's all been sorted out."

"And what about the other murders?" Sean reacted as the men turned to leave.

"There were no other murders. You've been warned. Both of you." The head of security left with his entourage.

"We'll see about that. We'll see what the news has to say about your great Wessex Cruise Line."

The head officer turned back, and added, "I guess you haven't been checking the news? The unfortunate deaths have been taken care of by our Wessex liaisons with a little help from your MWW president. And Mr. Hawthorne, a/k/a Mr. Brodsky, or whatever he goes by, will be too . . . by tomorrow morning. Too little, too late for your little NYPD friends."

Sean didn't respond. The security officers left and the door slammed shut.

He had been checkmated and so had I.

Or had we?

* * *

Sean and I were left in the cabin. I picked up my high heels and the cashmeres that had almost been the death of me. Sean picked up my black sequined bag, which had saved my life— along with him of course— and handed it to me.

"That's unnerving,' I said.

"I didn't like it, either. A little power goes a long way out here on this ship."

"What do you expect from a multi-national corporate

machine like this?" I tossed my sweaters back in the suitcase.

"The battle's not over though, by a long shot," Sean sat in a nearby chair. "They can't cover things up that easily."

"It wouldn't be the first time. They're fighting for their financial survival."

"They've never fought me. Come on." Sean had gotten his fight back. "Let's get to the Internet. We've got to check the damage they've done."

"Yeah, Elias and Mary can wait. I don't like being threatened, either."

I spoke with conviction despite the threat of arrest for Brent's murder—after all, I had been accused of murder before, at the Valentine Theatre. I had simply detected and exposed the real murderer.

I followed my leader, but with some trepidation.

* * *

We went to the library. It was empty at this hour. We searched through the New York and London newspapers, blogs and Internet for news on the deaths. We found the media called them just that, deaths, not murders.

We scrolled through one screen after another, silently reading what Wessex's mighty publicity machine had done with its cover-up.

As Sean did a new search, he said, "I know I transmitted enough evidence to the NYPD at least to get Amy detained when she gets off the ship whether she disposed of the other evidence or not."

"Then she will be." I gave Sean the reassurance he was looking for.

"Shh. Just a minute." He peered at the screen.

"Look. Frederick's own publicist announced his death was the result of a heart attack, too."

"Well, what else, if Wessex got to him first?"

"Yeah." Sean flipped from screen to screen.

"And there's the video Sean found of Mendel on the floor in the dining room."

We played it.

"Well, that helps explain the uphill battle on my partner's part. That looks like Mendel was partying and out of control."

"Too bad."

We opened a few more sites.

"Stop . . . there . . . see?" I pointed to a New York Times article from today and read it out loud. "'The New York Police Department confirmed last night in a statement that there was no reason to suspect foul play in the death of Otto Stein. The deaths at sea of Frederick Larsen, Oscar winner and prominent writer in Hollywood, and Mendel Weitzman, famous novelist appear to be from natural causes. Although the police investigation remains open, the NYPD can confirm that, at this stage, there would appear to be no suspicious circumstances surrounding the death of either man on the Wessex cruise liner the *Queen Anne*.'"

"No wonder my ex-partner has been hemming and hawing on the phone."

"Did he say they were reopening Otto's death?"

"Side-stepped the subject."

"My God. We're ensconced in this . . . *Queen Anne* microcosm steaming across the Atlantic with corporate thugs and, of all people, *Esther* filtering what goes out into the real world."

"You do have a way with words. I want to read one of your books, published or not."

"Thanks."

"You're welcome." Sean signed off the Internet and stood. "Look. I don't care what's on the Internet. I know my partner, and I know at a minimum he's going to get Mendel's and Frederick's murders investigated. Don't worry. Scotland Yard has to pick up Amy for questioning with what we forwarded and what my partner can do."

"We have motive down solid."

"And opportunity."

"Yes."

"That's enough to sweat her," Sean stood. "And she could break. Let's get going. Mary and Elias are waiting. We've got to fill them in . . . about Brent too, if they haven't already heard."

I followed, but not with Sean's motivations. After my near jettison off the balcony, I wanted to find Curtis before he went to his dinner. My heart already missed him. I needed to be comforted by him.

As I walked with Sean, I worried about that need—but not enough to put on the brakes.

CHAPTER 39

Angst and Appletinis

At the bar, Elias and Mary were just ordering another round for themselves. Our drinks sat untouched, waiting.

"There you are," Elias called. "We were just going to send in the troops. We got you appletinis."

Sean nodded. "Fine by me."

"Me too." I really would have preferred a glass of wine, but sat next to Mary and took a sip.

"Took you a while to get Curtis-worthy?" Mary whispered in my ear as I sat down.

"Unfortunately, no." I put the small black sequined bag that had helped save my life on the table.

Sean and I recounted Brent's attack in my cabin and my save by grabbing Sean's ankles. Both of them vented their anger and shock. They were glad we were alive and then enjoyed some bantering to relieve the gravity of what had just happened.

"So that little purse and our Sean saved your life?" Mary sipped her Martini.

"Yes." I looked over at Sean with gratitude.

"And our little Veronica saved Sean's ass, so to speak." Elias's mustache popped with his smile. "'Tini's are on me."

There were smiles all around.

"And the captain? Did he finally make the leap to murder or did he conclude Brent accidentally tried to toss you overboard?" Elias smirked.

"Yeah," Mary chuckled. "Or are they arresting you for murder, Sean?"

"They all said I acted in defense of others."

"Well, that's a change of tune." Mary shook her head.

"Not quite. He did say to back off our investigation or he might decide it was first-degree murder, with me *and* Veronica as the defendants. He accused us of avenging Helga's death!" I said.

"That's absurd. Forget it," Mary said. "He's a bag of wind. No one would avenge Helga's death!"

We all laughed. Me, not so much.

"The doctor said . . ." Sean halted mid-sentence.

"What?" Mary asked. "What did he say? Spit it out."

"It's hard to quote that incompetent whiskey-saturated quack, but he finally hit the nail on the head," Sean said. "Brent landed on his head . . . snapped his neck."

"Huh . . . too bad. In a way, he was charming." Mary said. "But a man like that deserves what he gets. He married that witch for money and couldn't stand it. Very much like the character I'm making the centerpiece of my new book when I get home."

"We shouldn't be pleased with this. It was horrible," I said.

"Oh, I'm not. Don't get me wrong, but ideas for new books are ideas," Mary insisted. "He was inspirational in more ways than one."

I found this ghoulish aspect of Mary quite off-putting. She could at least let the idea percolate privately. Then I smiled to

350

myself. Maybe I would beat her to the plot and the really amazing Brent character. I started thinking of a serial marriage murderer called *The Merry Widower*. Suddenly, Mary didn't seem so ghoulish.

"You did what you had to do, Sean." Elias ignored Mary's plans and observations. "You had no choice. If you had hesitated, Veronica wouldn't be here."

"I know. But he was a fun guy and he didn't deserve Helga's crap. Believe it or not, I have only had to take out two other people. It's hard no matter what."

"Don't feel too bad," I said. "But for you, I'd be in a body bag with Frederick, Mendel, and God forbid . . . Helga!"

Elias added, "What a wretched thought."

"But the frosting on the cake is that the captain said the MWW can't cruise on Wessex again," Sean interjected.

Mary laughed. "I'd like to see Esther's face when she finds that out."

"Speaking of murderers," Elias interrupted. "There she is . . . our other little problem."

Amy sauntered in and slid into a barstool by Heather, who was settled in and surrounded by a clique of men vying for her attention.

* * *

We watched the two. I suddenly caught a glimpse of Curtis in the hall headed toward the dining room with his group of investors. He scanned the bar. But I was buried at the back. Then, he disappeared down the hall toward the dining room. I felt cheated. I knew I wouldn't see him at dinner because we had our awards banquet. I wanted to run after him, but didn't. I couldn't have caught up with him with any modicum of grace anyway.

351

I relied on the fact that our *modus operandi* was to meet in the bar after dinner. I had to have faith our ritual hadn't changed in less than 24 hours, especially after last night.

I turned my attention back to my friends. Each of them watched Amy with eyes of cold analytical steel, but there was something else in them, too, an overlay of fear. The fear that emanates from deep within. It makes prey fight even in the hopeless face of death. I had proved that with Sean tonight. I recognized their fear because I was afraid of her, too.

"Speak of the devil. Are they at least looking into Amy for Otto's murder?" Elias asked. "Have you talked to New York?"

"Oh, yeah. Veronica and I looked at the internet and the news reports." Sean replied.

"Otto's murder is moot and Mendel's and Frederick's are being neutralized, too," I said.

"But I know my old partner will come through for Mendel and Frederick's murders. I know him, and he's still trying Otto's. If he finds anything, he'll reopen that," Sean said.

Sean explained what we had found on the Internet that afternoon. Our table was deflated and Mary was angry.

"So that little bitch is going to get away with it?" Mary seethed.

"Not if I can help it," Sean muttered. "It's not over until the fat lady sings. My former partner has a channel to Scotland Yard. And I have tipped my stewards to find me here and at the banquet when he contacts me."

"*Enai kallo.*" Elias rubbed his hands together. "Sorry. Good. It's good."

"*Enai kallo.* I'll remember that." I smiled.

"Come on guys, let's focus. Amy and Heather are thick as thieves." Mary observed the two at the bar. "And Amy's laughing and flirting like she doesn't have a care in the world."

"She doesn't know us!" I said. "Most of the hard evidence may be gone and she thinks she has outsmarted us. But we have cards left to play."

"You're tenacious, Veronica. That's good," Elias said.

"That's *kallo*." I smiled.

"Right," Elias said. "We have circumstantial evidence and even though Amy's motive is remote in time, it was rekindled by the Oscar show and the book. Veronica's right about that."

"But Sean's NYPD didn't help by closing Otto's case," Mary lashed out.

"I know. I know," Sean agreed. "Confidentially, it's a hard uphill battle for my partner . . . ex-partner. The labs are overworked and all those crime investigation television shows where the techs eat, live, and breathe their jobs are bullshit. They are nine to fivers, at most, and all lazy as a dog lying on the porch in a summer heat wave."

"But you think we have enough to get her picked up and questioned on Mendel and Frederick?" Mary asked.

"I do. I'm sure of it." Sean stood up. "But it's time for the cocktail party, And drinks are free there. Elias, Let's go. Esther asked me to present Otto's life-time achievement award tonight. I'll need the liquid support to keep a straight face.'"

Free cocktails motivated this group. But, in point of fact, my motivation was that I might still catch Curtis outside the dining room. Our table group was now just rehashing the self-evident, and starting to implode by attacking each other instead of Amy.

"Why you, Sean?" I knew Esther had asked him from my eavesdropping, but I didn't know why.

"I think because she caught me in the hall after lunch and couldn't find anyone else," Sean replied, as he signed for the bill. "She's over her head on this trip."

"Good luck," Mary said. "I would have said 'no way.'"

"I should have."

"Keep it short," Elias volunteered. "Short and sweet."

"I will."

"Sean, just a warning," I said. "I heard Amy is doing your introduction to present the award, not Esther. I overheard Esther tell Mavis that just a while ago."

As my three co-conspirators absorbed what I had told them, Sean remarked "I'd better not touch the water on the podium! Amy is going to go for us whenever the opportunity arises.."

"*Na pari i eychi*! That's 'damn it' to the rest of you. I'll be on my guard. All of us have to be, now more than ever."

As we walked by the bar, Heather caught my eye.

"Veronica, hello!" Heather called with liquored cheeriness. "Time for the awards?"

I turned to answer and locked eyes with Amy. She was defiant and confident. I pulled my eyes away from her and smiled at Heather.

"Yes," I answered cheerily.

Heather jumped off her stool and grabbed her handbag to follow us to the gala.

But an audible protest by the males around them fortunately made Heather and Amy linger in their popularity.

⌘

CHAPTER 40

Cocktails and Churlishness

As Sean, Elias, Mary and I made our way through the ship to our MWW festivities, I kept an eye out for Curtis. Passing the line going to the dining room, I lagged behind and looked at every tall man in a tuxedo.

Mary eyed me. "Looking for Curtis?"

"It's our last night. But he must already be in there."

"Too bad. Death seems to be trumping romance on this crossing."

"At least it wasn't our own."

"Not yet. Just don't get careless tonight. We still have at least twelve hours."

"And then Amy gets taken into custody."

"Right!"

I gave up my search.

* * *

When we got to the cocktail party, it was in full swing. It was the prelude to the biggest event in the mystery writers' world. It was, in fact, also one of the biggest events in the entire writing world because it had been expanded over the years to include awards for mainstream novels and other genres.

But, more than that, the revelry was heightened because the bar was hosted by MWW. Free liquor was always a powerful draw and a great social lubricator.

The crowd gravitated to the long bar lining one side of the banquet room's large cocktail and hors d'oeuvre area. Chatter and laughter swelled and undulated throughout.

The nominees needed the liquid courage to get through the night. The hangers-on needed it to embolden themselves to touch the auras of the nominated, to motivate themselves to write better and get nominated themselves next year. Agents and publishers were sucking up equally to all nominees, and savvy writers were genuflecting to their best guesses for the winners in each category. Friends are friends, but friends of value are golden.

Abutted to the cocktail area was an array of round tables with a stage and a podium beyond. Next to the podium was a table of sparkling gold pen-and-quill trophies to be awarded that night. In the center sat a very large one, obviously Otto's lifetime achievement award.

The array of tables before the podium had black tablecloths, white china, and bright red napkins. The centerpieces were of red roses and in the middle of each were a lit candle and a dagger protruding upward. The room was dimly lit and low background music oozed mysterious notes through the air. It was impeccable and beautiful.

"My God," I marveled. "I have to hand it to Esther, she has done a top-drawer job."

"Yes, she has," Elias said.

"This is amazing. All these heavy hitters in one room."

"It's a real fawn-fest," Sean chuckled. "Everyone trying to guess who won. The nominees acting oh-so-humble, but hopeful. I remember the year I was nominated. I was the darling . . . until I didn't win."

"Right." I ratcheted down my amateurish enthusiasm.

"There's a lot of tension in this room," Mary observed. "The nominees, the agents, the publishers. Everyone has a lot at stake."

"That's why the MWW plies them with free liquor," Sean whispered. "It makes the evening go smoother."

"Not always," Mary warned. "Remember the year when the best thriller winner got decked by that drunk proctologist? He thought he should have won with his first book. Imagine an amateur who spewed out one halfway decent book thinking he should have won."

"Yeah," Sean smirked. "I was a judge that year. I only got halfway through the doctor's derivative tripe. I don't know how he got published or nominated. His book was a knock-off of every hospital serial killer book ever written."

"There's no end to the M.D. ego." Mary shook her head.

"Amateurs," Elias mocked. "They have no craft and no discipline. They all write only one aberrant publishable and saleable product. This guy is lucky enough to get nominated and he punches someone out over not winning. Really?"

The word "amateurs" rang in my ears. I cowered and kept quiet. I knew I had the discipline to write more than one book; I had already proven that. But not to edit. Not yet. I knew I had to take the leap to edit, fully to master the writer's craft, to submit to an agent, and to demonstrate real discipline. If I had learned one thing on this journey, it was that writing was a business: a real, hardcore, competitive, indeed cutthroat business. But the horror stories about self-publishing and the huge chunk Octopus takes and the control it has over just giving away your books scared me, too. Too bad it was the only game in town—practically speaking.

"He thought he was going to win, get a movie deal, and retire," Sean added. "I don't blame him. Who would want to be a proctologist? Obviously, that's what motivated him to write in the first place. But we're all good, and all of us standing here are still waiting for our movie deals. All but Mary, of course," he grinned.

"Hey, I can always use more," she retorted, with an even bigger grin.

I knew that the winning writers in each category tonight would double and triple their sales. They could plaster their award wins on their web pages, on their book covers, book backs, and even their foreheads if they wanted. The losers, just as readily, would follow suit and advertise that they were nominated, if they hadn't already.

Many of the winners had a good chance of getting movie deals to put them on easy street, especially if that led to a second or third deal for other books. All savvy writers knew that writing series was where the big money was. And in movie deals, they always wanted a sequel or two optioned out in case the movie grossed well.

"Let's go get the Martinis, Elias," Sean said. "Remember . . . free."

"I want a sour apple Martini." Mary smiled. "Love them."

"Sure," Sean said. "The rest regulars all around?"

I agreed—to be part of the whole.

"You two keep an eye on our drinks," Mary warned. "We've got to be vigilant with Amy's Prolixin still around."

"Of course," Elias called back as he and Sean made a beeline for the hosted bar.

* * *

"Do you see Amy?" Mary looked around to see if she had come from the bar. "Is she . . .?"

"Veronica!" Mavis ran up, interrupted Mary, and pulled me aside.

"Esther wanted me to tell you that we tried to keep it on the QT, but the cat is out of the bag."

"What are you talking about?"

"I'm so sorry I wasn't still in the room to help you. But, then, I don't know what I could have done. You must have been terrified."

I realized Mavis was blathering about Brent and, true to her nature, lying by saying that she ever tried to keep it on the Q.T. Even now, her voice was ramped up to attract attention. She had undoubtedly told anyone and everyone who would listen that she was the roommate of a murder victim—or almost murder victim. I realized that she had tracked me down here for the intimate details in order to repeat them, particularly to Esther. It was all about *her*—again.

"Mavis, can you keep your voice down?"

"Oh, sure. I get it!" Mavis blurted, attracting stares and ears.

"Shh."

"I suspected Brent killed Helga," Mavis lowered her decibel level, but only in half. "Did you have proof? Was that why he went after you?"

"Who told you all this?"

"The doctor reported to us, of course." Mavis preened in the limelight.

"'Us?"

"Esther and me. And Esther sent me to talk to you first hand. She doesn't trust anything the doctor says. Who would?"

"You could have fooled me." Sarcasm laced every single one of my words.

Mavis didn't care that I was still here and alive; she merely wanted to trade on my information to ingratiate herself further to Esther.

"This is an ongoing investigation and I can't talk about it." I quoted a line from many a mystery book, including mine.

"But . . ."

I cut Mavis off mid-sentence with a quick exit and went back to Mary, who was schmoozing with Anne now.

Mavis retreated. She had gotten the public flurry of self-importance she wanted and knew she was not getting any information from me.

* * *

With Sean and Elias intent on the free liquor, I stepped back to where Mary was and stayed with her now, as close as two peas in a pod. Amy's expected Southampton detention tomorrow morning would not keep us safe tonight.

"It should be a great banquet," Mary said. "And . . ."

"Veronica!" Anne interrupted Mary. "I am so glad to see you with us. I hear we almost lost you."

"Oh?" I knew who she had heard that from—my *dear* Mavis.

"And poor Brent," Anne Britished at me with crisp consonants. "I can't believe that handsome gentleman would have done you harm."

"Neither could we," Mary added, "Until we saw Helga in a puddle of blood."

Anne damned her proper British manners and just bulled ahead. "Imagine the utter horror of living with a woman like Helga, though. She always pushed him so. Remember, we only saw the tip of the iceberg at our dinners. She attacked everyone, really. And I shan't forget her discourteous, not to say nigh unforgivable, abuse of my offer to pay for wine for the table at dinner. Still, she didn't deserve death for that, and such a hideous one!"

"Yes." We were going to be subjected to this woman's crisp English drivel whether we liked it or not. I agreed with this disconnected old British bag who had the nerve to have said *poor* Brent to the person he almost threw off her own balcony.

"Pushed?" Mary chided Anne. "Poor choice of words."

"Quite so," Anne acknowledged with a wry little smile, exposing her oh-so-British yellowed teeth with receding gum lines. "Well, anyway, all of us were with Helga and Brent, if only for a few evenings this cruise, and I for one was almost ready to kill her, too. What an arrogant, unpleasant woman."

"That's putting it mildly," I smiled, thinking "You stuffy British twit."

"I just don't understand, though," Anne ruminated, oblivious to everything and everyone else. "The news reports said Helga fell because of the storm. Obviously, you knew more or Brent wouldn't have . . ."

"I'm sorry. I really can't say. This is all under investigation."

"Oh?" Anne was offended that I wouldn't analyze Helga's demise with her.

"Well, I'm sure they'll sort it all out. Isn't that the quaint British euphemism you all use?" Mary did some British bashing to get rid of the woman.

Anne left in a huff for chattier pastures.

"She can take her flower murders and stuff them." Mary said.

I laughed.

"This is going to be a long . . . long evening." Mary shook her head.

"I am starting to view British accents as speech impediments . . . for that matter, brain impediments, as well."

"Crack observation." Mary mocked in a stilted British accent.

"Funny!" I nodded toward the door. "Over there. We have company. Amy at three o'clock, with Heather. Just entering."

"What in the hell is a nice girl like Heather doing with Amy, anyway?" Mary studied the incongruous duo.

"Maybe she's not such a nice girl."

Heather led the way to the bar while Amy followed, scanning the room. Amy spotted Mary and myself and glared at us. She whispered to Heather. Heather glanced over but did not smile.

"Maybe," Mary said. "Hey, do you think Amy's going to represent Heather's mystery books?"

"I wouldn't think so. Heather has one of the best literary agents in the business. He's gotten all her science fiction sold. Authors usually don't trade down, especially down to Amy's mid-level."

Elias and Sean came back with Martinis all around.

* * *

Elias handed Mary her Martini. "No sour apple. Only the usual."

"Too bad."

"I got yours very dry."

"Thanks. This is the only way I'm going to get through the night." Mary took a drink. "Mmm, that hits the spot, but sour apple would have been nicer."

Sean handed me mine. "Liquid courage."

I took a sip and involuntarily winced.

"It's an acquired taste," Sean laughed.

Elias tapped our Martini glasses all around and toasted, "To us. May we disembark safely, and most importantly, alive!"

"And may death not disembark with us." Sean did a second toast.

"How poetic," Mary initiated an enthusiastic interactive universal glass clicking.

"You are a surprising man, for a cop."

"Detective. And I'm counting on Amy being in custody tomorrow so I can enjoy my stay in London."

"Me too," Elias agreed.

"But first we have to get through the open seating here tonight," Sean said. "We have to stay clear of Amy's Prolixin, stick together, and disembark tomorrow devoid of body bags . . . our own, that is."

"Sean's right," Elias added.

"I changed my mind. You are not poetic. Just gruesome," Mary said.

"You should talk, Mary," Sean said. "Ms. Slasher of the Year."

"Let's grab a table up in the front now." Elias led the charge

⌘

CHAPTER 41

The Devil Comes to Dinner

As we caterpillared through the array of empty round tables to the front, Esther stepped up to the podium on the riser. She was stunning in her silver sequined evening gown literally painted on her older, thin and fit body. She was coiffed and her makeup impeccable. Her eyes sparkled as she looked out over the assembling diners. This was her moment.

"Testing, testing," Esther's microphoned voice boomed through the room.

As Esther struggled to adjust the microphone, it emitted an equally loud high squeal. A server rushed to her rescue, but not before I covered one ear with my non-Martini'd hand. Other lookers-on followed suit.

The sound was quelled and Esther proceeded in a moderated boom—feedback squeals squelched. She was poised as always and spoke in her slow, self-important cadence, enunciating every word.

"Welcome everyone to our biennial gala awards dinner. As you know, I am Esther Nussbaum, the master of ceremonies for tonight, and it's that time! The time you have waited for these two long years."

There was a thunder of cheers and applause.

"If you will all be seated, we will begin our banquet and then proceed with the all-important presentation of the awards. The recognition we will bestow on our fellow writers is reported worldwide. Each award recognizes great works, great careers amongst us. It also launches new careers to carry on the MWW torch after the old guard is gone—and, as we know, our present losses are great."

There was a murmur through the gathering.

"We do mourn the untimely loss of our fellow writers. Mendel Weitzman, a stalwart amongst us for many years, Helga Brodsky, the successful and incredibly prolific luminary, both winners of several past MWW awards, and the accomplished Hollywood screenwriter and double Oscar winner Frederick Larsen. And, it goes without saying that we suffered an especially untimely loss with the death of Otto Stein, whom we will honor with a posthumous Lifetime Achievement Award tonight. They will all be deeply missed."

The applause rose. As it receded, Esther's voice rang from the microphone again. "But we must begin. Begin in order to finish, recognizing those most deserving in our difficult and challenging profession, even as we grieve for those we have lost before their time. Dinner is about to be served. And don't worry. The bar will remain open throughout the evening and there is wine at the tables. In that vein, can you all please take your seats?

There was a smattering of approval voiced at the confirmation of free booze all night, especially from the already imbibed attendees, including Sean.

Sean called out. "Hear, hear!"

The crowd followed their leader's orders and herded into the tables for seats.

"Grab that table by the stairs." Mary moved her chubby body forward with incongruous speed toward one of the front row tables. "Easier to get up and down to present."

"Not that thirty feet make a difference," Elias mocked.

Elias helped lead the charge, circling around in a second path to assure we got our chosen table and our four seats. Most of the heavy hitters in MWW and other presenters followed suit and started filling up the front tables.

We procured seats facing the podium, which was always a plus at an awards dinner. Mary sat next to me with Sean and Elias beside her. I was happy. I hated having to twist my neck the entire night to see the recipients get their awards and make their predictable speeches.

The adjacent tables filled fast with groups that had bonded, and optimistic nominees who also wanted to be close to accept their hoped-for awards.

As the tables formed, the sound level was rising with the excitement of the evening and anticipation of who would win.

Our table remained empty, but for us four. After all, with our activities we had not had a chance to get to know many of the other writers. Not to mention that three of our original dinner companions were dead, Heather was now friends with a murderer, and we had insulted Anne. But that dotty old Brit deserved the affront after she sympathized with Brent who had tried to toss me in the Atlantic.

We were a quartet—alone.

Mavis eyed two seats for her and Esther directly under the podium at the table next to us. They were between Anne and a tuxedoed man with his back to me. Mavis always went for the men. However, there were dinner napkins draped over the back of the chairs to reserve them. Mavis started to remove them, but the man stopped her with a glance and his hand on the nearest chair.

Mavis retreated, looked over at our table, and caught my eye. I ignored her and looked straight ahead at the stage. I didn't want to spend my last evening with her demeaning comments about my amateur status. However, I was out of luck. From the podium, Esther signaled Mavis to take seats at our table.

Mavis did as directed and I was stuck. Mavis sat next to Sean and grabbed the napkin for the seat immediately to her left. She shook it with a flurry and placed it ceremoniously over the back of the chair for Esther.

"Good evening, all. Esther is coming to sit with us," Mavis announced with pride that was wasted on us. "This is going to be a wonderful evening, isn't it?"

"Yes," Elias agreed, ever the pleaser.

Esther's amplified voice silenced our greetings. "We had 'Reserved for Presenters' signs for the front tables, but Mavis forgot them. So can you other presenters please fill in the seats down front? It will help move the ceremonies along later."

No one obeyed. Why should they leave their friends and colleagues and fill in the few seats smattered up front? In point of fact, they were not nominated for an award and had no real investment in moving anything along, especially with the open bar. Esther should have asked the nominees to come forward; they might have obeyed to assist the progress of the proceedings.

"I left the signs here at the bar," Mavis defended herself to our table, as if we cared. "And someone threw them away. How could I have known?"

"Understandable." Elias remained the proverbial peacemaker and pleasant dinner companion. "But a shame."

"Yes, you see my point. Thank you." Mavis was grateful that someone had acknowledged her plight.

"Of course."

Elias sympathized with such insincerity that I thought Mavis would have seen through him. But she didn't. She simply smiled warmly and gratefully at him.

Esther concluded at the podium. "Enjoy your meal and we'll begin our ceremonies with our coffee and dessert."

Esther stood at the steps on the riser until a nearby server offered her his hand. She came down gingerly in her tight sparkling dress.

* * *

Esther joined us at our table and continued complaining about anything and everything that had gone wrong or probably would, whether imagined or actual. She intermittently gave Mavis a Helga-esque evil eye. Despite our differences, I felt badly for Mavis.

"Well, thank God you didn't misplace the awards envelopes," Esther glowered at Mavis.

Mavis, cowed, picked up the basket of rolls, with the usual seeded flat crackers and cheese-drizzled bread sticks.

"Would you like one, Esther?"

"No, I don't see any whole wheat." Esther turned her nose up.

"Neither do I. What poor form." Mavis passed the basket the other way without partaking either.

"Well, it looks like it will be a marvelous evening." Elias eased the tension. "We have several presenters here excited to do their parts."

"Indeed." Esther glanced condescendingly at me.

Elias took the basket. "*Efharisto*. Thank you," Elias took two rolls, Greeking happily—never to be defeated. "We Greeks love our bread. It's not a meal without it."

I sat quietly. I was at the table with my friends and at Mary's side. We had all made a mutual pact of protection. I did not want to attract more Mavis attacks and would not be forced out if she started.

Just then, to my horror, Agnes, Jody, and Herbert came running up.

"Veronica," Agnes boomed. "We were looking for you. What happened with Brent?"

"Is it true? That . . ." Jody joined in.

"Did he really . . ." Herbert interrupted in his irritating, nasal, tenor voice.

I replied, "What?"

All three of my classmates focused on me in unison, like three baby birds chirping for a worm dangling from their mother's beak.

". . . try to kill you?" Herbert finished his question.

"And murder Helga?" Agnes prodded.

"What happened?" Jody demanded.

"This is a celebration tonight and . . ." Elias tried to stop them.

"But we want to know if . . ." Agnes insisted.

"It's an ongoing investigation," Mary interrupted with a booming voice tantamount to a judge's gavel. "No more questions. Period."

The three shut up and I ignored them. I busied myself with my roll. I poured olive oil and balsamic vinegar onto my plate, broke a piece, soaked it, and enjoyed it.

Mavis, who always wanted to be the authority, ignored Elias and Mary's shutdown of the subject. She took center stage and explained.

"Evidently, Brent might have had something to do with his wife's death and . . ." Mavis looked directly at me ". . . someone knew it! And so . . ."

"Excuse me," Amy interrupted Mavis and shouldered Herbert aside. "This is my seat."

As if the night couldn't get any worse, Heather and Amy arrived. They descended on our table from behind without warning.

Of course it wasn't her seat, but Amy pulled out the chair next to me and sat down.

"Huh?" Herbert was bewildered. "But I was going to sit . . ."

Herbert could not stand his ground and solidify his claim on the seat.

My body stiffened as Amy settled next to me. I instinctively moved my water glass to the left away from her. I grabbed my Martini, took a drink, and did not put it down. I needed it now, without a Prolixin kicker. Images of Mendel and Frederick's horrific Prolixin deaths flashed across my mind. Amy had sat next to me assuming I was the weak one of our quartet and could be culled from the herd. There had already been one attempt at culling and she obviously presumed she could do a better job than Brent.

I was afraid. I scooted my chair back to leave. Then, I felt Mary's fingers hard on my knee. We glanced at each other for a microsecond. She was brave and true to our plan. Me? I was a coward ready to run and she knew it.

I obeyed Mary's fingers and relaxed into my chair again. We had to stick together. More than that, it was a perfect set up for Amy to get caught in a mistake if she was emboldened enough and stupid enough to

I stayed. I recommitted to the role of investigator and author extraordinaire. I held my ground with my associates. We were together in this to the end. Body bags or buddies forever. I personally didn't like the fact that I was the one sitting next to Amy, but that is how the hand was dealt.

"Sit," Amy ordered Heather, who hesitated after Herbert's objection.

Heather sat next to Amy, right under Jody's nose.

"But . . . ," Jody grabbed the dinner napkin from the next place setting and sat quickly.

It was musical chairs. Agnes grabbed the last chair and Herbert lost the game. There were ten little Indians at the table and Herbert was the odd man out.

"We'll fill you in later, Herbert," Agnes told Herbert, who stood there dismayed. "There's a seat over there."

Agnes pointed to a table with a single seat nearby. Two attractive women, one younger and one Herbert's age, book-ended the seat. Herbert's lips turned up in a smile of his yellowed crooked teeth as he honed in on it.

He raced over to grab it, having learned that speed was of the essence—a quality he generally lacked, both physically and mentally.

* * *

Our table settled down in silence.

Elias, ever the pleasant host, greeted Agnes and Jody and then introduced them all around, even though it was essentially unnecessary.

Mavis then grabbed the limelight and filled in everyone about Brent's death. I was silent even in the face of Mavis's half-truths.

Amy zeroed in on Mavis with piercing and quizzical eyes. She listened with the intensity of a judge conducting a trial in a pivotal legal case. But she was not guaranteeing justice; she was evading it. She was evaluating just how effective our foursome could be.

"So . . ." Amy turned to me. "Why don't you tell us the reason Brent chose now as the time to off his wife, whom he had endured for years?"

"Uh . . ." I froze under Amy's predatory glare.

"How could Veronica know what was in his mind?" Sean came to my rescue and then baited Amy. "As you know, murderers can lie in wait even for years and then act at the slightest provocation when they think the time is right."

"That's for sure," Elias said. "The killer's mind is something that has been studied for centuries. Look at my people's ancient Greek tragedies written by the greats: Aeschylus, Sophocles, and Euripides. We mystery writers do that in our own way as well."

Mary spoke up and completed the trio's frontal assault on Amy.

"But then, of course, maybe Amy can analyze a killer's mind better than all of us. I mean, as an agent, she must have a well-honed critical sense about that after reading so many submissions."

A vacuum of shrill profound silence fell on our table. Amy did not answer Mary. Instead, she studied the four of us.

Fortunately or unfortunately, the dependably oblivious Jody took this opportunity to machine-gun questions at me about why I suspected Brent had murdered Helga.

She was cut short by none other than Esther, who had been detached and aloof from the conversation. She took charge and turned the subject to the awards. She was going to have no more talk of murder at her exalted table. Her purpose and that of the MWW was not going to be waylaid by some amateur like me taking center stage at *her* event.

Esther had, unknowingly, and I was sure, unintentionally, done me a service. I didn't want to answer Jody, Amy or anyone else.

"Esther's right," Mavis expectedly parroted Esther's sentiments. "This is a celebratory night. Let's recognize our fellow writers and enjoy the evening together. Even if all of us may not have the credentials."

I just shook my head. The comment went over the heads of Agnes and Jody, who were pleased with anything that came out of the gospel mouth of their teacher.

I had to admit, Mavis was in rare form trying to rehabilitate herself with Esther. However, Esther just looked down again and reviewed her note cards for the awards. With her head down, I caught a glimpse of gray roots at her part. I smiled at the one imperfection.

Whether wise or not, my friends had confronted Amy. I kept my peripheral vision on this triple murderer sitting next to me and looked for any sign of the Prolixin. When she started fumbling with her evening bag on her lap, my heartbeat and my flight-or-fight adrenaline pumped.

Amy finally put her small gold evening bag on the table between her and Agnes.

I knew her last opened vial of Prolixin was in that bag, or, possibly, in her hand below the table now.

I finished the last of my Martini and set it down—never to drink again at this dinner with Amy.

⌘

CHAPTER 42

All Hands a Wreck

I missed the *Queen Anne* gourmet menus with sumptuous descriptions of dinner choices. We all did. Tonight was banquet style with a menu picked by Esther.

"Yuck," Mary whispered to me. "Salmon or vegetarian pasta. I suppose Esther or Mavis arranged this."

"Mavis," I grumbled. "She's so pedestrian."

We chose, begrudgingly. The servers poured our choice of red or white wine and left bottles on the table. Then we got a generic salad of assorted baby lettuce, arugula, spinach, orange and red tomato slices, and Parmesan croutons.

"Even the salad is dull," Mary murmured.

"But colorful!" I replied.

Mary grunted.

Observing the salad serving, I decided there was no way Amy could have Prolixined my salad or those of my cohorts. Nor could she have laced the dressing, because the servers drizzled dressing for us. But, even though Amy had not touched my salad or the dressing, I couldn't take one bite. Objectively,

I knew it was safe. I had watched mine and presumed Amy was not into mass murder, at least not aboard the *Queen Anne*. But I still just shoved it around on my plate while my associates ate heartily. I couldn't drink my wine or my water, either. I just couldn't.

"Don't care for the salad?" Amy whispered to me.

"What?"

Amy then spoke past me to Mary. "So did you go to the afternoon panel discussions or did you write all day? I understand there are several on board vying for the most prolific authorial throne . . . now that Helga is gone. I presume you're one of them."

Mary did not jump to the bait. "I enjoyed the panel discussions, but I didn't see you at any."

"I didn't, either," Sean added.

"No?" Amy smiled. "I might have been doing some housecleaning!"

"Housecleaning? On board a ship?" Jody intruded with a loud incongruous laugh awkwardly trying to impress Esther and the heavy hitters at this elite table.

"She means work." Agnes clarified with the authority of a schoolteacher. "Not literal housecleaning."

"Oh." Jody was unabashed, as usual.

I kept a poker face, but I knew what Amy meant. Agnes and Jody did not. Amy was referring to the literal *house cleaning*—of the evidence. She was telling us that all the evidence in her cabin had been destroyed—except, of course, the Prolixin she kept close.

"Beautiful bag," I said to Amy.

I wished I had x-ray vision to confirm that the last vial of Prolixin was in there and also not in her hand. It would be solid evidence. In addition, I would feel safer, at least from the Prolixin, which was apparently Amy's murder vehicle-of-choice this cruise.

"Thank you," Amy gloried in patting it lightly. "The minute I saw it, I bought it. It literally takes your breath away doesn't it?"

"Yes. It's *killer,*" I defied Amy.

Amy had her left hand on her lap under the table. She could be holding the Prolixin. She only brought one hand up at a time to eat her salad or drink her wine. I wished she had taken a roll, instead of a cheesy breadstick, and needed to do a two-handed tear to dip in the olive oil.

"So do you like being an agent?" Agnes asked Amy.

We all knew where this inquiry was going.

"It has its moments." Amy was not pleased to be the focus.

"Are you looking for new clients?" Jody smiled.

"No. My plate is full." Amy was blunt.

Jody's face fell and Agnes looked down. Another vacuum of silence filled the table, like a black hole surrounded by the cheerful chatter at other tables.

"It can't be that full, can it?" Heather was embarrassed for her new friend.

Elias came to the rescue.

"Are you agent shopping, Jody?"

"I will be. I haven't finished my book yet."

"You just started it?"

"Oh, no I have been working hard for years . . . editing and stuff."

"Ah, interesting." Elias fumbled for his wallet and handed Jody a card. "Then call me when it's done. I'll connect you up with someone. And you too, Agnes. I presume you're not quite finished yet either?"

Elias knew hangers-on when he saw them. Writers who wrote and wrote and wrote—never to finish anything.

"Not quite," Agnes admitted.

Jody beamed as she reached across and took the card and Agnes covetously took the second.

I knew Elias was making an empty gesture, and so did everyone at the table except Jody and Agnes. "Working on it for years" was code for *never* finishing in amateur-author speak. Everyone has a story they think is worthy of a book or even a film. And everyone in L.A. is working on a book or a film script. L.A. is ground zero for "talking" about books and scripts, not writing them. Or, if the writing has begun, never finishing it. Or, if finished, never polishing and editing and publishing. I was the poster child for all of the latter.

Elias was savvy. He knew his offer was empty. He knew it was very unlikely that Jody or Agnes would ever finish their in-progress books. And, the chance either would edit it or get it ready to submit with a good query letter and synopsis was even more remote. Naturally, I knew *that* more intimately than anyone else at the table.

Elias had hit a home run and slid safely to the plate pleasing everyone, with absolutely no cost to him.

* * *

The wine flowed as the salad plates were cleared and dinner came with no other incidents.

Esther quietly peeked at her presentation cards. Jody talked her book to death, encouraged by Elias sharing his card. Heather listened politely and Amy ignored her. Agnes watched Jody like a hawk. She wanted to get in on the Jody amateur-hour bandwagon. The bandwagon where novices bored everyone to death with the details of their books. They think people are actually interested in their undeveloped characters, unexecuted plots, and embryonic drafts.

I knew in the professional company at this table there were only two kinds of books—the published and the unpublished. And it was clear no one was listening to Jody. They also ignored Agnes trying to derail Jody by interjecting

377

her Italian-American family novel into Jody's oration about her coming of age American frontier novel.

The four of us were actually busy keeping an eye on Amy. And Amy felt and was enjoying her power. She had not been neutered by our comments.

Agnes couldn't stand being back-seated by Jody and terminated Jody's lecture on how to write authentically about frontier life.

"So who's going on the British writers' tour after the cruise?" Agnes asked.

"I am." Jody raised her hand with wine-induced enthusiasm.

"Besides you and me and Herbert. Obviously."

No one else acknowledged going. Nor did I. I decided I was canceling my tour no matter what the cost. Being on a bus tour for three days with the three stooges was not my idea of anything other than torture. I would stay in London and do the play circuit until my flight left. I could pleasantly, and by myself, relive my past as a college theater arts major and my amateur endeavors in Hollywood with old college friends. Then, Curtis popped into my mind. Perhaps he had the time—this man who had become my sexual renaissance—this man I was falling, plummeting, for.

"Too bad," Jody said. "It will be fun."

I sensed that the entire table shared a collective shudder at the thought of being with those three doing anything—even the ever-kind Elias and accommodating Heather.

Esther signaled our server—her hand and wrist, as usual, adorned with diamonds marking her recently acquired status as a married and wealthy woman. I knew her past mystery series had not earned her such baubles.

* * *

"Can you get the tables cleared and serve dessert? Tell the maître d' to do it quickly. It's time for our program. And I want a coffee now, please."

"Yes, ma'am." He took Esther's half-eaten plate and then went for Mary's.

"Hold up." Mary seized it. "I'm finishing."

He let it go.

Sean's plate was empty and gone, but he grabbed one more roll as the server cleared the basket.

"Another, sir?"

"Nope, just this one and my dessert and coffee."

"Certainly, sir"

"I'll have Earl Gray tea." I dutifully released my uneaten dinner, which had probably remained Prolixin free.

I hadn't been able to do more than play with my food sitting next to Amy, but I downed several rolls and a seeded flat bread.

"Certainly. Decaf or regular?"

"Regular."

Heather followed suit. "The same for me, thank you."

Amy got a caffeinated double espresso. Caffeine all around was the consensus. Obviously, the table, and probably the entire room, were hyping themselves for a long-winded ceremony, at minimum, given Esther's unfortunately predictable and numbingly methodical droning.

Agnes finally wedged her way into the conversation again and nattered on about her unfinished book.

"My husband loves my take on the Italian-American experience in Long Beach," Agnes basked in the limelight—once Jody's. "He says that I caught the flavor perfectly, especially the religious overlays."

I leaned over and whispered to Mary, "How can you eat?"

"I can always eat. Besides she's next to you, not me!" Mary finished the last of her salmon, put her fork on her plate, and let it be cleared.

She was right. Brent's attempt on my life, however unconnected, made me an acceptable target. And I was within Amy's orbit. Within easy reach of being surreptitiously Prolixined.

"Your husband edits it?" Elias asked Agnes.

"No. I just tell him about it."

"Ah," Elias responded robotically.

"It does sound interesting," Heather smiled, salvaging the moment.

Agnes was encouraged and prattled on to Heather until Jody bent Heather's other ear stereophonically. I noticed in the cacophony of the evening that being amongst adults, instead of her elementary school students, had speeded up Agnes's speech, and perhaps even elevated her vocabulary.

As our desserts and beverages came, I marveled at the elephant in the room. No one mentioned the deaths on the *Queen Anne,* including the little-old-death-purveyor Amy. It was also the end of the meal and nearing the end of Amy's chance to use her Prolixin. I was wound tight waiting for her to act. Her window of opportunity was narrowing.

Tonight was progressing and tomorrow we landed.

The server placed Amy's double espresso in front of her. Then, he put my teacup with a nice sized teapot of the Early Gray before me. I poured a generous hit of the caffeine into my cup. I was confident this was a Prolixin-free offering. This entire cruise I had been delighted that the Brits' individual teapots were huge, unlike the tiny restaurant ones. The Brits knew tea lovers because they were a nation of them.

"I'll just grab the cream." Amy suddenly reached across my dessert and cup of steamy Early Gray for the creamer.

"No." I grabbed her wrist.

My teacup toppled and the creamer fell from Amy's fingers. Tea and cream splattered the table, Amy, Heather, Agnes, Jody, and me. I didn't care. I was not going to have Amy reaching over my tea, my last chance to consume anything.

"What was that?" Agnes exclaimed, taking her napkin and stopping the flow of tea towards her on the table. "You two are worse than the kids in the lunch room at school."

"I'm sure there's enough cream on this boat to get more," Jody mediated.

"Ship," Agnes corrected her.

"Yes, you're right . . . ship," Jody said. "We'll get more."

"Let go," Amy seethed at me.

"What?" I realized I still had my hand clenched around her wrist. "I . . ."

I started to apologize but stopped. Instead, I twisted her palm up and looked to see if she had the vile of Prolixin in it.

"Ow." Amy objected. "Let me go."

"You're hurting her," Heather said.

I looked down at Amy's hand. It was empty. She had set me up.

"Let go," Esther commanded. "Are you crazy?"

"No, I'm sorry. I just . . ."

"Just what?" Esther was incredulousness.

I released Amy's wrist.

"She was just trying to pass the cream." Elias defended me with diplomacy.

"Yes," Heather agreed.

"It could have happened to any of us." Elias said.

"Not to any of us who were table-trained," Mavis muttered.

"I'm sorry. I was trying to pass the cream." I took Elias's lead.

"Here, madam."

Our server brought more cream and then cleaned up the tea and cream from the table efficiently, handing the splatter victims new napkins.

"Of course." Mary took her queue from Elias. "I've collided with the creamer many a time."

"But Veronica grabbed Amy's arm and . . ." Jody stopped when she saw Agnes's teacher-like evil eye.

Amy smiled, showing her properly bleached teeth and two small evenly matched dimples. She had achieved her purpose and played a chess piece that fully discredited me. She had made a fool of me. She was playing cat and mouse with our quartet.

I cowered back into my chair. I didn't say another word. Fortunately, I didn't have to. Esther got up and started the ceremonies.

The room lights dimmed and the riser spots went up at the podium.

With every presentation, all I could focus on was Amy. She had demoralized me. I was even more vulnerable now because I was unsure of myself. I couldn't act so precipitously again. She knew it. All I wanted was for her to be detained tomorrow morning when she disembarked.

But would she be? And would I be alive to see it?

CHAPTER 43

An Unexpected Honor

The awards ceremony was just that, an awards ceremony, with its own dull rhythm—broken up with vapid remembrances of our fallen comrades; couched in regret, not outrage, at their murders. The audience of mystery writers was buzzing, but attentive and even somber when required.

In truth, however, the room pulsed with desires to win, regrets at not being nominated, hope for next year, and hopelessness at muses gone missing.

As the ceremony unfolded in all its repetitive nature, the presenters, being writers, tried their best to be interesting. And at the correct moments, they were sad and respectful about the recent deaths.

The presenters were word wizards and masters of storytelling. Each speaker added jokes, sarcasm, witticisms, quotes, and a mention of our fallen fellow authors as they rattled off the names of the nominees. However, in the end these people, all of them, were ultimately handicapped by being word crafters and not entertainers—and they were not charismatic speakers. They necessarily lived an isolated existence with their characters and their plots. Thus, they flopped more than they succeeded and elicited only minimal smatterings of polite laughs. What had been so unique about Frederick was that he had triumphed in Hollywood, not only because of his talent, but because he had a high social IQ. Mendel had reason to have been jealous.

The acceptors, much to everyone's regret, did nothing unique. They abounded in cookie-cutter "thank you's" to the deserved and undeserved. It was serial brown-nosing to the writing world and to families who didn't sincerely support these financially draining insular writers, at least at first, anyway. Every speech was a meaningless monologue of rapid-fire and unfamiliar names—unfamiliar particularly to me and every other newcomer here.

I listened like a trapped animal as the redundant accolades for Mendel, Frederick, Helga and Otto trickled through the speeches while the evening painfully wore on. I also endured the occasional more iconic references to Frederick and Otto. I knew too much of the back-story to join in the applause at the pauses the speakers took just for that purpose.

Mary, Elias, and Sean were enjoying seeing their colleagues recognized. Mavis managed an artifice of interest. Agnes and Jody were in awe. I believed Jody would have taken notes if she had pen and paper with her. Amy was on autopilot doing timely, appropriate and mime-like silent claps throughout the program. She was a picture of control and blending in. Heather's eyes sparkled either from the wine or perhaps because of genuine interest. It was clear why she was such a success and so popular.

I whispered to Mary, "Why does Heather like Amy?"

"No clue."

"And look at Amy. She has no fear."

"She feels invincible."

"Is she?"

"No. Sean's done his work. Scotland Yard will get her. You'll see tomorrow."

Amy slowly turned her attention from the speaker to our soft buzz of whispers. She put her hand on her evening bag. A shiver went down my spine as I clapped for the winner walking up to the podium.

Maybe because I was an amateur, I had faith in justice and in our investigation. I had faith that law enforcement actually wanted to get the murderers. I put my faith in the system. Past experience should have taught me something different. I suppose I just could not become a total cynic.

"Well, I'm next at the podium. Best unpublished mystery novel." Mary smoothed her hair back into her bun. "Tell me, why didn't you enter this category?"

"I don't know. I . . ."

I was tired of lies. I stopped midsentence. I was just pleased I had talked a good game. Mary actually believed that my books were edited and ready to be entered, I guessed. I hadn't thought of the contest for myself because, of course, I knew I was an unabashed liar when it came to my authorial life. I desperately wanted to get at least one of my books edited for the next MWW awards contest, though. I would try because I would lose my credibility with my new friends if I didn't.

"I could do it," I thought. "I could".

"You're just going to have to submit next time. If you're worried about Esther, don't be. The submissions are anonymous, so Esther can't get you black-balled."

"That's good." I wanted off the subject.

"Yes." Mary shook her head. "Oops! Here I go."

Mary got up to and went forward to stand at the steps at the side of the riser for her entrance and presentation. I looked over at Sean and Elias. They were enjoying themselves. Amy whispered intermittently to Heather. Agnes and Jody clapped starry-eyed with loud alcohol-punctuated vigor every time they had a chance.

Agnes called out to Mavis across the table, "That could be one of your students next year winning. One of us!"

"Yes," Jody raised her glass of wine to Mavis and took a drink. "You're the best and so are your students. Right, Veronica?"

"Of course." Too bad Herbert wasn't here to round out the idiocy of the trifecta.

"Thank you," Mavis preened. "That would make me proud."

She glowed at the recognition because she knew she wasn't going to get any other accolades tonight, especially for her stale and defunct writing.

Before I upchucked, I stood and went back to the bar. I wanted a fresh glass of wine that I wasn't afraid to drink. Needless to say, I had bothered neither with the table wine nor any more of the Earl Grey tea in my teapot.

* * *

At the bar, I got a glass of Cabernet. I studied the platform, the diminishing number of trophies yet to be awarded, and the spotlighted pageantry. It looked less important from the bar so far away. And, concomitantly, the writer's world I aspired to was diminished proportionately at this particular moment. Why wouldn't it be? This cruise had turned from an authorial adventure into a string of murders and a fight for my life. Death was too close, too physical, and too personal.

"What time is it?" I asked the female bartender.

"Half past ten, ma'am." She sparkled at me with her plump cherry-glossed lips and a smile with rounded, full cheeks that signaled her fertile, ready years.

"Thanks."

The word *ma'am* shot *old lady* through my anxious, fear-riddled mind. I gulped my wine to take the edge off.

The loudspeaker hurled Esther's voice in all its prodding monotony at me.

"And now Mary O'Connell! She is our own very successful suburban housewife who writes those bestselling graphic slasher sex crime novels. She will present the award for best unpublished mystery novel. One of these lucky unpublished authors, judged anonymously, will win a contract with a publishing house. We have no idea who this new rising star will be, but he or she will officially be one of the elite amongst us. I wish all the nominees well. They are our future."

I laughed to myself. I knew with Esther's unadmitted ghostwriting and Mavis's writer's block that neither one of them were our future.

Mary headed up to the podium with surprising agility. Her secret? The sensible shoes peeking from under her long dress. She was as frumpy in her dressy evening clothes as she was during the day. I took my glass of wine and headed back to our table.

It would be Prolixin free as long as I didn't set it down. And I wouldn't. I needed it—all of it.

* * *

At the podium, Mary grabbed her audience with her first sentence. Unexpectedly, she was an amazingly entertaining speaker with impeccable timing. Unlike most of the other writers, she was humorous and charismatic with a marvelous array of personal anecdotes and jokes. She woke up the entire flagging audience. And artfully, before her presentation, she said a few seemingly heartfelt words about our departed colleagues.

"And, now, I am so happy to present this token of recognition to the next generation of mystery writers—not to mention the prized publishing contract."

There was a wave of chuckles.

"We all know that a nomination is noteworthy. So congratulations to all of them and best of luck in the future. And, of course, we wish the winner much success with his or her soon to be published book. Everyone here will support you and embrace you as one of us. Whether for good or for ill, you will be a member of this circle, this family made up of the well-known and the too well-known, the famous and the infamous, the friendly and the reclusive."

There was a smattering of laughter and Mary paused. I drank my wine and listened. She was a brilliant, unassuming woman.

"The first nominee is Thomas Heitel, a Professor from Bakersfield State, for *Death in the Farmlands,* a mystery about a serial murderer raised in Bakersfield, California. Our second, Shanisa Moore, is a lawyer . . . turned ice cream parlor owner . . . turned author who has used arsenic as her vehicle for murder in a fresh new book called *The Ice Cream Murders: Pistachio.* It's clear we have many flavors to go! A great hook for a series. Our third nominee is Thomas Coyne, M.D. who has used his medical knowledge in *Global Mutants* to create a unique virus that threatens mankind globally. And our fourth . . ."

As Mary continued her illumination of the nominees, I was startled at the mundane, prosaic and derivative nature of the nominated mysteries. I knew mine were better. At least, they were more original and had more unique settings. My theatre mystery was set in the sordid small theatre world of Hollywood with stars and hopefuls intermingled. It was unique and well written. I needed to get serious. I really did. Again, I committed myself to avoiding the neighborhood coffee klatch and entering this category next time—two years from now.

But then, when Mary announced the final nominee, I realized that not all of these unpublished authors were without originality and talent.

"Our fifth and last nominee," Mary read from her list." Is Niall Littlemill for *The Fatal Firth of Forth,* a noir serial murder mystery set in his home city of Edinburgh, Scotland. The bodies are all found in the Firth of Forth near the Fourth Bridge, and traditional Scottish haggis is implicated. The murders are investigated by a tattooed, spike-haired, punk pub bartender and her regular customer, a retired Sergeant Major from the famous Black Watch."

"And the winner is," Mary paused dramatically, opened envelope, took out the card, and stared at it.

Her face lit up with a huge grin.

From the audience a man shouted, "Well, who is it?"

"Niall Littlemill for his mystery *The Fatal Firth of Forth*. It appears some evildoers did not get off *Scot-free*! And now that his novel will be published, I am sure the author is glad the victims were *kilt*."

There were friendly boos from the audience.

"Just a harmless pun," Mary chuckled. "Now, Elias Vlisides will have competition from another published author in his food-murder category."

The whole room burst with applause. It was strangely fitting that an author from the British Isles would be honored as we cruised toward that very destination.

Up on the risers at the front of the room, Mary handed Niall the pen and quill trophy. He hugged Mary, whispered in her ear, turned, and then stepped up to the podium. My mouth dropped open. That was the man whose balcony Brent's body had landed on. I looked at Sean and Sean looked back and shrugged.

As the thundering applause waned, Mary rushed her large body down the steps, sensible shoes popping out prominently, and sat in her chair.

Niall stood with his award in the spotlight and in his moment of triumph.

"Thank you. This is such an honor."

Niall gazed alternately at the trophy and then out into the audience. The standing-o's sat and a smattering of applause still popped through the room. All were poised for a heartfelt acceptance speech commensurate with the honor. Then— Niall's eyes met mine. He recognized me, but couldn't place me. I glanced at Sean. Seeing us both gave him context. He was startled and losing his words that had probably been rehearsed a million times alone.

"Thank you . . ." He started haltingly.

"Thank you . . . from the bottom of my heart. I feel a wee bit sheepish. I . . . I never . . . ah . . . thought . . . well that I would win! The other four nominated were grand. Cheers to my fellow competitors!"

Niall had a reprieve as the audience applauded the other nominees. Sean and I had disconcerted Niall, but when he saw Amy next to me, his eyes shined.

"Maybe now I can get a meeting with Ms. Amy Miller . . . here in the front. Hello! I hear you do murder . . .

Amy's eyes popped wide. She gave our quartet the evil eye and looked up at Niall.

". . . with your deals, I mean," Niall laughed. "I know you're a stellar agent and perhaps we could share a blood pudding one day!"

Amy nodded and raised her glass.

". . . and my thanks to the judges and all of you."

I sat dumbfounded.

"Do murder!" Elias whispered to Mary as she sat. "An unconscious but apt public accusation."

"Yes." Mary's eyes sparkled. "Did you see that look? We had better be careful until she is taken into custody."

"Only a few hours more," Sean said.

"We'll make it," Mary said.

I didn't say anything because I wasn't as sure.

"What the hell did he whisper to you?" Sean asked Mary.

"He just asked me "'What the hell do I bloody say now?'"

"He seems to have figured that one out," I said.

"And, finally," Niall gushed, "I want to thank Otto Stein, who so many years ago taught me how to write in his renowned writing program and helped me sow the seeds of this mystery and, hopefully, many more to come."

Niall basked in the limelight and, having succeeded, puffed advice. "Writing can be lonely. But having a class with a great teacher and other writers can inspire you. I am sure Ms. Miller does not remember me but for the blink of an eye, I was in the class, with her and her close friends, the late Frederic Larsen and Mendel Weitzman."

"Ah, a source!" I said to Mary.

"Don't let anyone distract you from your goals and don't stray from your path. To be a writer is to be dedicated, focused, and to believe in *yourself.* Above all, you must believe in your *own* talent and future. I know that growing as a writer means growing as a person and being mature enough to filter through your lessons in life without letting anything or anyone get in the way of your creativity and craft."

Sean, like the class bully, was sizing up Niall and Amy as well. He was looking for vulnerability on Amy's part and loose lips on Niall's.

"Bully on!" I thought.

* * *

I scanned the audience. They were spellbound. And why shouldn't they be? Niall was almost as charismatic and funny as Mary, and this was his moment. He didn't know the woman he had lauded and bantered about was a murderer of three men—nor did his appreciative audience. And *that* was the truth behind her smiles. No matter how justified in her mind, Amy was the brutal bludgeoner of Otto in New York and the lethal poisoner of Mendel and Frederick on the high seas.

She was the murderer amongst us. Brent was not one of us, and though an abused husband, had been every bit as much a murderer.

I scanned our table.

Jody was obeying all of the award-etiquette rules and focused on Niall's every word—he was where she wanted to be and never would.

Mavis was properly attentive, but the vapid look in her eyes revealed that she was listening to nothing. She was blinded by jealousy. But to be fair, with her financial problems, I might be as well.

Heather was bright-eyed and proud that an MWW award winner had mentioned her new friend.

Elias and Sean were both stoic, like Buddha book ends. Their arms were folded on their ample bellies as they glared at Amy-the-man-killer, basking in reflected glory, and not appearing to have a care in the world.

Agnes picked at her dessert, obviously bored because she was not talking about her own writing or being the center of attention.

And I just listened to Mary humphing and grumping next to me as Amy maintained her charm and demeanor, giving no hint that anything Niall had said had disturbed her in any way.

"They'll get her smug ass in Southampton," Mary whispered.

Jody scowled at Mary for daring to whisper again while Niall had the floor.

Sean ignored Jody's reprimands and whispered to us, his fellow murderer chasers, "I'm going to get her tonight."

"How?" I asked.

"You'll see."

⌘

CHAPTER 44

A Whiff of Wickedness

Niall finally began to bring his remarks to a close.

"Best I conclude, before ye all are completely scunnered, though I may already be a wee bit late for that. I mourn the recent loss of the wonderful members of our family and valuable MWW members along with you. Especially the marvelous Otto Stein who, as I mentioned before, was my teacher, mentor, a great man, and a great friend."

Amy's pasted on pleasant face did not change or even twitch.

"But all our recently and untimely departed colleagues would want us to look forward and not back. That is what I have learned to do on this cruise where we are commemorating them. Thank you again, everyone."

There was loud, uninhibited applause as Niall returned to his seat. The audience applause of adoration and expectation for the new, upcoming writer, someone who now had a publishing contract, and maybe an agent in Amy Miller. They all knew that such notables as Helga, Mendel, Frederick, and Mary had gotten this award in past years and were prepared to embrace Niall into the fold instantaneously.

I couldn't stay next to Amy any longer. Already, I had given her too many opportunities to get to me, and had made a fool of myself in the process. I was going in search of Curtis at the bar, our regular meeting place. I was sure if we had seen each other at dinner, we would have made arrangements again for the last night of our voyage.

"I've got to get out of here," I whispered to Mary.

"No. That's what she wants—to get us separated and vulnerable."

"But . . ."

"Stay . . . please. If Curtis wants to be with you tonight, he will wait." Mary smiled. "He's not worth your life."

"Perceptive . . . and right, but I don't have to like this." My mind screamed at me that another night with Curtis *was* worth my life—I ignored it and stayed.

"Neither do I . . . but it's almost over."

Esther relieved my immediate concerns. She nodded at Amy to come up begin the presentation of Otto's posthumous lifetime achievement award by introducing Sean, the presenter.

Amy rose and looked at our table triumphantly, especially after Niall's public choice of her as an agent. She strode to the podium followed by the eyes of the audience members, especially the males.

Over the loudspeaker, Amy did a more than creditable job waxing effusive about how deserving Otto was of the award. Indeed, she went on at length, bathed in the limelight, and, in the process, made a good portion of Sean's planned award speech duplicative.

"Well, she's shortening my speech!" Sean said. "Good."

"Shh," Jody hissed.

"I've had just about enough of her shushing." Sean frowned and shook his head.

Amy continued. "Otto, as you know, lost his life in that terrible burglary at his home in New York before this cruise. He gave so much to this profession and mentored so many great writers that his death is a great loss to us all. Mendel Weitzman was going to present the award posthumously, but unfortunately, as most of you already know, Mendel had a heart attack here on board the *Queen Anne*. We mourn his death as well. But Sean O'Flarity has graciously consented to do the honors this evening in Mendel's stead. And appropriately so. As you know, Sean is an internationally famous best-selling detective author and has lived a lifetime in Otto's beloved New York. Sean needs no further introduction to any writer here or any mystery loving reader worldwide. Sean?"

We "conspirators" knew that Amy was baiting Sean and us, gloating in the belief she had bested this seasoned detective and all of us.

Applause rose as Sean straightened his cummerbund and scooted his chair back.

"Here we go," Sean whispered to us. "Maybe Amy will be afraid after this!"

"What is he going to do?" I asked.

We all looked at each other as Sean went up to the podium.

"After what?" Elias whispered. "We didn't authorize any assault from the podium. Is it wise?"

"Lord above," Mary murmured. "What could he do in front of all these people?"

Spotlights overshooting the stage washed our table. Amy was clapping at the podium along with all the others. The charade was more than I could bear. I wanted to flee to Curtis and be with him, but I couldn't.

Amy returned to sit with us, like a black widow hovering at the edge of her web. A web spun for us, the only ones who knew what she had done. Amy knew that she had won, as she had planned and hoped. She now had gotten a last victorious moment, if an unexpected one, through Niall's speech and her own, before her three dead men were interred. She was dancing on their graves. She had revenge, admiration, acknowledgment and, she thought, immunity from murder.

But, notwithstanding that, Mary was right. Until Southampton, *the game was afoot,* as the unassailable and impeccable Sherlock Holmes aptly would have put it.

Sean began the presentation speech that Mendel had originally been slated to give.

* * *

"I am honored to present this lifetime achievement award to Otto Stein. It is just tragic that I have to do it posthumously."

Sean took a folded sheet from his breast pocket, opened it on the podium, put on his glasses, and began to read.

"I have had the good fortune to have had two careers. One as a NYPD homicide detective for over thirty years and the other with you as a mystery writer. You have accepted me into your fold and the public has faithfully bought my books, one after another. Otto only had one career, molding and helping young writers to succeed. But he did it superlatively. He did this in the face of great personal sacrifices—including never marrying. Instead, he devoted every waking moment to establishing, improving, and promoting his writing program. He did so until it slowly became the premier and world-renowned launching vehicle for accomplished and award-winning writers in every genre, including books, magazines, film and television. He then nurtured and promoted his graduates' careers with great pride. He kept his program relevant to the changing publishing platforms over the years by including the new indie world which we have all embraced."

Sean proceeded to read a condensed version of Otto's biography, glancing around the audience over his glasses. He skipped the substance Amy had usurped. Then he listed the monumental writers Otto had mentored in his writing program.

Then, unexpectedly, Sean paused. He studied the tiring audience. He peered over his reading glasses, slowly removed them, and looked straight at Amy. He folded his speech and put it back into his jacket pocket.

"Oh, no," Mary whispered.

Sean spoke extemporaneously.

"Otto was not a perfect man. He may not even have been a nice man . . . at times. But then, who is perfect? Who is always nice? I put it to you that the answer is . . . none of us. Otherwise, we could not so realistically weave into our manuscripts the dark side of humanity, and so readily rationalize the crimes and murders we commit on paper. We are here to celebrate Otto Stein's leadership and contributions to the writing world. Yes, the *entire* writing world. There are those who believe that mystery writers, like us, are at the bottom of the barrel of that world—aside from romance writers, of course."

There was a chuckle and smattering of applause, and one jeer. Obviously, one romance writer had stowed away masquerading as a mystery writer amongst us. The jeer was met with another smattering of chuckles.

"But not Otto," Sean's voice rose and he scanned the audience to discipline its unruliness. "Otto made it his mission to help writers of all genres. He helped make the MWW a worldwide and respected institution. And what did he get in return? Bludgeoned to death."

Sean paused and zeroed in on Amy again. He did not take his eyes off her.

"I submit to you that no man who has helped so many deserves to die in a pool of his own blood. I also submit to you that Otto's killer is amongst us tonight."

The audience sat, stunned into silence. Amy scooted her chair to run—but then hesitated and looked nervously around the room. She realized all eyes were on Sean and not her. She remained in her seat and glared back at Sean—her eyes narrowed and her jaw set defiantly.

The mystery writers began to murmur and then rumble. They needed Sean's next words. So did we. Was he going to name Amy? My cohorts and I looked at each other in expectation, fear, surprise, and, yes, pride.

"Can he name her with no proof?" Mary whispered to me.

"Apparently he can do anything he wants."

"Has he just sealed our death warrants?" Mary panicked.

"He has a plan." I whispered. "He'd better."

"He does, doesn't he, Elias?" Mary asked.

Elias shrugged his shoulders.

At that moment, I really believed Sean was nuts. He had gone off the reservation, but I was the one sitting next to Amy and her Prolixin—he wasn't. I had already barely escaped being pitched over my balcony this evening. I wasn't up to being poisoned, too!

Sean continued. "His ultimate killer was his trust in and love for all of us here tonight . . . his trust in opening his door that night . . . and his love of his profession and for each and every one of you, as writers. His door was, unfortunately, always open."

The room applauded and cheered. Amy scooted her chair back in, crossed her legs, and glared defiantly up at Sean. Sean had failed to force Amy's hand and had to cover instead.

Amy's eyes shone bright, and beamed white-hot anger at Sean.

Sean concluded: "He trusted and mentored and tutored all those who came to him. It was that openness that got him in the end. Thank you, Otto. We just wish you were here, alive and in person, to receive this award."

Applause overwhelmed the room. In unison, each and every writer stood. The standing ovation swelled and cheers were scattered about.

Our table stood also—all but Amy.

"Good try," Mary whispered in my ear.

"Yes," I lied, and thought only of the Prolixin Amy still possessed.

Amy finally stood, but it was to leave.

"Excuse me." Heather said. "Amy's upset. She owed so much to Otto."

Heather followed the still unexposed murderer out of the awards ceremony.

⌘

CHAPTER 45

Champagne Gone Flat

After the ceremony, our quartet made for the bar. I wanted an explanation from Sean. What was his rationale for stirring the beehive that was Amy—especially after Niall's unexpected comments had lulled her? However, any explanation would have to wait until we had found a table and some privacy. It was the last night of our cruise and the bar was crowded.

As we wove our way into the celebratory bar, I spotted Curtis at a large table across the room entertaining his usual clients. My heart leaped. Of course it did. I had fallen for him. He was smiling and talking animatedly to an attractive woman with short graying hair. Her eyes twinkled as she listened. I knew that twinkle. And I knew the twinkle tingled down into her body.

I thought of throwing caution to the wind and going over. But then, we had not integrated our groups. Or, more accurately, I unexpectedly realized he had consciously not integrated me into his group. I quickly rationalized that his business of finance was serious and perhaps my quest for a murderer might be considered frivolous or, possibly, less than credible to his group.

I smiled. I must appear to be an exciting woman to him with the constant interruption and overriding necessities of death and murder—not to mention my world-renowned friends. Then, as Curtis turned his head to signal the server for another round, he saw me.

Instantaneously, his face crinkled into a broad smile. That was the look of a man captivated by me. I was delighted. Delighted by Curtis and that my authorial persona had assumed another dimension, the dimension of an alluring, magnetic *femme fatale*.

"We'll find a table," Mary said. "Go ahead with your knight in shining armor coming."

"Thanks."

Sean, Elias, and Mary went to the back to grab a table for four.

I waited as Curtis excused himself and came over. The graying-haired woman glowered at me. I nodded and smiled at her. I had emerged as the conqueror woman.

"Veronica! It's all over the ship. Brent's dead."

"Yes, I . . . I . . ."

"Speechless?"

"A little . . ."

"Come on. Does your little group always have bodies popping up, or should I say, plummeting?"

"Well, I . . ."

"What happened?"

I *was* speechless. I did not want to blurt out the truth— that I was lucky not to be one of the bodies he was mocking. And, I also I didn't want the evening to be about Brent or death sailing the Atlantic with the MWW. I wanted it to be about us, Curtis and me.

Curtis marshaled me to a small window table abutted to the black expanse of night sea beyond. The ship's reflected lights hit on the intermittent white foam popping where the sea clashed with the ship's hull. Curtis signaled for the server.

"Champagne?"

"Wonderful!"

Curtis ordered a bottle of 2002 Louis Roederer Cristal Brut. He was certainly going all out tonight.

I noticed he cast the same winning smile at the server that he had at the woman with graying hair and was now shining down on me. I didn't care if it seemed indiscriminate. It was for me now.

I was enthused. Champagne signaled more of what I had wanted since we first met at the airport and what I got on shipboard—romance and lovemaking beyond my experience, beyond my fictional fantasies. I downplayed the Brent incident and Curtis seemed satisfied after expressing his male protective reflexes and outrage. I did not want the focus to be on all of that.

"Enough about death," I said. "Tell me, did you pick up more investing or clients or whatever you call it?"

"I can take a hint. And I agree. Enough about the morbid. And the short answer is 'yes'."

"That's wonderful."

As we drank our Champagne, I enjoyed the successes of his day as I had with my husband for so many years.

"Tell me more," I said. "How do you reel them in?"

I wanted to be a part of Curtis's life. I wanted our relationship to be more than a shipboard romance. I thought he wanted that too. But it was transparent to me that he was captivated with a woman of intrigue of excitement, of danger. I needed him to know the real me and me to know the real him. I needed him to share my real self with him—the me that didn't trade on murders because I knew the sad truth of my daily routine.

403

"It's not that hard . . . for me. I'm an expert *reeler*," Curtis touched my hand and leaned forward. "Now . . . give me the inside track on Brent."

Curtis's dark eyes searched for the excitement of a murder mystery and not the excitement of getting to know me. Disappointed that my attempt at deflection had failed, I gave it to him because he was indeed a *master reeler*.

"Pony up, Veronica. And don't leave the Heather angle out."

"Heather angle?"

"You mean you never noticed? You're the one with the investigator's mind, the detecting nose!"

"I . . . I . . ."

I was at a loss. I thought back to the interaction and contact between Heather and Brent. It was arguably too familiar, but only on his part. Helga was right about that. To me Brent's attentions were well costumed in politeness and appropriate wine-enriched, evening dinner banter. Heather's reactions were charming but only polite.

"You're the mystery writer and keen observer of human nature." Curtis set down his flute and took the bottle to fill his glass and top off mine. "You mean you never noticed the heat between them?"

"Of course . . . from Brent . . . but . . . but I didn't realize it was requited heat."

I reran the Heather-Brent moments in my mind. Curtis was wrong. But, then, he was not one of us. I didn't argue. I didn't want to.

"Oh, it was requited." Curtis leaned close to me over the table and whispered, "Much like ours."

"Like ours?"

"Well, not like ours. In my entire life, I have never been so completely and fascinatingly *requited* as with you." Curtis's deep bass tremolo voice vibrated through my body.

"Nor I." I put down my champagne and looked at him for a very long, and very short, moment filled with expectation, but also disappointment that his ardor was feeding on a woman—a persona that I was not.

My whole body felt the sense memory of our three nights together. My surprise that the momentum had spurred each of us to try new territories of experimentation. It was as if the cozy cocoon of Curtis's cabin isolated in the wide Atlantic took on a passionate, new life of its own. I attributed it to our chemistry, our pairing, our hunger, and our loneliness. Or, at least, my own loneliness.

"To tonight and more r*equiting*." Curtis clicked his flute on mine.

My heart and mind raced to find a colorable compromise that would let the me that Curtis wanted, the me disguised as an exciting writer, slip into his world for another night of love. I picked up my champagne flute and drank in hopes of finding that compromise. Then, I put it back down with a hollow heart. He did not feel the same about me as I did about him. I recognized the gamesmanship, the insincerity, and hated his cute use of the word *requited* when it came to us.

"I'm sorry. I've got to get back to my friends. Mary and I have to stick together. The murderer is still free and we want to disembark without being shrouded in a body bag." I decided right then and there that the solidarity of my cohorts was the most important thing, as well as being with Mary who had no one in her stateroom.

"I . . . I thought . . ."

"I'm sorry, but we have London."

"London?"

"Yes. I'll be staying three days. Theatre and all."

"I have a few business meetings and then I have to get back."

"Oh."

"Tonight?"

I looked over at my friends and used them as an excuse to depart with my deflated heart. If he felt about me like I did about him, I would hear from him back in California.

"I can't."

"I understand."

"I just wanted a chance to say good-bye and thank you for all your help. I didn't want to miss you tomorrow and not have said goodbye."

I thought, "And give you a chance to make a date for when we were home, you idiot. This is the moment."

"Sure." Curtis was disappointed and his winning white smile disappeared. "I understand. I've got to get back to my clients anyway. I shouldn't abandon them on the last night, either."

I saw him look over at the woman with the short gray hair who he had been charming.

"Yes, I can see that." I glanced at the woman who had kept an intermittent eye on us. "I'm sorry. I . . ."

"I am too, Veronica," Curtis said. "You were the only thing that made this cruise bearable."

"Bearable?" I was incredulous at the word choice.

"That isn't what I meant. I meant you're the only person on this cruise who I found . . . and still find . . . interesting." Curtis smiled and then emptied the champagne bottle into our flutes. "Here's to a woman I find not only interesting, but intoxicating, intriguing, attractive, and very, very charming."

He picked up his flute and added, "Maybe we can go sailing back home and have dinner at the yacht club?"

"I'd like that."

"Bingo," I thought. We would be seeing each other at home. I knew there had been a deeper connection.

I lifted my flute slowly and held it out and he touched his rim very gently to mine and held it there.

Our eyes locked. Suddenly, the sparkle came back into his eyes. He smiled that smile as he put his card on the table. I picked it up.

I took a long drink of my champagne. The card and seeing each other back home turned my disappointment into elation.

The night had been negotiated, but the stakes had changed—there was a connection. He liked me.

I had changed my mind about being with Curtis and said, "You know, my friends can take care of themselves tonight."

* * *

Or, could they? Sean ambled over to our table. There were greetings all around.

"Champagne?" Sean remarked. "Veronica, I hate to interrupt, but we have plans to make."

"Right."

"Plans?" Curtis asked. "More bodies popping up?"

"No," Sean laughed. "But the night is young."

"Ah, sounds intriguing," Curtis said.

"Not so much, but we do need Veronica."

"But . . ." All I thought was that Curtis wanted to see me back home and now I wanted to be with him tonight.

"Veronica, please," Sean insisted in his most polite police directive.

"I have to go." Even in my bubbly state, I knew I had to go with Sean and did.

Curtis called, "Let me know if you find another body!"

The night had been negotiated and renegotiated, but was now lost to Curtis and me.

Curtis went back to his table and the animated, attractive woman with short graying hair.

As I sat at their table with Sean, Elias and Mary, I watched as Curtis and the woman started another bottle of champagne. I feared that their own night was being negotiated.

* * *

"Veronica, pay attention here," Elias said. "We have to keep you girls safe until morning."

"I haven't seen Amy since the banquet," I said. "I think she's had enough. She's gotten what she wanted."

"I don't." Sean had the authoritative presence that came from his years on the force. "Elias and I are moving into the same cabin and that is what you and Mary have to do."

"Okay." That was a far cry from waking up with Curtis.

"And no one is to open their door or order room service or anything else tonight." Sean looked directly at me. "We don't know how far her tentacles reach."

⌘

CHAPTER 46

No Morning After,
But No Mourning Either

The next morning, I awoke early in Mary's luxury stateroom. I was still alive and so was Mary, who was showering. I peeked out the balcony curtains and saw the Southampton dock lights through the mist. I had to have my suitcase out by five a.m. for it to be transported ashore.

I left Mary a note that I'd meet up with her in the cafeteria for breakfast. I disobeyed Sean's orders and went back to my stateroom to pack. But I carefully replaced Mary's Do Not Disturb sign on the door handle, where it had been all night.

As I made my way down the passageway, the cold Atlantic wind invaded the warmth of the *Queen Anne's* halls. The crew willy-nilly opened doors, racing about preparing for our landing and gathering suitcases.

Back in my stateroom, Mavis was in the bathroom.

I peeled off my evening clothes, very glad Mavis wasn't front and center to question me about where I had been last night. I didn't want any more of the attacks Mavis inflicted on me. I put on my light travel robe and saved an outfit for the disembarkation. I threw everything into my large suitcase and rolled it outside the cabin door. I left it next to Mavis's oversized suitcase already out in the hall. A half-full luggage trolley was being pushed down our hallway from the elevators. I made it just in time.

As I stepped back into the cabin, Mavis was hanging up the phone.

* * *

"You're here!" Mavis was dressed and ready for disembarkation at Southampton. "When did you get back?"

"What?" I murmured as I packed my small roller case with my remaining things. Given our fears about luggage loss had proven unfounded, I put it next to my large suitcase outside our stateroom. So much for "The Power of the Luggage." I did not want to have to drag it up or down any steps when we disembarked, an added incentive.

"Well, that was Mary. She wanted me to remind you to meet her at six for breakfast in the cafeteria."

"Thanks." I started for the bathroom.

Mavis stepped up, blocking me in the small hall. "Where were you?"

I ignored her question again. I was through with her. I had no intention of answering her queries "Done with the bathroom?"

"Curtis again?" Mavis demanded again as-of-right—posturing with her teacher-student voice, as if I had a duty to respond.

"Excuse me. I can't be late." I started to walk right through her.

"Humph," Mavis snorted and moved. "I told Mary I was meeting Esther at five-thirty, so we couldn't join you. We have to get out the awards press releases we did last night."

"Too bad."

I closed the door, locked it, and turned on the shower. Any relationship I may have had with her was over, whether it was teacher-student, mentor, or friend. I knew Mary had not asked her to join us. I also knew Mary must have been amused as Mavis slathered on her self-importance over reasons why she and Esther could not join us.

Mavis called out, "Someone has to take care of the business."

As the warm water washed over my head and body, Mavis was drowned out. This was the last time I would be cornered into a conversation with her. We would have encounters of the formal kind at future MWW meetings, but that's what I would keep them, formal. I would fend off any familiarity she might try to inject after I won the best unpublished mystery novel award. I didn't wish her ill, but I couldn't forget or, frankly, forgive her demeaning, brutal attacks on me.

The warm water relaxed my entire body and my thoughts went from Mavis to Curtis. I flashed on that attractive woman sharing what should have been my champagne and, I hoped, not my night with him.

I stayed in the shower until I was sure Mavis was gone.

"Mavis," I called through the bathroom door to make sure she had actually left for her five-thirty obsequious breakfast with Esther.

There was no answer.

* * *

I cracked the bathroom door and peeked out. No Mavis. She was gone for good with her carry-on that she had so expertly advised me always to keep with me. It was good advice, except that my large suitcase had arrived timely for our first dinner.

On the electric clock the minute number rotated to five-forty. I was late. I blew dry my hair for two minutes and brushed it to air dry. I put on blush and mascara. Then, I crammed all my toiletries into their case and stuffed it and my robe into the carry-on.

I put on my disembarkation outfit; my cherry red wool pants and matching red sweater. The cafeteria was the only place to coffee-up this morning and Curtis had to be there. I anticipated a warm good-bye, one that wasn't really a goodbye at all. I paused from my flurry and looked at myself in the mirror. I was pleased. Curtis would be enticed to follow through on our dating arrangement post-cruise. After all, last night, he had offered to take me sailing and have dinner at the yacht club in Marina del Rey.

I paused in fantasy for a nanosecond and then renewed my departing flurry.

I threw my small, folding travel umbrella into my purse. This was England, the land of rain and greenery, despite global warming.

It was a few minutes before six by the cabin clock. I checked the cabin for anything I might have left. Nothing. I grabbed my purse, black jacket, and carry-on. I would make it to the cafeteria almost on time if the elevators were not too full.

I was looking forward to Amy's arrest. I relished being a witness to her demise. After that, I would be on my way to London. I would sit and have coffee in Leicester Square until the last minute; discount theatre tickets went on sale there for the best theatre scene in the world. Too bad Curtis had to go straight to Heathrow and home.

But, face it; I was happy my cohorts and I were getting off this ship alive and kicking—which I believed to be certain now. Too bad it had cost me my last shipboard night with Curtis. It was a large price but worth it for Mary's and my safety.

With just a glance back, I left our stateroom. It had indeed been an "eventful" voyage.

⌘

CHAPTER 47

An Anxious Disembarkation Day

In the cafeteria, I spotted the ever-social Elias sitting at a table with Sean and Mary. Three award winners, and some hangers-on, clustered around Elias.

Sean and Mary conferenced together, ignoring Elias's boisterously festive congratulations and heartfelt good-byes.

I caught Sean's eye and waved. I pointed to the cappuccino station where I detoured to get activated. I grabbed a strong double cappuccino. As I went to our table, I scoped out the food stations and densely packed tables for Amy. She was nowhere to be seen. But Curtis was in a cluster of passengers down the way at the Belgian waffle station.

Amazingly and suddenly, I craved a waffle to go with my cappuccino.

I sidled up behind Curtis and tapped on his shoulder.

"Hey there."

Curtis turned and his smile disappeared. "Veronica, good morning, I . . . uh . . ."

I was unfortunately face to face with the attractive gray haired woman from last night.

I looked from Curtis to the woman—the woman with a face emanating that unmistakable fresh-fucked glow. It was the same glow I had after my first night with Curtis. She had the sparkly eyes of a woman who had possessed and enchanted a man, a man who she made want her in every way. She had the aura that should have been mine this misty morning in Southampton—that would have been, but for the multiple murders and the protectiveness of my new friends.

Suddenly, I was angry with Mary, my other new friends, Amy, Brent, and myself. At that moment, I didn't care about solving multiple murders or Amy's arrest.

I salvaged the situation and my pride. "I . . . I just wanted . . . to pop over and say goodbye and thanks for all the . . . help."

"You're more than welcome." Curtis recovered his winning smile. "I'll call."

"Sure. See you Stateside."

The last thing I wanted was to linger and be introduced to my usurper. The female who had gotten the things I had bargained for and charmed for and planned on having yet again.

I walked away, head held high, but feeling like a deflated balloon crash landing in lava.

"Who cares?" I muttered, flushing him down and out of my mind and heart, or, at least, trying to.

Then I answered myself, fighting back my tears, "I do."

* * *

I joined Sean and Mary at our table and avoided Elias's carnival. I was heartbroken. I didn't want to be a catalyst for yet more happy, congratulatory conversation. Besides, we had business to discuss—the business of murder.

Mary and Sean were debating where Amy's actual arrest would take place. I was heartened they were debating where and not if.

I buried my disappointed heart and focused on our murderer's apprehension. I realized I needed this victory and these friends, since my Curtis endeavor had apparently floundered. I put him on the back shelf for now, a teeter-tottering one, but a shelf. Southern California would be the test with a phone call from him using just the right words. After all, I rationalized, there was no spoken commitment between us, and last night the champagne had flowed along with that predatory woman's estrogen—or what she had left of it.

I thought that my propensity to male forgiveness was embarrassing even to myself. Like any woman, I parsed circumstances and found distinctions without differences when it came to men. Especially men to whom I had given myself, given myself in ways I had never imagined. I considered it a genetic flaw in the female of our species, designed to keep the family unit strong and the offspring fed. I tuned out the static roar of passion in my mind distracting me. I had to deal with the Amy problem at hand.

"I think they'll take her at the customs desk when they scan in her passport." Sean was analytical and confident.

"I don't," Mary countered. "They'll wait until she steps off the gangplank onto British soil."

"I think on British soil, too," I jumped on board with Mary. "It'll be less of a spectacle."

"That's true." Sean agreed.

"And with more legal authority." I was on a roll.

"That's true, too. A good point," Sean said. "But the nearer she gets to disembarking, the more likely she could slip away."

"Are you kidding? The Brits have taken care of that," Mary sniped. "The U.K. is the land of surveillance. London has surveillance cameras on every corner. I wouldn't be surprised if we were on camera now."

I involuntarily glanced around, but saw no obvious surveillance. As we conferred, the loudspeaker announced that disembarkation of group one would begin in ten minutes and that everyone should use the stairs to get to the departure deck and customs if possible.

With that, the social flurry around Elias waned. Other breakfasting passengers downed the last of their coffee and started out.

"Congratulations, again," Elias handed one of his Greek dancing-man cards to the author who had won for best published short story. "We'll have lunch when I'm in New York. I'm taking some time in London and then Mykonos, but I have meetings in New York next month."

"Wonderful." The ecstatic author pocketed the card. "I'll e-mail."

The remaining groupies unglued themselves from Elias's charm and wandered chatting toward the door.

Then, just as Elias joined our debate on Amy's detention, Anne flurried by our table—a blue floral burst from head to toe. She was the quintessential British woman crowned with an absurd, silk-flower-bearing hat—a throwback to the early 20th century.

"Good morning all." Anne paused. "See you next awards cruise. I'll give you a call, Elias."

"Yes. Wonderful"

"Cheerio. Splendid crossing, all things considered, of course," Anne gave Mary and me the evil eye as she left.

"Good bye," Elias boomed for our group.

"Forget her," Mary whispered to me.

"I will."

"Sean, have we gotten any word from your partner?" Elias asked.

"No. Could be the on-board communications or the time difference. I tipped the steward. He'll keep checking and get me here. So . . . if something comes through, we'll know."

"Not to change the subject, but what about Brent? Even if he's dead doesn't the NYPD have to look into that too?" I didn't want to sound like an amateur, but I had a personal interest in Brent—dead or alive.

"It's a judgment call," Sean answered. "You see, Helga's . . ."

"Forget Helga," Mary interrupted. "What about him throwing Veronica around like a rag doll and your jettisoning him overboard?"

"Look, he's dead and . . ."

Elias interrupted. "They shouldn't drop anything. I have one book where the cops . . . excuse me . . . the detectives . . . investigated a deceased serial killer and they found cold cases years back. The book was based on true police work and the killer was dead. I think . . ."

"I know that case," Sean cut Elias off. "And I read your book. It was good . . . the detectives were a little cardboard, but . . ."

"Of course, you would think they were cardboard, Mr. Thirty-Year homicide detective," Mary mocked.

We all laughed.

"Seriously," Sean added. "Brent was not a serial killer. There is no trail of bodies. Veronica and I are alive and kicking. Helga's the one dead and the word is, Helga has no one who cares enough to push the department. My partner said it's a nonstarter. They are busy enough. And the Wessex Line and the MWW doing the cover-up dance doesn't help."

"But he tried to kill Veronica," Mary fumed.

"It'd be a civil suit against his estate," Sean said. "Sorry, Veronica."

"He was penniless!" Mary blurted. "That's why he married Helga in the first place."

"Men like that always start pilfering and stashing money away from the honeymoon. Veronica could get some of that, but he has relatives and I bet there's a poor one somewhere!" Elias suggested.

"You're right," Mary agreed. "If there is a penny in the estate, some obscure relative will crawl out of the woodwork to fight you."

"Besides," I said. "I was stressed out enough when I filed in small claims for a deposit I had stupidly paid a contractor who walked out on my bathroom remodel. No lawsuits. I . . ."

"Now. Let's focus," Elias interrupted. "What about Amy, Sean?"

Sean recapped the options we had discussed while Elias played host.

"Bottom line: My partner said Scotland Yard was going to detain her."

"And they might find the Prolixin on her," Mary added.

"Yeah, but too bad Amy deep-sixed all that other stuff we had," Elias said.

"And too bad the bodies are stale," Sean added.

"Agreed," Mary said. "The *Queen Anne's* refrigeration was obviously not designed for bodies . . . just food . . . and rightfully so."

"They'll find the cause of death, won't they?" I interjected. "The Prolixin!"

"Maybe," Sean said. "At least, they'll sweat her."

I stopped. I bordered on being the overly enthusiastic amateur. I was just so frustrated. I also worried that Amy would come after us if she went free. She knew that we knew. We were loose ends—a lingering threat to her freedom, if she somehow managed to keep it.

Over the loudspeaker the first group was announced for disembarkation.

"What are we doing sitting here? Let's go watch Amy get taken down." Mary gulped the last of her coffee.

We got up, grabbed our things, and followed Mary.

⌘

CHAPTER 48

Just Us

Mary led our caterpillar line of four through the mingling passengers to the elevators. Her unkempt bun bounced down on her neck as she maneuvered through the crowd. When she reached up to replace a loosened bobby pin, her purse slammed into a man competing for the elevator ride.

"Hey!" He protested.

Mary ignored him and beat him and everyone else as she squashed herself into the full elevator going down. She ignored the grumblings of her elevator fellows as they pressed together to accommodate her substantial presence.

"I'll meet you below. Hurry," Mary bellowed.

"Which floor?" Sean called out as the doors slammed shut.

"It's on . . ." Mary's voice disappeared down the elevator shaft.

"Shh," Elias said. "The loud speaker. Listen. Instructions."

"Down the main stairs to the customs floor," I repeated the announcement.

"Let's go." Sean led the charge for us three down the jam-packed, chattering hallway to the main stairs.

Sean called back to Elias, "Hurry."

* * *

We bounced down the stairs with the stream of excited passengers. Far ahead, Mavis was affixed to Esther, as she had been the entire trip. Now, of course, I knew it was a parasitic coupling. Mavis needed to extract some kind of living as a ghostwriter from Esther or her contacts. Not far behind them were Jody, Herbert and Agnes—parasites of another type.

"Hold up, Mavis," Agnes bellowed, reverting to schoolyard behavior yet again. "Where are you staying in London?"

"Where are you staying?" Jody parroted Agnes with the unfortunate perfection born of the days they had spent together. "We can have dinner."

Esther and Mavis ignored the trio and pushed their way into a short customs line. They were intent on disembarking before the three stooges could catch up. Who could blame them? I would do the same. In fact, I realized I had better hide in case they looked my way.

As we neared the last landing, I marveled at the frantic herding of these people.

"Really? Seriously?" I mumbled to myself. Did they think the cruise line was going to keep them aboard for an all-expense paid kidnapping back to New York?

Then I spotted Amy at the bottom of our staircase, working her way into the overcrowded customs room. Her shiny honey blond hair stood out and I recognized the mustard pants suit she had also worn at the embarkation in New York.

She moved with her usual smooth grace while all the passengers surrounding her were jostling packages and each other with awkward and unnecessary fervor.

"There she is. Down there," I called to Sean who was now just ahead of me, in the staircase waterfall of passengers.

"I see her. But there's no one here to detain her."

"I don't see any cops either," I added.

"It's bobbies." Sean proceeded to barrel through the crowd with the skill of a detective in hot pursuit of a suspect.

"She's down here," Sean yelled back to Elias who was closer than I was.

"I see her." Elias was unexpectedly swept past Sean in an unimpeded ribbon of people hugging the right hand rail. "But what do I do if I get to her?"

"Just stall her. Until someone shows up."

Sean stopped cold on the steps to survey the lobby below. I bumped into his back and but for his strength we both would have started a domino fall of passengers.

"Sorry." The very British and proper woman behind me peeled herself from my back.

"No. No. My fault," I insisted, letting British politeness rule out by accepting responsibility when in fact it was Sean's fault.

"That's right. Your fault," a typical American chimed in. "Keep it moving lady. I have a tour bus to catch."

Sean turned back to me, took my arm, and kept it moving.

"Come on," Sean whispered. "We've got to catch up to Elias. I can at least stall her by acting like a cop."

Sean and I descended, again. I couldn't help but think that Elias would be more effective stalling her with his sociability than Sean strong-arming her.

"Just remember," Sean whispered to me. "I'm retired. And we're in England. I have no real authority. Just follow my lead. Back me up."

"Back you up? What the . . ." I had only seen back up in the movies and it always ended in guns and blood and death.

"Yeah, just confuse the hell out of her."

"Okay. Okay," I agreed.

Unexpectedly, the crowd loosened. We got halfway down the last flight of stairs before it slowed again. I now saw the total expanse of densely packed passengers below in the large foyer. I figured Amy was not going anywhere anyway unless she cut in front of everyone. And that wouldn't happen in Britain. They are famous for the rigidity of their *queuing*.

* * *

The jumble of people disembarking was quite unceremonious compared to the gala boarding process. Wessex Cruise Line had gotten their money and was focused on the gala boarding of more paid customers at the other end.

There were rows of customs tables that stalled the departure. They needed more. Everyone in line policed those trying to get ahead. A couple tried to slip in front into a line and they were cold shouldered to the end. With that, I was assured that Amy could not speed the process for herself.

"She's moving toward the short line at that customs table," Sean observed. "Damn."

"But look, there's Heather waving at her."

"Good. That'll slow her down."

It did. Amy waited for Heather as other passengers trickled around her in line. The two greeted each other like long lost sisters. As they chatted, the crowd funneled past them to the table. Then, they rejoined the line of disembarking passengers.

"There they go," Sean muttered. "And no Scotland Yard anywhere. I don't understand."

"Wait. There's Mary coming off the elevator. She'll stall her."

Mary spotted me and thrust up one of her usual big, uninhibited, and enthusiastic waves. She fought to get to us against the throng of exiting passengers, chomping at the bit to get on with their lives or their vacations.

It was the wrong way. I reached my hand above the woman's brittle blond hair in front. I pointed and directed Mary to Amy and Heather.

"Over there," I mouthed.

Mary looked confused.

"Over there. Amy. Amy." I mouthed again.

It worked. Mary turned and saw Amy. She steamrolled through the other passengers to get to her. Elias was close at hand, but not close enough.

I grabbed Sean's arm.

"We have to get there too. You'll have to fake a detention," I urged. "There's no one anywhere in sight."

"Okay!" Sean agreed, much to my surprise.

But Sean and I were stuck tight on the last flight of stairs. There was nowhere for the people to go in the packed disembarkation foyer. The forward undulation of the crowd had stopped.

Our advance had ground to a complete standstill. Worse yet, we started to be pushed back to the stairway. I looked. Fortunately, Amy was halted too.

The passengers began to rumble in loud dissatisfaction.

"What's going on?" I asked Sean as I looked with my bird's-eye view around the foyer.

"There. Over there," Sean whispered in my ear as he pointed to the gangplank entrance. "Scotland Yard."

"For Amy!" I cheered.

"I'd bet my bottom dollar on it." Sean dredged up a saying I hadn't heard since my parents used it in my childhood.

"Thank God."

We both watched. Elias and Mary were within an arm's length of Amy, but had been frozen in place also.

The two suited Scotland Yarders, followed by four blue uniformed Bobbies, pushed the passengers back into a sardine pack as they crossed.

"They're heading right for Amy," I said. "Justice!"

"My partner must have gotten through to someone," Sean bragged.

A woman from a few stairs up blurted out, "What's going on? I see cops."

"We call them Bobbies, madam," a man with a Cockney accent corrected her.

"What is happening?" she replied.

"I don't know," another woman chimed in.

"Drugs?" a man guessed.

There was a rumbling about a drug bust around us.

Another man volunteered, "I heard some people got sick," "Oh?"

The rumblings of speculation did not stop. People buzzed about smuggling, drugs, bad food, or trouble with the crew. The passengers apparently followed the recent news reports which were rife with international shipboard problems. These stories got out despite every cruise line's efforts at cover-ups of any and every shipboard mishaps and crimes. It was fascinating that no one thought of terrorists. It was just not associated with cruises like these.

"No one knows about her but us," I whispered to Sean.

"They will." Sean smiled and kept his sharp hawk-like eyes on Amy. "Look at her. Amy knows."

I watched from above, but afar, at the culmination of all our efforts. I thought of the hard fought proof we had found, my superb detective instincts, and my friends. I reveled at the vindication I would have against Mavis and Esther. I was proud.

I was ready to rub all this in Mavis's face if I ever saw her again, which I might make happen now just to make a point--and get a little payback.

"Yeah, look at her face," I gloated. "She sees them . . . She sees the uniforms."

"She's looking around for a place to run like they all do when they get caught. Predictable. That's what criminals are . . . predictable."

I said, "Heather's oblivious."

"She doesn't know who her newfound friend really is."

I smiled. "She will now."

I studied the panic written all over Amy's delicate face, normally flawless and serene. I enjoyed the fear in her usually calm hazel and gold eyes as she searched wide-eyed for an escape; an escape from justice for the three murders now bearing down on her.

Then unexpectedly, Amy's eyes met mine as she calculated the probability of an escape up back up the staircase. Her eyes blazed at me with hate. If she could have killed with them, she would have. I was afraid but was at this moment invincible and out of reach.

As pride and joy at our victory filled my heart, the corners of my lips moved up into a smile at this trapped animal. She would pay for her murders, no matter how justified in her mind. I would go to my neighborhood coffee place with a new story. My stories about solving the Valentine Theatre murders had gotten a bit worn. I would give myself three weeks grace to glory in this new headline murder case at my coffee place and my social events. Then back to writing in earnest for me.

"She's going down." Sean interrupted my negotiations with myself.

"Yes." I watched Amy—her head now swiveling around, desperate for a getaway with pin-wheeling radiantly. "We did it. All of us. And I for one am—"

427

"Wait. What's happening? What is . . ." Sean interrupted. "They are passing her by."

"Passing her by?" I parroted.

We both watched the ribbon of suited Scotland Yard men and Bobbies move past Amy slowing with the packed crowd.

Amy's face calmed back to its flawless saucer-eyed charm. Her eyes looked up at me again. Their deep calm pool of gold was alive with a victorious glint. She flashed a dimpled smile at me and then turned gracefully back to Heather at the customs table. Amy's charm returned and she chatted with Heather. Heather hadn't noticed that Amy's façade had ever faltered.

* * *

Sean whispered, "Are they just here for the bodies?"

"The bodies?"

"Yes. To transport them." Sean spit out, "God, damn it!"

I said, "That can't be."

"If they were here for murder—" Sean didn't finish his sentence.

In the crowd beyond Amy, one Scotland Yard detective put his hand to his ear. His lips moved. Then he moved with his men directly back to Amy as two gray suited women bookended her. In an instant her face contorted, and her eyes shot up looking directly at me with fear and hate. Then, instantaneously, the men from Scotland Yard and the bobbies encircled Amy. With one swift move the scrum of officers moved her and her fury to the exit and off the ship.

"She's in custody," Sean mumbled. "My partner pulled it off. She'll be extradited and the evidence we got will do the rest."

The passengers funneled through the tables and on to exit once again. Elias and Mary moved against the tide of passengers toward the stairs and us. We stepped down into the foyer from the last flight of stairs and joined Elias and Mary. The crack quartet of investigators was reunited in victory.

"We did it." Elias said shaking Sean's hand.

"Yes," Sean smiled. "We did."

"It was so quick, Veronica." Mary was flushed with excitement and hugged Veronica.

I said, "Yes, I can't believe it."

Veronica and Mary shared hugs with Sean and Elias.

Then, Sean put on his dry professional hat on. "When I get back to New York, I follow through just to make sure justice is done."

As we moved towards customs, a collective cementing relief and joy at a job well done bonded the group.

"I was worried because she got the evidence from my room," Elias said.

"Not your fault really," Mary said.

"We all write enough about desperate murderers so we should have known." Elias chuckled.

"Hell, I'm NYPD . . . well, retired NYPD. I should have realized."

"She'll be convicted won't she?" I asked.

"Yes," Sean said. "So many bodies. And the NYPD is on it. Wessex's corporate machine won't bury this one."

"And at least it wasn't one of us in those body bags." Elias flashed a mustached smile. "Or you, Veronica."

Elias gave me a big Greek hug.

"We'll see each other next cruise?" Mary asked. "I've never had more fun on this dumb awards thing. Oh dear, that sounds so terrible!"

Sean said, "I feel the same way."

Elias announced, "And, in two years we'll be presenting an award to Veronica."

I gulped.

* * *

After customs, I paused on the gangplank. I looked out to the dock and the morning gray—overcast and misting but not raining. It was British gray, deep and solid. It wasn't like my Santa Monica misty mornings that always had the promise of sunshine behind them. I took a deep breath of the sea's salted air.

EPILOGUE

Southampton

At the port in Southampton, the body-bagged and decomposing remains of Mendel, Frederick, Helga, and Brent were taken off, escorted by England's finest. At Sean's urging and with his NYPD clout, the modern advances in forensic science were able to put the Humpty-Dumptied, compromised evidence back together again. The group of four would get justice for the murders of Otto, Mendel, and Frederick even in the over-peopled, over-worked Big Apple—and even when the perpetrator was sailing on the high seas and protected by the corporate power, money, and vested interests.

As Anne disembarked, she was greeted by her lady friends from Bath—outfitted in floral wear from hat to toe in celebratory homecoming. They were as stout as Anne was slight, and they embodied the fairy godmothers in Disney's animated movie *Sleeping Beauty*. That year, Anne published *Foxglove Afloat*—a deadly family reunion Hawaiian cruise where a rival inheritor kills off the rich relatives with the ever-popular, poisonous Foxglove plant. Anne's inspiration was obvious—her result mediocre. Were she in our quartet, it would have been so much more.

Elias Vlisides and Sean O'Flarity left the *Queen Anne* and made a beeline for London and a pub lunch with good English ale. Elias's muse came back with a vengeance in a mystery about yacht deaths in Greece. Sean added more books to his best-selling detective series—as if the prolific Helga had possessed his fingers.

Jody, Agnes, and Herbert went on the British writers' tour, *sans* me. Back home, they stayed in Mavis's writing classes. I, of course, never crossed paths with the three stooges again. However, I did occasionally look for their publications. And, not surprisingly, there were none.

Mary went straight to Heathrow Airport to return to her suburban Farmington Hills life, her four kids, and her slasher books. After farewells, she trotted away, bun bouncing at the nape of her neck and sensible shoes moving her ample body through the crowd. Her next book was stellar with its vicious slasher plying his trade on a Mississippi River cruise.

Mavis left the *Queen Anne* trailing after Esther Nussbaum—good riddance to both of them. Esther remained a visible and popular president of the MWW for years. Mavis and her agent republished her old series as e-books. The effort bombed, except for a smattering of five-star reviews, clearly elicited from friends or students. Mavis never published again. Instead, she edited for a living and enticed new suckers into her classes by trading on fictitious friendships with fabricated stories about Otto, Mendel, Frederick, and Helga—the dead can't protest. Obviously, no one will ever know if she resorted to ghostwriting gigs.

* * *

I took a bus into London and stayed for three days waiting for my flight home. My refund from cancelling the English writers' tour was paltry, but well worth it to avoid Agnes, Jody, and Herbert. I found an economy hotel near the theatre district with no *en suite* bath. I spent my mornings at Starbucks in Leicester Square waiting for the discount theatre ticket stand to open. There, I eavesdropped on the candid exchanges of artists, business people, tourists, locals, and—yes—writers bemoaning their writers' block. I was a voyeur into a Santa Monica-like coffee klatch transported to London. I lunched at Harrods in the *crêperie* and at the Harp Pub, saw several plays on the cheap, took in the National Portrait Museum, and attended choral evensong one night at the beautiful and famous St. Martin-in-the-Fields. It was a wonderful experience, free of my cruise mates and asserting my own persona and interests.

* * *

Back in America Otto's, Mendel's, Frederick's, and Helga's funerals were celebratory of their contributions to the writing world, not their actual lives, as is true of many artists. They rose in popularity commensurate with their well-publicized untimely deaths. They, of course, were never to write again. But, as often happens, their royalties mounted in trust accounts for the people fighting over their estates. As usual, death turned a tidy profit.

Brent Hawthorne's funeral freed him of his millstone and brutalizer, but unfortunately for him, not the way he wanted. He and Helga were buried together forever in the side-by-side plots Helga had very efficiently bought. She had even pre-ordered headstones—hers monumental, his a pale shadow beside it.

Otto Stein lived on after death. But his memory survived not in the crude, sexualized, credit-mongering manipulative reality that was truly his. Instead, as often happens to the dead, he lived on in a fictionalized, posthumous alternative reality. That manufactured reality was one of a mythical, sage, fatherly, and nurturing icon. His canonization materialized because of a void felt in the authorial world, a marketing need on the part of his writing program at Greenwich University, and Esther's search for a tragic, noble figurehead for MWW's own aggrandizement. With the increased membership dues from the publicity, Esther now claimed an annual salary—not that she needed it, of course.

Upon Sean's return to New York, he and his partner fine-tooth-combed all the forensics and evidence. The district attorney had a sound case with Amy's revenge motive. Her criminal defense attorney tried the case in the news media. With Amy's beauty it played well. But to the jury in the actual trial, it did not. There were simply just too many bodies. The thumbnail of the novel I had taken from Amy's stateroom of the thinly disguised murders of Otto, Mendel and Frederick did not help. The deaths of the men who had tormented her fictionally paying the ultimate price. The cruise quartet had nailed her with her own words.

Heather's books combining mystery, murder and science fiction were original and sold well, but, as I had predicted, not as well as her science fiction. As I had observed, she was missing the *je ne sais quoi* that all elite mystery writers possessed. Heather kept her old agent, but she and Amy remained a duo—strikingly attractive, talented, and popular. Thanks to Heather's husband and the partner he worked for, they each landed a movie deal—or at least, they sold the rights. It remained to be seen if Hollywood would back the options with money and produce them. But Heather's husband rose in his law firm along with those deals. Heather continued to apply to the Poetry Society of America, but never got in—famous or not, her poems remained mediocre. To me, they were excellent.

But then, I believed that poets, as a literary group, produced an inbred snobbery—and not necessarily good poems.

* * *

Once home, our crime-solving quartet kept in touch by e-mail, at first in frequent flurries and then intermittent bursts. I personally appreciated my life much more after nearly losing it. Plus, I had learned a great deal from my new friends and worked hard to publish. I, of course, shared my shipboard adventures at my Santa Monica coffee klatch. Admittedly, I feigned professionally intimacy with each of the celebrity dead, since, after all, who could challenge me?

Even more exciting—my muse erupted from the shadows. I finished the theatre book and started a cruise ship blood-bath book that rained bodies nightly. Why not? Everyone else had used the murders on our cruise in new novels in some fashion and cruise mysteries were good sellers. I planned to edit and finalize one of my books for the MWW contest, but I had almost two years to do that.

I had learned that writing and editing product was only one-third of the work of a published author. The business of publishing and promoting was the other third. I took workshops on getting an agent and e-publishing. Mary offered me her agent but a polite email let me know he didn't want to take on any new authors, or specifically me. I certainly forgot about Amy's shipboard offer.

E-publishing with Octopus Books looked better and better. But I balked when I learned its new program gave books away for free if customers joined their ten-dollar-a-month Readers Club. It left thousands of Indie authors with a small piece of a communist-style pot-of-money—in other words, pennies! Worse it came to light in the authorial world that Octopus Books did a secret deal with the Big Six publishers to promote their books in the algorithms—thus, relegating to oblivion and starvation the small publishers and Indie authors. But I had no practical choice. Either way, I needed to get concrete authorial validation before the next awards cruise. I joined the Octopus Books demeaning oppressive programs.

At home, with the cruise murders and strategic name-dropping, I was even more popular at my coffee place, lunches, invitational speaking engagements, and writers' conferences. I considered it promotion, but never let it interfere with the time I devoted to writing. I discovered I could promote myself at my usual coffee place with a whole other population of squatters to thrill with my exploits. Then, I learned of other nearby coffee places with yet other potential fans. I was having a great time name-dropping, mystery solving, and just generally being popular. After all, I had now solved the Valentine Theatre murders and the MWW cruise murders single-handedly—well, almost.

* * *

Curtis and I never got together. I waited months for his call. In late fall, I called him at his office. He was married—with grown children and even grandchildren. He was encrusted in a life he liked, but not enough to stop his dalliances—frequent dalliances I believed. I rationalized that I was special to him. I rejected the possibility that he simply knew I was vulnerable, susceptible, and perhaps naïve—an easy target. Besides, although admittedly I was also a liar of sorts, Curtis lied to satisfy his own ego. I did not. I was sincere and simply exaggerated. I hurt no one. At least, that is what I told myself.

Interestingly, the MWW cruise was scheduled again with Wessex. The Wessex marketing team had somehow spun gold from our web of murders and deceit. The MWW body bags and

Amy's conviction at trial were a positive not a negative for the cruise line.

With my heightened prestige, I devoted my time to my new friends, to my promotional activities, and to finishing a book to win an MWW award on the next cruise. I also spent a great deal of time drafting a unique and witty acceptance speech for my future award. I believed that I would inevitably need it. It was my destiny, after all.

Reviews Appreciated

http://www.amazon.com/Death-Sets-Sail-Veronica-Kennicott-ebook/dp/B00R3DP4K8

Sign up for a Mailing List [NO SPAM ONLY SPECIALS]

https://dalemanolakas.com/sign-up

Audible Audiobooks

Hollywood on Trial: A Legal Thriller

https://www.audible.com/pd/B08Z4FGJ3S/?source_code=AUDFPWS0223189MWT-BK-ACX0-244908&ref=acx_bty_BK_ACX0_244908_rh_us

Rogue Divorce Lawyer: A Legal Thriller

DALE E. MANOLAKAS

**More Books by Dale E. Manolakas—All Books on Kindle
Unlimited— View Book Trailers and Buy**
http://www.dalemanolakas.com

About the Author

DALE E. MANOLAKAS

After a lifetime of writing poetry, books, nonfiction, and legal documents, it was author Ray Bradbury's friendship and encouragement that finally inspired Dale E. Manolakas to pursue writing as a career. Raised just outside Los Angeles by a surgeon father and a homemaker-author mother, Dale E. Manolakas earned her B.A. from the University of California at Los Angeles, and M.A., M.S., Ph.D., and J.D. degrees from the

University of Southern California. She is a member of the California Bar, had the privilege of clerking for the Honorable Arthur L. Alarcón at the United States Court of Appeals for the Ninth Circuit, was a litigator in two major Los Angeles law firms and a senior appellate attorney at the California Court of Appeals, as well as an Administrative Law Judge. She is also a member SAG-AFTRA and Actors' Equity Association.

Dale E. Manolakas

Author's Official Website

http://www.dalemanolakas.com [Find portal to free books at *your local library*.]

Author's YouTube Channel View Book Trailers & Limited Time FREE Audiobook

https://www.youtube.com/channel/UCac1mJynScdPGd2FVz1987A

Amazon Author's Page with Videos

https://www.amazon.com/Dale-E.-Manolakas/e/B00H0FMRX6

Click through to sales channels on Author's Official Website – All Books on Kindle Unlimited

http://www.dalemanolakas.com

Sample of
HOLLYWOOD ON TRIAL

Chapter 1

The sunset burned across the stormy Pacific Ocean. On the beach, director Nick Claren paced in the wet sand eyeing the horizon. For his last shot of the day, he needed the surging November squall to hit shore before nightfall.

Waiting for the cameras to roll, actors Cristian Alba and Tiffany Simms fought the windswept swells near the Santa

Monica Pier on a submerged platform. The two leads, nude waist up but wet-suited below, struggled for their footing.

Tiffany yelled, "I'm freezing. Why don't they start?"

"Don't know. Night'll kill the long shot from the beach." Cristian studied the wind flurries battering the two drone cameras above. "And those drones are wacked."

A wind shear diagonaled a drone down at them.

"Watch out!" Cristian, a veteran action star, covered Tiffany with his broad back.

Tiffany screamed, "I can't take this."

"Just hold on." Cristian waived at the drone operator in the surf. "Hey! Get control of those damn things."

Cristian's shouts were lost in the wind and so were Tiffany's protests.

As a mound of ocean hit them, Tiffany clung to Cristian and screamed, "Don't let go!"

Cristian wrapped his arms around her as the wave battered them and then crashed on the pier pylons beyond.

* * *

On the beach, Nick ran to the drone operator—knee high in spent, foamed waves.

Nick muted his headset. "What the hell happened?"

"The gusts. They're worse."

"Deal with it. We're doing the take."

"The storm is here … it's too dangerous."

"You mean too perfect. What a shot! The red sky … black clouds."

The operator fought with the duo-drone control box. "No. I'm telling you—"

"You're telling me nothing … we're doing it *because* the storm is here."

"Cristian will walk out."

442

Nick smiled. "Walk out? Hardly ... Cristian never quits and she's too green to leave."

"It's too damn risky."

"So's being over budget. We're not coming back tomorrow." Nick unmuted his headset. "Everyone, it's time."

* * *

On the pier, the assistant director Quinn Kolberg whispered into his headset. "It's too late. We're losing control out here."

Nick ignored him. "Ready on the set!"

Nick's order blasted through the crew's headsets. His orders were law; the buck stopped with the director.

Quinn turned to see yet another wave pummel Cristian and Tiffany.

I should get them out, Quinn thought, but instead followed orders.

He signaled Cristian and Tiffany to get on their marks.

⌘

Chapter 2

Nick jogged up the dry sand to his cinematographer Floyd Tyson, a friend since their U.S.C. Film School student-project years.

"Ready Floyd? This is a once in a lifetime. One take. That's all we get."

Floyd said, "Mother Nature may not give it to you."

"She will. We can do it."

"Remember the helicopter that killed—"

"Yeah. Yeah. But little drones can't kill anyone." Nick left and enthroned himself in his director's chair.

* * *

The wind plopped scattered rain bursts onto the dry sand. Nervous sweat seeped down Nick's forehead from under his tan, tattered lucky cap. He hated Floyd resurrecting the helicopter crash in the *Twilight Zone* movie. Three actors died. He had known two.

Nick watched the orange sun filtered behind the low, blackening clouds dropping rain.

But that was a lightning thing with the helicopter, he thought.

Then from the pier, Quinn dropped a headset word bomb, "*Stein.* Behind you. Three o'clock. Stein and a new one."

"Damn. Not now."

"Play nice."

* * *

Nick glared across the sand to the secured entrance at Josh Stein, the most powerful entertainment lawyer in the business.

Nick took off his tattered good luck cap from his U.S.C. days and wiped his sweat. "Like clockwork. That ass never forgets a nude scene and never comes alone."

Josh Stein was the gatekeeper to the highest grossing industry talent—feared and respected by studios, directors, producers, and agents alike. He always showed up, as of right, at his female clients' nude scenes—scenes he bullied them into putting in their contracts.

444

* * *

At the entrance Bruce, the bulked up head of security, stepped aside for the infamous entertainment lawyer to the stars. "Mr. Stein, welcome."

"Bruce," Josh said. "She's with me."

Following Josh was Kaitlin O'Keefe—a tall, lean, striking woman.

The security guards pushed back the gawkers and paparazzi. Then, gawked themselves at Kaitlin prancing in the sand behind Josh—the man who was going to "make her a star."

A young man in a black hoodie ran by the distracted guards. "Kaitlin. Kaitlin."

They caught him ten feet in and muscled him back into the crowd.

"I'm with her. She's my girlfriend." The man struggled. "Kaitlin. Kaitlin, wait for me!"

Kaitlin glanced back and mouthed, "Get lost."

This was her big break and Ted Ripple, ex-acting partner, loser, and stalker, was not going to ruin it for her.

Bruce got into Ted's face. "Get out of here or we'll call the S.M.P.D

"No. No cops." Ted slithered away.

* * *

Nick took the requisite minute to genuflect, greeting Josh like they were *brothers*—shaking hands, touching shoulders, patting backs.

"We're here in time?" Josh asked.

"Just barely." Nick flipped off his headset. "How's Miriam?"

"Fine." Josh slapped down Nick's domestic probe in front of his new Y & B, industry jargon for *young and beautiful*. "This is Kaitlin O'Keefe. Kaitlin … Nick."

Josh was always accompanied by the new talent he was grooming—today a sultry, long-legged beauty with a red mane glazed by the sunset.

Kaitlin purred, "Love your pictures, Nick."

"Oh?" He was transfixed by her eyes—light gray and lustrous, even in the fading light.

Kaitlin sat in the sand. Nick was gripped by the elegance of her tall porcelain body. As she nestled into a comfortable spot, her white tube dress hiked up to reveal no undies.

Nick thought, *They're films, not pictures, honey. But with those assets who cares what comes out of your pouty mouth.*

Josh looked out toward the pier, "So this is the beach nude scene I put in the contract?"

"Yeah, we moved it into the ocean." Nick twisted his wedding band, watching Kaitlin's delicate touch dusting the sand and rain droplets off her thighs.

"Hell, I see more skin when my housekeeper bends over."

Josh smoothed his thinning hair whipped by wind flurries. Then, he asserted his prerogatives by plopping his silk-suited, high-maintenance pint-sized body into the assistant director's chair. He represented both stars on the ocean platform—Cristian, whose Hispanic machismo Josh had molded into a seasoned action adventure star, and Tiffany, the blonde bombshell he had stolen from her C-list lawyer.

A storm gust forced Nick's attention back to his take. The windblasts now carried strings of airborne foam and salty spray from the pounding waves.

He flipped on his headset. "Are we ready?"

Affirmatives came from all positions.

"One take. No mistakes."

446

* * *

"Places," Quinn, megaphoned and headsetted, was thinking, frustrated, *It never rains in L.A. ... except today.*

The readiness and anticipation were shattered by Fire and Rescue sirens sounding up the cliffs along Palisades Park.

"Hold. Let them go by." Nick listened to the sirens passing on Ocean Avenue, turning left on Wilshire, stopping in three blocks at the trendy Third Street Promenade.

For a film location, the world-famous Santa Monica pier was always challenging, but sterling if you got your shots. Nick had planned on a sunny L.A.-rainless-November shoot with no sirens, summer-sized crowds, helicopters, or small planes dragging banner advertisements. Instead, Cristian and Tiffany drew numerous onlookers and paparazzi and, worse, Nick got an un-L.A. rainy day, the earliest and wettest in fifty years.

He took the challenge head-on. That's what made him an A-list director. He embraced the heightened drama and danger of the storm and was unthwarted by the crowds and the emergency sirens.

* * *

As Cristian and Tiffany held their position, the storm swells hit faster—cresting and crashing harder into them and the pier pylons nearby. Cristian's powerful legs fought the heavy undercurrents. He kept them on the platform built to make the shot look natural in the unnatural depth.

"I can't stay." Tiffany shivered uncontrollably wiping the salt water and rain from her face.

"Yes, you can." Cristian tightened his grip around her.

"Let me go. I'm quitting."

"No." Cristian lost his temper and along with it his subtle Hispanic accent—an affectation adopted years ago. "I'm not coming back here tomorrow."

The sirens stopped.

"Quiet on the set. Ready." Nick adjusted his lucky cap against the storm.

Cristian smiled at Tiffany. "You see. They're ready."

Quinn megaphoned. "Quiet on the set. Take one. Action."

⌘

Chapter 3

This was the money shot—Cristian's and Tiffany's ostensibly nude, passionate kiss in the ocean.

As their lips met, Quinn blurted into his megaphone, "Cristian, duck."

Cristian, who had worked with Quinn and Nick before, trusted them implicitly in dangerous action shots. When a command came, he reacted without question. A wind shear pushed one drone down toward the platform. Tiffany held on to Cristian, frozen, terrified, and screaming. The machine sucked their hair into its airstream as Cristian pulled them under water to safety.

"Cut," Nick yelled into the headphones. "Get control of that drone. One more time. The light's turning."

Quinn announced again, "Quiet on the set. Ready. Take two. Action."

Cristian placed his lips on Tiffany's again. Then, with cold calculation and experience, he cheated his face into the drone cameras mosquitoing around their heads—giving him prime exposure over this ingénue. Cristian dominated the scene in both the long shots and the close-ups. He gazed at her, as his face carouselled around into the lens of the close-up drone. He flexed his biceps, popping every pumped-up trainer-honed muscle above the water.

Tiffany was unaware that Cristian had been upstaging her in every shot—long, short, and in between.

In this scene, she simply closed *her* eyes and kissed Cristian, throwing her arms passionately around his neck and pulling him into her. Cristian, the savvy pro, held her back to optimize his presence on the big screen. The public wanted him, and he made sure they'd get him.

The wind whipped the swells, but Cristian maintained his pose, the now-burning red, sinking sun contouring his striking face and high-definitioned body. As the drone came in fast and low, he held still for the close-up.

He pressed his lips harder on Tiffany's, feigning passion but preserving his professionally advantageous position. He vice-gripped her in place to ensure his limelight.

As the drones and wind swirled around and the water sprayed over them, Cristian heard Quinn yell, "Down. Get down."

But before Cristian could go underwater again, a downdraft slammed the high hovering drone into Cristian's head—a gush of blood blinding his right eye.

The drone blades spinning out of control sliced through Cristian's cheek. He shrieked as his severed cheek flesh fell to his jaw—blood poured down his neck and salt water seared through the open wound. He dropped Tiffany and pressed his cheek back into his bloodied face.

"Help! Hel…" Tiffany gurgled as another drone blade rapiered into her neck.

Blood spurted from her jugular, and she flailed as the white-capped, red-stained sea sucked her under.

* * *

Extras screamed. Nick yelled piercing headsetted orders and ran to the pier. Josh and Kaitlin followed. The crew mobilized at the pier with Nick. Sirens sounded up Ocean Avenue again, but this time for them.

The S.M.P.D. backed the crowds to the east side of Ocean Avenue: the rapid-response parasitic media, voyeurs, and paparazzi.

First responders clamored at each other, getting Cristian out alive. Then, the organized chaos turned funereal as Tiffany's body recovery blanketed tense silence over the film set, the beach, the pier, and Nick, Josh, and Kaitlin.

* * *

When Tiffany went under, so did Nick's filming of *Deranged*.

⌘

Kallias Publishing also presents a limited time FREE audiobook on YouTube—
https://www.youtube.com/channel/UCac1mJynScdPGd2FVz1987A

Portal to Free Books at your Local Library on Author's Official Website
http://www.dalemanolakas.com

Author's YouTube Channel with Book Trailers
https://www.youtube.com/channel/UCac1mJynScdPGd2FVz1987A

Sign up for a Mailing List [NO SPAM ONLY SPECIALS]
https://dalemanolakas.com/sign-up